The Nessman

The Nessman

Alasdair Campbell

Birlinn

First published in 2000 by
Birlinn Limited
8 Canongate Venture
5 New Street
Edinburgh
EH8 8BH

www.birlinn.co.uk

The publisher acknowledges subsidy from The Scottish
Arts Council towards the publication of this volume

ISBN 1 84158 090 2

British Library Cataloguing-in-Publication Data
A catalogue record for this book is available
from the British Library

Typeset by Palimpsest Book Production Limited,
Polmont, Stirlingshire
Printed and bound by Creative Print and Design,
Ebbw Vale, Wales

Na luin

T HE TWO OLD MEN were sitting outside Flory's house, in the sun, Sharp was with them, and he moved off the road in order to give them all a wide berth. The two old men burst out laughing as soon as they saw who it was, and started trying to stick Sharp on him. 'Whiss, Sharp!' they urged the dog. 'Look who's here! Whiss! Go and bite him!' Colin shifted the screwtop of milk from his right hand to his left, in case he had to make a run for it. But Sharp never moved; he lay where he was, flopped over on one side, with his tongue hanging out and his side heaving. It was too hot. Colin crept warily past on the far verge, keeping an eye on Sharp all the time. 'Get up, Sharp!' the old men shouted, laughing, and prodding at the dog with their sticks. 'Get up and bite his head off!' But Sharp never moved.

At John the Battler's shed, the laughter of the two old men still following him, he turned out towards their own house. The road out to the house was the same reddish-brown clay dirt as the village road, but narrower between the verges, in one place a culvert ran under it, weeks of no rain had left it dusty and dry, full of stones and small, dried-out potholes and the intersecting ruts of cartwheels, baked hard by the sun. He walked along, kicking at a loose stone as he went with the open toes of his sandals, raising small spurts of dust with every kick. Their house was the first in the village on the right hand side, coming in from the main road; long and low, with a flat, tarred roof and walls of roughly plastered cement, it stood on its own at the top of the brae. Across from it, on the other side of the road, was John the Battler's house; and over from John the Battler's, set in its own parks and enclosed by high drystone walls, the biggest house in the village, Angus John Tully's, where the Macleod family lived (Roddy Macleod was on the same class as him in school; John Norman was on the same class as his brother). He closed the gate behind him, pressing down on the wire loop with both hands over the shiny-smooth top of the gatepost, and waited in case the loop began to slide up the post again. Along the side of the house facing in to the village it was cool, out of the sun – a bluish shadow. He was panting after his climb.

His mother wasn't in the scullery, she wasn't in the kitchen. The door of the partition that separated the kitchen and the front bedroom was open a little. 'Is anyone in?' he whispered, above the ticking of the kitchen clock. The silence hummed in his ears.

Back in the scullery, he put the screwtop of milk into the dank interior of the water-barrel to keep it cool, then dipped the new tin mug into one of the pails of water on the trestle and took a long, gulping drink. The water, from the well at the loch, was clear white, and so cold it made his teeth ache and his forehead go numb. He stopped drinking, snorting into the mug through his nose as he waited for the pain to subside, not taking the mug from his mouth; brown spots of rust, which had already started to appear on the bottom of the mug, seemed to move as he looked at them, quivering through the bright water; as he tilted and drank again, twin streams ran trickling from the corners of his mouth, onto the front of his jersey. He put the mug down, gasping, and went out, brushing at the beaded wet on the front of his jersey as he went, around by the front of the scullery, skirting the broken wheelbarrow of peats, ducking under a line of limp, new-smelling washing, to the front of the house. At the corner, he stopped dead – he couldn't believe his eyes. His father was at the front of the house. On the camp bed. Colin couldn't believe his eyes.

He stood open-mouthed at the corner, staring.

His father, looking up, saw a small, sun-freckled face with large eyes and close-cropped hair at the corner, regarding him. The face vanished like lightning.

2

'Come on,' he heard his father say.

He peeped out warily, with one eye; the rest of his face flattened against the cement. His father beckoned to him.

'Come on.'

Colin went forward, keeping his head down. He stopped beside the camp bed and scuffed on the grass with his sandals.

'Where have you been?' his father asked.

'Down in my granny's.'

'Where's John?'

'I don't know,' he replied, startled. He glanced guiltily upwards. John was his younger brother. But it was all right – his father was smiling at him. 'It's all right,' his father said, smiling. 'Don't look so alarmed . . .' His father's voice was very soft and quiet now – you had to strain in order to hear it. And his eyes were so blue! Colin had never before noticed how blue his father's eyes were. He felt shy and happy, those eyes smiling at him, and ducked his head away and down, and then his own face started to smile, and it wouldn't stop, and he laughed out loud, into the damp front of his jersey, with a small, happy, shrugging movement. He couldn't believe it!

He had never seen his father outside the house before. Except a long time ago.

He sat cross-legged on the grass beside the camp bed, and watched his father, on the camp bed, reading.

His father sat on the camp bed, propped among cushions, reading. He had a bonnet on his head, the peak shadowing his forehead. And a yellow cardigan on top of his pyjamas, with round leather buttons. He had shoes on his feet, and the socks granny Alan had knitted for him, for a present, the month before. His father had made a song for granny Alan, to thank her for the socks, and granny Alan, when she heard the song, had put her face into the shawl and cried. He had trousers on. A scarf round his neck. He looked just like anyone else. Beside him, on the camp bed, were his cigarettes and matches, a pair of binoculars, a tartan rug and a pile of *Bulletins*. He sat in the sun, reading a *Bulletin*. He looked just like anyone else.

'Dad, is Mr Shinwell a footballer?'

'No.'

He put down the *Bulletin* and took a cigarette from the packet of Capstan beside him. Holding the cigarette with his left hand – the index and middle fingers stained yellow by cigarette smoke – he raised it to his mouth. As he did so, the shadow of the cap bill fell away from his face, and Colin saw that his father's face, even in the sun, was a strange greyish-white colour, the colour of lard, of candles, and full of lines and hollows; and his eyes, so blue when you looked into them, were rimmed with black and set deep in his head. But that was because his father lay in bed all the time, in the back room, for as far back almost as Colin could remember, with the door closed and the clock taken away. And Colin and John were not allowed to make any noise in the house, or play games outside the windows of the room, and they weren't allowed to go up into the room to see their father, but sometimes they were – when Mrs Stanton the teacher sent Colin home, after giving him the strap, with a letter to his father, Colin was four hours up in the room, in a corner, with his face to the wall, not moving; until his mother came back from Stornoway on the seven o'clock bus. Granduncle Norman said it was the illness that made his father do these things. There was a small bell on the table beside the bed with a pearl button on top like an inverted collar stud that his father pressed down on, to make the bell ring, when he was too weak to speak. There was a zinc bucket under the bed, always. And one night Colin woke up, terrified, to hear his father, through the wall, loudly groaning and vomiting, and then his mother came down from the room carrying the zinc bucket in both hands, it slopped in the dark as she passed through the partition door on her way to the scullery, and he heard the front door opening, and got up, holding his breath, and tiptoed awkwardly to the kitchen window, and from there, standing barefoot on the cold linoleum, watched as she buried what was in the bucket in an old ashpit beside the peatstack. And when she had finished, she stood for a long time in the mouth of the peatstack, the spade still in her hand, in her wellingtons, an old waterproof thrown on over her nightdress, looking in to the village that lay hushed and sleeping at that hour – for what was she looking? – where all was dark at that hour, unmoving, with no light anywhere except in the window of the room where his father lay now as quiet as a mouse, making no sound at all. Then, in a while, she came back in, he heard the scrape of a match and the pop of the methylated spirit as she lit the small primus stove in the kitchen to make tea, and pretended to be asleep when she went past the foot of the bed, carrying two cups, on her way up to the room, and through trembling eyelashes he saw the black stains on the front of her nightdress. That was just before morning. And that morning, and every other morning, she would tell them, brushing vigorously at their hair with a spiky wire brush – 'Now if anyone asks how your father is today, say he's just the same. He's just the same, say . . .' And here his father was, up and outside and dressed in his clothes. It was like seeing a miracle.

Mr Shinwell wasn't a footballer, he was in the parliament. He was Labour. His father, when Colin asked him the question about Mr Shinwell, had looked down at the face of Mr Shinwell and smiled. In the picture, Mr Shinwell had on a collar and tie. That told you he wasn't a footballer. Footballers all wore jerseys with the collars open at the neck. Billy Steel was a footballer. But maybe Mr Shinwell was a footballer once upon a time.

'Were you a footballer, Dad?'

'No.' His father smiled. 'I was a boxer, though.'

He was a boxer, though. That was true enough. That was his father's nickname: The Boxer. And he got that nickname when he was small, in the primary school, because he was so good at fighting, and he could beat everyone else in the school at fighting.

The grass was warm to sit on; bright with daisies and buttercups. An old smell rose from the green canvas of the camp bed; it was hot under his hand. He felt so happy! So proud, he could hardly breathe! And he wished that all the other boys in the village could be there as well, to see his father; he wanted them to be there, to see his father – Ivor Macleod's boys from across the road, Donald and Roddy and John Norman, who lived in a big white house, Angus John Tully's, with stairs and storm windows and slates and a bathroom, their father went to sea and came back from Australia with a serious brown face and presents for all of them out of his suitcase – he wanted them to be there; and Donald Ishbel, from Aird, on his new bicycle; and he wanted the Barneys to be there, the Big Barney especially, it was the Big Barney who said, seeing the doctor going into Colin's house with gloves on: 'There's the doctor going in to box the Boxer!' – the Barneys' father went to sea too, but not serious when he came back, but singing and laughing in the back of the boat bus; and he wanted John Angie to be there, and the Rebel, and John Angie's brother Donald, and Snooks, and the three Pongos, Shamus and Calum and Tom-Tom, whose father was sometimes the roadman, and wore faded blue dungarees, full of patches, and could lift you above his head with one hand, easy as anything, and laugh as he held you there, haw haw haw, his face purple and red, bristling with grey bristles, laughing up at you, and you could see his Adam's apple wobbling, and his teeth all black and yellow, his bonnet was lined with newspaper, his breath would make your head reel – he wanted them all to be there, to see his father; and when they were all there he would say to them, he would say, he would point to his father and say, 'Look! Look! My father is up and outside and dressed in his clothes, just like anyone else! Look! Look at him!' And they would look, and be silent . . . Or else he wouldn't say anything, he would sit where he was and not say anything . . . And the older boys in the village would be there too, to see his father, everyone would be there to see his father; and his father would speak to all of them, softly and quietly, and they would all listen, looking at him, and the Big Barney would shift from one foot to the other, listening, and the grin would slowly leave his face . . .

The day was like a Sunday; so heavy, so quiet. He leaned his back against the wall. The sun beat solidly on his face; beat back, like a furnace, from the wall of the house behind him. Everything went black when he tried to look at it. Leaning against the wall was his father's stick, yellow and knotted; the number of their house – 6SD – burned into it, near the top. He remembered his uncle John doing that with the branding irons in granduncle Norman's house; the hiss and smell of the stick under the red-hot iron; the thin, blue smoke rising from it, turning, as it rose, to yellow. Along from the stick, at the corner, was an old tar bucket. The tar was melting. He could smell it. Out on the main road it came bubbling up in blisters between the chips; you could burst them with your thumbs. The tar brush was still in the bucket. Bluebottles hummed round it, coming and going. One of them had flown into the kitchen, through the open window; now it was banging against the pane from the inside, trying to get out again. Farmer Jack fell asleep after his dinner one hot day because of the drowsy noise of a bluebottle in the window, and the little mouse came out of her hole and ran across the floor and up Farmer Jack's leg and onto the table and ate all the cheese. That was a story in his brother Alan's reading book. His brother Alan was older than him. He was on Class Five. He stayed down in their granny's house all the time. That was the noise the bluebottles were making at the bucket: drowsy. He leaned his back against the rough cement of the wall, feeling the heat from it through his jersey, hearing the drowsy noise of bluebottles, smelling the afternoon smells, the hot, green and yellow, windless afternoon smells – grass, and melting tar, and canvas and sunwarmed stone. He looked up at his father. His heart started to beat more quickly.

The newspaper was still between his father's hands; but he was not reading it any more. Instead, he was gazing out to the moor, to the ben, blue in the distance, against the sky; far, far out, beyond the telegraph poles, their cups and wires flashing, that lined the main road. He sat very still. The newspaper, forgotten, was between his hands.

'Isn't it hot?' Colin said. His voice sounded strange in the silence. He felt awkward at having spoken.

His father came back from far away.

'What?'

'Isn't the sun . . . hot?' Colin said again. Squinting up uncertainly as he spoke and puffing out his cheeks – whew!

His father smiled at him.

'Open the buttons on your jersey.'

Colin started fumbling at the three glass buttons on the neck of his jersey.

'Dad, why is the top of the ben moving like that? Where it meets the sky?'

'That's a heat shimmer,' his father said.

Together they looked out at the ben.

7

'It's like . . . at the edge of a bonfire. When you look at the edge of a bonfire.'

'There's a Gaelic name for that,' his father said. 'Na luin.' He said it very softly. 'Now you say it.'

'Na luin.'

'Will you remember it?'

'Yes.'

'Look over there,' his father said. From the road a small column of dust rose, whirling, into the air, travelled a little way and settled. 'You won't see that unless you have a long spell of good weather.' He stopped speaking and closed his eyes, and Colin could hear the breath coming and going in his chest with a thin, weak, whistling sound, like kittens mewing; his breath seemed to go only a little way down in his chest before it stopped and came back up again. Then he coughed quietly, several times, into a hankerchief. Holding the handkerchief to his mouth, he went on: 'The old people had a name for that too . . . that little whirlwind. They called it Maighdean Fhionnlaigh.'

'Maighdean Fhionnlaigh,' Colin repeated, and laughed.

'Isn't that a good name?' his father said, almost in a whisper.

'Yes,' Colin said. 'O yes. And the sky is almost white, isn't it?'

He waited; but his father didn't answer. He was breathing that way again.

'I can do the dictionary at school,' Colin told him.

His father nodded, holding the hankerchief. Colin waited for him to stop coughing. He made no sound coughing; his shoulders moved, and his eyes filled with water. He dabbed at his lips with the hankerchief.

'I can look up words. I looked up murmuring.'

'Did you?' his father whispered, glassy-eyed.

'I looked up all the words for "If I were Lord of Tartary". Athwart means across from side to side. Their fins athwart the sun.'

His father sank back among the cushions with a sigh. The world shimmered on in silence. Then he turned his head and smiled:

'You're a clever boy, Colin,' he said.

The gate gave a high squeal on its hinges, gave a wooden thud as it swung back, rebounding, from a heavy hand, and then, around the corner of the house, came his mother. Bare-armed and bare-legged, in a brightly coloured overall, her red face shining, black hair loose and flying, she came charging down on the camp bed like a swelling sea wave, shouting at the top of her voice, and seeming to set everything – the grass, the air, the very stones – into a stir of tremulous agitation as she came. 'I never meant to be so long,' she shouted. 'That woman kept me talking an hour and a half. Could I get away? No fear!' She halted in front of his father. 'Are you all right?' she asked. Hands above her knees, she bent down and peered into his father's face, under the cap brim. 'I came back as quick as I could. All out of breath – look at me! That woman wouldn't let me go!' His father said something Colin couldn't hear. 'Is it me?' she exclaimed, straightening. 'I never opened my mouth hardly. I never got the chance. What are *you* doing here?' she asked Colin. Before he could answer, she asked, 'Did you bring the bottle of milk from your granny's?' Before he could answer that, she said, to his father, 'Norman was saying the weather will break before tomorrow. "The white wave is on the skerry," he was saying. "We'll have bad weather by nightfall".' She raised his father to a sitting position, telling him what else Norman had said as she did so, and started tidying up around the camp bed, putting things in order. She put all the cushions to one side, pummelling them into shape with the flats of her hands. She arranged the *Bulletins* in a pile, and placed the binoculars on top of them. She folded up the tartan rug. 'Give me that stick,' she said to Colin. Colin handed her the stick. She put the stick into his father's hand, folding his fingers around the crook. Stooping, she put her left hand underneath his shoulders, and hauled him to his feet. She took his free arm and put it around herself, holding it in place by the wrist. His father looked very frail and unsteady beside her – a thing of sticks. 'Come on, now,' she said.

Carefully, they moved off. Colin watched his father – he never took his eyes off him. They took two steps forward – faltered and stopped. His father's head hung down; he dabbed feebly at the ground with his stick. But when he tried to put his weight on it, the stick, and his whole arm with it, trembled violently. They went forward two more steps; halted. Two more; halted. His mother kept talking all the time, encouraging his father, urging him on. With growing rage, Colin watched them go – the thin, bowed back, held up so effortlessly by his mother's arm, the muscles of which moved, tightening, under the smooth white skin, with every step they took. The yellow cardigan had ridden up under her arm, and he could see the upside-down V of his father's braces at the back, the blue and white striped pyjamas underneath. 'Don't you touch anything on that bed,' his mother said to him, over her shoulder, before they went round the corner – meaning the binoculars. Colin stared at her, red-faced with rage and shame. He didn't answer. His father was trying to turn round as well. Colin turned his face to the wall.

Useless . . .

He heard them moving on again, going round by the scullery. The clap of a blanket pushed to one side, as they went under the washing line.

He couldn't even walk. He couldn't even do that . . .

Colin's face burned with shame . . .

And he was glad the other boys in the village hadn't been there to see him. He was glad – *glad* – they hadn't been there . . .

Useless . . .

He pressed his face against the rough cement wall, and sometimes it was black before his eyes and sometimes red, with a noise in his ears like faraway singing.

In the kitchen, the bluebottle banged against the windowpane, over and over again . . .

The clock in the kitchen gave a long, preliminary whirr, like someone with bad asthma, then struck four times. Sullen-faced, he listened. Four strokes meant it was five to three. It was the stupidest clock in the whole world. Sometimes the long hand fell off. At five to twelve it struck once . . . Out of the corner of his eye he saw Roddy Macleod slinking along beside Angus John Tully's garden wall, dragging a tea-chest behind him. Going down to the loch! 'Hui!' he yelled, jumping to his feet and starting to run, 'Hui, *Roddy!*' racing past the window of the back room and round to the gate – it was wide open – as fast as his legs could carry him, 'Wait for *me!* . . . Hui, Roddy, *wait!* . . . Wait for *me!* . . .'

The Borve wedder

COLIN AND HIS GRANDUNCLE Norman stood at the door of the barn. They were waiting for uncle John to come. The wedder was tethered inside, to an iron loop in the wall.

The barn was called the Old House in Gaelic. It was on the other side of the road from Norman's house. Maggie lived in Norman's house as well. She was Norman's sister.

Norman's house was number 14 in the village. Down from it, in number 13, lived Chrissie Alan and her mother and her sister Catherine. Flory and the old man lived in number 12. They would all get a piece of the wedder, and Flory and the old man would also get the trotters. They ate Waddell's sliced sausages, raw.

The Old House was where Norman and William and his grandfather and Maggie had lived when they were young.

William lived in a big white house at number 23. He sat by the fire all the time. He was his granduncle too.

His grandfather had been drowned in the First World War, on the third of March, 1915, on HMS *Clan MacNaughton.* The government gave his granny a pension for that, and she still got it, and the king, George the Fifth, sent her a round, heavy disc, reddish-brown in colour, like a large medal, much-polished it glowed on the sideboard, with his grandfather's name – Murdo Maclean – on it, and *He Died For Freedom And Honour,* and a woman with a helmet and a shield and a three-pronged spear and a lion at her feet, looking out to sea. Maybe it was the queen that sent it. Queen Mary. The other side of the medal was as flat and smooth as the bottom of a cooking pot.

A photograph of his grandfather, taken when he was in Egypt in the Seaforth Highlanders, hung on the wall of his mother's bedroom. It was taken in Cairo. In the photograph, his grandfather is staring straight ahead; not smiling. He has a moustache. He was a sergeant.

Days before he died he had sailed within sight of home, when the *Clan MacNaughton* steamed through the blue and green and grey turmoil of waters off the Butt of Lewis, on her way north to Scapa Flow. In his last letter home he had written: *Today, through the telescope, I could see the ben, there was snow on the top of it. I kept thinking of the poor sheep . . .*

Maggie would sometimes tell him stories about Norman and William and his grandfather, and the Old House where they had all lived when they were young. Then their father – Colin's great-grandfather – had built a new house – number 14, Dell, Ness – on a stance across the road. All that was left standing of the Old House of sticks and stones that he didn't cart or manhandle across the road and incorporate into the new dwelling was the barn. Or rather, half the barn; the end wall, facing south east, had never been rebuilt and closed up again, and a gap remained, three feet wide and less than four feet high, which was blocked up, windily but effectively, by rolling a rimless old cartwheel across it from the inside. Years later, a small fank was built alongside the barn. A cement trough for dipping sheep, set into the ground, with stances on either side for two men in their oilskins; a cement ramp, an extension of the trough itself, with raised steps every foot or so, leading up to a stonewall pen. The floor of the pen was of cement also, and sloped slightly downwards, so that as the sheep, drenched and bedraggled, dropping green pellets, scrabbled desperately up the ramp and into the pen, the tawny flood of dip water, pouring off them, would run back down into the trough. From there (the cartwheel rolled aside; Colin and Roddy Macleod on guard at the gap) they were herded into the dank, creosote-smelling gloom of the barn to shake themselves dry.

Uncle John should have come at eleven o'clock, with the knife and the killing board. The basins, the two enamel buckets, and the rope for tying the wedder's legs, were waiting in the mouth of the peatstack, out of the wind. Maggie had put them there herself, clumping across the road in her unlaced man's boots and jutesack apron, trailed by a garrulous squad of brown and white hens. Chrissie Alan spoke from the door of number 13:

'Isn't this a morning?'

'Keep that dog inside the house,' Norman said to Maggie, 'till we're finished out here.'

The barn was windowless. The only light came filtering in through the spokes of the cartwheel, across the gap at the bottom.

Through a chink in the rotting, greenish door, Colin peered in at the wedder. He'd been tethered in there since the night before. He stood nuzzling at a sheaf of corn that hung, tied with hairy rope, from another iron loop in the wall. His eyes, in the half-light, were like glass marbles.

Uncle John's knife was like a razor for sharpness. A man from the west side of the island had given it to him. The man got it in South Georgia, at the whaling. It looked the same as any other knife. But it wasn't.

'John? *He's* in no hurry,' granduncle Norman said, in reply to a question from Chrissie Alan. 'He took his time coming into this world, and he'll take his time going out of it.'

Willie the Carrier, speaking of uncle John, once said:

'Has anyone told him the sun also rises?'

Norman and William were uncle John's uncles. Maggie was uncle John's aunty. Colin's grandfather was uncle John's father.

The rest of the family – his granny's family – were: aunty Annie, his mother, aunty Isobel and aunty Margaret.

Norman's house – the house great-grandfather Murdo built – was a black house with thick walls (you could shelter three deep in the doorway, under the stone lintel) a thatched roof, and a fire in the middle of the floor. A small square window, in which hens roosted, was set far into the wall; one pane, the bottom left, looking out, had a curved crack going all the way across it; putty had been thumbed into the crack on both sides of the glass to keep the wind out, a line of whorled, overlapping thumbprints hardened into the putty, and the glass itself had turned a smoky yellow colour, like the windscreen of

Charlie's lorry. There was a wooden bench, an oatmeal kist, Maggie's box bed and a dresser full of dishes. There was an anvil. Maggie's box bed had heavy purple curtains, with facings of yellow, hanging across the front. That was the living room. Up from the living room was a partitioned space called the closet, and up from the closet was Norman's bedroom, where he kept his books in English and Gaelic (all covered with brown paper, and smelling of peatsmoke and must; the *History of the Clans* sewn up at the back with cobbler's thread), his seaman's chest, his toolbox, and in a frame above his head, his certificate from King Neptune, king of the arctic regions, of mermaids and polar bears and icebergs.

Instead of proper wallpaper, the wall of the living room was covered over in places with pages from the Scottish *Daily Express*, smudged and smoke-blackened. One page had a picture of Bobby Brown, Rangers, leaping high and punching clear. Colin, sitting on the anvil, wanted that picture more than anything else in the world. Maggie wouldn't give it to him. She didn't want to make a hole in the paper. A ginger tomcat curled in her lap. She crooned over him:

> Hush-a-bye, hush-a-bye,
> Hush-a-bye, Polo . . .

The three-toed prints of hens – Jojos and Light Sussexes – were all over the floor, in and out of the ashes; stooping, she made swirling passes at them with a brush made of bound heather switches.

She liked the king and queen – King George the Sixth and Queen Elizabeth – and the rest of the royal family. But her favourite was old Queen Mary. Her favourite princess was the Princess Louise. A picture of Queen Mary and Edward, Prince of Wales, taken from the *Illustrated London News*, was pasted inside the glass door of the clock in the wall recess. A small square had been cut out at the bottom of the picture, in the centre, so that you could still see the yellow meniscus of pendulum bob going back and forth, inside.

'Stop looking at that footballer, and tell me who was in the shop . . .'

. . . Late afternoon sun, slanting through the small, square window, flung bars of smoky gold across the blue haze of the living room, lit up Bobby Brown punching clear, and dazzled so brilliantly on the glass door of the clock that Queen Mary, in her purple robe, and Edward Prince of Wales, in his red coat and silver breeches, disappeared in the reflection of light.

The cattle and sheep were in the front part of the house. You came out of the fire-lit, lamp-lit peatreek, closed the door behind you, shuffled across the stone flags with one hand out in front of you until you found the sneck of the connecting door, went through, and you were down among the animals. It was warm from their breath, and smelled of dung and straw. It was dark. You had to wait for a while, in the warm, steaming dark, before you could make anything out. The animals stirred and stamped restlessly; butted the boards of their pens. They knew you were there.

The cow – Starboard – had only one horn: she lost the other one in a fight. The horn she lost was on top of the wall outside. It was the left horn she lost; that was why she was called Starboard.

The dog's name was Delse. The cats' names were Polo, The Winterman, Kruger and Leddy Liza.

All the sheep had names. All the hens. One sheep was called Crooked Marion. She cropped the grass in the ditches round the houses, and wouldn't run away even if you went up close to her. Blackbirds perched on her back.

Donald Dod was with them now.

'Which one are you killing?' he asked Norman. 'The three year old?'

'No. The Borve wedder.'

'Where did he come from this time?'

'Shader. One of Telfer's lorries dropped him at the door two nights ago. All the way from Shader. Right, said I, my fine fellow, when I saw him, your gallivanting days are over . . .'

The Borve wedder was so called because he grazed far out on the Borve moor, at a place called the Blackwater lochs. That was where he was born (where he got the milk, as the old ones said), and that was where he always returned. Borve was a village five or six miles to the south. Every time they held a fank in Borve, a message was sure to come down to Norman that his wedder had turned up there, as usual, and for someone to come and collect him. Sometimes he turned up at the fanks in Shader, a village even further to the south. Once he turned up in North Tolsta, on the other side of the island. Colin liked the idea of the Borve wedder, and always went to have a look at him in the backyard on his return – a large, brownfaced animal with quiet eyes, waiting to go away again.

Donald Dod was talking. He took the pipe from his mouth, looked up angrily at granduncle Norman, pursed his lips and spat.

'The world?' he said. 'The world's gone to the dogs.'

Donald Dod was a small, round man, red-faced and querulous. All the year round he wore a cap called a hard weather cap. It had a shiny black bill like a sea captain's. His belly came over the belt of his trousers.

'Look at them in this day and age,' Donald Dod shouted, 'and then go ahead and tell me I'm wrong. For my dinner yesterday, what did I have? – a piece of cod you'd be ashamed to throw to the cat. Where did it come from? The back of a fish lorry. Where did the fish lorry come from? Stornoway. One and six she paid for it. Yet less than three miles out from that shore there – what? – as much ling, cod and haddock as a man could desire. Bred for the handlines. Will they go for it? No. Why? I'll tell you why . . .'

His voice, as he spoke, went higher and higher – he sounded very angry. Chrissie Alan appeared in her doorway again, came out as far as the gate, stood with her head thrust forward a little and cocked to one side, listening.

Granduncle Norman, his hands dangling by his sides and a little way out from his body, laughed at what Donald Dod was saying. He made no noise when he laughed; his mouth opened, you saw the sole, yellow tooth, you heard his breath: *aaahrr-ah*: an ancient, crackling exhalation: and you knew granduncle Norman was laughing. Granduncle William, when he laughed, made no sound either, except a low, winding-down whistle at the end, like a kettle coming off the boil; and his eyes used to water. In his leather armchair by the fireside, all conversation over for this morning, he would sit looking from Colin to John, and from John back to Colin. Side by side on the clear-varnished bench (it had a row of little cupboards underneath, with tiny double doors and brass doorknobs), Colin and John, aged four and three, wearing pixiehoods, looked expectantly back at him. Minutes would pass. No one speaking. The tall clock groaning. Then granduncle William, his face starting to crease, would heel over slowly in the chair, always towards the fireside, raise his right haunch and ponderously break wind . . .

Donald Dod took off his cap and examined the inside. At a line going all the way round his head, wrinkles and weatherbeaten skin ended, smooth white skull began. He put the cap on again. It had a high front, and a hard, shining bill like a sea captain's.

'Idlers!' he shouted. 'Idlers and layabouts, the whole pack and parcel!'

In the trenches, in the First World War, he murdered an officer on their own side. Murdered him first, then buried him.

'Who's idle?' Chrissie Alan asked.

The officer had been bad to his own men. He wanted to put a young boy who had fallen asleep on sentry duty on report. That was why Donald Dod had murdered him.

'The world's kaput,' Donald Dod said.

To steal turnips out of his field was highly dangerous; his doors and gates were given a wide berth by children at Halloween. And Roddy Macleod told Colin that when Donald Dod caught the Big Barney stealing his turnips, Donald Dod dragged the Big Barney by the scruff of the neck to a drainage ditch at the end of the field, held him upside-down over it, and informed the Big Barney that he, Donald Dod, was sorry there wasn't enough water in it to drown him.

One of the big enamel buckets was for catching the wedder's blood; the other was for the stomach and intestines. And later that day, after cleaning out the stomach and intestines at the rainwater barrel at the end of the house (turning the large and small intestines inside out as cautiously as Colin had once seen her handling a silk scarf – 'Feel, lady! Feel it!' – from a traveller's black case), Maggie would take the great yellow mixing bowl from its press in the bottom of the dresser, push the table up against the window to catch the full afternoon light, and start to make black puddings. Shredding the suet into the bowl, into the oatmeal, the salt, the chopped onions – the suet crumbling thinly from the edge of the knife; pouring in the blood, a little at a time, from the ewer-shaped milkjug, and stirring the mixture with a wooden spoon; finally plunging both hands into the bowl (the sleeves of her woollen jersey rolled up above her elbows) and kneading the mixture in the same way as, at other times, on a flat baking board, she would knead and pummel the dough to make oatmeal or barley bannocks; breaking up the larger bits of suet and blood-clotted lumps of oatmeal with quick, reddened fingers. Meanwhile, over the fire (as with her fingers and with the spoon handle she poked and prodded the churned red mixture down into the glistening, balloon-like skins, tying the open ends afterwards with heavy white thread – in the case of the round pudding, running a steel knitting needle through the gut, to close it up), the black, three-legged pot would be on the boil, its round, wooden lid, formerly the lid of a herring barrel, on to which Norman had tacked a wooden handle, clattering loudly on top, lifting and falling, in spite of the two round, flat pebble stones, taken from the seashore, identical in shape and contour, that weighted it down on either side of the handle.

Black puddings took hours to boil, and you needed to watch them all the time; otherwise they would burst. ('*Too old, a ghraidh,*' she sighed, handing the silk scarf back to the traveller. '*Too old, too pretty for me ...*') You had to stick a darning needle into them from time to time. Otherwise they would burst.

Colin didn't like black puddings. He didn't like onions. He used to pick the bits of onion and fat out of the fried slices of black pudding with the blade of his knife. Grownup voices railed at him:

'At it again, are you?'

'How do you expect to grow up into a big, strong man if you won't eat black puddings?'

'No wonder you're so thin!'

A raw egg, beaten in milk, with a teaspoonful of sugar added, put a new drop of blood in you. White meat was better than red. ('*But lady!*' the traveller pleaded, rolling his eyeballs. '*Lovely lady! ...*').

Best of all for young, growing boys was warm milk, straight from the cow's udder. It was also good for sciatica. His granny held out the bowl with both hands. It frothed, pale yellow. Her mouth tightened. She set down the bowl again.

'Why won't you?'

'I can't.'

'It will put a new drop of blood in you.'

'. . . can't . . .'

Uncle John, in his place at the head of the table, scraping at a cold muttonbone he'd taken from the drawer of the dresser, although it wasn't teatime or anywhere near it, now spoke up. 'Let him be,' he snorted, clutching the muttonbone in one hand, and in the other, unclasped, the west side man's knife, all the way from South Georgia, that was like a razor for sharpness. 'Let him be. He wants to grow up a – a *puny* – that's *his* lookout. Won't have this, won't have that. Won't drink milk, warm or cold. Whoever heard of a growing boy that wouldn't drink milk?'

'What *will* you drink,' his granny asked, 'poor thing?'

'Tea,' said Colin.

'I go to Jerusalem,' said uncle John.

The plant in the porch window was called a geranium. Aunty Isobel looked after it. The one in the bedroom was called a begonia. His granny put her ear close to the small electric wireless. *Kirrrr. Ere I sleep.* The word of God and prayers at the close of the day.

'Where's my Super-duper annual?'

'Be quiet!'

'Ssssh!'

Round the back of the sofa on all fours. Into aunty Annie's ear, whisper:

'Where's my Super-duper?'

Finger to mouth, aunty Annie also: Ssssh! Head half-turned; hair in a bun. Wait.

Fffpweeee. Krak. Blipliplip . . .

. . . They saw a whirlwind one afternoon, through the window, Colin and his granny. They were alone in the house. Everyone else was at the hay. Suddenly a tarpaulin went sailing past the window, followed by a hen, followed by a patched cooking pot with no handle.

Chrissie Alan came out again.

'Not here yet?' she asked.

'His mother's people,' said granduncle Norman.

'His father's too,' said Donald Dod.

The door of number 12 was flung open, and out with a rush came Flory, a griddle of black, smoking scones held at arm's length in front of her. The old man's high, thin laughter followed her out. She dumped the burnt scones into the roadside ditch. 'Isn't this a morning?' said Chrissie Alan. 'Ho!' said Flory, straightening. 'I've done it again. Mary! Ho! Mary!' Across the stream, Colin's mother appeared in the doorway of their house, wearing a bright overall. 'Look!' – holding up the empty griddle. 'I've done it again!' Crooked Marion nosed warily at the charred segments. 'Sharp!' Flory shouted. 'Here, Sharp! Here here here!'

'Did you ever,' granduncle Norman murmured mildly, 'see a bull cook the likes of her?'

'Ho!' Flory shouted, pointing at Crooked Marion. 'This is the lop-eared tinker's bitch you should be putting under the knife.' 'Ah, dashity, Flory . . .' granduncle Norman began reasonably, but she wasn't listening. Swinging the griddle, she scuttled fussily back up the path, a tiny woman dressed all in black, and disappeared under the low lintel. High, thin laughter greeted her incoming. Their house was even lower and darker than Norman and Maggie's, grass ran wild along the tops of the walls, dockens sprouted through the thatch, but at least, as Colin's mother used to remark, at least their fire was no longer in the centre of the floor, at least, she would continue, giving uncle John a look, if they'd done nothing else, the seagoing nephews had built a proper fireplace for them at one end of the livingroom, where the old man sat all day, in his bonnet and gansey, and his waistcoat with the two rows of silver buttons on top of the gansey, smoking black twist and laughing at Flory through his long, white old man's beard. Except on sunny days, when Flory would put him out to the front of the house in a wooden chair with arms, and another old man, Dolly from number 7, would come up to keep him company, and the two old men would sit in front of the house all afternoon, in the sun, smoking their pipes and laughing so loudly that people working on their crofts at the backs of the houses would stop whatever they were doing in order to listen to them, and listening, would smile themselves, and shake their heads, before bending to their work again. They could be heard as far down as Disher's shop in the middle of the village – Dolly's deep, trolling rumble, like a bullock coughing, and the old man's thin, high shriek which, according to Flory his sister, would drive horses out of the corn; their mother, when she was in a good mood, could imitate them. Chrissie Alan and her mother and sister, on the other hand, lived all by themselves in a big white house with a whitewalled garden in front where a rhododendron grew, and where now were the three fine sons who smiled down so bravely from the wall? In Canada, New Zealand and the grave. Granny Alan, too, sat by the fire. A white house between two black ones.

'Send Colin for him,' his mother shouted.

'Colin!' said granduncle Norman. 'Is it the man that went to the Mill for a dozen eggs and fetched up in his uncle's house in Swainbost?'

'Is it the man,' said Donald Dod, 'that once jumped into the river after a trout?'

'Why isn't he in school?' Chrissie Alan asked. 'Why aren't you in school, Colin?'

'I've got scrips.'

'Scrips?'

'Impetigo,' his mother shouted. 'Show Chrissie your arm!' she shouted.

Colin pulled up his sleeve and showed Chrissie Alan the scabs with the gentian violet on them.

'He can't go back to school until they clear up,' his mother shouted. 'In case anyone else gets them. You've no idea . . .'

'Here he comes,' Donald Dod said.

'Keeps picking at the scabs, he won't leave them alone. Scratch scratch scratch, day and night. Even in his sleep . . .'

Uncle John was at Tam's house and coming, the killing board over his shoulder, striding along.

'. . . tie his hands to the bedpost . . .'

'Well,' said Donald Dod, 'but this won't do it. She doesn't look so promising to the south west,' he added.

'Where?' said granduncle Norman. 'What did you say?'

They stood looking to the south west together. Uncle John, striding his stride, was almost upon them.

'Mackerel sky,' said granduncle Norman, shielding his eyes with one hand. 'Good weather.'

'I doubt it,' said Donald Dod.

'Good weather for three days.'

'I wouldn't bet on it,' said Donald Dod.

Uncle John had the killing board over one shoulder. It was the same as an ordinary trestle table, but with two boards fixed along its sides and raised slightly from the horizontal.

'You're here at long last, John,' Donald Dod greeted him.

'Here I am.'

'You made it.'

'What time of day do you call *this*?' their mother shouted at uncle John from across the stream. Uncle John reared at the sound of her voice as if he had been bitten. His face went red and started to swell up with anger. 'Bloody woman,' he snorted.

'Keeping other people hanging about all morning waiting for *you* . . . !'

'Bloody woman . . . Is everything ready?'

'He's in here,' granduncle Norman said.

'Well,' said Donald Dod, 'I'll leave you to it.'

He went off down the road, puffing blue clouds.

'What was he after this time?' uncle John asked, as soon as Donald Dod was out of earshot. 'Another hammer?' He dragged open the rickety door of the barn, scraping back a heap of dried mud and small stones, and propped a larger stone against it, at the bottom, to keep it open. From his place by the wall, the Borve wedder looked out at them. Colin and granduncle Norman went to collect the buckets and basins from the mouth of the peatstack. He stood with a bucket in his hand. 'Take the rope,' said Norman. 'We'll need the rope.'

'He's a big beast,' uncle John said. He had already positioned the killing board in the middle of the barn. 'We'll have to sit on him.' The roof of the barn leaked, water seeped through the thatch all the time, and the earth floor was black and muddy. Uncle John took a bundle of old sacks from a corner and started spreading them on the floor, around the killing board. He snorted through his nose as he worked. For all his size and easygoing ways, he could move quickly when he wanted. Taking the enamel bucket from Colin's hand, he placed it carefully on the sacks he had laid down between the splayed front legs of the board, then took two paces backwards and tilted his head, to consider if that was the best place for it. 'Where's the rope?' he asked. Numbly, Colin handed the rope to him. Up to now, he hadn't thought about what was going to happen. He hadn't thought about it. He'd thought about black puddings – about Maggie making black puddings. He hadn't thought at all about what was going to happen. Now, with the nearness of it, he suddenly felt panicky. He wanted to run away. Where could he go? 'You'll stand at that door,' uncle John was saying to him – uncle John, who could carry two cartwheels on their iron axle across his shoulders: what chance did the Borve wedder have? 'You'll stand at that doorway – at it, not in it – and if a hen or a dog or any other creature on four legs comes along, you'll keep them out of here. Till we're finished. Understand? Do you think you can manage that without making a . . . a ballocks of it?' The wedder stood quietly by the wall. He hadn't done anything. What had he done? *Let him go,* Colin wanted to shout. *He hasn't done anything. Please don't kill him.* 'Well?' said uncle John. Colin nodded. 'Don't stand in the light, remember,' granduncle Norman said. 'Stand at the edge of the door, outside.'

Uncle John now removed the tether from the wedder's neck, and felt him with his hand along the back. 'Fine and dry, anyway,' he said. 'He's a good beast. Put another two or three sacks down. I don't want him all muddy.' Norman fetched some more sacks from the corner and spread them at uncle John's feet. Colin, from the door, couldn't stop watching. What was he going to do now? What he did was bend slightly at the knees to give himself more leverage, reach underneath the wedder and take hold of him by the front legs. His other hand cupped the wedder's jaw. He steadied; then, in a single movement, he jerked the wedder off his feet and upended him, belly upwards, upon the sacks; clamped the head between his knees, reached for and caught one of the kicking hind legs, and working swiftly, gripped the forelegs and hind leg together in one hand and tied them tightly with the rope. As he was straightening, he gave a sudden yell of pain and lashed out at the wedder, twice, on the side of the head, with his clenched fist. His fist, against the wedder's head, made a sound like hitting a car tyre with a stick. 'Now will you stay still?' he bawled. He stood rubbing at his knee, where a horn must have caught him. The wedder jerked and struggled at his feet. Heart heaving, Colin turned away. Maggie's face was on the window pane. 'Get hold of his other leg,' he heard uncle John saying. 'Bitch's bastard of an animal. Get him up on the board . . .'

Maggie was waving at him through the window. She rapped on the glass, to attract his attention.

'What?' he shouted peevishly, although Maggie couldn't possibly hear him from where he was.

She mouthed through the glass: *Have they started?*

He shrugged his shoulders and turned again quickly. They had arranged the Borve wedder on the killing board. His head hung forward, over the front edge of the board, facing the door and staring straight out; uncle John straddling him at the front, and granduncle Norman behind; both bearing down on him with their full weight. Under the weight of the two men, the Borve wedder seemed quite content; he had stopped struggling; his eyes, in the big brown face, were passive and calm. For a long moment, after Colin turned, the three in the barn paused in what they were doing, as if interrupted in the middle of a private game; then uncle John scowled, indicated with savage, sideways jerks of his head: *Get out of the doorway, out of the light.* Colin went away.

He stood loitering at the peatstack. Maggie's face had gone from the window. You couldn't see into the barn from the peatstack.

He looked all round him. But not even Crooked Marion was anywhere to be seen. So he could keep guard from here.

Noises were coming out of the barn, hoarse scraping noises, out of the dark entry. And then a tinny dripping.

He shouldn't be at the peatstack. Uncle John had said at the barn door, at the side. But there wasn't an animal to be seen.

He could keep guard from here.

In a sunless cove behind the Toe of Galson, Colin and Roddy Macleod once saw a grey seal pup down below, whimpering and sprawling among the slime-covered stones, trying to get back out to sea. Only it kept on going the wrong way, it kept heading in the direction of the land. Roddy Macleod threw stones at it, stone after stone, in front of it, to make it turn around. But it wouldn't. After a long time, granduncle Norman came out. 'You're doing a good job there, Colin,' he said, and started to laugh.

'Is he finished?' Colin asked.

'What would we have done without you?'

'Why is he skulking over at the peatstack?' Uncle John had also come out, carrying a bucket in each hand. His hands were streaked and spotted with red, as though he had been working in paint.

'Did you kill him?'

'What do you think?'

Granduncle Norman laughed.

'Did he?'

'Go and look.'

'He'll eat him all the same, though,' uncle John said. He had set the buckets down and gone back into the barn. Now he had reappeared, wiping his hands on a piece of sacking. 'Put a lump of gigot in front of him and watch his nose turn up . . . *what?* No fears!'

He picked up the buckets, snorted and shook his head.

'Catch Paddy,' he said.

'Never you mind him, Colin,' said granduncle Norman, as they watched uncle John, with the buckets, striding across the road and into the house. 'Never you heed a word of it. You stick to the pen and paper, that's what to do. They'll serve you better in the long run. Take out an education – that's the ticket. Leave butchering to the butchers. What do you think, then?' he continued in the same slow, kind voice. 'Will we give him a helping hand with the rest of it?'

'All right.'

They went into the barn. Headless and skinned, the pink carcass of the Borve wedder hung, turning, by the hindlegs from a rafter. It shone with a suety sheen; the stubby forelegs, the bloody stump of neck between with its trailing filaments of blood, thrusting downwards towards the earth, almost in supplication, as if imploring the black muddy floor of the barn to open up and hide them. So it would hang for a day and a night. Then uncle John would come back and carve it up with his hacksaw and cleaver.

'Here.' Granduncle Norman handed him a basin of suet. 'Have you a proper hold of it? Off you go, then.'

Stepping carefully, the basin held tight with both hands against his chest, Colin crossed the road. He felt proud now: he was helping. He hoped Chrissie Alan was watching him out of her small porch window. But he didn't dare to look. He went into the house. Delse whimpered from behind the door connecting the house and the byre. In the front room, Maggie and uncle John were arguing loudly.

'My dinner's waiting for me at home.'

'But I've a dinner here for you!' She took the basin from Colin's hands without looking at him, and dumped it on the dresser. 'Salt herring and potatoes. Who's going to eat it?'

'Colin,' said uncle John. 'Colin'll eat it.'

'No he won't.'

'Colin with his white face'll eat it. Colin'll eat anything.'

He ducked out of the door. Maggie clumped out after him.

'What about the head?' she shouted. 'Are you taking the head?'

'Don't you want it?'

'Take it! Where is it?'

'Here it is.'

'Don't show it to me. Put it in a sack.'

'Bloody women . . .' uncle John muttered to himself. Then, out loud: 'What's wrong with you *now?*'

'The Borve wedder,' she cried, in a high, quaking voice. 'Don't let me see his head. Don't let my eye settle on it.'

'I go to Addis Ababa!' said uncle John. The middle part of his body, tight in a dungaree jacket, went past the window, briefly blotting out the light. Maggie clumped back in. She looked at Colin. Her eyes were shiny with tears. 'Ah, ghraidh,' she keened, sitting on the bench and rocking herself backwards and forwards. 'The Borve wedder! Ah, ghraidh!' She stopped rocking and pointed to a plate beside the fire with two herring and a semi-circle of potatoes in their jackets on it. 'Eat that,' she said. 'That was for your uncle John. You eat it.' The skins on the potatoes nearest to the fire had wrinkled and turned brown from the heat; the tails of both herrings had curled up. Colin shook his head.

'Why won't you? What's wrong with it?'

'Nothing.'

'I'll give you that footballer if you eat it. I will.'

'No.'

'Who'll eat them, then, the good herrings?'

Meanwhile, across the road, granduncle Norman had made everything shipshape and Bristol fashion. He had rolled up the pelt of the Borve wedder, wool side inside, tied it with hairy rope, and stowed it away in the driest corner of the barn for the time being, along with the muddied sacks and the killing board. He had closed the door of the barn from the outside, propped the large stone against it at the bottom, and also an old iron cart axle, between the jambs. Now, instead of coming into the house, where his dinner was waiting for him, he was on his way down to the door of number 12, with his pipe in his mouth and the trotters tucked under his left arm.

Christmas Eve

U NCLE DAN CAME UP from Swainbost to see them on Christmas Eve, in the afternoon, in the middle of a snowstorm. Colin and John first saw him from the kitchen window, out on the main road, a small black figure on a bicycle, pedalling against the wind, and when Colin shouted to his mother to come and have a look, she left what she was doing at the range, and – putting her face close to the glass (as though she wanted to butt her forehead through it) – said: 'Now who on earth is that poor soul, or where does he think he's going in weather like this? Tch tch tch! Let's see if he turns in at the village road or carries on up to Galson.'

Through a swirling blizzard, they watched the figure making slow progress between the telegraph poles – watched and waited. He kept disappearing and reappearing; for a long time, between successive flurries, he seemed to be poised in one position and making no headway at all, curved like a small black questionmark over the handlebars of the bicycle; at the head of the road, he vanished into a thick, grey and purple avalanche, so prolonged they thought he would never come out of it. 'He's gone to Galson,' their mother said, but she was wrong – when they caught sight of him again, he was on his way in to the village. '*Aha!*' she said. 'I thought so! Look at him! It wouldn't surprise me, you know, if that wasn't your uncle Dan from Swainbost coming on a visit – him or his brother the Palmy. Only the Palmy is in Peru. That's their style, you know, your father's people, to be gadding about and abroad while the rest of the world is housebound.' She went back to the range, where a

28

dumpling was rumbling in the big green pan – a round, metal patch was studded to the bottom of the pan at one side, which caused the pan to tilt whichever way you turned it, and she had inserted a poker underneath the other side to bring it back to level, and stop the boiling water from splashing out at the top and chasing, in frantic, hissing beads, over the glossy dark surface of the range. 'People with no sense at all!' Raising the black enamel lid, she bent down and peered into the pan, huffing back with her own breath against the issuing clouds of grey steam. The dumpling burped and rumbled heavily inside. She replaced the lid with a clatter and came back to the window. 'It *is* him!' she exclaimed, her head almost going through the pane. 'Didn't I tell you! Look how white one side of him is! Is that a parcel or what is it he's got tied to the handlebars? The Palmy –' she went on in the same happy, excited voice '– The Palmy was in an earthquake in Chile. Your uncle Calum. An earthquake! Houses going bodily up in the air! The ground opening under his feet! He lay where he had landed, anyhow, in a ditch, watching the upheaval through spectacles, and when it was all over he stood up – Look at me! – went like this –' with fastidious fingers she brushed imaginary dust from herself 'blinked all round and said, "*O dear me!*"' She nodded towards the window. 'Here comes another version of the same. You –' she turned to Colin '– go and open the gate for him. Put your coat on, hurry up. And remember to close the gate again after you.'

But by the time Colin had closed the kitchen door, and struggled into his coat and wellingtons, and kicked aside the sacking for keeping out draughts from the bottom of the scullery door, and then, after a series of fierce, two-handed tugs, managed to pull the scullery door open, uncle Dan was already on the other side of it, framed in a white whirlwind of snow, and untying a large cardboard box from the handlebars of the bicycle. 'Colin!' he yelled, above the howl of the wind. 'You saw me coming!' 'We saw you from the kitchen window,' Colin shouted back, and burst out laughing. 'What is it?' uncle Dan asked. 'Your eyebrows!' Colin yelled. 'They're full of snow!' 'Are they?' Uncle Dan looked up, wrinkled his forehead. 'So they are! What a day! But never mind about that. Come and give me a hand with this box here. Hold it up . . . that's the way . . . from underneath . . . that's it . . . both hands under it. Take the strain off the knot.' He smiled at Colin. 'I'll bet you she never expected anyone at the door today, in weather like this.' By she, he meant Colin's mother. Colin smiled back at him and shook his head. Uncle Dan was a small, dark man, but he was as hardy as the steel! He went about in all weathers in a striped blue jacket of one of his brother Myles' old suits (sent to him through the post by uncle Myles' wife; uncle Myles was a minister in Inverness-shire), a pair of corduroy trousers and wellingtons; today, in addition to these, he was wearing an army greatcoat, much too big for him – the points of the collar flew above his ears like wings, the hem almost reached to his ankles. A woollen scarf, wound over his head and knotted under his chin, was only to keep his bonnet on against the wind. He looked like Captain Oates; like the Russian soldier in granduncle Norman's history book after the Battle of Inkerman. Colin watched uncle Dan's hands, red-knuckled, with black hairs on the backs of them, going steadily at the knots on the string. Why weren't they cold? All the fingernails had black crescents under them. One thumbnail was flat; the other curved yellow, like a hoof paring, with an ugly split going down the middle. The clean mark of a recent sticking plaster on another finger; and on the middle knuckle of his left hand, a raised brown scab, the size of a halfpenny, going pink at the edges where it met the skin. Their mother was right about uncle Dan – he didn't seem to feel the cold. As a boy in Bernera, Harris, he fell asleep in a quarry one winter's night, woke up to find one side of his head frozen to the ground. His hair among the grass, stuck solid. He never even caught cold as a result. He was as hardy as the steel! And there was a place on the Swainbost river, at a bend, where he had leapt across without wetting his feet, and no one else could do it, lads from other villages in the district used to come and try, leaving their bicycles at the bridge, but none of them could do it, until at last one or two started to say that maybe uncle Dan couldn't do it either, someone the size of him, that maybe it was a story spread about by the Swainbost folk, who were notorious liars anyway, and when they heard that, four lads from Swainbost went to uncle Dan's house one evening after work, and made uncle Dan put on his sandshoes, and fetched him down to the bend at the river, where by now a crowd had gathered, and he did it again.

When they appeared in the kitchen doorway, Colin in front of uncle Dan, cradling the cardboard box in his arms, their mother was standing in the middle of the kitchen floor with both hands on her hips and her elbows sticking out like a Highland dancer's. Her face couldn't stop smiling. Uncle Dan didn't come all the way in because he was so wet – he stood in the doorway, on the scullery mat. 'I knew it was you!' she shouted at him. 'We saw you out in it.' 'Hello, Mary,' said uncle Dan. 'Who else could it be? I said to the boys. Didn't I? Look at the state of you!' 'Go and put the box on the table,' uncle Dan said to Colin. 'What's inside it?' John asked. 'Groceries,' uncle Dan said, to their mother. 'Take the coat off at once, whatever else you do,' she said. 'My God! Where did you get the coat?' 'From Donald John,' uncle Angus said, grinning up at her. 'Donald John! I thought, my first sight of it, it had come off an army warhorse. When I saw you through the window. Then I said to myself, "No," I said, "it's a relic of the Giant MacAskill's, the family must have acquired when they were in Bernera."' 'What's inside the box?' John asked again, with a whine in his voice. 'First thing I'm going to do,' their mother told uncle Dan, 'I'm going to clip those eyebrows of yours with the scissors. I see you've managed to lodge two small snowdrifts in them since you set out from Swainbost.' 'And Margaret sends her blessings and a happy Christmas and so forth,' uncle Dan said. 'And the same to herself, tell her from me. What's she thinking about, anyway, letting you out of the house with eyebrows like that? Just wait till I see her! Now stop dangling down there, take your wellingtons off and come up into the heat. Hang the coat on a nail where people won't see it and take fright. Are your feet wet?' Behind her, John started crying. 'What's wrong with you, John?' uncle Dan asked. 'Pay no attention to him,' their mother said. 'What's always wrong with him?' 'He wants you to open the box,' Colin told uncle Dan. 'Don't you?' John, his face twisted up, wailed and nodded. 'Well then,' said uncle Dan. 'Why don't we do that? What do you say, John? Will we open it now?' Between hiccuping sobs and gulps, John spoke to uncle Dan. 'I want to see . . . what you . . . *brought* me . . .' he said.

By eight o'clock in the evening, the storm was over. They were all in the upper room – the new room, as it was called – the room in which his father had died; uncle Dan on a high-backed chair in the centre, facing the fire; to the left of him, filling two armchairs with their bulk, uncle John and John the Battler from next door; and to his right, with their long legs stretched out across the carpet, granduncle William's sons, Malcolm and Dolly. Beside them, on the sofa, was Angus Gunn from Aird, who had a brown mahogany face and never said anything; and next to him, on another high-backed chair, their mother, sitting up very straight with her arms folded across the front of her cardigan in such a way that only her two thumbs were visible, sticking out from under her armpits; happy to see so many faces in her house at the same time, and frowning only when her eye happened to land on uncle John. The peatfire in the grate blazed brightly, set quick shadows moving along the walls and ceiling, was reflected in miniature in the glass panels of the bookcase by the door. Two tall oil lamps at either end of the mantelpiece made yellow circles on the wall behind them. It was cosy and warm. Outside, behind the curtains, the night was hushed and still.

Someone asked uncle Dan who Cramanas was.

'Cramanas,' said uncle Dan, bringing his eyebrows together – what was left of them – and the other men stirred and sat forward in their seats like five large schoolboys round a diminutive master. 'Cramanas was the name of a man who lived in Swainbost over two hundred years ago, beside the seashore. There's a small stream – Allt Chramanais – near the shore there, named after him. This is the story. A woman from Uig set out to visit her married sister in Ness. The woman was pregnant, and near her time. She walked all day, following the coastline. By nightfall, with the weather turning to wind and rain, she had reached as far as the shore at Swainbost, when she felt her birthpains starting. She made for the nearest light – Cramanas' house – and begged him to let her in. Cramanas refused;

and the child was born soon after, on the open machair, before she could make it to another house. Another version has it that as she wandered about in the rain and the dark after being turned away from Cramanas' door, she stumbled across the body of a horse, tethered above the shore, struck dead by lightning in the storm – that she hacked open the still-warm belly of the horse with a stone, crawled inside and gave birth to the child there. In any case, she survived the night, and the child – a boy – survived also.

Now this boy, when he grew up, was one of the Lewismen pressed by the Earl of Seaforth when he set up the first Seaforth regiment. He was abroad for a long time, first in the Mahratta wars in India, and after that on the island of Java. And in all that time there was one thing, more than any other, that he kept turning over in his mind – a saying of his mother's that he remembered from childhood. On nights of wild wind and rain, she used to say, "Pity any poor soul tonight who goes to the door of Cramanas." After many years, the soldier returned to Uig. He asked his mother what the saying meant, and she told him. The soldier set out for Ness. Before going to Cramanas' house, he went down into the foreshore and selected a hard staff out of the tangle. It was with this staff that he killed him.'

When the story was finished, no one said anything for a while. Cousin Malcolm and cousin Dolly stared into the fire. Then uncle John said:

'He must have been a big man, the Uigeach.'

'Why?' their mother snapped at him. 'What's his size got to do with it?'

'To do what he *did!*' uncle John said, going red in the face. 'He must have been a big, hefty man to take someone's life with a . . . a *staff!* Big men, the Uig men,' he added, looking round the rest of the company. 'Big, strong, tall men. Hefty.'

'I don't believe that part,' cousin Malcolm said slowly.

'What part?' their mother asked.

'About him killing Cramanas. I don't believe that part.'

'Why *not?*' uncle John exclaimed. 'Man alive! A staff of seaweed would kill a . . . a horse, never mind a man. *What?* In the hands of an Uigeach?' And he motioned with his own hands, as though he were holding a staff in them.

'Do you believe it yourself, Dan?' cousin Malcolm asked.

'Yes.'

'H'm . . .'

'Why not?'

'H'm . . .' Cousin Malcolm's nose twitched, as if a fly had settled on it, and he stared into the fire. With exactly the same expression, Colin had seen him staring into the backs of clocks and watches that people brought along to him to be mended. He could put ships into bottles. 'I don't know,' he said, after a silence. 'It seems to me . . . somehow . . . I don't know . . .'

'What?' their mother asked him. 'The murder itself, or how he did it?'

'I don't know.' The fly had settled on cousin Malcolm's nose again. 'Both, I think.'

'A lot of murders in them days,' John the Battler offered. 'They were forever at it in them days, the Nessmen and the Uigeachs, murdering one another.'

'Look at Mac an t-Sronaich,' uncle John said.

'Mac an t-Sronaich wasn't an Uigeach,' their mother snapped. 'Mac an t-Sronaich wasn't even a *Lewisman!*' she said.

'Was Mac an t-Sronaich before or after Cramanas?' cousin Malcolm asked, before uncle John could start.

'After,' said uncle Dan.

'How many is he supposed to have murdered?' John the Battler asked. 'Fifteen? Twenty-one?'

'Too many,' said cousin Dolly.

'My grandmother saw Mac an t-Sronaich,' their mother said. 'My Uig grandmother. When she was a girl, sixteen years of age, herding cattle on the sheiling. A rainy day, she crouched under the lip of a peatbank when she saw him coming, and he strode by, right over her head. So close, she could hear the rain pattering on his oilskins.'

Cousin Malcolm raised his head slowly. 'He had *oilskins* on?' he asked.

'Yellow ones!' said uncle John.

Cousin Malcolm blinked his eyes doubtfully, and concentrated on the fire again.

'Maybe it was a ghost she saw,' John the Battler suggested. 'A ghost ahead of its time.'

'It was Mac an t-Sronaich,' their mother said. She waited for cousin Dolly to stop laughing. 'He came out of the Uig hills, where one of his caves was. She saw him as plain as I'm seeing you.'

'A big, powerful man,' uncle John said.

'*Big – powerful – man,*' their mother repeated, imitating uncle John's voice. 'Have you ever met or heard tell of anyone in your entire life that wasn't a *big – powerful – man?*' She rounded on cousin Dolly. 'What are *you* laughing at?' she asked him.

'Nothing,' said cousin Dolly. 'Nothing at all.' He blinked frankly at her with his round, watery eyes. 'Not a thing, Mary.'

'Stop that wheeking and whistling, then, every time I open my mouth. Like an old melodeon that's been left out in the rain.'

'I wasn't –' he began. He looked across at John the Battler and the corners of his mouth twitched, but he managed to control himself. Then, because everyone was looking at him, his face went unnaturally solemn. Everyone was still looking at him. 'Ghosts,' he muttered awkwardly, shifting his legs about.

'What's that?' their mother asked. 'What did you say?'

'Ghosts,' cousin Dolly muttered. 'Don't hear much about ghosts these days.'

'True,' said John the Battler. 'At one time in this village itself, dammit, there were ghosts at every turn of the road – you couldn't set foot outside the house for fear of them. Where have they all gone to? That's what I'd like to know.'

From the back of his mother's chair, Colin grinned over at cousin Dolly, trying to catch his eye. But cousin Dolly pretended not to notice that Colin was grinning at him, he kept his eyes fixed on the polished black points of his own shoes, gleaming in the firelight, although Colin knew he knew, because once, in the loomshed, without turning his head, he told Colin to stop sticking the ends of the cardboard bobbins into one another; and another time, during a road tide, when he caught the great crab in a cleft among the rocks, he didn't ask Colin to carry it separately from the ones already in the canvas sack. And when at last he looked up, he didn't wink at Colin as he usually did, but only nodded his head twice, briefly, as much as to say: *Yes, I know, your mother gave me a row, but that's all over and done with now.* Like his father, granduncle William, like his brother Malcolm beside him, cousin Dolly had round, red-rimmed eyes which filled up with water in windy weather or whenever he laughed, and he always spoke to Colin not as a grownup but as though Colin were the same age as himself (although he was as careful as everyone else when speaking to John). He had been a commando in the war. The people at home thought he was in the navy, but he wasn't, he was in the secret commandos – a man from the district saw him on D-Day jumping out of a landing craft and running up the beach over the dead bodies. It was hard to believe that about cousin Dolly, looking at him. But it was true. And not everyone could be a commando. You had to be specially chosen, and then you had to go through trials and ordeals. Iain Red's uncle was a commando. You had to know eleven different ways of killing a man with your bare hands. You had to swim a loch in the middle of winter with all your clothes on, full pack and battlegear, and afterwards climb a mountain. It wasn't Iain Red's uncle, but his sister's husband's brother. And Colin remembered again the Sunday afternoon he came upon cousin Dolly in a loch out on the moor, miles from anywhere, called Loch Ullabhat, and cousin Dolly was swimming in it, up and down, like a seal, first on his face and then on his back, breaking the Sabbath, and not at all afraid of the bottomless hole in the middle of the loch, lair of a black beast, the reason why it could never be drained. Flattened out among the heather on a small hill overlooking the loch, Colin lay watching him; he could not have gone closer for anything on earth. A long, uneasy shiver went through him as he watched the naked man below, at his lonely and private activity; far out from the village, and the sight of other men and all wise people. He seemed to Colin then like someone out of another time, that he would never know; out of the olden times, the long ago, before there were Sundays and net curtains and ministers in motor cars. And he was afraid of approaching nearer. And he was afraid in case the man below should see him. Another long shiver went through him, and he crept back the way he had come. He could not have gone closer for anything on earth.

'All I know is they're gone,' John the Battler was saying. 'Where's the Old Woman of Brae? Where's the Old Man of Loch Bharabhat? What about the ghost at the White Cairns that was so active he used to terrify the very horses in the middle of the daytime? What happened to *him*?'

'Have *you* ever seen a ghost, Dan?' cousin Malcolm asked.

'No,' said uncle Dan. 'I thought I saw the Old Man of Loch Bharabhat once. But it wasn't.'

'When was this?'

'When I was on the day-labouring with Tawse three years ago, over in Stornoway. I used to travel every day then, back and forth, between Ness and the town! –'

'I remember you,' their mother said.

'– on an old motorbike Dubba gave to Donald John next door, after he lost his licence.'

'I used to watch out for you every morning, from the window –'

'Did you?'

'Between seven and quarter past every morning – puttering up the road –'

'That was me. And one morning of weather, much like today's – snow driving down, blowing back up from the ground before it could settle – I was coming to the bend in the road there at Loch Bharabhat, trying to keep the bike to the middle of the road, when a long, gangling figure suddenly materialised out of the blizzard in front of me. *Ah God!* I thought, *it's the Old Man!* – every hair on my head rose on end, the motorbike bucked under me like a live thing, and do you know what it was? – only Angus John Norman's son from this very village, the one you call The Gannet, coming back from having his bollacks tickled for him all night by some girl in Shader.'

John the Battler erupted in his chair and threw his arms and legs in the air. 'Ha ha ha!' he roared.

'Wheesht, Dan,' their mother said, trying not to laugh also. 'The children.'

'Martin the Missionary's daughter!' John the Battler roared. 'He married her an' all!' Everyone was laughing loudly. Colin looked eagerly from face to face. He started laughing too.

'I'll tell you all a good one about her,' John the Battler shouted.

'No you won't,' their mother said.

'No I won't,' John the Battler shouted.

'Remember who might be listening.'

'Right you are, Mary, dammit. Point taken.'

'Look who's laughing his head off!' cousin Malcolm exclaimed, grabbing Colin behind the leg, above the knee, and pulling him, hopping backwards, across to the sofa. 'What are you laughing at, MacGinty?' he asked, putting his other arm around Colin and rubbing his bristly chin against Colin's cheek.

'Nothing!' Colin yelled. 'Aaagh! Nothing!'

'Wheesht!' their mother told cousin Malcolm. 'He doesn't understand anything.'

'Eh, MacGinty?' cousin Malcolm asked, tickling him between the ribs. 'What do you say now?'

'Nothing! Nothing!' Colin screamed, kicking and squirming out of his grasp, almost losing his jersey over his head as he landed, with a thump, on the mat at their feet. He couldn't bear to be tickled.

'Be quiet!' his mother told him. 'And get up from there. Where's the other one?' she asked, turning her body around in the chair, first one way and then the other. 'Where's he gone sneaking off to now?'

'Who? John?' uncle Angus asked.

'Who else?'

'He *was* up here,' uncle Angus said.

'I saw him with these two eyes not a minute ago,' uncle John said.

'Where's your brother?' his mother asked Colin.

'*I* don't know.'

'Where is he, I said. Answer me properly when I ask you something.'

Colin shrugged.

'There he is,' uncle Angus said, pointing underneath the bed. Their mother bent down.

'What are you doing under there, John?' she asked. No answer. She straightened up. 'What's he doing in there?' she asked Colin.

'*I* don't know.'

'You didn't say something to him, did you?'

'No.'

'Are you sure?'

'Yes, I'm sure.'

'Hmf!' She bent down again. 'Come out of there, poor soul,' she wheedled. 'Before you're eaten up by the spiders. Come out and I'll give you a slice of duff.'

'Aah . . . leave him be,' said uncle John. 'He made his own way in there, he'll make his own way out.'

'He's an odd one, isn't he?' cousin Malcolm said. 'Not at all like MacGinty here.' He made another sudden sideways grab for Colin's leg, not looking at Colin as he did so. But Colin was on the alert for him this time, and dodged laughing out of reach. As he did so, he bumped into the back of his mother's chair. She turned on him in a fury. 'Are you going to stop your carry-on?' she shouted. 'This instant?' Behind her wrathful face, he could see the faces of cousin Malcolm and cousin Dolly, both grinning at him, and felt his own face go hot and silly. He hated them. 'Do you want to go down to the kitchen?' his mother shouted. 'Do you? Do you want to spend the rest of the evening down there? Because that's where you'll go, my fine lad, double quick, if I get one more piece of nonsense from you. I won't tell you again.' With a last frown at Colin, she turned to uncle Dan, pointed underneath the bed and confided in a whisper:

'It was the fits he had in the cot when he was a baby.'

'Fits?' said uncle Angus, following the direction of her finger. 'John?'

'Wheeesht!' She gestured a warning towards the bed, then continued: 'When he was a baby. He was never the same after them. That, and falling out of the pram.'

'He fell out of the *pram?*'

'Head first. And the strange thing was, he never cried when he did it. You know how he cries all the time?' Everyone nodded. 'How his face sometimes screws up if you as much as say *Good morning* to him?' Again everyone nodded. 'This time, not a cheep. When my uncle Norman and the other old duffer that was supposed to be keeping an eye on him, Sandy, went over to check was he alive or dead, he looked up at them and said, "Cocoa."'

'*Cocoa?*' said uncle Dan.

'And that was the first word he uttered in his life.'

'Weird,' said cousin Malcolm.

With a great squealing of springs and sighing of cushions, John the Battler sank back into the armchair. 'The Gannet,' he said. 'Dammit, Dan, but that was a good one.'

'Good?' said uncle John. '*Good?* Man alive! That was . . . that was one of the best I heard this year.' He looked round the rest of the company. 'One of the best that *ever* I heard.'

'And did you *say* anything to him, Dan?' John the Battler asked. 'Once you realised who it was?'

'Not a word, John. All power of speech had deserted me.'

'Alarming enough to look at The Gannet in the flesh,' their mother said, 'with that nose and Adam's apple, without the additional anguish of thinking he's a ghost as well.'

'Ha ha ha!' roared John the Battler.

'Will you sit at peace for once in your life,' their mother scolded John the Battler, 'and mind the springs in that chair?' She was only pretending to give him a row; her own face was bright red with suppressed laughter. 'Do you know this?' she continued in a high, trembly voice, turning her back on John the Battler and speaking straight into uncle Dan's face. 'Soon there won't be a chair left intact in this house, with that man's backside bumping up and down in them.'

'Ah yes . . .' said uncle John. (No one was listening to him, they were all laughing.) 'Yes, but there *was* such a man. As the Old Man of Loch Bharabhat. O yes!' He swept his hand out as though he were skimming a stone across a pond, then shook his head and goggled so solemnly at Angus Gunn that in the end Angus Gunn was forced to nod back to him.

'There *was!*' uncle John repeated, shaking his head. 'I *know* there was!'

Angus Gunn shifted in his chair and nodded.

'What?' their mother asked.

'An old man in Loch Bharabhat.'

'So we're told,' cousin Malcolm said.

'He was there!' uncle John cried. 'I know he was!'

'How do you know?' their mother asked scornfully. 'Did you see him? Tell us about him, then.'

'No, I didn't *see* him –' uncle John began.

'Was he a big, hefty man?' A strangled wheek of laughter escaped from cousin Dolly. 'Did he have big hands on him?'

'Are you going to shut your mouth two . . . two *seconds?*'

'Oh, go *on* then. With your tale.'

'Bloody women . . .' Uncle John scowled at the ceiling and bared his teeth so far back that someone coming into the room, not knowing any better, might have thought he was having a quiet laugh to himself at something that had happened a long time ago, when he was in the aluminium smelter in Kinlochleven, perhaps, or on the road between Fort William and Foyers, and Colin could see the black gap at the side of his mouth where he had pulled the tooth out of himself (going *Ngaaa!* into the small square mirror on the sill of the kitchen window, tugging at the tooth, nagging it back and forth, his fingers wrapped in a small facetowel in order to get a better purchase on it, the thumb of the other hand pushing his top lip up and out of the way – *Ngaaa!* – as aunty Annie and aunty Isobel and his granny watched in a huddle from the far side of the kitchen table, and only aunty Isobel daring to speak. 'Why can't you go to a dentist like everyone else?' . . . *Ngaaa!* . . . 'Who's ever going to use that facetowel again?' . . . *Ngaaa!* . . . 'Why don't you –?' . . . *Ngaaa-ha!* . . . and he turned, snorting loudly, the towel held between thumb and forefinger, and showed them the tooth, yellow and black, crowned at one end with pale tusks, that he had just torn out of his own head. Hawking a gob of blood and saliva into the facetowel, he then wiped his mouth with it. 'Dentist my arse!' he said.)

'Go on with what you were telling us, John,' uncle Dan coaxed him.

'What I was saying was . . .' he glared at their mother, 'what I was saying was, of *course* I didn't see him. That's what I was saying. How could I see him and him no longer *there?*'

'Big John's right,' said John the Battler. 'He was never seen again after Dan Nick killed himself at Loch Bharabhat with the car.'

'The Talbot,' cousin Malcolm said.

'I remember the day it happened,' their mother said. 'I was a little girl at the time. He was having a race with someone, wasn't he?'

'With Dan the Post's son,' said uncle Angus. 'There were two cars in this district at the time – Dan the Post's car, and Dan Nick's Talbot. Dan Nick bet Alex Dan the Post a five-pound note that his car was the faster.'

'He was a reckless man, by all accounts,' their mother said.

'Wild,' said cousin Malcolm.

'And what else would you expect?' uncle John exclaimed. 'What else would you expect of a son of Red Finlay from Eorodale? Married to Calum Fox's daughter out of the Pennylands? Her mother smoked a clay pipe. What else would he be but . . . but reckless, him and all his tribe?'

'Anyway, the Old Man of Loch Bharabhat was never seen again after that day,' John the Battler said.

'Yes he was,' said uncle John. 'People were still seeing the Old Man of Loch Bharabhat in the 1920s.'

'Who saw him, then?' their mother asked.

'Stuffan, for one.'

'Rubbish!'

'Didn't he, Angus?' uncle John appealed to Angus Gunn.

'He did, yes,' Angus Gunn replied, and coughed.

'And so did Callan Bobs. On his way home from a fank in Galson. And Murdo Last, who was with him. Go on now.'

'Well . . . I never knew that.'

'You know it now.'

'Stuffan?'

'And Callan Bobs and Murdo Last.'

'O, you can keep *them* for witnesses,' she snapped. 'I wouldn't rely on that pair to see the road under their feet properly, never mind a ghost. Coming back from a fank in Galson or anywhere else on God's earth for that matter. But *Stuffan?*'

'If Stuffan saw him, he was there,' said John the Battler. 'Definitely!'

'No two doubts about it, Mary,' cousin Dolly said. Their mother eyed him suspiciously.

'When they were still plying back and forth between Ness and Stornoway with the horses and carts, that's the generation that mostly used to see him,' said uncle Dan.

'Exactly!' said their mother. 'The end of the last century, and the beginning of this one.'

'The Oats,' said cousin Dolly.

'They used to see the Old Woman of Brae around the same time,' said John the Battler.

'Yes and throughout the war,' said cousin Malcolm. He sounded annoyed as he spoke. 'Yes and *after* the war, during the emigrations to Canada at the start of the 20s. She was still going strong *then*, the Old Woman of Brae.'

'Calum Don's son emigrated to Canada because of her,' their mother said. 'Young Calum Don, the carrier. He couldn't go up or down the Dell brae, alone or leading a horse, but she would appear and start walking alongside him. Not only that, if he was coming from the Ness side, she'd dog him all the way down the brae, until he crossed the mill dam at the foot. She wouldn't go further than that.'

'Ghosts can't cross water,' John the Battler told Colin.

'Anyway, the day he was leaving for Canada, never to return, he was in the back of a cart taking him to Stornoway, and when they came to the Dell brae Murdo Stob's son, who was in the cart with Calum, turned to him and said: "Well, Calum," he said, "small comfort, but at least she isn't putting in an appearance today." "O yes she is," Calum said. "She's just climbed into the cart and is sitting beside me."'

Cousin Malcolm frowned into the fire.

'Some people used to see her all the time,' he said, sounding more and more irritated. 'Now why was that, do you suppose? The same with the Old Man of Loch Bharabhat. He used to stand in the island in the middle of the loch, and certain people – Cleedy from Habost, for example – used to see him all the time. There would be a trail of carts, six or seven carts, one after the other, all going the same stretch of road at the same time, and no one else would see a thing. But Cleedy would see him, every time.'

'It must have been a nerve-racking stage of the journey, this village, in the old days, when you think of it,' uncle Dan said. 'Sentinelled by ghosts at both ends. Hardly were you over the shock of not seeing the Old Woman, coming *into* the village, before you'd be getting keyed up again at the prospect of not seeing the Old Man, less than half a mile *out* of it.'

'There wasn't another village in the island like it,' said uncle John. 'The *island?* No, nor anywhere else in the . . . the *world!*'

'Famous for ghosts,' said cousin Dolly.

'We never had the same class of apparition in Swainbost,' said uncle Dan. 'A small ghost used to appear at the back of Nellie's once in a blue moon, but he was nothing special to look at or speak of, and he didn't do anything, and people mostly ignored him.'

'You couldn't say that about *our* two,' said uncle John proudly.

'*Hundreds* of people saw the Old Woman of Brae,' their mother told cousin Malcolm. 'What's the *matter* with you? Waddo saw her. Mary Bella MacFarquhar. Your own great-aunt *Isobel* saw her. From Melbost. And they all said the same thing. That she was a tall woman –'

'A big, tall woman,' said uncle John.

'– wearing a long, striped skirt, and a plaid fastened at the front with a pin –'

'Big, big in the bones,' said uncle John.

Their mother closed her eyes.

'Why doesn't someone strangle him?' she appealed to the middle air. 'Shut him up once and for all? Why didn't my mother smother him at birth, when she had the chance? Make life that much less trying for the rest of us?' She opened her eyes, took a deep breath, and enunciating each word very carefully, continued: 'A tinker's child died in the quarry. The mother ran demented down the Dell brae looking for help, and then across MacFarquhar's park to the big house. She was a tall woman. *A big – tall – woman.* She was wearing a long, striped skirt and had a plaid over her shoulders. People who saw her running recognised her for the Old Woman.'

'And was she?' asked cousin Malcolm.

'Of course.'

'And the Old Woman was never seen again?'

'Never.'

'She wasn't half mobile, the Old Woman of Brae,' said John the Battler defiantly. 'What?' he looked in surprise at cousin Dolly. 'I'm telling you! She could spring out at you anywhere, dammit, between the township gate at the top of the brae and the corner of MacFarquhar's park at the bottom. You had to be on the alert all the time. Why are you laughing? Why is he laughing, Mary? Now the Old Man of Loch Bharabhat, give him his due, always stayed put in the one place – the middle of the island. Never moved out of it.'

'He moved out of it once,' their mother said.

'When was that?' said John the Battler.

'When Doolan went to throw the stone at him.'

'Doolan?' said John the Battler. 'Is that –?'

'John Murdo Doolan's grandfather, from Lionel. Your own relations, as a matter of fact, on your mother's side, if you didn't know it before. Are you going to sit still now, till I tell you what happened?'

'Fire away, Mary.' John the Battler settled himself back noisily in the armchair and folded his arms high up on his chest, like a footballer in the back row of the team picture. 'I never heard this one before.'

'Listen then. A line of carts was returning from Stornoway to Ness one evening, and Doolan was in the second cart, he was a young man then, and he was drunk. On the haul up from Galson bridge to the loch, he was on his feet in the cart and shouting at the top of his voice that if the Old Man was there again tonight, on the island, he, Doolan, would prove, once and for all, whether it was a real man or not. People in the other carts kept telling him to sit down and shut his mouth – an old man in the leading cart, Tomas, warned him not to interfere with something that wasn't interfering with him – but by this time he was too far gone in his own head to listen to advice from anyone. When the first cart came round the bend at the top of the brae – the loch to their left now, in full view – a shout came back down the line that the Old Man was there again, on the island. "O, is he?" said Doolan, leaping out of the cart, into the ditch at the side of the road, "Then we'll see what kind of a man he is," and he bent down to pick up a stone. "Don't bother to straighten up," Tomas advised him. "He's standing in front of you."'

'God keep us!' said John the Battler. 'What happened then?'

'Even as he spoke, the Old Man – ghost – whatever – seemed to go through him, half-crouched where he was, and dissolve into the air behind him. The stone fell from Doolan's hand –'

'No wonder!'

'– but the three fingers that held the stone never straightened again. He carried them, cramped like a claw, to the grave.'

A red peat detached itself from the fire and disintegrated in the hearth in a bright scatter of sparks and ashes. Cousin Malcolm picked up the the fragments, their glow already fading, one by one, with the tongs, and put them back on the fire. There was a silence.

'I'll send Colin down to the scullery for another armful in a minute,' their mother murmured.

Still no one spoke. They were all looking into the fire. The firelight moved on their faces in a mingling of red light and black shadow.

'I know a story like that,' their mother said, 'and it's a true story. When the long line fishing boats were still working out of the villages at the beginning of the century, they used to clean and cure the skate on the leas above the shoreline, at the foot of the crofts, and this work was usually done by the old men and young girls of each village – old men no longer able to go out in the boats, and young girls not yet old enough to follow the herring fleets to Shetland and the mainland. So that the work would proceed more quickly, an old man and a young girl were usually paired together – they wouldn't have so much to say to one another. In the village of Shader, a young girl was paired in this way with an old man who happened to have six fingers on his left hand. The old man was a slow, deliberate worker, far too slow for the girl's liking, and she started to speak insolently to him – she was a quick-tongued, arrogant girl. Among other things, she said to him: "You'd think, with the number of fingers *you* have, you'd be twice as fast as anyone else." To which the old man made no reply, but a woman from the village, overhearing, came to where the girl was and told her that, sure as what is most sure, a day would come when she'd have cause to regret the words she had just spoken. The girl answered this woman back insolently as well. Years later, the girl emigrated to Canada. She met and married a man from the district of Lochs over there, a fisherman on the Great Lakes. Their first child was a girl. The child was perfectly formed except for one thing. She had no left hand.'

'Man alive!' said John the Battler.

'Her left hand ended in a stump at the wrist.'

'I go to . . . to . . .' said uncle John, and he shook his great head slowly from side to side.

'A terrible tale,' said cousin Malcolm.

John the Battler surged forward in his chair.

'Do you know this?' he said. 'That story sends the shivers through me. To the very marrow. And I don't mind admitting it.'

And Angus Gunn's mouth, too, was open, in the shape of a small O, as though he might say something in a minute, given the chance, or blow out a perfectly formed bubble of spit at the very least. Only cousin Dolly, of the listeners, seemed not to be bothered by the story; a grin had come over his face when John the Battler was speaking, then their mother's eye must have fallen on him, for his face suddenly went straight again as quickly as the Reverend Morrison's face in Flory's house when he raised the teacup to his mouth and saw the lump of soot floating in it. But Colin, too, had felt a shiver go through him at the story of the little girl's hand. It was a terrible story. It was a punishment on the mother for mocking the old man. But it was also a punishment on the little girl, and she hadn't done anything. And that was horrible. But he mustn't say that, or even think it, because God knows your inmost thoughts, and God is not mocked. And if you mock someone who has something wrong with them, you are mocking God. There was a boy in Melbost with white hair and a blue face. But no one ever mocked him. And if you mocked someone with a cleft palate, or someone who was daft, you were mocking God's children and you would be punished for it. And the children who mocked Elisha were eaten by a bear.

Cousin Dolly took a packet of Capstan cigarettes from his pocket and offered them round. 'Haven't seen a Capstan for weeks,' said uncle Dan, taking one. 'Nothing in Swainbost but Kensitas.' 'Kensitas?' said cousin Dolly. 'With the cork tips and the fat, bald butler on the front of the packet? That's not a smoke for a man.' 'Craven A you're thinking of,' said John the Battler. 'The red packet with the cat? They're even worse,' said cousin Dolly. All the men took a cigarette except uncle John. Uncle John didn't smoke. He'd smoked a crab's claw filled with black twist when he was a boy, himself and another boy, Solomon's John, dead of consumption in Canada, and he'd been as sick as a dog, and he'd never smoked again, it was pure poison to his system, he said; whereupon their mother remarked that it was also a good way of not spending money, especially for someone who never put his hand into his pocket in the first place, if he could possibly help it. 'I don't suppose there's anyone in the village who might be willing to sell me two or three packets?' uncle Dan asked. 'I tried Disher's shop on my way up, but he hadn't any.'

'Disher?' said cousin Malcolm. 'I don't know why he bothers to keep a shop.'

'*He never has any*,' their mother mimicked Disher's voice. '*Of anything.*'

'I wouldn't say that,' said John the Battler. 'Run out of Snowfire or galvanised collars, and Disher's your man.'

'*I've just this very day ordered some*,' their mother mimicked Disher's voice again. She could do anyone's voice. 'Mind you,' she said then, in her own voice, 'he wasn't always as slack.'

Uncle John snorted loudly.

'Is it Disher?' he said. 'There was a time Disher would try and sell you the scruff off his own head. That's all there is to say about Disher.'

'I don't know,' cousin Malcolm mused out loud, 'who might have some cigarettes to spare.' He looked at his brother. Cousin Dolly shrugged.

'Dodo, maybe?'

'He hasn't,' said John the Battler promptly. 'I've been, and he hasn't.'

'In that case I don't know,' said cousin Dolly.

'Why do you smoke so much anyway?' their mother asked uncle Dan. 'Your brother was the same. Couldn't go two minutes without a fag in his mouth. Threw things about the room when he couldn't get any.'

John the Battler laughed.

'Remember the little tin washbasin, Mary? When you were nagging him to shave off his moustache?'

'And there's the dent in the wall where he threw a hairbrush.'

'You can see it better in daylight.'

Angus Gunn took the cigarette from his mouth, made a fist and coughed.

'Uh . . . how many . . . packets want . . . buy?' he asked.

Uncle Dan raised his shorn eyebrows, and his eyes widened. 'Did you speak, Angus?' he asked cautiously, staring at Angus Gunn.

'Cigarettes . . . could sell . . . want buy?'

'You've *got* some!' said John the Battler. 'I'll be damned!'

'Heesht, John . . .' their mother frowned at him.

'But he's got fags, dammit!' John the Battler shouted. 'He just said so.'

'Where'd you get them?' cousin Dolly asked Angus Gunn.

'Didn't know *anyone* in the village had fags,' said cousin Malcolm.

'Come on,' said John the Battler. 'Tell us where you got them.'

'That's it,' said Angus Gunn.

And his mouth moved at the corners in a small smile. He had a thin, wide mouth, which he hardly ever opened, going far round on his face – Colin thought it resembled a sea-trout's or a salmon's – and when he spoke, his lips seemed to disappear altogether, seemed to tighten and turn in over his teeth, so that people always had to ask him to repeat himself, uncertain whether he had spoken or not, and then concentrate on the line of his mouth, to try and catch the words as they came out. Only once in his life had he spoken to Colin – when he caught him climbing over his rylock fence instead of using the gate. 'Would you . . . do that . . . own fence?' he had barked out of a brown mahogany face, expressionless as peat, from which the lips had entirely disappeared. 'Then don't . . . do it . . . mine.'

'Could sell you . . . sixty,' he said to uncle Dan.

'Sixty!' said John the Battler. 'I'll be double damned!'

'John!' their mother said.

'That would be fine, Angus,' uncle Dan said quickly, his round, dark eyes still staring at him. 'Fine.'

'Go over . . . Aird now . . . fetch them.'

'You'll do nothing of the kind,' their mother said. 'Send Colin for them.'

'Colin?'

'Who else?'

'. . . he go?'

'He'll do as he's told. Where is he?'

'I'm here,' said Colin.

'What are you doing at that curtain?'

'Playing a game.'

'Come out from behind that curtain, and go and put on your coat and wellingtons. Wait!' she said. 'Dashing off before you know where you're going or why. Now, Angus. Tell him.'

'Go over . . . our house . . .' Angus Gunn began.

'Look people in the face when they're speaking to you!'

'. . . over . . . our house . . . tell Ishbel . . . sixty fags. Say to her I said. Tell her . . . suitcase . . . top wardrobe.'

'Is that all in your head now?'

'Yes.'

'Off you go, then.'

'Can John come with me?'

Their mother bent down, raised a corner of the counterpane and peered under the bed.

'Do you want to go over to Aird with Colin, a ghraidh? A nice walk over to Aird?'

'No.'

'Can I go and ask Roddy Ivor, then?'

'If you want. And remember to behave yourself in other peoples' houses.' She bent down again. 'Do you want a slice of duff, then, a ghraidh? Come out and I'll give you a nice piece of duff.'

'I know why MacGinty wants someone to go to Aird with him,' cousin Dolly said.

'Why?' cousin Malcolm wanted to know.

'He wants someone to go to Aird with him,' cousin Dolly said, 'in case he meets the Aird ghost on the road over.'

Their mother let drop the counterpane and straightened up.

'That's enough of that talk,' she told cousin Dolly. 'Putting things into the boy's head. Now then –'

'In case the Aird ghost creeps up behind him when he's not looking and gets him in the neck.'

'Shut your mouth, I told you. I won't tell you again. Never you heed a word of it, a ghraidh,' she said to Colin. 'There's no ghost in Aird, never was, never will be. All out of his own head. Now tell me again what you're going for.'

'Fags.'

'How many?'

'Sixty.'

'Where are they?'

'Top of the wardrobe.'

'Inside . . . ?'

'A suitcase.'

'Off you go, then. You won't need a torch, there's a moon. Remember to stay on the road. And put a scarf round your neck – the green one on the kitchen pulley –'

'Remember the ghost,' said cousin Dolly.

'Didn't I tell *you* to shut up?'

'You'll know him by his long goat's face and the horns on his head . . .'

'Wheeking *pest!*'

'Colin isn't afraid of ghosts,' said uncle Dan. 'Are you, Colin?'

'Never!' said John the Battler.

'He knows there's no such thing.' said uncle Dan.

'You can go on all you want about ghosts,' cousin Malcolm told his brother. 'You won't frighten Colin.'

'Is it Colin?' said uncle John. 'Colin would go to the . . . the *moon* and not be afraid!'

'As long as he goes to Aird first,' their mother said. 'And no loitering on the way, mind. Straight there and back.'

Going out of the door, he heard cousin Dolly's voice calling after him:

'Have a good look at his feet as well. See if he's got horseshoes on them . . .'

Ivor's house was behind John the Battler's, on the other side of the road. It was known as Angus John Tully's house (after the man that built it. He was a cousin of Ivor's; or his wife was; that was how Ivor got the house) and it was the biggest house in the village. It even had an inside bathroom. To get to it, Colin had to pick his way between the heaps of stones in front of John the Battler's house. The night was quiet, after the storm; the air muffled and soft. It wasn't cold. The snow creaked under his wellingtons as he crossed the road. Everything was still. The world seemed to be holding its breath, after the storm. Even the sea at the back of Aird was still. The moon was shining overhead, with a misty circle round it. It looked blurred and out of focus, as though viewed through a badly adjusted telescope. The moonlight seemed to be melting in a misty blue vapour over the houses and walls and peatstacks. A beam of yellow light, slanting from the window of John the Battler's house, spilled out over the snow and lit up one side of a pile of stones on the far side of the ditch, before fading into the bluish darkness beyond. Inside the house, John the Battler's mother was in her usual chair by the fire; as Colin passed the window, he saw her lean forward and snatch the lid from a small, soot-blackened teapot boiling over on the hob. Streams of tea leaves ran down the sides of the pot; a sluggish brown clot of them pushed out at the spout. With both feet on the bottom rail, hands gripping the spears at the top, he swung himself in on Angus John Tully's iron gate until it stopped with a jarring thud against the roughcast cement pillar. He let it swing back by itself, listening, as he walked up the path, for the noise of the latch scraping back up the catch and chinking into its slot. No one had been in or out of Ivor's house at the front. The kitchen curtains were drawn. A light was on in the scullery as well, but the window was misted over and running with steam. He looked back at the dark prints of his own feet on the path, in the snow. Then he went in.

At first, he thought the kitchen was empty – he had opened the glass-panelled door and advanced as far as the dresser before he noticed Roddy's father, Ivor, sitting in the warm corner beside the range, under the hot water boiler, his feet up on the rail, and reading a book with a brown paper cover on it. A teatowel that had been hanging on the rail to dry was on the floor. Ivor lowered the book before Colin could back out again, and waited for Colin to speak. A stern look came over his face, as though he had just swallowed a spoonful of breadsoda.

'Can Roddy come out with me?'

'At this hour of the night? What for?'

'Going over to Aird.'

'What for?'

Colin told him.

'Cigarettes?' Ivor frowned. 'He's got *cigarettes?*'

'Yes,' said Colin eagerly. 'Hundreds of them.' His voice stammering with eagerness, he went on: 'They're in a suitcase on top of the wardrobe. That's what I've got to tell Ishbel. That's why –'

Ivor jerked his head violently at the ceiling. 'Roddy!' he shouted. At once there was a sound of running feet overhead. Colin stood where he was. He felt stupid.

Ivor had raised the book to the level of his eyes again. The blood raged in Colin's face. Why had he opened his mouth?

He stood in front of the range, feeling embarrassed and stupid.

He wanted to pick up the teatowel from the floor. But if he did that – or stirred in any way – Ivor might lower the book and look at him again.

He knew Ivor wasn't reading. He could tell. Why was Roddy taking so long?

His mother was always telling him not to speak in front of grownups. She was always telling him off for that. Keep your mouth shut. Don't speak where there are people. Speak only if you're spoken to. Yet he'd done it again. Roddy appeared silently at his elbow. He had the knack, when he wanted, of coming and going without making a sound. He looked at Colin and then at his father.

'Do you want to go over to Aird with . . . ?'

Roddy looked at Colin.

'Yes.'

'You don't have to if you don't want to.'

'I want to.'

'Watch yourself, then,' his father said. 'Remember who you're with. And don't be long, do you hear?'

'No.'

'Half an hour, no more.'

'We won't be long,' Colin said.

'D'you hear me?' Ivor said to Roddy. 'Half an hour, I said.'

'How long were you at the kitchen door before you came in?' Colin asked Roddy, as soon as they were out of the house and making their way along by the garden wall at the back.

'Why?'

'No reason.'

He gave Kate Stanton, their teacher, a bad fright once by appearing from behind the blackboard while she was standing at the classroom fire with her clothes hoicked up, warming her backside – she thought she was on her own in the room, and he'd gone back for his dinner ticket, and the scream she gave brought the headmaster's wife, whom very few had ever seen before, to the front window of the schoolhouse, facing the playground, and everyone in the queue for the canteen saw her, Colin among them, a small woman with a blue dress and a cardigan and beads.

'I knew he'd do that,' Colin said to Roddy.

'Who?'

'Your father.'

'Do what?'

'What he did. When I told him Angus Gunn had cigarettes. Didn't you see his face?' He laughed, imitating a grownup laugh; shook his head in the dark, as he had seen grownups do when something amused them. 'I thought he was going to fall off his chair, when I told him.'

'But he's *got* cigarettes,' Roddy said.

'Who?'

'My father.'

'Has he?'

'Plenty. He takes them home from sea. Capstan Navy Cut, bonded.'

'O?' said Colin.

'I've tried them,' said Roddy.

'When?'

'Plenty times.'

'I bet you haven't,' said Colin. He didn't speak again till they were going through the Aird gate. Then he said: 'Maybe he was surprised because he thought no one else in the village had cigarettes, and then I told him Angus Gunn had some.'

'What are you on about?' Roddy said. He started walking in front of Colin, arms curved, legs bowed, like a monkey, padding along.

'I think that must have been it,' Colin said. Now he was talking in a grownup voice as well. His face went stern in the dark, considering.

'Yes,' he assured the back of Roddy's head. 'That would have been it, all right.'

'I tried black twist too,' Roddy said. 'Flory's old man gave me a shot of his pipe.'

'When?'

'It made me dizzy.'

'I bet you never.'

'I nearly fell down. It burnt my tongue.'

'When was this, then?'

'I'll sell you a cigarette, if you want.'

'What?'

'I've got some hidden. In the barn.'

'You haven't.'

'Capstan Navy Cut, bonded. I'll sell you one.'

'How much?'

'Twopence.'

'When'll I get it, then?'

'Any time.'

'I bet you haven't.'

'Come to our house tomorrow. Round the back, so my father won't see you.'

'How many have you got, then?'

'Plenty.'

They came to the first house in Aird. The light from the lighthouse at the Butt had just completed a circle, and they halted on the road, waiting for it to come round again. It glimmered faintly in the sky above Eoropie, like a star on a rainy night, almost fading from sight altogether; then, just when it seemed on the point of expiry, it started to gather strength again, prickling the night sky, it flickered more strongly, growing brighter and brighter, and 'There she goes!' said Roddy, as a long, solid beam of light suddenly shot out over the sea behind the Butt and began to sweep in a steady, raying circle back towards the land, the light from it, at its uttermost extension, passing like a failing shadow of breath over the backs of the houses in Aird, before cutting itself out at the darker land's edge below them.

'I wish the foghorn was going,' said Roddy.

'Alex Dan Handy put his ear to the foghorn when it was going full blast,' said Colin. 'Alex Dan Handy from Port.'

'I would do that,' said Roddy. 'If someone paid me.'

'It nearly blew him off the Butt,' said Colin.

'For a pound I'd do it,' said Roddy.

'He has to have cottonwool in his ear all the time now. The one that was next to the horn.'

'I'd still do it,' said Roddy.

Angus Gunn's house was at the back of Aird, away from the other houses, near to where the peatbanks began. It didn't have a path to it. Across the ditch by the roadside, a wide plank acted as a footbridge. For some reason, it had a round hole drilled through the centre of it. Roddy and Colin followed the prints of wellington boots and a bicycle over this plank, going in towards the house. First they passed a henhouse, brooding under its thatch of snow, and then a peatstack and barn. One side of the peatstack was plastered white, the other side was black. The house was behind that, the outline of a tilley lamp sharp against the window blind downstairs, and an oily yellow square of lamplight on the window of the room upstairs where Red John Gunn, the old mad seadog, stayed all the time, bellowing curses at the crew of the oceangoing transport and thinking Sunday was Wednesday and Wednesday was Sunday. 'That bike was going out, not coming in –' Colin had started to say (he had seen Angus Gunn's bicycle propped against the wall of their own house), when Roddy came to an abrupt standstill. 'Get back!' he whispered fiercely, warding off Colin, who had collided clumsily with him from behind, with a backward swing of his arm. 'Hurry up!'

'What is it?'

'Heesht!' Roddy shoved him hard in the chest, back towards the barn, out of sight of the house. 'Don't make a sound!'

'But what *is* it?'

'Angus Gunn's wife and someone. Don't look yet,' he whispered. 'Wait'll I tell you.'

'Where are they?'

'Heeesht! In the doorway of the byre. The back door.'

'What are they doing?'

Roddy looked at him.

'I mean . . . Who's with her?'

'Purdy, I think.' He looked at Colin again. 'Don't move,' he said. Going down on his haunches, he peeped cautiously out. They were on the sheltered side of the barn. He took a long time. He stood up. 'Now you,' he said. Taking a hold of Colin's jacket by the arm, he pulled him to the corner. 'Don't let them see you,' he said. Colin peeped out. Roddy's hand was tight on his jacket, ready to pull him away. He could hear voices coming from the doorway. He heard a happy laugh. It was Ishbel, Angus Gunn's wife. He narrowed his eyes until his vision trembled. 'I can't see anything,' he said.

'We're in the wrong place,' said Roddy. 'I'm going round to the other side of the house,' he said. 'You stay here.'

'I'm coming with you,' said Colin.

'They'll hear you.'

'No they won't.'

'They will.'

'Not if I stay close behind you.'

'All right then. Stay close behind me and keep your head down.'

'Right.'

'And don't speak. Don't open your mouth.'

'What about the dog?'

'Never mind the dog. Just do as I do.'

'Right.'

'Don't speak, remember, whatever you do.'

'No.'

'Otherwise we're finished.'

'I won't speak,' he said.

'Come on, then.' He dipped into the monkey crouch and sped back the way they had come, as fast as Oliver Twist in the pictures in Galson schoolhouse running away from the orphanage – faster – his shadow on the wall of the barn keeping pace with him. Colin followed, crouching as well. He came round the bottom of the peatstack, breathing hard, to catch a glimpse of Roddy's back already disappearing into a shadow of moonlight between the house and the garden wall at the back. As he scuttled anxiously after him, over the open ground at the front of the house, Roddy's arm appeared at the corner, beckoning impatiently. Colin arrived, panting. 'Through here,' Roddy said, pointing to a gap in the wall. 'Why are you running in that funny way? Come on!' He vanished through the gap and waited, squatting, on the other side, for Colin to appear. 'Now this way,' he said. 'On your knees. Come on!' Thrusting his backside into the air, he crawled noiselessly away, like a large, scampering puppy, following the line of the wall. He could crawl almost as fast as he could run. Colin laboured clumsily after him, on wet hands and knees, straining his head forward to keep him in view. Lumps of snow went down the tops of his wellingtons, his hand flattened a soft, warmish mound of currants; Roddy had stopped at a place in the wall and was peering through it, one hand cupped against the side of his head to keep out the moonlight. Voices were coming from the other side of the wall. He moved over when Colin came up and put his mouth close to Colin's ear. 'Purdy,' he breathed. Colin felt a tickly shiver run down his neck. 'Go on and look.' Colin put his eye to the wall.

He saw them at once, clearly, through the narrow chink in the wall, they were straight in front of him, in the back doorway of the byre. Purdy's back was to him, and Ishbel Gunn was inside the doorway, facing him, her head looking out over Purdy's shoulder. The dark green coat she always wore outside the house was open. Underneath it, her skirt was pulled up above her waist, and she was holding it there with both hands. Her legs were wide apart, and Purdy was standing between them and butting himself against her. In the clear dark of the doorway, her long legs and thighs, thrust out on either side of Purdy and bent forward a little at the knees, looked startlingly white, much whiter than the snow. She had wellingtons on, with the tops folded down, and with every butt forward that Purdy gave, her knees straightened, and her feet, in the wellingtons, seemed to lift off the ground a little. 'I hope you don't do this to your other girlfriend,' they heard her say in a strange, gasping voice, and her head jolted forward on Purdy's shoulder. 'Never,' Purdy grunted. His boots scraped and scrunted on the stone doorstep. 'Poor girl if you do. Now I know what she has to suffer.' 'Never,' Purdy grunted again. 'He's well up her,' Roddy's mouth whispered at Colin's ear. Colin swallowed, but couldn't speak. A queer, sick feeling was going through him, together with a roar in his ears like the sea going back down a pebble beach. The back of his head was trembling.

'I bet you've never seen a woman getting it before,' Roddy whispered.

'Wuh?'

'Better go now, while they're still hard at it.' Colin shook his hand off; his eye still pressed to the wall. Roddy pulled him away. 'Come *on*,' he whispered. 'Before they hear us.'

'You go first.'

'Come *on*, you daft peeping tom.'

'All *right*,' Colin snapped at him in a sudden fury. He crawled away, offended. They didn't speak again until they were back through the gap and standing at the corner of the house. 'Well?' said Roddy. 'What did you think of that?'

'Who's a peeping tom?' Colin asked.

'Nobody.'

'If I'm a peeping tom, what are you? Who was in the lead?'

Roddy grinned slyly at him.

'You're a bigger peeping tom than *I* am.'

'I know.'

'Your breath smells of boiled turnips, do you know that?' He couldn't keep it up. His face broke into a grin, in spite of himself. Flaring his nostrils, he inhaled the soft night air, then started to pace up and down restlessly. He was bursting to talk about what he had just seen. But the words wouldn't come. At the same time, he was beginning to feel vaguely ashamed of himself, now the excitement was over. He scooped up some snow from the ground and started rubbing his hands with it.

'Did you see her legs?' Roddy said. 'In the wellingtons?'

'Didn't I half?'

'I could see right up. All the way.'

'So could I.'

'Did you see the hair on it?'

'Sure!' They nudged one another happily.

'Purdy,' said Roddy. 'What a weapon!'

'Yeah!'

'Like a – a –'

'Like a –'

'What a weapon! I bet you he's still going strong.'

'Do you think?'

'I bet you.'

'Let's go back and look.'

'Don't be daft.'

'What'll we do now?'

'*Do?*' said Roddy. He sounded surprised. 'We'll go into the house, of course.'

'Do you think?'

'That's why we came over.'

'But Ishbel's not *in* the house yet. We'd've heard the door.'

'No, but the old woman is. Angus Gunn's mother.'

'I don't want to see *her*.'

'Keep your eyes closed, then.'

'With her warts and her trembling chin. I don't want to talk to *her*.'

'*I'll* talk to her.'

'And her teabreath and whiskers. Yeeach!'

'What do you want to do, then?'

'Wait here. Till Ishbel goes back in.'

'And when'll that be? I've got to be back in half an hour. And what if Purdy comes round that corner, once he's finished?'

'I never thought of that.'

'Come on. We'll give the scullery door a good bang on the way in. Loud enough for Ishbel to hear it. That'll bring her back in.'

'So long as you go first.'

'Why?'

'The dog.'

'The dog's in the barn at this time of night.'

'Maybe not.'

'Want to bet?'

'No.'

'Here we are.'

'You go first.'

'Give the door a good slam after you, remember.'

'No sign of the dog anyway.'

'I told you that.'

A smell of rotten straw and manure, wafting in from the byre, mingled with the reek of peatsmoke in the kitchen. Ishbel must have left the connecting door open. They edged sideways across the cement floor, towards the yellow line of light at the bottom of the livingroom floor. 'Who's there?' a cracked voice shouted from the other side. 'Is that you, Ishbel?' Roddy found the thumblatch, pressed down on it and pushed open the door. Half of a floursack, used instead of a towel, hung from a nail behind the door. Kelvin Brand, 140 lbs was printed on it in blue letters. There was a sour, damp smell from it. 'Come in if you're coming,' the voice crackled. 'And close that door behind you.' The walls and ceiling of the livingroom were lined with wooden V-panelling, unpainted, blackened by peatsmoke (Angus Gunn's chimneys were notorious for blowdowns, they never vented properly); where the wall wasn't black, the further away from the fire you got, the wood had turned a tawny brown colour, like bogwater in spate going over the stones. Angus Gunn's mother was crouched on a low pouffe by the fire. In a blue haze, she sat tending a line of drying saithe that sagged across the fireplace between two yellow brass knobs screwed into the mantelpiece. Other lines, strung on cuphooks, criss-crossed the ceiling, the salt-stiffened saithe hanging from them by their tails in bunched, orderly rows. 'Little boys from the village,' the old woman crackled feebly, turning her head round far enough for Colin to see the long, yellow face under its black, knitted skullcap, the moustache – stained orange by tea at the ends – scalloping her upper lip, the brown warts on her chin and cheeks with hairs as long as cats' whiskers curling out of them. 'Little boys from the village, I know them by their noses. Roddy Ivor, the bonny boy, and Colin the skulker behind him. I thought you were Ishbel when I heard the door. Gone to Katy Mary's an hour since and more, leaving me here on my own, and only the creature upstairs if I take a turn, and no one to make a cup of tea or fetch my balsam, only the creature upstairs, an hour and more, an hour and a half, and I can't with my bones, the Lord knows what's keeping her . . .' Munching her lips until the point of her nose almost met the point of her chin, she turned back to the fire and picked out of her lap a triangle of steel knitting needles from which the top of a furry grey sock was growing. A fourth needle glinted behind her ear, under the skullcap. 'But what do the young care about the old?' Between her liver-spotted hands, the needles began to click steadily.

'*We* never saw her,' Roddy said loudly. 'Did we, Colin?'

'What?' said Colin. He was staring at the face of Angus Gunn's grandfather, the great church elder and friend of Macbeth, in its large oval frame on the wall. Wherever you went in the room, the eyes of Angus Gunn's grandfather followed you.

'We never saw Ishbel, did we?'

'No,' said Colin, from the window.

'We never saw anyone, did we?'

The only other thing on the wall was in a square wooden frame above the mantelpiece. It was a text: *Hitherto hath the Lord helped us.*

Something – a heavy object – clattered on the floor above, and the old woman stopped knitting. 'Here he goes again,' she moaned into the fireplace. Scarcely had she uttered the words when over her shrinking head, to an agonised creaking of joists and floorboards, six heavy footsteps suddenly tramped across the ceiling, turned and came thudding back, turned and tramped forward again. 'Back and forth,' she moaned, 'day and night, without rest, without ceasing. Creak creak, back and forth, day and night, night and day . . .'

'Red John,' Roddy whispered to Colin. 'Look out for squalls.'

'What if he comes down?' Colin whispered back, gazing fearfully at the ceiling.

'What if he does?'

'I'm getting out of here.'

'And where is Angus, my one and only,' the old woman moaned, 'to go up there and batter him back to his senses? Or the gaddingabout harlot he married, to sweet-talk him back into the armchair with her crooked mouth and serpent's tongue? Campbell by name and Campbell by nature. You'll clear off to the asylum!' she shrieked at the ceiling in a sudden frenzy. 'They'll know what to do with you there! You'll go in the morning, do you hear?'

'It's all right, tell her,' Colin whispered to Roddy. 'I think I heard the byre door.'

'Tie your hands and feet with an iron chain! Put a jacket with no arms on you!'

'It's all right,' Roddy shouted to her. 'Ishbel's coming.'

'Who?'

Colin moved forward into the room. Behind him, the kitchen door opened, and Ishbel came in. Her black hair was down to her shoulders. 'Well!' she exclaimed, when she saw Colin and Roddy. 'Would you look at the pair of them! Large as life and twice as handsome!' She spoke a little breathlessly, as if she'd been running. Her cheeks were bright red and glowing.

A loud yell came from upstairs. The tramping had ceased.

'Go and see to that . . . *creature!*' the old woman quavered. 'Before he brings the roof down on us.'

Ishbel looked up at the ceiling, and her face softened.

'Awww . . . is he on the bridge again?' she asked, in a fond, gentle voice. 'Has he let go fore and aft again, the old seadog?'

'Why are you standing there?' the old woman crackled at her. 'Where were you, anyway, till this hour of the night?'

'None of *your* business,' said Ishbel. The skirts of her dark green coat swinging, she strode across the room and opened the door that led to the stairs and bedrooms. 'Ahoy, up there!' she cried. 'Hallo, the ship!'

'Shitehawks!' a voice roared back at once. 'Call themselves seamen, the ragged-arsed dockside scum! Ha!'

The tramping recommenced, louder than ever.

'Where's she bound, skipper?'

'Useless louseridden bastards, bum peddlers and false alarms! Sheet bend their bollacks to the stern hawser! Lash their mangy hides!'

'You tell them.'

'Skewer their arseholes on red-hot harpoons! Let go slack! Run 'em out sideways, the whole pack and parcel!'

'That's the stuff!'

'Sons of dogs, sons of bitches . . .' The voice subsided, rumbling.

Ishbel cautiously eased the door to, but didn't close it, and drew her head back into the room.

'Well now,' she mused. 'I don't think I ever heard him that loud before . . .'

'Go *up!*' the old woman quavered viciously at her. 'Go up *now!*'

'I think there's a mutiny on board . . .'

'Bastards!' the voice roared out again. 'Is it Dolan Disher? Ha!'

'Who?' said Ishbel. 'Who's he on about?'

'Go *up!*' the old woman quavered. She gestured feebly with her hand. 'Take a stick to him!'

'Is it slant-eyed Sandy from the boglands, Marion the nettle pisser, and all their pox-riddled progeny? Who killed the brown cow? Ha!'

The voice came nearer, to the top of the stairs. Ishbel went through quickly and closed the door behind her.

'Hallo, love,' they heard her voice. 'You don't want to come down here, do you?'

'Dolan Disher!' Red John raged. 'May he be visited with the plagues of Pharoah and the boils of Job! May all the maggots of King Herod and their Harris relations hold a Fast Day prayer meeting in his ringpiece!'

'Yes, love. You go back up now. Back on the bridge.'

'May all the mangy, starving strays of the township slobber and snarl among his entrails on the day of his death, in the absence of driftwood to cobble a coffin for him! Scummy outscourings of an old whore's pisspot! Ha!'

'And I'll bring you a cup of tea and one of his lordship's fags. You'd like a fag, wouldn't you, love?'

'Dolan Disher!' Red John's voice reverberated through the house, shrank the roof, shrivelled the walls, penetrated every nook and cranny:

'May the Lord batter and bugger and blind him! May he be roasted and toasted on the black brambles of hell! And may the greyhounds of hell chase him to utter damnation!'

The knitting fell from the old woman's hands. Jerkily, she raised her head to the ceiling.

'God forgive you!' she gasped, her breath coming and going in quick, unsteady pants. 'Foul-mouthed blasphemer! God . . . forgive . . .'

Ishbel came back into the room. She closed the door behind her carefully, like someone coming out of a sickroom, and turned to the old woman.

'Who's Dolan Disher?' she asked quietly. 'Why was he so angry?'

'You heard him,' the old woman gasped. 'Blasphemer!' She clutched at her chest. 'Fetch my balsam.'

Ishbel narrowed her eyes and looked more closely at her.

'You weren't annoying him again, by any chance, while I was out?'

'But you wait! . . . Just you wait!'

'You didn't go to the bottom of the stair again, by any chance?'

'He's not staying here, hide nor hair of him. You wait till my Angus gets back –'

'You *did*, didn't you?'

'I'll tell him. You wait! Everything!'

'The devil doesn't get tired.'

'Everything! I'll clear him yet, bag and baggage, the red-haired loony. And you with him. You whore.'

'You evil old bitch –'

'You whore! Think I don't know your goings-on, you whore?'

'Evil, merciless old bitch –'

'Grinning Campbell whore!'

'And you look it! God knows, you look it!'

'But I'll tell Angus, you wait. My one and only. I'll open his eyes.'

'I'll close yours, you mouthy old bitch. If you don't shut up.'

'Fetch my balsam, you whore!'

'Fetch it yourself, you old bitch! And not another word out of you, do you hear me? Not one other word.' She turned to Colin and Roddy, her face bright red with anger, and tossing her head as though she'd just walked through a spider's web. 'Poisonous old bitch!' she muttered. 'No end to it.' Gradually, her face cleared. 'So?' she said, smiling at them. 'And what brings the pair of you over to Aird this late at night? Who's the spokesman?'

'Him,' said Roddy, giving Colin a nudge with his shoulder.

'Do you know this?' she said to Roddy. 'Colin's eye hasn't come off me since I came in. Following me everywhere. As bad as the whiskery old sot and hypocrite up on the wall there . . . I wonder why?'

Roddy shrugged, grinning round at Colin. Colin felt the blood rushing into his face.

'Staring, did I say? . . . Do you think he's in love with me?'

'Whore!' came the crackle from behind her.

'Don't know,' said Roddy.

'I think he is, you know . . . Anyway, a ghraidh,' she asked kindly, 'what is it you want?'

Carefully, Colin repeated his message. All the time he was speaking, Ishbel looked straight into his face, without blinking, moving her mouth along with his own, silently shaping the words. When he had finished, she burst out laughing.

'*Where* did he say they were?' she asked, laughing loudly. 'On top of *what*?'

'The wardrobe.'

'That's all *he* knows.'

'She smokes my Angus' cigarettes on him,' the old woman crackled, out of the haze.

'Inside a suitcase,' Roddy added.

'That's what *he* thinks.'

'Gives them to the loony . . .'

'Sixty was it you said, a ghraidh? Wait two ticks.' She went out, not up to the bedroom but down to the kitchen, leaving the door open behind her to give herself light. The old woman moaned into the fireplace, munching her lips; prodded a saithe with her fingers. In less than a minute, they heard Ishbel's footsteps, hurrying back.

'Here we are!' she cried in a high, ecstatic voice. She had three blue packets of Capstan in her hands. 'Have you got pockets, Colin? Wait! I'll do it!' She started shoving the packets down into his coat pockets, one in each pocket. 'Do you love me with all your heart?' she whispered, peering into his face. 'Do you? One to go.' He tried to keep still as her hand, with a packet in it, went under his coat and slid into his trouserpocket. 'Goodness!' she cried. 'How tickly he is!'

'Leave the child alone,' the old woman groaned.

'Now out of here with us!' she cried, ushering Colin and Roddy ahead of her down to the kitchen. 'Step we gaily! Do up the buttons on your coat, Colin, before you catch a cold and start going achoo!

Wait!' she said at the front door. She took a packet of Capstan out of her own pocket, opened it and counted the cigarettes inside. 'Eight!' she cried ecstatically. 'I've got eight! What do you know! Two for Roddy, two for my new sweetheart, two for the old seadog and the rest for myself. Compliments' – pulling a face in the dark – 'of the one and only. Little does he know. Don't smoke them all tonight, boys, keep one for tomorrow, for after the big dinner. So . . .' she stood in the doorway. 'Away you go, then.'

'Cheerie,' said Roddy. 'Thanks a lot.'

'Thanks,' said Colin.

'That circle round the moon means more bad weather.' She looked towards the village. 'I wish I was going with you,' she said. All the laughter had gone out of her voice. 'I wish I was in Saint Kilda,' she said. 'I wish I was dead.'

The door closed in their faces. The kitchen window went dark.

'Well?' said Roddy. 'Are we going to stand here all night?'

'Huh?'

'I'll have to run. Are you coming?'

'I wonder why she said that.'

'She's fed up . . . how would *I* know? Listen –'

'Didn't *sound* fed up . . .'

'Watch your feet going over the plank . . . Listen, I'll buy those fags off you.'

'How much?'

'Threepence for the two.' When Colin didn't answer, 'Fourpence, then. That's a smasher bar.'

'No.'

'Go on. Four penny caramels.'

'No . . . I don't want to.'

When they were back on the road, Roddy said:

'I'll have to put a spurt on it. See you tomorrow.'

'When?'

'See you in our barn, after dinner.' He dipped into his crouch and sped away, silently, like a monkey. Colin ran after him a little way, and then slowed down to a walk. He couldn't have kept up with him anyway. No one could; he was too fast. He was the fastest boy on Tammy's class. Yes, and in the whole school. The older boys never let him into any of their races, because they knew he could beat them. Boys on the Qualifying, like Nero and the Missionary's son and Don Al Graham, who practised in the long playground where all the girls could watch them, and went to the Rural Schools Sports in Goathill Park in Stornoway where they competed against schools with names like Lochcroistan and Fidigarry. But Roddy could beat any of them at running. He could run like the wind. Even Dubba, the long-legged janitor, couldn't catch him, the day the slate fell on his head. Someone had put a slate from the roof on top of the WC door, leaving the door ajar, and the slate fell on Dubba's head and broke neatly in two. And Dubba chased Roddy for it (because Roddy's was the first face he saw, popping up from behind the ashpit), down the length of the school garden and across the allotments at the bottom, then along the bank of the Cross river as far as the bridge, then over the bridge and out to the old slaughterhouse, round that twice and back towards the main road, the pair of them zig-zagging in furious tandem between henhouses and telegraph poles, and up the Cross brae as far as the nurse's cottage, before Dubba finally gave up the chase, coughing and heaving, at the Cross pump, halted heavily with one hand on the pump for support, and with the other scooping handfuls of cold water from the permanently whining tap against his face and forehead; while a little further up the brae, at Dancer's gate, Roddy stood watching him. And Dubba had chased the wrong man in the first place, because it wasn't Roddy that balanced the roofslate on top of the WC door for it to fall on him, he was too small to reach, but John the Coat from the New Road and his pal Watty. John the Coat and Wicked Watty. But Colin knew how Dubba felt then, stalled and spluttering over the Cross pump, his chest on fire, head in a mist and the taste of red cough mixture at the back of his throat, while a little further up the brae, so near yet so far, Roddy Macleod stood watching him. Catch me if you can.

A faint iron clang came over the snow. There he was, at the village gate already and climbing over it. He never opened a gate if he could help it.

But Colin's brother Alan would beat him in a race, if ever they tried. Colin was sure of that. His brother Alan was fast. He ran differently from Roddy, keeping himself very upright, and with his head tilted back. Alan was in the big school in Stornoway now, himself and Calum Pongo. Two lads from the one village in the big school. Mrs Ferguson, old Peter's wife, who was English, had put it into the *Stornoway Gazette*, in the Ness news. Alan was on 1A and did French and Latin, and Calum Pongo was on 1B and did French and Gaelic. They stayed in the Boys' Hostel in Stornoway, and came home on the bus every fortnight. His brother Alan could probably beat Roddy in a race, if ever they tried. Colin was sure of it. Not that Alan would ever have a race against someone younger than himself. He had other things to do. He was better at football than running. If Roddy and his brother Alan ever had a race against one another, Colin wouldn't be able to watch.

Why had Ishbel said that she wished she was dead? Why had she said that? Because she was in Angus Gunn's house? But she was Angus Gunn's wife. Did she want to be with Purdy instead? But Purdy was only fourteen years old, he was still in school, in Lionel. He thought of what he'd seen in the doorway: his heart shrank. What people did with one another. In the night, in the dark. He had seen it now with his own two eyes. His mind refused to come to grips with it. Again he saw Ishbel's head, over Purdy's shoulder; her long, white legs scissoring the dark. Again the faint tremor of sickness went through him; his legs went weak, his breath lurched in his throat. And the next time he saw Purdy in the shop, among the other boys, he wouldn't be able to keep his eyes off him, he would watch him, on the sly, how he stood, how he held and smoked his cigarette, and he would remember everything Purdy said and did, and think about them afterwards and imitate them. And if Purdy happened to say anything to him, or winked at him, how happy that would make him! Or if the chain on Purdy's bike broke, as it sometimes did, and he asked Colin to take the bike home for him! He wanted to do things for Purdy, so that Purdy would take notice of him and let him be near him. He was a hero worshipper. He wanted to adore.

The moon, blurred hub of a misty great wheel, shone down on the world. God was up there. Behind where the moon was. In Australia just now, his aunty Annie would say, they'd be putting the kettle on for the morning sly cup . . .

He was off school with tonsillitis. The nurse had painted his throat yellow. He stood at the window of the front bedroom. Water licked and lapped under the sill, over the white-painted wood. In the dull, weakening daylight, John the Battler's mother passed slowly by, a black shawl covering her head. If there was no world, there would be nothing. No earth, no people. There would be nothing. He tried to think what nothing would be like. The thought was too big for his head to contain. It fretted him, like a vague pain. And if the world had never been, nothing would ever have been. There would have been nothing, ever. The thought almost took his breath away. But God made the world, and all that therein is. But where did God come from? What was there before God? And he made man in his own image, which meant we were like God, and he made the fowls of the air, fish of the sea, and all that pass through the same. The work of creation is God's making all things of nothing, by the word of his power, in the space of six days, and all very good. And when Colin asked uncle Calum who God was, and where did he come from, uncle Calum, seated on the wheelbarrow, said that God simply was, and had been, from always, without beginning or end, ever-present, everywhere. And uncle Calum was a missionary, home on holiday from Chile, who wore his Sunday suit every day of the week, and a collar and tie and polished black shoes, even to the peats, where he would take the suit jacket off, as a concession to the sun, and push the barrow in his waistcoat, which had a shiny silk back and two tapes, one with a metal buckle attached, dangling down. So that was who God was. And the Spanish for God was dios.

Uncle Calum was in Peru now. He was nicknamed the Palmy. Before that, he had been in Chile. He went from the one to the other. Peru was above Chile in the atlas – it was yellow, and Chile was pink – and uncle Calum went from the one to the other, being a missionary. He had been down to the Straits of Magellan ('The Magairlean straits,' John the Coat called them one day, in Tammy's class), and he had been up in the Andes. Letters in his dense, curled, sinister-sloping handwriting used to arrive regularly from wherever he was, thin blue letters with Par Avion on the envelope, hoping everyone was keeping well at home as this found him, and going on to tell the name, in Spanish, of wherever he happened to be just then, the size and population of it, the height above sea level, the summer and winter temperature, the average rainfall and what the main crop was. 'Nothing again today from Oxendale,' their mother would complain, barging back into the house after answering the postman's whistle. 'Another letter from your uncle Calum, but nothing from Oxendale. I haven't time to read this now,' she would add, holding the blue tissue paper at diagonal corners and glaring at it. 'Who can read writing like this anyway? They should have kept his left hand tied behind his back in the infant school.' But Colin used to read all of his uncle Calum's letters, counting the fat-bellied 'a's, following the loops of the consonants, and he often thought of uncle Calum, down there in South America, going from Chile to Peru and from Peru back to Chile, in a black suit and a white Van Heusen shirt and tie and black, polished shoes. Outside a whitewalled house with black, square holes for windows, he sat at a table in the sun, writing a letter home. Behind the house rose a green mountain, capped with snow. But in the street, it was hot. Men went by, riding on donkeys, their legs dangling down. They wore wide-brimmed hats and brightly coloured blankets. It was blindingly hot. A bell tonged in the churchtower. Uncle Calum did not look up from his writing.

He climbed over the village gate, as Roddy had done; let go of the bar at the top, then caught it quickly again as he felt the gate wobble under him. The bolt rattled in its hole. Which way now?

He could stay on the village road, keeping beside the houses with their lighted windows, until he turned out to their own house at John the Battler's loomshed. Or he could take the short-cut across the stream. But the stream was under snow now; you couldn't tell where it was. He didn't want to go into the stream, or into any of the holes of rising water that Smeets had dug out there to clean the cement from the wheel of his barrow. The Big Barney had slid into one of these holes, and gone right under, after stealing turnips out of Smeets's plot ... So he would stay on the road, where all was plain before him. And when he came to their own house, he would not go along the side of the house and then turn the corner blindly, he knew better than that. No, he would take a wide swerve out into the snow, away from the house, and approach the door that way, lest any creature happened to be lurking in the deep-angled dark between the wall of the house and the scullery, waiting to pounce on him the instant he turned the corner and tear at his face with steely, hooked fingernails.

When

JOHN STOOD BEFORE THE fire in granduncle Norman's house. He had taken the new satchel off. Their mother and Maggie stood behind him, looking down at the top of his head.

'Come away now, John,' Maggie said. 'Everyone has to go to school.'

John scowled into the fire.

'Even I went to school,' Maggie said. 'I'll give you a butterscotch if you go,' she said. 'Look!'

'I'm not going,' said John.

He started crying again.

'What'll we do with him?' Their mother appealed to granduncle Norman.

'I'm not going,' John cried, 'and I'm going to drown myself in Geo a' Gharaidh and I'm not going.'

'Man alive, John,' said granduncle Norman. 'This is terrible news.'

'I'm going to drown myself,' John repeated. 'In Geo a' Gharaidh. I am.'

'I've a better idea,' said granduncle Norman. 'Will I tell you what it is?'

John, sobbing softly, nodded his head.

'Take out an education first,' said granduncle Norman. 'Drown yourself afterwards.'

Jacob's cup wasn't a cup at all but a thick, white mug with two maroon lines going around the top. Stamped on its base was a spiked crown with knobs at the end of each spike, and the hole in the handle was so small you could only get one finger through it, which meant, when the mug was full, that you needed both hands to lift it. It came in a parcel from uncle Myles' wife, May; also in the parcel were a dark red herringbone tweed coat with one button missing and the other hanging off a single long thread, a striped jersey and stockings, a pair of brown sandals, and pinafores and anklesocks for Annie. The sandals and stockings went to his brother John; so, although it was too big for him, did the striped jersey. But the mug and the tweed coat were Colin's; and the first day he went to school, Jacob's cup, as it was called, went to school with him, and sat on a shelf in the cookery room between Peggy Ann Macritchie's cup (red and yellow flowers) and Donald John Graham's mug (A Present From Wick). This was before the canteen was built, when they still got cocoa at playtime, out of a gleaming white boiler that made your face go small and long if you looked at yourself in it. Before Bella Babs, in her green overall, one sleeve rolled up past the elbow, took the lid off the boiler, plunged her arm in and started filling the cocoa cups, the class had to sing a psalm. *I to the hills will lift mine eyes.* 'After three,' Kate Stanton said, spreading her arms wide. The windows of the cookery room needed a long pole to open them. Poised beside the boiler, Bella Babs waited patiently, soup ladle dangling. Through the high windows, the blue sky went far away. *Behold, He that keeps Israel, He slumbers not nor sleeps.*

Jacob was their first cousin, uncle Myles' son. He was also the son of Isaac in the Bible, whose father was Abraham, and he lived on the mainland, in Inverness-shire, in a place called Knockglass, where uncle Myles was the Free Church minister. They'd never seen Jacob, except in photographs. There were two photographs of him on a chest of drawers in their house – one, on his own, in a chair, smiling, with a tartan tie and freckles on his nose, his hair flattened to one side but crested at the top of the parting; two, in the same chair, with the same smile, but with his sisters on either side of him. His sisters had identical dresses on; they were standing. They were older than Jacob, and the younger one, Catherine Grace, was bigger than the older one, Margaret Joy. Uncle Myles called Jacob after Jacob in the

Bible; his other names were Manson, after his mother's father, and Walters, after the doctor who brought him into the world. 'JMWS,' mused John the Battler, when Colin told him. 'You wouldn't catch me trying to carve that on a henhouse door.'

Kate Stanton –

('Everybody's teacher,' said John the Battler. 'Since time began.')

– had a squashed, jowly face, black hair that sprang in places out of the hairnet, brown eyes that seemed darker than they were because of her eyebrows and eyelashes, and a trick, while writing on the blackboard, of scratching her left buttock with her left hand, simultaneously. She was his fourth teacher in primary school. ('She taught Angus of the Bens,' said John the Battler. 'She taught your grandfather.') In the infants' class they had Miss Maciver, who shouted in English all the time at everyone except Alasdair Angus Morrison, who was related to her. Then they had the headmaster's wife, who didn't count, and then a small, soft-spoken woman from Carloway who told Colin to stop nagging her for another book, please, as the rest of the class hadn't finished Book One yet, and he'd already had Book Two home with him, and Books Three and Four, and he couldn't have another book because there wasn't one. *Now go back to your seat, please, and stop following me about the room and tugging at the back of my cardigan.* After the small woman from Carloway they had Miss Murray.

Miss Murray was lovely. She had black hair, not like Kate Stanton's, but going down to her shoulders, and little pearls in her ears, and she was lovely. She was from the next village but one. Colin wanted Miss Murray to be related to him, because her surname was the same as his father's, but when he asked in his granny's house one afternoon if she was, they all started talking at once, aunty Annie at the stove, his granny at the dresser, uncle John in the doorway that connected the house and the barn, aunty Isobel (unseen) from the livingroom, arguing and putting one another right, raising their voices, and Maggie Dods, who happened to be in the house at the time, putting in her spoke from the armchair next to the stove, the best seat in the kitchen (a cushion at your back and a small rug his granny had made doubled under you), and they were still at it when

Colin went home for his tea, but he gathered amid the hullaballoo that he wasn't related to Miss Murray at all, or if he was it was far removed, and likelier to be on Miss Murray's mother's side than the Murrays, or his own great-grandmother's people in Eoropie, if they were the same Macleans. Then he got scrips.

Scrips was impetigo. Colin's skin went on fire, red watery lumps appeared all over him which turned to scabs, he had to be dabbed three times a day with gentian violet, and wore woollen gloves in bed at night to stop him scratching himself in his sleep. It didn't stop him rubbing his face in the pillow, though, gently at first, then more and more urgently, until John, who was in the bed with him, would sit up smartly in the dark and shout peevishly through the wall to their mother: 'I can't sleep. He's doing it again.'

He wasn't allowed to go to school; and when the other boys came home from school he wasn't allowed out to play with them. It was a long time. He spent it in the new room. Roddy Macleod would sometimes appear at the window facing in to the village, stare in at him and laugh, because of the gentian violet, which was purple, and the scabs, which were yellow. Colin would glare out at him, ask him what he wanted, tell him to clear off; then he would start laughing himself, and the two of them would stand laughing and pulling faces at one another through the glass. Another time, the Big Barney appeared at the same window, with a boy from Galson whom Colin had never seen before, who had a white patch on one side of his head where the hair should have been. The boy from Galson didn't want to look in, but the Big Barney made him. When Colin crouched behind the bookcase to hide from them, they left the window facing in to the village, walked round the end of the house, and started staring in at him through the window facing out to the main road. And John told him that when Miss Murray now took the register for the big class, instead of shouting 'absent' at his name, the boys all shouted 'scrips'.

The brown corduroy polka jacket came in a parcel from J.D. Williams, The Warehouse, Manchester. It had a picture of a warehouse on the label, and their address, and the letters COD in red underneath. Full of excitement, he stood at the wardrobe mirror.

'Stand still!' his mother told him, brushing at his hair with a spiky wire brush. Grey short trousers; grey woollen stockings, turned down at the tops. His brown shoes gleamed with Cherry Blossom shoe polish. But the neck of his jersey was too slack; the collar and top two buttons of his shirt were showing. The jersey had belonged to his brother Alan, and was still too big for him. 'Wait,' said his mother, and she took a safety pin from her overall and fastened it at the back of the jersey, to keep the neck tight. 'That'll do till you come home,' she said.

Back in school, he was put on Kate Stanton's class. Miss Murray taught the little and big infants; after that you went to Class One and Kate Stanton. She also had Class Two. Class Three was Miss Mackenzie, who was beautiful, classes Four and Five were Tammy. The last class was the Qualifying, taught by the headmaster. When the bell went, he'd gone into the big infants' line as usual and followed the little infants into the school, past the headmaster's room and Kate Stanton's room and the boys' cloakroom across from it that didn't have a door (a brown corduroy polka jacket, identical to his own, among the little infants, had his brother John's head on its hollow stalk of a neck emerging from it), and he was on his way up the steps to the infants' room when the headmaster called out his name and told him to stay where he was. Everyone else went in, and he was left alone on the steps. The headmaster went into the infants' room, and came out with Miss Murray. They stopped in front of Colin and the headmaster said to Miss Murray didn't she think so, and Miss Murray looked at Colin and said *Yes, O I'm sure, yes,* and went back into her room, leaving him out there with the headmaster. Goodbye to Miss Murray.

Kate Stanton never said a word when the headmaster took him into her classroom. She didn't even look at him. Without taking her eyes off the headmaster, she pointed to an empty desk, then followed the headmaster out of the room. The door closed behind them.

'What are you doing here?' a boy called Snitchy asked, as soon as the door had closed.

'Yes, what's leaving you in our class?' another boy, John the Coat, wanted to know.

'I don't know,' Colin said.

The whole class was looking at him. The ones at the front had turned round in their seats. Some heads on Class Two were looking across as well. He sat down in his seat. He was pleased.

He didn't know why, jumping the big infants' class, he had been put in Kate Stanton's class.

'Because he's so clever,' Cathy Fat from his own village said. 'He is,' she said. 'He can read the newspaper.'

'He can't tie his shoelaces,' Roddy Macleod said.

'Yes I can.'

'He can't put his wellingtons on the right feet. His mother has to show him how.'

'Clever Colin,' Joan Handy said, sniffing through one nostril and tilting her head to one side like a hen in a doorway. She was from his village too. She was a year older than him.

Everyone on the class was a year older than him.

He studied the top of his desk, the clean, grainy surface of the wood. It was a new desk. Were they still watching him?

Roddy Macleod was a year and five months older than him. So was the Yank. Yet here he was, on the same class as them.

He took his schoolbag off, and put it under the desk, between his feet. He felt very pleased with himself.

Kate Stanton came back into the room, and a lesson began. It was Arithmetic: sums. Kneading her left buttock with her left hand, she wrote six sums with a chalk on the blackboard. Colin had never done sums before. Bewildered, he copied down on his slate numbers with two figures, numbers with three, that he didn't understand. Once he'd done that, he couldn't do any more. He sat staring at the sums, and the two lines under each sum with the spaces for the answers. His face went hot, a hollow fluttering started in his stomach. But Kate Stanton would know he couldn't do sums. She was with Class Two. Maybe she'd forgotten he was new in the class. Flora Annie in the next desk put down her slatepencil, briskly sprinkled water from a small bottle that had contained veganin tablets onto her slate, stopping the mouth of the bottle with her finger to make the water come out in drops, briskly cleaned her slate with an old facecloth, began again. Kate Stanton came down the room from Class Two, and moved slowly between the desks. She was old. She had been his mother's teacher. She went past his desk, then came back and stood over him.

'Well, my friend?'

She bent down, creaking under her clothes, and wrinkled her forehead at his slate, peering and frowning. Her breath smelled of tea and peppermints.

'Well?' she said. 'Are you still on holiday?'

Colin's heart started beating very fast. He couldn't speak.

'Why haven't you done any of your sums?'

'Please miss,' he said at last, 'I can't.'

'Why not, my friend?'

'Please miss, I don't know how.'

She straightened up, making a different creak under her clothes, and he felt her fingers removing from the back of his jersey the safety pin his mother had put there in the morning to keep the neck tight. 'What's this?' she asked, holding up the open safety pin in her hand. Without waiting for an answer, she jabbed the pin into Colin's shoulder, through the corduroy polka jacket. Frightened, Colin jerked away from her, and put his hand on his shoulder. She jabbed the pin into the back of his hand. 'Aobh!' he yelled out, before he could stop himself. One or two on the class laughed when he yelled out. Class Two was silent. 'Put it in your pocket, my friend,' Kate Stanton said, closing the safety pin and handing it to him. She caught up his hand in hers, examining where she had stuck the pin in it, peering and frowning. 'Blood of the black March cockerel,' she said. 'It'll heal before you marry.'

She went to the cupboard and came back to his desk with a reading book, a Simple Arithmetic book and a speller. 'Tell your mother to put covers on all three before tomorrow, my friend,' she said.

One other thing happened, at the end of the day. Miss Mackenzie's class, through the partition, burst into song.

'O nach aghmhor . . .' they sang.

Instantly, Kate Stanton was on her feet.

'Are we going to let them do this to us, my friends?' she shouted, waving her arms about.

'No miss,' Classes One and Two shouted back.

'Listen to them!' Kate Stanton shouted.

> le cridhe suamhnach,
> bidh mi ri gluasad,
> gu eilean suairce,
> nan cruachan monach . . .

'We have a better song than that,' Kate Stanton shouted. 'Haven't we, my friends?'

'Yes miss,' both classes shouted back.

'What song have we got that's better?'

'Leis a' Lurgainn!' both classes shouted.

'On your feet!' Kate Stanton shouted, and with a terrific clattering of wooden seats, everyone stood up.

'After three!' she shouted, waving her arms about, her face squashed and distended in a smile as if a giant tongs were squeezing it.

> Leis a' Lurgainn, O hi,
> Leis a' Lurgainn, O ho . . .

'Louder!' Kate Stanton shouted. 'Let them hear you!'

> . . . beul an ainmich, O hi,
> 's fheudar falbh le cuid sheol . . .

'Verse two!' Kate Stanton shouted. 'Tarsainn Eirinn, O hi . . .'

> . . . Chan fhaic mi 'n fhaochag,
> no 'n duilisg chaomh ann . . .

Miss Mackenzie's class sang sweetly on the other side of the partition. '*Now!*' Kate Stanton shouted. 'They still can't hear you!

> Tarsainn Eirinn. O hi,
> Muir ag eirigh, O ho . . .

'Louder!' Kate Stanton shouted. 'We'll show them!'

Why did you take the pin out of your jersey?' his mother asked him when he got home. 'Where is it?'

'I'm on Class One now,' Colin told her. 'Kate Stanton's class. I've got three books, and you must put covers on them before tomorrow.'

'How did you manage to take the pin out of your jersey?' she asked. 'Where is it?'

Later, on his way to granduncle William's house, he was stopped by Alice Arabella Finlayson from the manse. She had a bony red face, a loud joyful voice and a big nose. Her spectacles had no rims on them. She was holy.

'Wasn't I going to come up to your house after the gale, tell your mother!' she yelled – her voice between a laugh and a scream. 'But I didn't. What a night! What weather! Were you afraid in that wee flat house? But God is good. "O protect the wee flat house and all that therein is through the wild watches of this night." I prayed to Him, and brother Evander prayed too. "Get up, Evander!" I said to him, "Get up and get down on your knees!" and God heard our prayers, and in the morning, lo and behold, not even your ashbucket was missing!' She caught Colin by the arm and looked straight into his face. 'Not a scrip to be seen!' she yelled. 'Are you glad?'

Cousin Dolly was working on the wall at the front of the house.

'Yes, I had Kate Stanton in school,' he said. 'Everyone had Kate Stanton in school.' He laid down the trowel and grinned. 'Why?'

'Where's Malcolm?' Colin asked.

Cousin Malcolm was in the scullery.

'MacGinty!' he said. 'Come here till I show you this plan.'

Colin took the Simple Arithmetic book in its brown paper cover from under his arm and put it on the table, on top of the plan.

'Can you show me addition and subtraction?' he asked. 'Before tomorrow?'

Milly moved between the scullery and the kitchen. She put pancakes with butter and red jam in front of them, cups of tea. Malcolm's finger moved slowly up the column of figures. It stopped at the top and carried one over to the next column.

'Do you see now?'

Colin stared numbly at the page.

'Go on,' said Malcolm. 'Tell me what you do next.'

'If you would be so good, boys, as to shift your books and paraphernalia to the other end of the table,' said Milly, 'I need to get to the range. Just a minute!' She picked up the blue writing-pad with lines from the table and glared at cousin Malcolm. 'Is this my writing-pad you're using?' she asked.

When Milly went to Glasgow to visit her sister Agnes, she brought all the Kitty's Favourites back for Colin and John. These were picture cards of famous footballers, numbered from one to forty-eight. The cards came in packs of five, enclosed in rice paper which was double-stapled on one side, and they weren't in any particular order – a pack, once the staples were prised open and the rice paper removed, might contain Peter Docherty (Ireland), Willie Woodburn (Scotland), Tommy Lawton and Stanley Mortenson (England) and then Peter Docherty again. The rarest card was number forty-eight – Tommy Lowry (Wales). Only one boy in school had Tommy Lowry – D.M. from Swainbost, who, showing them Tommy Lowry in the playground, wouldn't let the card out of his own hands. But among the Kitty's Favourites that Milly brought back from Glasgow was a single Tommy Lowry! Colin and John found themselves with a complete set of cards, including Tommy Lowry! They also had four George Youngs (number one, captain of Scotland), and three of Wally Barnes (Arsenal and Wales) with his bald head. One day Colin asked John for a look through the cards. Tommy Lowry was missing.

'Where's Tommy Lowry?' he asked.

John had given him to Alan.

By trickery and deception, Alan had taken Tommy Lowry from John. Now he had a full set of Kitty's Favourites and Colin didn't.

Ever since his appendix burst and he'd nearly died, no one was allowed to touch John or raise their voice to him. He had a scar on his belly from the hospital going right across.

Colin went down to his granny's house. Alan was standing at the peatstack, between the wall and where the cart was. 'Where's

Tommy Lowry?' Colin cried, 'I want Tommy Lowry back,' and rushing at Alan, he started pounding him on the back with both fists. Alan, trapped between the wall and the end of the peatstack, half-crouched away from him, with one arm across his face, not fighting back. Uncle John and Old Peter the Captain stood happily watching. 'Let them fight, woman!' Old Peter bawled at their granny, who, from the door of the byre, was shouting at uncle John to put a stop to it, before Alan came out of his crouch and hit Colin in the face, knocking him backwards over the trams of the cart. 'On your feet, Colin!' Old Peter shouted, and when he got up from the ground, where he had so suddenly and unexpectedly found himself, Alan looked him in the eye and then hit him in the stomach. Colin lay on the ground, on his side, curled up, his knees touching his chin; all the breath knocked out of him. The world was very small. On a blade of grass before his eyes, a tiny black insect teetered and clung. Alan caught him by the forelock, hauled him to his knees and asked was he going to stop it? *Say yes! Yes,* he gasped. *Again!* Alan twisted the forelock. *Yes yes,* he screamed, tears scalding his eyes. 'You've got plenty of temper but not enough beef,' Old Peter the Captain said, giving Colin a consoling pat on the shoulder. 'Fighting someone three years older than himself!' uncle John snorted. His grandmother appeared with a cup of milk. 'Drink this,' she said, in a trembly voice. 'Drink this for the good of your body and of your soul.' And that was the story of Tommy Lowry.

Old Peter the Captain's beard was yellow about the mouth and going grey further out. Wiping clots of buttermilk, slobbered straight from the bowl, out of his beard with the flat of his hand, he spread his arms wide and sang:

> O God of Bethel, by whose hand,
> Thy people still are fed . . .

His voice, surging, tremendous, came back from the walls, soared up to the ceiling of their granny's kitchen. It was the Communions time; the kitchen was full of cooking smells and Christians. 'Never a singer like him,' said granny's cousin Daniel from Uig, when Old Peter the Captain had finished. 'Glorious! A gift from God!' said

Alice Arabella Finlayson. 'To hear you sing, Peter,' said Murdoch of Melbost, 'is to be granted a foretaste of Paradise. When the tongue of the dumb shall sing, and the lame man leap as an hart. When of our earthly vanities, naught but singing shall remain.' In Murdoch of Melbost's beard, streaks of soft-boiled breakfast egg coagulated downwards from his nether lip to join bits of lint, crumbs of crowdie, mahogany teastains. Aunty Annie, after shaking hands with him, excused herself and vanished through the barn door. It was Communions Friday. The Christians were in their Sunday clothes. Loud retching noises came through the barn door from the direction of the byre, where aunty Annie, one hand on Maddy the cow's rump, the other folded across her body, was vomiting into the stone drain. 'Cold in the stomach ... not been too well ...' aunty Isobel whispered rapidly into the silence, and they all started talking at once. 'But that's terrible! Terrible!' said Alice Arabella Finlayson. 'Has she tried breadsoda?' Murdoch of Melbost wanted to know. 'Away with your breadsoda!' said Old Peter the Captain. 'A bowl of hot milk with butter and black pepper in it! That's what she needs.' In the byre, aunty Annie straightened up, glassy-eyed, but kept her hand on Maddy's rump. 'I didn't make it outside,' she said feebly to Colin. 'O Lord! Go to Noony's house –' (a neighbour who had a weak stomach) '– as fast as your legs can carry you, and tell him that Murdoch of Melbost is in the village, and could be heading his way.'

'If you think Kate Stanton is bad,' said cousin Dolly (although Colin hadn't said a word about her) 'wait till you get to Tammy's class.'

'Why for once in your life can't you take these boots off in the porch?' Milly complained.

'Tammy?' said cousin Malcolm. 'I remember him once firing a blackboard duster at Maggie Bell's daughter, it nearly took the head off her.'

'*Scum of the earth!* he used to call the Dell boys,' said cousin Dolly. 'Mind you –' carrying his cement-whitened boots, enemies of beetles, strangers to dubbin, in one hand, and heading on stockinged feet for the porch '– with one or two of us, he had his reasons.'

'Which ones?' Colin asked. From the black doorway of the porch, silence.

'Which ones?' he asked cousin Malcolm.

'The ones that couldn't do arithmetic,' cousin Malcolm replied.

Two boys from the tinkers' encampment in the Dell quarry came to the school. They were brothers. Their names were Jacob and Isaac, and they were put into Kate Stanton's room, Jacob on Class Two and Isaac on Class One.

Separated by the length of the schoolroom, the tinker boys kept looking for one another, and there was nothing Kate Stanton could say or do to stop them. She wound a yellow duster with which she sometimes cleaned the blackboard round Isaac's hand, to make him stop biting his thumb; and when a transparent skein of snot emerged from Jacob's nose, lengthening like elastic, until it almost reached the top of the desk, with no effort on Jacob's part to snuffle it back up or wipe it away on his sleeve, she stood before him (he was in a front seat), moved her feet as if pedalling a bicycle standing up, made a sparring motion with her hands, then rushed out of the room and returned from the cloakroom with a scouring cloth out of Dubba the janitor's bucket. 'Wipe your nose in that, my friend,' she told Jacob. 'And keep wiping it.'

'Jacob,' she said then, in a gentler voice. 'Jacob is a name in the Bible. Can you tell me, Jacob, who Jacob was, in the Bible? . . . Isaac, then?' she said, when Jacob didn't speak. 'Isaac is in the Bible too. Who was Isaac in the Bible, Isaac? In the Old Testament? . . . He was Jacob's father, wasn't he?' she said, when Isaac didn't speak either. 'And who was Isaac's father? Anyone?' Donald Finlay on Class Two put his hand up. 'Abra-*haam*,' he said, pronouncing it the Gaelic way.

'*Abe*-raham,' Kate Stanton corrected him.

And speaking in the same gentle voice, she told them the story of Abraham and Isaac.

God told Abraham to sacrifice his son Isaac to Him. It was a test. God was testing Abraham to see if he feared Him enough to kill his only son. But also to see if he loved Him more than his only son, because you must love God more than anyone or anything in the whole world, because God loves you. So Abraham took Isaac with him up into a mountain, Isaac carrying the wood, Abraham carrying a knife and a light for the fire, and up they went into the mountain and Isaac said, 'Where's the lamb for the sacrifice?' and Abraham said, 'God will provide the lamb,' and he bound Isaac and placed him on the pile of wood, and he was just going to slit Isaac's throat when God stopped him. Abraham had passed the test. There was a ram nearby with his horns caught in a thicket, and he sacrificed the ram to God instead. God was always testing people in this way, Kate Stanton said, to see if they feared Him and were obedient and loved Him. Little children too. So even when you think God is being cruel, He isn't really, he might only be testing you, or letting the Devil tempt you, as he did Job, because God is good, He made you, and He can do what He likes with you, visit you with boils or scrips if He wants, out of His mere good pleasure, and just as your father and mother and even your teachers sometimes do things to you which you think are bad and cruel, but are really for your own good, so it is with God; and just as you obey your father and mother, even when you think what they are doing to you is bad and cruel, so you must fear and obey God, only more so, because God loves you more than your father and mother, and God loves everybody.

At the morning playtime, the two tinker boys stood by themselves in a corner of the playground; Jacob with his head lowered and turned towards Isaac, and Isaac looking out into the playground with eyes as quick as a bird's that went everywhere and stopped nowhere. Colin raced past them once or twice, doing Tweedie's lorry. Without letting on, he kept watching them, and once he saw the small one, Isaac, say something very rapidly to Jacob, and whatever it was he said made Jacob's head droop even more. Back in the classroom, Jacob was taken out of Kate Stanton's class by the headmaster, and put into Miss Mackenzie's class on the other side of the partition. He kept looking round for Isaac as the headmaster ushered him out of the room, and Isaac stood up, ready to follow his brother, until Kate Stanton told him to sit down again.

When dinnertime came, and the tinker boys didn't appear in the cookery room for cocoa, Kate Stanton sent two of the big boys out to look for them, but they were nowhere to be seen. It was the Rebel, standing first on the hotwater pipes, then on the radiator and finally in the big window itself, who first caught sight of them, the tops of their heads, running back up the road towards the Dell quarry; running not on the road but in the deep ditch beside the road with the drystone dyke on the far side of it; dodging from side to side of the ditch as it narrowed and widened like a pair in tandem, and Isaac was in the lead.

'We won't see *them* back in school again,' Joan Handy said, sniffing through her nostrils and tilting her head to one side. She took a sip of cocoa.

'Good riddance to bad rubbish,' she said.

Walking home from school at four o'clock, they saw Jacob again. He was standing at the mouth of the quarry, beside a bender tent, and seemed to be shyly waiting for them. A little girl was beside him. More bender tents of green and brown stretched canvas were inside the quarry. The peat fires in front of each tent were banked up on stones, cooking pots and kettles suspended over them on iron bars. In the peatsmoke that blew low over the gravelly floor of the quarry, lean snarly dogs loitered and scratched themselves; shaggy brown horses, their tails sweeping the ground, nuzzled and clipped one another's necks, and ignored the dirty-faced, barefooted children crawling and tumbling among their legs. In the ashes of one fire, a child with nothing on but a short jersey sat examining what looked like a tin whistle. And Colin saw the big girl who had been in their house with her mother, selling tin mugs and pails. She was still wearing the same light-blue frock she'd had on then, although his mother had given her mother a telling-off for that (*'Keeping the girl in a child's frock and her almost a woman!'*) and two dresses for her out of the big bottom drawer in the wardrobe. Black hair tangled down to the girl's shoulders; her face, arms, legs were brown as an Indian's. 'Walk faster!' Roddy Macleod told Colin. 'Stop looking at them!' They were almost past the quarry and starting down the Dell brae when they saw Isaac. He was on horseback; perched on the horse's neck, rather. Gripping the mane in both hands and kicking with his heels, he urged the horse into a trot, went around two springcarts at the back of the quarry, disappeared behind a bender tent, reappeared crouched over the horse's neck, and came up the quarry almost at a gallop to where Jacob and the little girl were. There, he brought the horse to a halt, and shot one glance out at them from under the man's cap he was wearing on his head; then, heels kicking, hands working, he turned the horse and went back down the quarry again.

'I'll speak to Jacob tomorrow, if they come back to school,' Colin thought to himself. 'I'll tell him I've got a cousin Jacob on the mainland . . .' But Isaac and Jacob didn't come back to school the next day, or the day after, or the day after that. They never came back to school again.

Abraham begat Isaac, Isaac begat Jacob. Begat was another strange word. It meant you were someone's father. In Colin's own family, Alan John (his Swainbost grandfather) begat Angus (his father) who begat Alan, Colin, John and Annie. In the Maciver family, number 4 Aird, all the men were called Donald, going back to the great-grandfather, so that Donald begat Donald begat Black Dan begat Donald, Donald and Donald, three brothers, known in the village as Big Donald, Wee Donald and Dolly, after the grandfathers on both sides and a granduncle. Wee Donald was a seaman, six and a half feet tall, the tallest man in the village. He once ate an entire cod and an ashetful of potatoes for a bet. And Dolly was taller than Big Donald, but not as hefty.

Why did the tinkers call the older one Jacob and the younger one Isaac? But uncle Myles also called his son Jacob, instead of naming him after his father or his wife's father or even himself. Why did he do that? Colin didn't like Jacob in the Bible. He was the one who tricked his brother Esau not once but twice, and then had to run for his life. But God preferred Jacob to Esau, just as He preferred Abel to Cain, and Abel's offering of yearling sheep to Cain's offering of the fruits of the ground – potatoes and suchlike. Why? Why was a shepherd better than a tiller of the ground? No wonder Cain was angry. He was wroth and his countenance fell. And King David, who made the psalms, including *I to the Hills*, sent Uriah to the front of the battle, where he knew he would be killed, because he wanted Uriah's wife for himself. Her name was Bathsheba. But God was still on David's side afterwards. Colin didn't like David either. He preferred Saul. He couldn't tell that to anyone. Not even to his brother John, who read *The Big Book of Bible Stories* with a scowl on his face and his lower lip out . . . He didn't like *I to the Hills*. A small weariness went through him every time Kate Stanton made them sing it. Standing up in class to recite a psalm or answer a question from the *Shorter Catechism*, the same weariness would sometimes cause the breath to stop in his throat and the inside of his head to sing like a telegraph pole, although he had the words on his tongue, he knew them off by heart. He couldn't tell that to anyone either.

Here and there in *The Big Book of Bible Stories*, between the pages with writing, were brightly coloured pictures on shiny, glossy paper; the picture on one side of the page, the other side shiny and blank, good for writing on with a pen and ink but not with a pencil. One of the pictures was of Abraham and Isaac up on the mountain. The ram was there also, with his horns stuck in the thicket, Abraham in a long brown and white striped gown looking at him, Isaac in a shorter white gown, with a load of twigs on his back, looking at Abraham, and a white cloud radiating golden beams down on all three of them. 'God in all His glory shining forth!' Old Peter the Captain shouted, jabbing a finger at the cloud. Whatever John said in reply was the wrong thing (maybe he felt sorry for the ram) because Old Peter suddenly hauled him by the shoulders out of his chair and started shaking him violently back and forth, at the same time shouting in the voice that, on Sunday evenings, leading the praise in the small village Church of Scotland, easily outsoared the larger Free Church congregation across the road: 'Belial! Belial! Come out of him, you fiend! Come out of the tender child!' Goggle-eyed, slack-jawed, too astonished even to cry, the tender child sat afterwards with Colin up in the new room, listening to their mother in the kitchen, trying to calm Old Peter down, ministering to him with bowls of milk and wedges of barley bread. 'I felt the malice and the mockery of him under my hands, Mary,' Old Peter shouted. 'But by the power of God I cleared him from your child and from your home. Keep an eye on that boy,' he shouted. 'On both of them.' 'I will,' their mother said. 'I do.'

With Miss Mackenzie, he learnt *The Laird of Cockpen*. They did *The Laird of Cockpen* out on the floor, in twos; Colin's partner was Effie Chumbo from Cross. Colin was the Laird and Effie Chumbo was Mistress Jean who was making the elderflower wine, and what brings the lairdie at siccan a time? He had to go down on one knee in front of Effie Chumbo and ask her to marry him, and Effie Chumbo had to say 'Na!' and make a lang curtsie and turn her back on him. Then he had to pretend he was riding up the glen, and stop his horse and say to the class, with a nod in Effie Chumbo's direction, 'She's daft to refuse the Laird of Cockpen.'

Effie Chumbo had different knickers from the other girls – not navy blue, but black and white squares like a draughtsboard. They didn't have elastic round the legs. In the porch outside Tammy's room, the Rebel put his hand up Dolina Macritchie's dress. She leapt into the air and hit her head on an iron coatpeg. *'Did you interfere with this girl?'* Mr Macaulay had come into their room with the tawse already in his hand. Dolina Macritchie was with him. She was crying. *'Did you? You rascal that you are!'* The Rebel looked at Mr Macaulay, puzzled. He didn't know what interfere meant. Mr Macaulay gave him six of the belt.

With Tammy, they learnt Psalm 95 off by heart in both Gaelic and English.

> O come, let us sing to the Lord,
> Come let us, everyone
> A joyful noise make to the rock,
> Of our salvation . . .

They didn't sing in Tammy's class. They learnt vulgar and decimal fractions. The lowest common denominator. They learnt the history of Ness.

A long time ago, in Ness, lived a race of people known as Na Lubrachain. They were very small people. They were dwarfs. They lived in underground dwellings, like the ones found in Habost, on the machair. How many on the class had been to the underground dwellings in Habost? Two boys from Swainbost. How many from Dell even knew there were underground dwellings in Habost? Just as Tammy thought. None. How many of them had ever been to Habost? A village in their own district? What about Lionel? Port? Hands up! How many of them knew where Eorodale was? Just as he thought. Fivepenny? Skigersta? Where was Knockaird? Selecting a piece of broken chalk from the ledge under the blackboard, he fired it at someone in the back seats. The chalk made a noise against the wall like a stick snapping, landed with a duller sound on top of a desk, went from there to the floor. On the other hand, Tammy mused out loud, cocking his bald head and stroking his chin with a chalky forefinger, how many savages from Adabrock and Eorodale had ever been to Dell, north or south? Apart from briefly travelling through them on Mitchell's bus? How many of them even knew where Baile Gloum was? Caulk the known boundaries of the world, you won't contain or confine the ignorance therein. The Beaker people were also in Ness. They were known as Na Caganaich. Both Na Lubrachain and Na Caganaich buried their dead standing up, in stone cells. Cnoc Chuidhir in Eoropie is an ancient cemetery of the Beaker people. Eilean na Lubrachain is at the Butt of Lewis. 'I saw their dwellingplaces for myself with the two eyes that are in my head,' said Tammy, starting to get agitated again, 'before the barbarians of Eoropie vandalised and levelled them. What's another name for the Butt of Lewis? No?' Selecting another piece of chalk, he wrote on the blackboard, in elegant copperplate: *Rubha Rodhanis.* He spun round, scrutinising the faces before him; his eyes stopped at John the Coat, his arm moved, jerked, wanting to throw the chalk. But he controlled himself. 'Even the Romans were here,' he said. 'When the Roman warships came round the north of Scotland, a Roman called Seneca came ashore in North Dell, and who could blame him! A geo there is named after him: Geo Shuineaca. He went ashore in the other Dell too,' Tammy added sourly, 'there's an island, Eilean Shuineaca, at the back of Aird. Though what prompted him to step ashore there, him or any other Roman with his wits about him, *I* don't know.'

Murdo Major from Aird found a sword in a peatbank at the White

Cairns. It was known as Murdo Major's sword. It was in the Museum of Antiquities in Edinburgh, under glass. Mairi Alan and her father found a bone necklace.

The Qualifying was Ham's class. Ham was Mr Macaulay, the headmaster. He was tall, and wore a Harris tweed suit with lumpy knees and elbows. In Uig, where he came from, he was known as Donald Ham, meaning Donald, son of Ham. Ham was his father's nickname. He had brothers and sisters, and they all looked like one another. They were all teachers. They were known as the Ham family, or the Tribe of Ham. In Ness, he was known as Ham. Men wearing dungarees, leaning against shop counters or sitting at peatstacks between loads, would sometimes call him Donald Ham (*'The black year I spent on Donald Ham's class . . .'*). But in the school – itself, he was always Ham.

Ham gave them handwork, sums, *Radiant Reading* 4, *Treasure Island*, the use of a leather football at playtime so long as they didn't put it into the river, geography (India was red on the big wall map; part of Africa, with a river running through it, was white), the history of Scotland (in Stirling Castle, the English governor's wife was crooning to her baby, *'Hush thee, hush thee, dinna fret thee, the Black Douglas willna get thee,'* when suddenly, from behind, a heavy mailed hand came down on her shoulder), gardening and Gaelic. Gardening was digging Ham's garden at the back; Gaelic a green reading book with pages that stank nauseously, opening at page 1 on a matchstick figure running full tilt, carrying a large envelope. The name of the matchstick figure was Iain. Iain was going to the post office to post a letter. Look at Iain. Look at the small dark man in *Radiant Reading* 4, forever about to putt the stone against Tearlach the laird. 'Glounagrianan!' a voice spoke to him close by; and no one needed to ask the result. When Black Dog ran out of Long John Silver's eating house, do you think the men who went after him really tried to catch him? Colin scanned Ham's face eagerly, trying to guess the answer. 'Yes,' he said. 'No,' said Ham. He didn't pay the score. What's another word for score? Twenty. Yes. But that's not what score means here. Here it means the bill. Fat snowflakes smudged the windowpane, slid down, turning to water. In the glow of the coal fire, in the darkening room, one half of Ham's face shone redly; the other half was in shadow. 'Why not church bells?' he asked out loud, and opened his eyes. 'Get on with your work,' he told the class. 'You, girl,' he said to Margaret Maclaren, who was nearest the door. 'Put the lights on.' She was the only one on the class to get vaccinated for smallpox.

'Wee Donald Maciver?' said John the Battler. 'He'd eat his own vaccination scab! He ate an entire cod once, and an ashetful of potatoes. I'll tell you a better one. When himself and myself were on the sherryboats between Glasgow and Spain – do you know what a squid is –?'

'That'll do, John,' their mother said.

'Like an octopus, only smaller –'

'Shut up, John,' their mother said.

. . . Back on the Qualifying, Murdo John Bullags was reciting 'The Cuckoo' in Gaelic.

> O failt' ort fhein, a chuthag ghorm,
> Le d'oran ceolmhor milis . . .

He stopped. Swallowed. Went on:

> 'S e seirm do bheoil 's a' Cheitean og,
> A thogadh bron om chridhe.

'Translate,' said Ham.

'Welcome to you, blue cuckoo, with your musical song so sweet. It is the . . . the . . .'

'Seirm? Yes? Seirm do bheoil?'

'. . . the . . . the . . .'

Ham seized the metre stick.

'. . . music or melody of your voice . . .'

'Go on! 'S a' Cheitean og . . .'

'. . . in the young May . . .'

'Or the young May *time*. Go on! A thogadh bron om chridhe?'

'. . . that would lift sorrow from my heart.'

Murdo John Bullags sat down with a clatter.

'Next verse!' Holding the metre stick like a paddle, Ham quizzed the faces in the back row of the class. His eyes widened, then narrowed.

'Roderick Macleod,' he said. 'Stand up!'

'That cuckoo's been on the go a long time,' a seaman called Brown Jack, from Aird, said to cousin Dolly. 'Not just on Donald Ham's class in Cross school either.' He offered cousin Dolly a cigarette, a Prize Crop, from a yellow packet. He started to offer Colin one, before he remembered that Colin wasn't grown up. 'I heard a screech of a woman trying to sing it on the wireless the other night –'

'Ethel Cameron,' said cousin Dolly.

'Talk about a rabbit in a snare. I remember this boy's father, on his deathbed, banging on the bell at the side of his bed for Mary to come and switch the wireless off if even her *name* was mentioned. And that,' Brown Jack turned to Colin, 'was a judge and a knowing man when it came to Gaelic singing. Your father. He used to sing at concerts himself, with Kitty Macleod. I heard him.'

'When?' said cousin Dolly.

'When what?'

'When did you hear him?'

'I heard him at a concert in Cross school – for funds for the Lewis hospital – when I was ten years old.' Brown Jack looked shocked by the question. 'You'd have heard him too, if you'd been there.'

'Why wasn't I there? If *you* were?'

'Because you haven't got a musical ear. I've got a musical ear,' Brown Jack said. 'This boy –' he clapped Colin on the shoulder '– has a musical ear. You haven't.'

'Yes I have,' said cousin Dolly.

'MacFarquhar's boar choking on a slice of turnip. That's your idea of a musical noise.'

Cousin Dolly coughed once, blew out a small explosion of smoke and took the Prize Crop from his mouth. He stood spluttering and laughing. Brown Jack looked at Colin with the same shocked expression, went to say something else, then changed his mind. He had a wide, flat face covered in dense ginger bristles and freckles. He was fat. Red John Gunn, the old mad seadog, was his uncle. He nodded frankly at Colin, then sideways at cousin Dolly as if to say: *Look at him! Listen to him!*

Shaking quietly, cousin Dolly wiped his eyes with the back of his hand.

Bright ginger hairs curled out at the top of Brown Jack's semmit. If he didn't have a cigarette in his mouth, he'd be chewing on a spent match or a stalk of grass. He was a seaman.

'You were probably scouring the dumps of the village for old jamjars to flog to the ragman,' he told cousin Dolly. 'That was another of your ploys when we were kids.'

His nose, flat anyway, had been flattened even more in a famous fight in Timaru, New Zealand, against the champion of Point, a fellow called Dempsey, after Jack Dempsey, the Manassa Mauler. Colin heard a cousin of theirs – Murdo Finlay – telling uncle John about it.

'I was sailing bosun on the same ship as Dempsey,' Murdo Finlay said. 'Dempsey was AB. Word had got round,' said Murdo Finlay, 'about a challenge fight between Dempsey and a boy from Ness – Dempsey was always challenging people to fight him – and by the time I got down to the quay – it was Saturday afternoon – they're already inside a circle, with every seaman and dockside bum in Timaru for spectators, plenty white collars as well and police on the q.t. – word had got round. I stood at the back of this crowd, craning my neck, and there's Dempsey, dancing up and down on his toes, stripped to the waist, squaring up to Brown Jack, who hasn't even bothered to take his jacket off, and I'll tell you this, John – I didn't want to watch. He was a hard man, Dempsey. We had three from Point on the ship, all hard as nails, and Dempsey was the hardest. So a minute goes by, and I'm hearing the thump thump of fists, and judging by the shouts Brown Jack is still on his feet anyway, and another minute goes by, and they're still at it, and I think to myself, *What's going on here? I'll have a look*, and I'm just in time to see Dempsey land one on Brown Jack that would have collapsed a horse, only Brown Jack doesn't fall down, doesn't even blink, he lands Dempsey one back and puts Dempsey on his arse.'

'Is it Brown Jack?' Uncle John was excited. 'Red John's nephew?

Man, they don't come any stronger! Big, strong men on both sides of that family! When I was in Crianlaraich with his uncle Kenny –'

'Dempsey had the skill for fighting, you see,' Murdo Finlay interrupted. 'Up on his toes, lead with the left, all the rest of it. The knack. That's how he came by the nickname. He used to take on people at fairgrounds and places for money, when he was on the bum. With Brown Jack, none of that mattered.'

'Big, strong men,' said uncle John. 'His uncle Kenny, man alive, that was with me in Crianlaraich, had shoulders on him like . . . like Samson! I remember one time –'

'He could be quite funny, Dempsey. I found him after the fight in the ship's galley, one eye closed, ear out to here, split lip, and his hands in a bucket of ice water. "Do you know what, Murdo?" he said. "The congregation of Garrabost Free Church is singing a psalm inside my head. Tune, Martyrdom."

"That'll learn you," I told him, "to steer clear of the Nessmen."

Dempsey shook his head.

"Never mind, Dempsey," one of the lads in the galley says. "It was a draw, after all."

Dempsey shook his head. "No it wasn't," he said.

He's opening and closing his hands in the bucket.

"I know what I'll do," he says then, "if I ever tangle with that ginger bugger again."

"What?" one of the lads says.

"Take a gun with me. And never mind about the licence."'

'Man,' said uncle John. 'I could have told him that.'

'The garden in front of the house,' cousin Dolly said to Colin. 'We dug that for Ham. Didn't we, Jack?'

'And the potato patch behind the school. That was our class too.'

'It was called gardening,' said cousin Dolly.

'Him and his gardening,' said Brown Jack. 'Him and his cuckoo. I'll tell you something about that cuckoo –'

'Yes, you're an authority on cuckoos,' said cousin Dolly. 'Everyone knows that.'

'Damn right,' Brown Jack agreed.

'You've rifled a few nests in your time.'

'What was that other one he made us learn off by heart?' Brown Jack asked, forgetting about the cuckoo. 'It wasn't *in* a book. About a dying soldier?'

'"The Burial of Sir John Moore at Corunna",' said cousin Dolly.

'No it wasn't – what's the matter with you? We learnt that one on Tammy's class. This one didn't have a patch on "The Burial of Sir John Moore at Corunna".'

'"Bingen on the Rhine",' said Colin.

'How does it go again?'

A soldier of the Legion lay dying in Algiers . . .

'That's the one,' Brown Jack said.

There was lack of woman's nursing, there was dearth of woman's tears
But a comrade stood beside him while his lifeblood ebbed away,
And bent with pitying glances to hear what he might say . . .

'Keep going,' said Brown Jack.

The dying soldier faltered as he took his comrade's hand,
And he said, I never more shall see my own my native land,
Take a message and a token to some distant friends of mine,
For I was born at Bingen, at Bingen on the Rhine.

Brown Jack stared at Colin, his mouth working on a matchstick, his eyes huge. 'What a memory!' he said. He turned to cousin Dolly. 'That's from his father's side,' he said, 'not yours.'

Cousin Dolly was shaking with silent laughter again.

'Laugh away,' said Brown Jack. 'No ear for poetry either. Me, now. I could listen to poetry by the yard. From dawn to dusk. How does the rest of it go, Colin?'

'It's very long,' Colin said.

'Give us the bit about his father's sword.'

I let them take whate'er they would, but kept my father's sword,

And with boyish love I hung it where the evening light would
    shine,
On the cottage wall at Bingen, at Bingen on the Rhine . . .

'Bingen on the Rhine,' Brown Jack repeated. 'Now the bit about
his sister.'

Tell my sister not to weep for me and mourn with drooping
    head,
When the troops come marching home again with glad
    and gallant tread . . .

'But to –' Brown Jack raised his arm. 'Wait,' he said. His brow
wrinkled. 'I know this line.' His lips moved, his finger went up
and down to the rhythm of words inside his head. He stopped,
annoyed. 'But to what?' he asked.

But to look upon them proudly, with a calm and steadfast eye,
For her brother was a soldier too and not afraid to die . . .

'Doesn't he tell his sister to marry one of the comrades?' cousin
Dolly asked, joining in.

'What if he does?' said Brown Jack, rounding on him. 'Why
shouldn't he? Ignore him, Colin,' he said, 'and give us the verse
about his sweetheart. That's a good one.'

There's another, not a sister, in the happy days gone by,
You could tell her by the merriment that sparkled in her eye.
Too innocent for coquetry –

'What's coquetry?' cousin Dolly asked.

'Keep going, Colin,' said Brown Jack. 'Don't let on he's there.'

– too fond for idle scorning,
Ah friend, methinks the lightest heart makes sometimes
    heaviest mourning.
Tell her the last night of my life, for e'er this moon be risen,
My body shall be out of pain, my soul be out of prison . . .

'That's it,' said Brown Jack happily. 'That's the bit where Donald
Ham's eyes would fill up with tears. He used to go behind the
blackboard to recover. Now say the last two lines.'

I dreamt I stood with her and saw the yellow moonlight shine,
On the vine-clad hills of Bingen, dear Bingen on the Rhine.

'What a poem! We had to write it down in a red ink exercise book.'

'Us too,' said Colin.

'He dies in the next verse, doesn't he? The soldier of the Legion?'

'Yes.'

'It's the last verse, isn't it?'

'Yes.'

'"He sighed and ceased to speak." Am I right?'

'Yes.'

Brown Jack accepted a cigarette from cousin Dolly. A Capstan. He took a deep breath.

'My memory isn't so bad after all,' he said.

When uncle John was rebuilding the old manse, Brown Jack was fetched over from Aird to help him lift the great stone lintel into place above the front door. They sat in Sandy's house afterwards, drinking screwtops of MacEwan's Pale Ale, and when the screwtops were finished, whisky, and when Colin went in to ask was uncle John coming home for his tea, uncle John replied, 'Never!' 'Come come come, John,' said Sandy, who was hump-backed and lived by himself. 'What about the domestic harmony?' 'I'll give them domestic harmony,' said uncle John, seizing the whisky bottle by the neck. 'This is defiance,' Sandy informed Brown Jack. 'Nothing but,' Brown Jack agreed, holding out his glass. 'I know what, John,' said Sandy. 'Give us "Dark dark in the morning on the face of the foe".' Colin went away then and didn't hear any more, and that was the last time he saw Brown Jack, because Brown Jack went back to sea not long after and was drowned in Brooklyn Harbour, New York, in the United States of America. The village went very quiet at the news of his death, everyone except Red John his uncle, the old mad seadog, who cleared the house of mourners with his carry-on during God's word (not even the elders could stop him), and paced the Aird road afterwards far into the night, shoeless and bonnetless, bawling curses at the white face of the moon.

Uncle Myles

FOR SOME REASON, UNCLE Myles was staying with them. It wasn't a Communions time or anything. He slept on the bench in the kitchen, with cushions under him and pillows at his head.

Their father was still alive then, in the bed in the new room; and every morning, after soaping and shaving his face in the mirror of the cabinet fixed to the partition, uncle Myles would go up to the new room to speak to him. Their voices would be low and even at first, but then their father's voice would start to get louder. 'You envy *me*?' they heard him say one morning: 'Would you like to change *places* with me?' – followed by a bout of coughing, and when their father had stopped coughing, uncle Myles' voice, low and even, then their father's voice again, 'Think of what you just said, you fool! Have you taken leave of your senses?' – then uncle Myles' voice again, still low and even, and at last their father shouting, 'Go for a walk along the seashore! Get out on the moor! Let the air to your head, you fool of a man!' Then, after a short silence, the door of the new room would open, and uncle Myles, shuffling on slippered feet, would emerge, his face, above the collarless striped shirt with the stud in it, white and sad; while behind him, a hand banged insistently on the bedside bell, summoning their mother. 'You sit yourself at the range, Myles,' she would whisper to uncle Myles, 'till I come back down. Tell the boys a story.' But uncle Myles couldn't do that; all he could do was stare into the bars of the stove, wordless, kneading his plump white hands in the warmth from the fire and sighing, until their mother came back down from the room and shifted the kettle on to the hot plate to make another cup of tea for him. Then, slowly lifting his head and looking like an old dog that wanted his head patted, he would say: 'His tongue has lost none of its violence, Mary, I'm sorry to say.'

Uncle Myles always stayed in the houses of other holy people, whenever he came to the district. So why was he staying with them?

He didn't have his minister's collar on either.

It was strange.

Their day began in the morning.

Newly risen and pacing about the kitchen floor in bagging grey long johns, a semmit with arms down to the elbows and thick woollen stockings, uncle Myles would halt and enquire of the partition (behind which the rest of the family had withdrawn while he got dressed), 'Where are my trousers, Mary dear?' He had no idea that Colin and John, on the other side of the partition, were watching him through the gaps between the boards. 'Where do you think? In the *moon*?' their mother would mutter under her breath, and then, in a slightly higher than normal voice, 'Are they not over the back of the round chair?' 'No they're not,' uncle Myles' voice complained. 'I looked and they're not.' 'The knob at the end of the mantelpiece,' Colin whispered to his mother. 'Are they hanging from the knob at the end of the mantelpiece?' she shouted. 'Yes yes,' uncle Myles' voice replied. 'He must have been up for a pee again,' she whispered. 'The only man in the world who puts his trousers *on* to have a pee ...' His eye at a crack in the partition, Colin watched uncle Myles trying to put his trousers on. Holding them in both hands, he bent the upper half of his body and lifted one foot. Immediately he started swaying and almost toppled head first on to the linoleum. He stood on both legs, frowning. He tried again. This time he had to put his foot down smartly to prevent himself falling sideways against the kitchen table. Colin and John looked at one another. 'Well?' their mother's voice hissed angrily at them. 'Are we going to be here all *morning*? Take that grip out of your mouth,' she said to Annie. When Colin looked through the crack again, uncle Myles had his trousers on and was standing in front of the range doing up the flybuttons. They were black trousers with thin, white stripes and severe creases. The braces were over his shoulders. 'Finished,' he raised his head and addressed the partition. 'You may all come down now,' he said.

On a morning, perfect for trout fishing, after a night of steady, drumming rain on the flat felt roof of the house, Colin came in from collecting worms to be told by his mother:

'Uncle Myles is coming with you.'

'What?' said Colin.

Even as he spoke, uncle Myles appeared in the kitchen door in wellingtons, brown corduroy trousers, an old tweed jacket, a grey scarf wrapped round his neck like Rupert Bear's and a tweed bonnet. Colin stared at him in astonishment.

'But he hasn't got a rod!'

'Yes he has.'

Mutely, uncle Myles showed Colin his father's folding rod in its brown canvas cover.

'And here's the fishing bag. He says everything you need's in it. Colin'll help you put it all together when you get to the river.'

Uncle Myles took the fishing bag from her. He stood holding it by its strap, as though it contained a ferret.

'Perhaps, Mary dear, if you were to . . .' he began. She shook her head.

'He won't hear of it, Myles. You heard him yourself. He says it'll do you good. O, go *on!*' she said then. 'Maybe it *will* do you good. Get you out of the house. I put pieces in the bag for both of you and a flask of milk. Stop you starving to death.'

'But . . . ?' Colin still couldn't believe this was happening. 'Does *Alan* know?'

'What?' His mother turned on him.

'That uncle Myles is coming fishing with us?'

'Never you mind about Alan. Now clear off out of my sight, the pair of you.'

'But I'll have to get more *worms!*' Colin protested.

'So?' his mother said. 'Get them down at your granny's.'

'But I haven't got another *tin!*'

His mother opened the small press beneath the scullery window. In a cardboard box inside it, full of clattering tins, crumpled cloths, small and large shoebrushes, she found an empty tin of Johnson's Mansion Polish.

'Here you are.'

'But . . .'

'What now? Clear off, I said.'

In his granny's house, the family was settled round the table at breakfast. The appearance of Colin, with uncle Myles in tow, caused a stir.

'O my goodness!' said aunty Isobel, jumping to her feet. 'It's the minister!'

'The minister?' said aunty Annie, turning her head slowly and looking up at uncle Myles.

A pet lamb, called Billy Steel because of his crooked front legs, trotted across the floor, maaing loudly, and went up into the livingroom.

'So it is!' said aunty Annie. 'Won't you come in?'

'Take that dog down from the table!' aunty Isobel whispered fiercely to uncle John. Uncle John was at the head of the table with Boy the dog in his lap.

From the livingroom came the sound of horns butting against wood.

'Put him into the barn!' aunty Isobel whispered. 'Hurry up!'

'I'll get the other one,' said aunty Annie. She went up to the livingroom.

'He jumps up on me, the rascal,' said uncle John, trying to stand up and push Boy from his lap at the same time. 'Just a young dog,' he explained.

'The barn!' aunty Isobel said to him. 'Get a chair for the minister!' she said.

'No no,' said uncle Myles. 'How *are* we?' He bowed over their granny's hand.

'Who have I here?' their granny wanted to know.

'*Who have I here!*' aunty Isobel repeated. 'The minister!' she exclaimed, and laughed.

'Open the front door, someone,' aunty Annie shouted from the livingroom, as Billy Steel trotted back into the kitchen.

Alan came round the table. He had been staring at uncle Myles since he came in. 'What's going on?' he asked Colin. 'Why is he with you?'

'The door!' aunty Annie shouted. 'Kish kish kish!'

'He's coming fishing with us,' Colin said, opening the door. Billy Steel went out. So did Boy, who had followed uncle John back down from the barn.

'No he isn't.'

'I've got to get more worms,' said Colin.

'He's going with *you*, if he's going,' Alan said. 'Not with me.'

'You sit here, minister,' aunty Isobel said, pushing a chair against the back of uncle Myles' legs.

'No no . . .'

Their granny had uncle Myles' hand trapped in both her own. Slowly, he sat down.

'I'm going now,' Alan told Colin. 'I'm not waiting for you.'

Outside, Boy started barking furiously.

'Who left the gate open?' uncle John bawled. There was a sudden silence. Everyone looked at uncle Myles. 'It's nothing . . . nothing at all . . .' uncle John muttered, plunging out the front door. 'Come *hee*–ar! . . .' they heard him shouting at Boy. 'Come a-*horse*, you . . .'

'There we are, minister,' said aunty Isobel, placing a dainty china cup and saucer that she'd taken from the dresser in front of uncle Myles. 'Help yourself to milk and sugar.'

'I'm going,' said Alan. 'I'll see you at the Mill dam.'

He went out.

Still holding uncle Myles' hand between her own, their granny said, in a stern, quavering voice:

'*Come unto Me, all ye that labour and are heavy-laden, and I will give you rest.*' But uncle Myles wasn't listening. He was looking up at the dresser and blinking his eyes.

'That's our Peter,' aunty Annie told him. 'Did you think he was an ornament?'

On the top shelf of the dresser, at one end, a skinny blue cat sat motionless.

'I did,' uncle Myles cleared his throat, 'in all truth.'

'He isn't really a tomcat, although he's called Peter,' aunty Annie said. 'He's had several litters.'

'Tea?' said aunty Isobel.

'He's a she,' said aunty Annie.

Between his granny's house and Noony's was an empty house with a corrugated iron roof, that had been used by airmen during the war. In the small garden behind this house, Colin knew, were lots of unturned stones, tumbled from the walls, where he would find worms. The village was quiet. No one about. Blue peatsmoke from the chimneys went straight up and hung, thinning, in the quiet morning air. The grey sky was very near the earth. It was a perfect morning for fishing.

With a handful of long grass, Colin cleaned out the thin circle of polish left in the bottom of the Johnson's tin. The grass was wet. The doorway of the empty house was trodden black by sheep, and smelled of mud and sheep droppings. There was no door. Wisps of fleece clung to the rough stone walls and the rickety doorjambs. Colin started turning over stones and filling the tin with worms. He replaced each stone carefully afterwards. When he had enough worms, he crumbled fresh black earth over them, distributing it among the worms with his index finger, so that they would stay fresh and unclammy in the tin. He replaced the lid on the tin and went to fetch uncle Myles.

'. . . and what was on the handline when we hauled it?' Colin heard uncle John's voice asking when he went back in. 'Dogfish!' the voice answered itself. 'Dogfish on every single hook! Well, I looked at Angus Coll out of the corner of my eye, and Angus Coll looked back at me. A small man, but hardy! What? Arms on him like . . . like . . . "Big John," said Angus Coll, addressing me to my face . . . and he had a smile on his own face . . . "Big John," and he winked at me behind Sanny's back . . . "What's your opinion?" Well, I looked at him . . .'

'Are you ready?' Colin asked uncle Myles.

'Ah!' said uncle Myles. He stood up.

'But –' said uncle John.

'To be continued,' said aunty Isobel.

'All morning,' said aunty Annie. 'If he could get off with it.'

'All morning?' said aunty Isobel. 'Yes and all day, with his hands in his pockets.'

'Come on, then,' Colin said to uncle Myles.

'Welcome home, fisherman,' their granny said. 'Fisher no fish.'

'They haven't *gone* yet,' aunty Annie said, and laughed.

'Well well . . .' said uncle Myles, nodding his head rapidly and backing towards the door.

'Good luck,' said aunty Isobel. She put her hand on her mouth. 'I shouldn't have said that,' she said.

'No you shouldn't,' said aunty Annie. 'But you said it all the same. It's bad luck to wish a fisherman good luck,' she explained to uncle Myles. She turned to aunty Isobel. 'Take it back,' she said.

'I'm always doing it,' aunty Isobel said, her hand still on her mouth.

'Did you take it back?' said aunty Annie.

'Yes, to myself.'

'Take it back out loud.'

'I take it back.'

'I'm off,' said Colin. Uncle Myles came out behind him. His wellingtons were too big for him, and made a flopping sound as he walked. They went out through the gate and uncle Myles closed the gate behind him. Colin carried his own rod over his shoulder and uncle Myles' rod in his hand. Uncle Myles had the fishing bag.

'They won't catch anything now,' Colin heard aunty Isobel saying, inside the house. 'And it'll be all my fault.'

He walked quickly out the village road, uncle Myles flop-flopping along behind him. At the head of the road, where it met the main road, he stopped and waited for uncle Myles to catch up. The Free Church was at the head of the road, and Charlie's garage across from it. The smaller Church of Scotland, with the black wooden bier leaning lengthways against its wall, was on the other side of the main road, a little further down. Colin and uncle Myles crossed the main road together and headed out into the moor. Colin went into the lead again. He was in a hurry to get to the river. He waited for uncle Myles to catch up. The river was down to their left, in the glen, about a quarter of a mile away. Between the Mill dam and the bridge, it flowed straight and glimmering, in full flood; further out, against the darker green and brown of the moor, the bends gleamed bright as sixpences in the grey light. If, from their granny's skylight, you could see certain bends out in the moor, you knew there was enough water in the river for fishing. The best pools were out in the moor. The further out you went from the Mill dam, the better the fishing was. Colin started to get excited, looking at the river. He wished uncle Myles would hurry up.

Alan would be at the Grey Knolls already. He wouldn't start fishing there, though. He'd carry on to the old sheilings, and start at the Black Pool. After fishing the Black Pool, he'd cross the river at the head of the Black Pool in order to fish the next pool. Between where the Black Pool began and the next pool upstream tailed into shallows. That was how you fished the Dell river. You had to keep crossing the river all the time, from bend to bend. The pools had high peaty banks on one side, a gravel spit on the other. You fished from the gravel spit, following your line all the way down the pool, keeping your float moving alongside the central current, but not in it. Or you could drop your hook into the foam-covered waterhole, resting place for large trout, formed at the head of each pool between the current and the high bank, and holding the tip of your rod upwards, let your float rest on the scummy, peat-flaked foam and wait for it to vanish suddenly. On hot afternoons, fishing like this, the bright babble of water over the shallows, the snoring of dragonflies against the peatbank, the silence of the moor beyond, would almost lull you to sleep where you stood. The waterholes were dark and deep, and there was always the danger, fishing them, of catching an eel instead of a trout. Long and brown, with yellowish underbellies and small, pointed heads, they lay in the still water next to the bank, and if your float, instead of disappearing suddenly, started to bob on the surface of the water as though moved by tiny, myriad wavelets, you knew that an eel was on the other end of the line and had taken not just the hook but most of the nylon gut as well down into its boneless, rubbery, inedible body. 'Dirty shites of creatures,' the Big Barney said, one wellington boot planted on the eel's head, as he sliced the rest of it, bit by bit, from the tail upwards, looking for Colin's hook. 'They can live on land, you know.' The eel's body writhed ceaselessly as he hacked and sliced through it; the bits that had been detached continued to move. 'Look at that,' the Big Barney said. 'Cut an eel into a hundred pieces, it will grow back into a hundred eels. Dirty, ugly shites of creatures. Here . . . !' He gouged Colin's hook out with the tip of his knife, sliding the blade underneath the line of gut, severed the eel's head from what remained of its body and pulled the line and hook out through its mouth. 'What are you doing *now?*' he asked – Colin had opened his tin of worms. 'Go and wash your hook and line in the river first,' the Big Barney told him. 'Then rub gravel on them, and then wash them again. A trout won't come near your hook if an eel's been on it. Don't you know *anything?*' He dug the blade of his knife into the gravel, pulled it out and tapped Colin on the chest with it. 'Do you still think your balls are up there?' he asked, a huge grin coming over his face. Because Colin had seen gallstones on the man in the front of Black's Medical Dictionary, and thought they were the same as stones in the Bible. 'Well?' The Big Barney lowered the point of the knife and prodded Colin in the stomach. 'Am I getting warm?' He had a face like a Mongolian. It wasn't his own knife but his father's. The same age as Alan, he was always falling off walls and bicycles, getting stuck in barbed wire, blundering into ponds and ditches. Nothing seemed to hurt him. Twice he fell into the sea rockfishing, twice the sea refused to have him and cast him back on to the rock. 'What'll happen,' his father asked, 'if the earth refuses him as well?' 'We can cut down to the river from here,' Colin told uncle Myles. They had arrived at a little stream called Allagro. There were trout in it, but not big ones. 'The river's just right for fishing,' Colin told him. 'We'll start at the Mill dam and work our way out from there.' 'Very good, a ghraidh,' uncle Myles agreed. His face was very white. He was out of breath.

'We're nearly there,' Colin said.

'You go on ahead, a ghraidh,' uncle Myles said, handing Colin the fishing bag, 'and prepare everything. I won't be long.'

What was wrong with him now? Why wasn't he coming?

'I must stay here for a while . . . in this place . . .'

They stood facing one another. Colin could hear the noise of the river, loud and steady, behind him. Maybe uncle Myles needed to open his trousers?

'You go on,' uncle Myles said.

'I'll be at the dam,' said Colin.

Thin patches of mist still clung to the ground on the North Dell side of the river, in the hollows. Colin put his own rod and the fishing bag down on the bank, and took the folding rod out of its brown canvas cover. The river had burst its banks sometime during the night; it was still in spate, but the water was clear. A line of dirty, broken reeds along the bank marked how high the water had come. Colin jointed up the folding rod, keeping the eyeholes in line. He fixed the reel on the rod, and threaded the line from the reel through the eyeholes. With every tug he took at the line, the reel gave a screech of protest. He tied a brown trout hook on its nylon gut to the line, using the knot uncle John had shown him, and put a cork float on the line, two and a half feet from the hook. The cork was from a castor oil bottle. All the time, he kept watching the river. The water came brawling and twisting into the Mill dam at its upper end and flowed in a silent grey sheet down the length of the pool, before falling in a smooth curve over the dam at the bottom. Once over the dam, the water started boiling and roaring again, turning and twisting in foamy, whirling knots, as though resuming a fight with itself that had started at Loch Langabhat and would continue until it reached the sea. Opening the tin of Johnson's Mansion Polish, Colin selected a fat worm, pierced its head with the point of the hook and threaded it down through the hook until its head slid over the nylon gut. The tail wriggled in agony, and then, giving up, wound itself languidly around the shank of the hook. Colin left it on, and after making sure that no part of the hook was showing, spat on the worm for good luck. The rod was now ready. He picked it up, testing it between his hands, and checked that the line was the correct length. He didn't try a cast. It was uncle Myles' rod. What was keeping him?

Colin didn't want to fish the Mill dam anyway. You could only fish the upper end of it with a worm. Further down was no use.

He had seen people – visitors – fishing it with flyrods and taking trout from it. A red-faced man and two big boys in blazers. But Colin had never worked a flyrod. He didn't have one.

A bamboo rod, that was what he had.

Alan was going to get a folding rod and reel for his next birthday, from aunty Isobel. His birthday was in December, the day after Christmas, so he would have to wait four months before he could try it out. Alan had asked her to get the rod for him now but she said no. Uncle Myles' head, and then the rest of him, appeared out of the moor, going the wrong way. Colin shouted to him, and he turned and came back. He walked with his head down, very slowly, as though looking for something he'd dropped. Colin felt his face going hot, watching him. His ears started singing.

'Here I am,' said uncle Myles.

'Your rod's all ready,' Colin told him, speaking very fast. 'Look!' He showed uncle Myles the rod; moved it up and down in his hands, demonstrating. 'I've already put a worm on the hook for you. It's all ready.'

'Yes,' said uncle Myles. He made no move to take the rod from Colin's hands.

Colin handed him the rod.

'And there's your tin of worms and the bag. I'm going to start fishing further along,' he said. 'That bend there,' he said, pointing. 'I'm going to start there.'

Uncle Myles didn't say anything.

'Well,' said Colin. 'I'm going now.' He hesitated. 'You start here,' he said, 'and then follow me along.'

Off he went, carrying the bamboo rod by its middle; it bounced with a spring in his grip as he walked. The bend where he wanted to start fishing was straight ahead. He had to keep his feet from running. What a day! Along the straight stretch before him, the river glinted grey with little gleams of silver; round patches of foam raced one another endlessly on the current. The banks were very green, close-cropped by sheep. Up from the bank on Colin's side, the heather started. The other bank steepened to become brown clay and loose stones as you approached the bend. He'd lost a trout here one time, when it flew off the hook as he jerked it ashore and landed in deep heather behind him. He could hear it struggling down in the heather, but couldn't find it. 'Yes,' said Alan, when he told him, 'and you once jumped into the river after a trout as well, didn't you?' No one else believed him either.

'You stay with uncle Myles,' his mother had said. He'd done that. 'Show him what to do.' He'd done that too.

'Both of you,' his mother had said. 'Tell Alan.' But Alan had taken off like a bullet as soon as he heard uncle Myles was coming with them. He'd get a good row for that, if Colin told on him.

He'd be at the old sheilings by now. At the Black Pool.

And uncle Myles was all right. He wouldn't have held them back. He was at the Mill dam, fishing. Colin looked over his shoulder.

No he wasn't.

He was standing as Colin had left him. Staring at the ground. The rod in his hands, idle.

He wasn't fishing at all.

Colin started back. He thought of leaving his own rod on the bank, to save him carrying it all the way back. But then he took it with him.

Uncle Myles raised his head when he heard footsteps coming. 'Are you –' Colin began, and stopped. Uncle Myles' eyes were full of tears. Colin stared at him, horrified.

'*But Lord to thee I cried.*' Uncle Myles wailed,

My prayer at morn prevent shall thee.
Why, Lord, dost thou cast off my soul
and hid'st thy face from me?

Tears ran down his face. He didn't try to wipe them away. He opened his mouth and cried loudly, above the noise of the river:

The dreadful fierceness of thy wrath
quite over me doth go:
Thy terrors great have cut me off,
they did pursue me so.

Colin didn't know what to do. He wanted to run away.

'What's wrong?' he asked.

He had never seen a grown man crying before.

The folding rod had fallen at uncle Myles' feet. Colin picked it up. Still crying, uncle Myles blew his nose loudly into a handkerchief, and started clumsily wiping his eyes with the knuckles of his hands, like a child. 'I must – go home – a 'raidh,' he said in a jerky, hiccupy voice, as though he were having a fit. 'Not well,' he said. His mouth had gone out of shape, over to one side; his chin was trembling. 'You stay,' he said to Colin. He didn't mean it. Even as he said it, his eyes pleaded, implored. 'It's all right,' Colin mumbled rapidly, looking away from uncle Myles' face and starting to reel in the line on the fishing rod. The hollow feeling that had come into his stomach when he saw uncle Myles not fishing had now moved up into his chest and throat.

'I don't mind, really,' he mumbled.

He took the worm from the hook, threw it into the river; took the nylon gut and cork float from the line; reeled in the rest of the line; took the reel from the rod. The day was over before it had begun. He disjointed the folding rod, put the three sections into their pockets in the canvas cover; tied the strings at the top and the middle of the cover with butterfly knots; handed the cover, with the rod in it, to uncle Myles. The river was loud in his ears. He hadn't even opened his own rod. He picked up the fishing bag.

'Ready,' he said.

He could still go fishing tomorrow, he knew that; there would still be enough water in the river. But it wouldn't be the same. No two days were the same on the river. And even if he went back to the river after putting uncle Myles home, it wouldn't be the same. The day was spoiled. Lost. He couldn't get it back now. It was gone forever.

Back at the main road, he waited for uncle Myles to catch up.

'We'll keep on this side of the road up to the old milestone,' he said, 'and cut across to the house from there.'

That way, they wouldn't have to go through the village. They could avoid the village altogether.

Uncle Myles looked at Colin with dark, sorrowful eyes, and mutely nodded his head.

They plodded across the inner grazing in silence, side by side.

'I'll say the river was too full,' Colin said.

Silence.

'That the water was too dirty.'

Silence.

Uncle Myles stumbled, and put his hand on Colin's shoulder to prevent himself from falling.

'Well, it was,' Colin said.

They plodded forward again.

At the gate of their house a black car was sitting.

'Whose car is that?' uncle Myles asked.

'The doctor's,' Colin replied.

Growing pains

*T*HE WOMAN IN THE cardigan put her head round the door of the rector's office.

'Next,' she said, and Colin and his mother went in.

The rector was sitting behind a desk. He was fat, but not solid fat, like a Westsider; his jowls, when he spoke, trembled like jelly. 'And who have we here?' he asked. He wore a hairy yellow suit, and a waistcoat of the same material.

'Colin Murray,' the woman in the cardigan said.

'Murray'. Puffing noisily, the rector leaned forward and looked at a paper on the desk in front of him. 'Cross School,' he read. 'I see, I see ... Of course,' he said, 'he already has a brother in the school, hasn't he?'

'Yes,' his mother said. 'Alan.'

'Alan J. Murray,' the rector read from the paper.

'Third year,' the woman in the cardigan said.

'Known to all and sundry as Jonah,' the rector looked up and laughed.

'Moby,' said the woman in the cardigan.

'Of course.' The rector consulted the paper again. 'Class 1A, I think,' he told the woman in the cardigan. 'Is he in the hostel or lodgings?'

'Hostel,' his mother said.

'Class 1A it is, then.' The rector made a mark on the paper.

He sat back in his chair, puffing noisily, and looked at the woman in the cardigan.

'Now who's next?' he asked.

LANGUAGES

In the big school in Stornoway, the brainiest ones went to 1A and took French and Latin, the not quite so brainy to 1B and took French and Gaelic, the not quite so brainy again to 1D (French and Technical Subjects) and the ones with no brains at all to 1C or 1T, no one knew what they did, they all left school at fifteen and had nicknames like Jackal and Pongo. Holding *The Approach to Latin* open at arm's length on the palm of his hand and screwing up his eyes, granduncle Norman studied the picture of Augustus Imperator.

'Who's the warrior with the semmit and the cropped head?' he asked.

'The Emperor Augustus,' said Colin.

'Look, Mary,' said granduncle Norman. 'A Roman.'

Their mother came out of the scullery. She stood in the doorway, her arms flecked with soapy water, and granduncle Norman held the picture of Augustus Imperator up to her.

'Katy Ann Nellie,' she said at once. 'Put a headscarf and a swagger coat on him, you wouldn't know the difference. Except that the Roman's legs are skinnier,' she added, and went back to the scullery.

'He'll have to know every word in this book off by heart,' granduncle Norman shouted after her. 'If he still wants to be a doctor.'

'How come?' asked John the Battler.

'How *come?*' Their mother had reappeared in the scullery doorway. 'Were you ever in Tolmie the chemist's?' she asked John the Battler. 'And if you were,' she continued, not letting him answer, 'did your eye happen to light on all the little drawers in there with the pearl button knobs for all the poisons and medicines, and the coloured glass bottles with the pointy stoppers?'

'What about them?'

'What language was on them? On the labels? Was it English? No. Gaelic? But I'll tell you what language it was ...' Taking the book from granduncle Norman's hand, she thrust it violently at John the Battler. 'That one.'

'No use to me, Mary,' said John the Battler, looking down at *The Approach to Latin* and shaking his head.

'There are words in Latin,' said Colin, 'and the same words are in Gaelic. Columba is one.'

'Saint Columba,' said John the Battler.

'Columba is dove in Latin,' said Colin, 'and calman in Gaelic. Columba, calman, calman, columba.'

'Do you know, I never knew that,' said John the Battler. 'Say that again.'

'In French too,' said Colin. 'Church in French is eglise, in Gaelic eaglais. Eaglais, eglise, eglise, eaglais.'

'You could win bets at sea, knowing things like that,' said John the Battler.

'Well,' said granduncle Norman, blinking placidly, 'it's a true saying, John, the longer you live, the more you learn.'

'Maybe he'll be a teacher of languages,' their mother said, 'and not a doctor at all.'

'Beer in Spanish is cervesa,' said John the Battler.

'And what other wonders are they learning you over there in the big school?' granduncle Norman asked Colin.

'He's doing a picture,' their mother replied. 'A big painting on a canvas. Aren't you?'

'For a competition,' said Colin. 'The Battle of Culloden.'

'Drumossie Moor!' Granduncle Norman sat up straight and shook his head sadly. 'A black day for Gaels and Gaeldom. Now if you were doing a picture of the Battle of *Falkirk* . . .'

Tipping back his head, he recited:

> Mar gun rachadh cu a-measg chaoraich
> 'S iad nan ruith air aodann glinne
> 'S ann mar sin a rinn iad sgaoileadh
> Air an taobh air an robh sinne.

He laughed silently, his eyes closed, head still back, and slapping his hands on his thighs. Little wheezing noises came out of him.

'That . . .' he wheezed, laughed, trying to speak, '. . . wait now . . .'
He went weak with laughter.

Colin asked him once about Bonnie Prince Charlie and the same
thing happened.

'Donnchadh Ban . . .' he wheezed, laughed. 'He was on the wrong
side at Falkirk.'

'Mind you don't start coughing again,' their mother warned him.

The year before, aged eighty-two, he caught whooping-cough
from their sister Annie, who was always going up on his knee, and
nearly died.

'He was with the . . . the . . .' granduncle Norman gasped.

'The Roundheads,' said John the Battler.

'The *Hanoverians.*' Granduncle Norman raised a finger at John
the Battler, correcting him. Colin picked up his bonnet, which had
fallen from his knee onto the floor. 'The Roundheads were another
army altogether, John. Oliver Cromwell.'

'Right,' said John the Battler.

'The New Model Army. They were never beat. But Donnchadh
Ban was at Falkirk with the Argyll Militia, taking the place of a man,
Fletcher of Crannoch, who gave him a sword, and in the general
retreat and scatter after the battle, didn't Donnchadh Ban throw
the sword away, and Fletcher refused to pay him because he didn't
bring the sword back. It wasn't much of a sword anyway . . .' He
tipped his head back again:

> 'N claidheamh dubh nach d'fhuair a sguradh
> 'S neul an t-suithe air a leth-taobh
> 'S beag a b'fhiu e 's e air lubadh
> Gum b'e diugha a bhuill-deis e.

'What a memory!' said John the Battler. 'How does the rest of it go,
Norman?'

Their mother frowned at John the Battler; mouthed at him to
shut up.

'Let's be having it,' said John the Battler, crossing his arms on
his chest and settling himself noisily in the armchair. '*What?*' he
mouthed back at their mother.

Granduncle Norman shook his head.

'There was a day for that,' he said.

'Now shut your mouth and keep it shut,' their mother told John the Battler.

''On chaill mi trian na h-analach . . .' said granduncle Norman. 'He knew about old age, Donnchadh Ban . . .'

'What's sagitta?' John the Battler had opened *The Approach to Latin*.

'Himself and Dughall Buchanan . . .'

'An arrow,' said Colin.

'Ged bhiodh an ruaig am dheidh-sa, cha dean mi ceum ro chabhagach . . .' granduncle Norman murmured sadly.

'"Alas! It is always raining on our island",' John the Battler read. '"Upon my word, how dirty the farmer is!"'

'That's the language he's doing instead of Gaelic,' their mother said.

'O b'ait a leig mi dhiom 'ad . . .' granduncle Norman murmured.

'Gaelic!' she exclaimed. 'What good is Gaelic to him anyway? What good did Gaelic ever do any of *us*?'

'You're right there, Mary,' said John the Battler.

'I remember what old Tomas used to say. "Gaelic?" he used to say. "Leave her behind you on the quayside the day you leave the island" . . .'

'True, Mary, true,' John the Battler agreed. 'He was a thinking man, the same Tomas.'

Clapping *The Approach to Latin* shut, he handed it to Colin.

'Forget about Gaelic from now on, scholar,' he said. 'This is the lingo for you.'

'Together after me,' said Struan W. Tainsh, stretching up and tapping on the blackboard with his pointer.

Small white dots with lines sticking out of them at one end ran along the board from left to right, on five thin parallel lines. It was a music blackboard. The dots went up and down quite a lot. Some of them were joined together by lines at the top, and one was facing the wrong way round and seemed to be larger than the others.

'Ta – ta –' said Struan W. Tainsh, tapping on the blackboard with
the pointer. 'Ta – tee – ta. Taffa-tiffi, taffa-tiffi, ta – tee – ta.'
He stopped and looked at Colin.
'Are you grinning, boy?' he asked. 'Is that a grin on your face?'
He looked more closely at Colin. Then, carrying the pointer like a
spear, he came up between the desks.
'Are you the boy who used to get under my skin in Cross?' he said.

ECONOMICS

Through the bars of the high iron gate of the Boys' Hostel, Church
Street, his mother (face wrathful), aunty Meg (face like uncle Myles)
and cousin Alex Norman (face pink) berated him. He'd been in the
hostel less than a month, and he hadn't any money left. He'd spent
it all. The money from aunty Annie and aunty Isobel. The postal
order from uncle Calum in Chile. Even the half-crowns his granny
had saved for him in the big Fry's Cocoa tin, that he'd sworn (hand
on the big Collins Bible) to put in a post office savings book against
a rainy day. It was all gone. He hadn't even his bus fare home to
Ness for the weekend. That was why his mother and aunty Meg
were over in Stornoway. He'd written a letter to his mother. Cousin
Alex Norman was over with a broken leg. He was uncle Dan's son.
He'd broken his leg attempting the leap across the Swainbost river
that his father had done and that no one else in the district could
do, although plenty had tried.

By their faces, as he explained to them how the money in his
locker in the downstairs study had been stolen, he could tell that
they didn't believe him. They were right not to. It wasn't true. He'd
spent it all downtown, in Woolies and Cabrelli's and Capaldi's and
the Cando's, on sweets and ice lollies and crisps and broken biscuits.
He stopped talking at last, and cousin Alex Norman, canted on a
wooden crutch, property of the Lewis hospital, offered the opinion
that spending all your money in one go was foolishness, nothing
but, since, after you'd spent all your money, you wouldn't have
any left, and would be unable, consequently, to go anywhere or
do anything with your pals, if money was involved, because you

wouldn't have any, whereas they, being wiser than you, would. The plaster coming out of his unstitched trouser leg had a bobban sock over the end of it. 'Listen to your cousin Alex Norman!' aunty Meg counselled him. 'He was in the hostel himself once.' 'And where's the Conway Stewart I bought you?' his mother shouted at him, pointing at the penless top pocket of his jacket. Her voice was the same as at home; she didn't try to keep it down. 'I bought him a Conway Stewart fountain pen,' she shouted. 'It came in its own box, wrapped in tissue paper.' 'It's inside,' said Colin. 'Go and get it then, this minute,' his mother shouted, 'till I see it with my two eyes.' Across the road, in the TA barracks, the young soldiers had stopped drilling and were beginning to take notice. A hissing noise started in Colin's head. He'd sold the Conway Stewart to a boy called Scratchy, who, when Colin asked him for a shot of it back, to show his mother, looked up from the game of push-meek he was playing and said, 'Perambulate, cove.' Back outside, the hissing in Colin's head increased to a roar. He spoke through the railings. 'I can't find it,' he said. 'It was in my locker in the downstairs study, and now it isn't there.' 'Liar!' his mother shouted. 'I've let a liar loose on the world!' Aunty Meg closed her eyes and puffed her lips out like uncle Myles. 'Well, I wouldn't go as far as *that*, Mary . . .' cousin Alex Norman began. 'Wouldn't you?' his mother shouted. 'What else is he but a liar and a fool? He's also a thief!' Across the road, in the TA barracks, the young soldiers were now lining the railings. 'I think,' said aunty Meg, puffing out her lips, 'we'll all go down town to the Square restaurant and have a nice tea. I think that's what we'll do, Mary, once Colin fetches his suitcase.' 'Suitcase, what suitcase?' his mother shouted. 'He won't have a suitcase either, you wait and see! His suitcase will have been snatched out of his locker in the downstairs study by a golden *eagle*!' Cousin Alex Norman laughed. 'Good one, Mary,' said cousin Alex Norman, laughing and hopping on one foot in appreciation. 'Golden eagle, what? Now that's a good one . . .'

'My name is Mr MacLachlan,' said Lachie. He wrote it on the board. 'I'm your French teacher.'

'*I don't care if you don't do any work in the French class,*' he said. '*That's the first thing I want to say to you. It's up to yourselves. I'm not the one who has to pass my exams. I passed my exams long ago. I did my work. That's why I passed my exams. You do your work if you like. Don't if you don't. What do I care?*'

'*Except for homework ink exercises,*' he said. '*You must do your homework ink exercises. Don't do your homework ink exercises,*' he said, '*and I'll thrash you.*'

DORM 12

The new Boys' Hostel was in Ripley Place. They moved into it when Colin was in second year.

The new hostel was very large, very bright. It had twelve dormitories; six beds to each dorm. One dorm had seven beds. Twelve six seventy-two plus one seventy-three.

Colin was in Dorm 12. Calman was the prefect. The other boys in the dorm were: Neeawgy, Angie Brommy, Snarler and Baggamealie.

Calman was a boy with spiky fair hair, a snub nose and a ramrod back, who sounded, whenever he spoke, as though the area at the top of his nostrils, between his eyes, was stoppered with glue. He came from the parish of Uig, and only went home on holidays. Keeping his person, his possessions and his general surroundings always clean and tidy was what Calman did best (he once twisted Baggamealie's arm up behind his back for sitting on his bed); that, and being an officer in the Air Training Corps, and marching along on Armistice Sunday in his blue-grey uniform and cap, straight-backed, arms stiffly swinging, and eyes fixed with petrified intensity on the neck of the boy ahead. Just as purposefully, he strode down the lower corridor of the hostel every morning after prayers, wheeled left into the cloakroom, left again into the toilets, and entering the first cubicle in the row (the one nearest the wall) closed and locked the door behind him. His shiny black shoes, cross-laced, tied with butterfly loops, and the turnups and part of his collapsed trousers, visible in the space between the bottom of the door and the floor. A ploplop, followed by an adenoidal snort, as he released another correct turd in the direction of Goat Island, via Newton. And plenty more where that came from . . .

Colin did not like Calman.

He sat at a corner of the dressing table in Dorm 12, writing an English essay. The essay was for Calman; half a crown a page. *My Favourite Pastime.*

'*Who among us,*' he wrote, '*has not, on one occasion or another, gazed out upon the vast ocean and observed the fishing boats bravely sailing forth to greet the far horizon? So it was that I found myself one fine summer's morning . . .*'

'Don't put a lot of your clever stuff in it,' Calman instructed from the back of the chair. 'I don't want too high a mark.'

'What mark do you *want?*' Colin asked him.

'Sixty per cent. And write smaller,' Calman ordered him. 'Your writing isn't as big as that.'

'I'll write the way I always write,' said Colin.

'Write your normal hand,' said Calman. 'That's not your normal hand.'

'I'll write any way I like,' said Colin. 'Never you mind about my writing.'

They scowled at one another's reflections in the dressing table mirror. They detested one another.

Neeawgy and Angie Brommy were cousins, from the west side of the island; one was from Bragar, the other from Brue. They sat side by side in the back of the same class – 2B – went about together at all times, spoke to one another in Gaelic, and emitted the same vaguely buttery smell from their clothes, as though they'd newly emerged from a haystack; and while they didn't look at all alike – Neeawgy short and fat, Angie Brommy long and skinny; Neeawgy yellow-haired and smooth, Angie Brommy black and hairy; Neeawgy round-faced and cheerful, a genuine Siarach, with a waddling walk and a neck like a bagpiper's, Angie Brommy hollow-cheeked and unsmiling, with sharp knees and an Adam's apple – nevertheless you thought of them as one person, and if you were speaking to Neeawgy, and Angie Brommy wasn't there, you still felt that you were speaking to Angie Brommy as well, especially as Neeawgy never said a word to anyone if he could help it, only grinned, whereas Angie Brommy had lengthy opinions on everything under the sun. Angie Brommy wanted to leave school at fifteen and go to sea; Neeawgy was going to leave school at fifteen and go to sea whether he wanted to or not. Angie Brommy held the hostel record for farts after lights out (seventy-six), and for farts in sequence while walking (corner of Robertson Road to Bill Soft's house on Scotland Street); Neeawgy held no records of any kind. Both smoked, fished for mogs off Number 1 Pier, supported Rangers and went home to the west side every weekend carrying identical small brown suitcases. They were cousins.

Baggamealie was on first year. He was from Lochs. He had a magnifying glass in his locker.

'This is a pig of a place,' he said.

Garyvard he was from. Or Caversta. Somewhere like that.

'Why did they call you Baggamealie?' Colin asked him.

'Ask them,' said Baggamealie, his voice muffled by the towel.

He was very small. He was the smallest boy in the hostel.

'After they nicknamed me, they put my head out of the window and poured cold water on it,' he complained, furiously working the towel. 'Jugful after jugful. If my big brother Dan ever found out, he'd come over to this pig of a place and stretch every one of them out cold.'

Snarler had a stammer. He told stories.

'It isn't a stuh-stammer,' he told a woman who came to the school with a chart and a contraption with earphones. 'It's a spuh-speech impediment.'

He told stories after lights out.

Lights out was at half past ten. The teacher who came round to switch the lights off was called Boily. Sometimes the other teacher, The Lisper, came round, but usually it was Boily. He would start downstairs at Dorm 1, go along the bottom corridor to Dorm 4, come up the broom cupboard stairs (also known as the sick bay stairs), go along the upstairs corridor from Dorms 5 to 8, and then from Dorms 9 to 12 on the other side of the main stair landing, before going down the baggage room stairs and back to the masters' common room and the Light programme on the wireless.

They lay in their beds: Calman, Baggamealie and Snarler on the windows' side of the dorm, and Colin, Angie Brommy and Neeawgy on the corridor side, facing them; Calman reading the Bible (like most bullies, he was a Christian), Baggamealie reading Biggles, Snarler grinding his teeth, Colin reading *The Old Curiosity Shop*, Angie Brommy farting and Neeawgy staring at the ceiling. The door opened.

'Goodnight, boys,' said Boily.

'Goodnight, sir.'

The room went dark.

In the dark, they listened to Boily's feet skipping down the baggage room stairs. A short burst of dance music as he opened and closed the door of the masters' common room below.

'Duh-did you ever hear,' Snarler began, 'abuh-bout the Liechten-steinians?'

'Shut it, cove,' said Calman.

'The what?' said Angie Brommy.

'I said shut it,' said Calman.

'Thuh-the Liechtensteinians. From Liechtenstein. It's a small cuh-country between Swa-Switzerland and Austria.'

'What about them?' said Angie Brommy.

'I'm warning the pair of you,' said Calman.

'Go on, Snarler,' said Colin.

'You an' all, cove,' said Calman.

'Thuh-the Liechtensteinians and the Austrians fell out one time and duh-declared war on one another. So thuh-the Liechtensteinians assembled an army of one thuh-thousand men, and off thuh-they went with buh-bugles blowing and muh-muskets at the ready to fight the Austrians. And thuh-they were away for a year in Austria, fighting the Austrians, and after a year thuh-they came back and thuh-there was a thuh-thousand and one of them.'

Silence.

'How come?' Calman asked finally, in spite of himself.

A muffled yelp came out of the corner where Neeawgy was.

'What were they called again?' Angie Brommy asked Snarler.

'Thuh-the Liechtensteinians,' said Snarler.

'I asked you a question, cove,' Calman whispered fiercely across the room. 'How could a thousand man go away, and a thousand and one come back?'

'Didn't any of the Lilliputians get *killed?*' Angie Brommy wanted to know.

'Liechtensteinians.'

'What kind of a war *was* it?'

'You two guys,' Calman warned Neeawgy and Colin. 'Cut out the laughing or I'll hammer you.'

'They couldn't have,' Baggamealie suddenly piped up.

'Whuh-what?' said Snarler.

'Come back with one over.'

'A lot of nonsense,' said Calman.

'Maybe they couldn't count,' Angie Brommy said.

'Maybe they recruited an Austrian to their cause,' Colin said. 'Gave him a bugle and a musket.'

In the corner, Neeawgy started moaning.

'Did any of the *Austrians* get killed?' Angie Brommy asked. 'Who won the war anyway?'

'A lot of rubbish,' Calman whispered fiercely. 'I bet there's no such place.'

'Yuh-yes there is,' said Snarler. 'It cuh-could happen,' he said then.

'How?' said Calman. '*How*, you bastard?'

'*I* know!' Angie Brommy sat up in the dark. 'One of the men who marched away was a woman dressed as a soldier. During the campaign she gave birth to a child. That's how. Well?' he asked Snarler. 'Am I right?'

'Nuh-no.'

'Tell us then, you bastard,' Calman screamed in a whisper. 'Before I go over there and bash your stupid face in.'

'*I* know,' said Colin.

'I'm asking *him*,' said Calman.

'They got lost in Austria,' said Colin, 'it's a big country. In the Alps –'

'What Alps?' said Angie Brommy. 'There's no Alps in Austria.'

'Yes there are.'

'The Alps are in Switzerland.'

'There's Alps in Austria as well.'

'Bullshit!'

'Are you all going to shut up? Now?'

'There's Alps in France and Austria. The French Alps.'

'What about Holland?'

'*And* in Italy.'

'*And* in Ireland,' said Neeawgy. 'The Irish Alps.'

'Right!' Calman shouted, erupting out of bed and feeling about in the dark for his slippers. 'I warned the lot of you.'

The door opened. The light went on.

'What's all the noise in here?' Boily stood in the doorway. 'Where are you going, Donald?' he asked Calman.

'They wouldn't stop talking, sir,' Calman said, blinking in the light and squirming the top of his pyjamas trousers around by the cord so that his prick wouldn't fall out. 'I was going to deal with it.'

'I see-ee,' said Boily.

Calman stood under the bulbous yellow lightshade with the dead moth inside it. He didn't know what to do next.

'The troubles that afflict the just, Donald,' Boily said to him, 'in number many be.'

A shush of leather slippers on the polished floor followed this remark. It was Calman, coming to attention.

'And which ones were doing the talking?' Boily asked.

'All of them, sir,' Calman replied promptly, rigid with respect and glaring at the picture on the side wall, yellow flowers in a red pot.

'*He* wasn't,' said Colin, pointing across the room at Baggamealie's bed.

'Did you speak, Murray?' Boily turned to Colin.

'Yes, sir, I –'

'Did I ask you to speak?'

'No, sir.'

'So why are you speaking?' He turned back to Calman. 'Well done, Donald,' he said. 'You can go back to bed now.'

'You, Murray,' he said to Colin, 'can get up.'

Colin started to get up.

'On second thoughts,' said Boily, 'stay where you are.' He came away from the doorway and leaned over Colin's bed. He put his face close to Colin's. The skin on his face was a dirty white colour, pitted like the surface of a semolina pudding, full of nearly erupting boils and pimples and the scars of ancient boils and pimples. He looked sour and resentful, as always. "I've got this," his face seemed to be saying. "What have *you* got?" He looked like the Mad Hatter in Alice in Wonderland, without the hat. Colin could see up into his nostrils. 'Always the same with you, Murray,' he said, speaking through his nose. 'Isn't it?'

'What, sir?'

'Get up,' said Boily.

Colin got out of bed.

'You think you're clever, don't you?' said Boily. 'Look at me when I'm talking to you.'

'No, sir.'

'*No sir*,' Boily repeated, through his nose. 'Where are your slippers?' he asked. 'Why are you standing there in your bare feet?'

'And of course,' Boily continued, when Colin, his feet in the Paw Broon slippers that aunty Meg had bought for him in Alan Martin's shop, was standing once again in front of him, 'the truth is that you're not really clever at all. Is he, Donald?'

'No, sir,' said Calman.

'He thinks he is. But he's not. Look at me when I'm talking to you! I'm cleverer than you are. As you found out to your cost that time you tried to dodge going to church. Didn't you, Murray?'

'Yes, sir.'

'*Yes sir!* Dodging past the main door through the shrubbery and then out of the seminary gate. You thought you were being very clever then, didn't you?'

'No, sir.'

'*No sir!* And speaking when you're not spoken to isn't very clever either.' Bringing his right hand up, he cracked Colin on the head with the knuckle of his middle finger. 'What do you have to say now, Murray? Look at me!'

'Nothing, sir.' Tears pricked behind Colin's eyes.

'You're learning,' said Boily. 'And there's plenty more where that came from. Now get back to your bed.'

He banged out. Banged back in.

'Goodnight,' he said, and switched off the light.

'Goodnight, sir,' said Calman, in the dark, after him.

You could play table tennis in Study One on Saturday mornings. All day Saturday, if you liked. So long as Boily didn't come skipping in from the masters' common room next door, looking for a game. No one could beat Boily at table tennis. He had a sponge bat, and played left-handed. Smash the ball as hard as you liked, pock it would come back, and there was Boily on the other side of the table, sandshoes squeaking, Fair Isle pullover tucked inside his trousers and sponge bat at the ready, waiting for the next one. And he spun the ball on his own serve, which he wasn't supposed to do. You hadn't a snowball's against him. After the third game it got boring. You wished you'd gone downtown. You wished you hadn't started playing him in the first place.

THE LISPER

'Murray,' said the Lisper. 'I am *in loco parentis*, and I command you to eat that tomato.'

'I can't, sir.'

'Do you hear me, boy? I command you.'

They were in the dining room, on their own. Everyone else had gone. As soon as tea was over, the other boys had followed the matron and Boily in an orderly manner out through the swing doors, fetched their coats from the cloakrooms and gone downtown. The hostel was silent.

Behind the kitchen hatch at the far end of the dining room the maids, too, were silent.

The Lisper pushed the segments of tomato around on the plate with a fork.

'Take it,' he said, waving the fork under Colin's nose. 'Take this fork from my hand.'

Colin took the fork.

'Now,' said the Lisper. 'Eat the tomato.'

'I can't,' said Colin.

The Lisper took the fork from Colin. He speared one of the segments of tomato on the fork and waved the fork under Colin's nose.

'Open your mouth!' he said. 'Open it!'

Colin shook his head.

'Take the fork from my hand!' the Lisper shouted. 'Take it!'

Colin took the fork.

'Now,' said the Lisper, 'put the tomato in your mouth. Open your mouth,' he said, 'and put the tomato in it.'

'I can't, sir,' said Colin.

'Do it,' said the Lisper. His breath went faster; his shoulders heaved. 'Do it now!'

'I can't.'

'Are you defying me, boy?'

'No, sir.'

'Then eat the tomato.'

'I can't, sir.'

'Are you defying me, boy?'

'I'll be sick, sir.'

The Lisper snatched the fork from Colin. The segment of tomato fell off it and landed on the table. Colin's hand went out to pick up the tomato. The Lisper, fork poised, looked at Colin's hand. Colin drew his hand back again.

The Lisper closed his eyes. 'Your grandfather was a missionary,' he said. His voice suddenly sounded weary. 'Your uncle is a minister of the gospel. Your father, before his passing, was a godly man. And you! . . . You! . . . How many poor creatures in the world this minute,' he asked, opening his eyes, 'would be glad of that tomato? How many poor creatures in the world this minute would raise their hands to

heaven and make a joyful noise at the sight of that tomato? And you!
... You! ...' He handed Colin the fork. 'Take it!' he said urgently.
'This minute!' Colin took the fork. 'Now,' the Lisper pointed at
the three remaining segments of tomato on the plate. 'That is a
tomato. But that is not any tomato. That is God's tomato. God's
gift, to you, of a tomato. What does God want you to do with that
tomato? Answer me, Murray!'

'I don't know, sir.'

'He wants you to eat that tomato. Eat it, and be glad.'

Colin didn't say anything.

'"Eat my gift of a tomato," God is saying to you. "Eat it now. This
minute. I command you to eat my tomato," God is saying to you.'
The Lisper's breath went faster; his shoulders heaved. 'Well?'

'I can't, sir.'

'Are you defying God, boy?'

'No, sir.'

'Are you defying God as well as me, boy? *Non modo sed etiam?*'

'I'll be sick, sir.'

The Lisper goggled at Colin, made a small noise in the back of
his throat, then strode down to the far end of the dining room and
knocked on the hatch. The hatch flew up at once. Bellann's face was
behind it, and Sheena the cook's.

'You may commence clearing up now,' the Lisper told them.
'We're finished in here.'

Without looking at Colin, he strode back up the dining room and
barged out through the swing doors. Bellann made a face after him.
The swing doors dodged one another briefly on their hinges before
coming to rest.

'He's raging,' said Sheena the cook. 'See the face on him!'

'Better go after him,' Bellann said to Colin.

'Why?'

'He'll only come back looking for you if you don't.'

'Could you no' have scoffed the bloody thing and be done with
it?' said Sheena the cook. 'Given us all some peace?'

Bellann jerked her head towards the swing doors.

'Go on.'

The Lisper was waiting for him in the front hall. Shoulders hunched, lower lip jutting out, eyes goggling, legs apart, arms crooked in front of his body and hands bunched into fists, he looked like someone about to make his third and final attempt in a high jump competition. The matron was beside him, talking into his ear. Her face was bright red. She'd started the argument about the tomato in the first place. The other teacher – Boily – was also on the scene, at the top of the stairs, leaning with both hands on the railing, listening.

'You horrible boy!' the matron exclaimed, as soon as she saw Colin. 'He's the worst boy in the hostel! In the school! In the island!'

The Lisper goggled at Colin.

'I shall punish him, Miss Ferguson,' he said.

'Punish him severely!' the matron urged. 'He deserves a good thrashing!'

'*Facta non verba*,' said the Lisper. 'What do *you* think, Mr Macaulay?'

'O ... *mura h-ionnsaich ris a' ghluin* ...' Boily intoned from upstairs.

'Murray,' said the Lisper, 'you have turned me into a vessel of wrath.'

'Spare the rod ...' Boily's voice floated down again. The matron reared her head at him. She didn't like Boily.

The Lisper had kept his eyes fixed on Colin. 'How should I punish you, boy?'

'Belt him,' said the matron.

'Detention,' said Colin.

'Both,' said Boily.

The Lisper brooded for a bit.

'Murray,' he said at last, 'there is a demon in you.'

'Horrible boy,' the matron said.

'Detention you want, detention you shall have. For the next month, you will not be allowed to go downtown after tea. You will not be allowed outside this building. Nor will you be allowed to sit in the wee study, as is your wont, listening to idle music on the wireless. No, for the next month you will carry out such tasks as Miss Ferguson and I might deem –'

'He can start by cleaning out the broom cupboard under the stairs,' the matron said.

'You can start by cleaning out the broom cupboard under the stairs,' the Lisper repeated. '*Laborare est orare.*'

'After that he can polish the corridors,' the matron said. 'Upstairs and downstairs.'

'Please sir,' said Colin, 'what about weekends?'

'How dare you!' the matron shouted. She rounded on the Lisper. 'How dare he!' she said.

'The same applies at weekends,' the Lisper said. 'Furthermore,' he said, 'you will not be attending St Columba's on Sunday from now on, as is your wont. A denomination to which you do not belong. No, you will attend the church of your father and of your grandfather and of your uncle. The Free Church.'

'Quite right,' said Boily.

'But sir –'

'And you will attend not once but twice. I'll see to that. Morning and evening you shall go.'

He goggled balefully at Colin.

'*Dixi*,' he said.

It was a physics experiment. On to small pans suspended by strings from twin pulleys, the Doc placed copper weights. One of the pans went down, the other one didn't. The Doc prodded a pulley wheel with his finger and equilibrium was restored.

'Eh,' said the Doc. 'Now pay attention.'

Through wire-rimmed spectacles, one of his eyes was much larger than the other; behind a pebbly lens, it wobbled like a bantam's egg. Snuffling up the dewdrop on the end of his nose, he wiped away the residue with a handkerchief that crackled when he used it. He restored the handkerchief to his trouserpocket, and a sudden stir went through the class. The Doc's flies were undone!

'In order to avoid parallax,' said The Doc, 'a small mirror was slipped behind each string in turn . . .'

'Someone should tell him!' Cathy Squeak squeaked at the boys behind her.

The Doc's flies were undone. Not just one button either, but all of them, revealing a piece of crumpled striped shirt and a hint of some sulphurous garment underneath.

'Care was taken,' said The Doc, 'to ensure that the pulleys were equidistant . . .'

'Excuse me, sir.' Sammy had materialised at the Doc's side.

'Eh?'

Taking him by the elbow, Sammy turned the Doc round, so that he was facing the radiator and not the class. Still holding him by the elbow, Sammy spoke rapidly into the Doc's ear, accompanying his speech with flowing, confident gestures of his free hand.

'Eh?' said the Doc.

Sammy pointed downwards. The Doc gave a little jump.

'Heh,' he said, and started frantically to button up. Viewed from behind, he resembled someone trying to knead dough while treading on water. Finished, he turned round. The dewdrop was back.

'Eh,' he said. 'Now pay attention.'

PENANCE

. . . up the wide path to the door of the great building, its jaws, like gigantic bivalves, gaped open to receive you. No turning sideways into the shrubbery here, no dodging through the grounds at the back. Already beginning to speak to one another in whispers; a heavy weight of oppression settling in. The smell in the vestibule of varnish and whitewashed cement, a holy odour, catching your throat, tightening your heart. Where two elders lower behind the collection plate on its marbled plinth, and your brown wing plays king of the castle upon the heaped paper and silver. *It's not much, but it's a contribution,* your aunty Annie would say. *As the wren remarked when he pissed in the ocean. They were not numbered among the host on the hilltop where the smiles were being handed out,* she would say. A head, long as a Clydesdale's, bland as a cheviot's, grey as a summer fog, swooping down, belches into your face the aroma of boiled mutton broth, boiled Sunday gigot; a spongy hand clammily enfolds yours. *And and and is this the Reverend Murray's nephew?* The Lisper, behind me, riding shotgun: Yeth. *Is that so? Well well. Well well.* Long grampus stare into my phizog. You'll know me the next time. I hate this. I hate this more than anything. Dried bloodspot on his collar, permanent tight knot in the shiny black tie. For Sabbaths and funerals. He hangs it on the wing mirror of the dressing table, slips it over his head like a noose. *And and is he . . . are we . . . a blessed boy?* The Lisper: No. Faces of the members turn to gaze on you in passing: feel my own face reddening. The adherents. And beautiful Annabel Graham among them, she passes with downcast eyes. Flanked by stern father, pudding mother. In a wine coat and white knitted toorie. Her legs in nylons. I saw under her armpit once, I saw the hair in it. When the girls were playing netball. It was light brown; glistening. *But perhaps God will open his eyes one of these days?* You bet your boots. You bet your three league bachles. And once I peeked over the wall of her house in Scotland Street to see the news of the day on the washing line. Who was that superannuated goof? Iain F. enquires in a whisper, as you creep like snails upstairs to the balcony. Haven't the foggiest. But I am Myles Murray's nephew. Here I am. In a side balcony of the Free Church, Kenneth Street, Stornoway, one Sunday evening (present), between the hour of my birth (past) and the hour of my death (never). Little dots in the grain of the pew. Wormwood. Varnish varnish everywhere. A silence like the hissing of a hundred tilley lamps. One fine Sunday evening comma my friends and I planned to go to the Free Church full stop. We took plenty of lemonade and sandwiches with us before we set off. Sonorous, the clock on the central balcony grinds out the time: *kreek-klunk* for every second. Only two and a half hours to go; two and a quarter, if he cuts it short. John Knox or Angus of the Bens was converted listening to the clock. *Kreek-klunk.* Buh-bring on the dancing girls. Who said that? Snarler. Stop laughing. O my bellybutton! The Lisper's watching you, Colin. Is he? Shite! He squeezed his hands between his knees, pretended to look for something on the floor. All right. I'm all right. Is he still . . . ? There's that woman (careful!) from Laxdale who comes on the early bus every Monday morning. Is it? Don't look at Snarler. Yes it is. No sign of a white knitted toorie below, among the shifting sea of hats, heliographing skulls, bowed and gleaming grey heads. God's people, down in the well, giving off naphthalene. They sit to sing and stand to pray. And I spy with my little eye the face of the hostel matron, flaming under a grey hat with a scrap of netting going across it. And Holy Porky, blessed boy, beside her, in a blue suit gone shiny at arse and knee and elbow. Bible and Psalmody on the pew before him, poke of bisected winegums in his pocket. Doctored goodies. He cuts them in half with a too blunt to shave with anymore blue Gillette razorblade. Have a burg. Have an undy. A tiny hag, all in black, flanking him to port (Have a po!) confidently gnashes her gums at his lug; he inclines his head, softly closes his eyes, the better to hear her. Pig in the middle. Pass it on. Between the two hats, his head shines like a seal's . . .

'Is he really your uncle, cove?'

'Sure.'

. . . The second psalm wailed and sirened itself to a straggling close, the precentor quit his small stance facing the congregation and settled himself among the front row of elders, and the Reverend Myles Murray, visiting preacher, uprose slowly from his place of concealment underneath the pulpit lectern (What was he doing under there? Checking his pools coupon? Carving his initials?), and hailed by a preludial barrage of coughing and unwrapping of goodie papers, stood, solemn and silent, conning the middle air, bidding the multitude be still. Beneath him, the obsequious deacon, two-handed bearer of the Book, opener and closer of pulpit doors, rose also, and semaphoring with his arms as he went, tiptoed tipsily across an invisible tightrope in the floor to a panel beside the vestry, where he switched off every second light in the building, to save on the electricity. To be switched on again at the close of the sermon. Waste not want not. Where was Moses when the lights went out?

Silent and solemn, his masked moon face surmounting a white clerical collar, over which the soft flesh at both sides of his neck bulged whenever he moved his head, uncle Myles waited until a silence, bated and profound, had fallen. Then, bringing his eyebrows together and puffing out his lips, he intoned sternly:

'We will now, in the brief time afforded to us together, turn to that portion of God's word from which we read ...' a hum and buzz started up again as the tardier ones leafed through the flimsy pages of their Bibles, pursuing the text '... The gospel according to Saint Matthew, chapter five, verse thirteen: "Ye are the salt of the earth; but if the salt have lost his savour, wherewith shall it be salted? It is henceforth good for nothing, but to be cast out, and to be trodden under foot of men ..."'

Watty was a huge man with a red, bristly moustache, who was always in a hurry. He had a trick, when entering a room, of flinging the door open all the way and backheeling it shut on the rebound. He taught English.

'Crichton,' he said, uncurling the strap he'd taken from his briefcase. 'Do you know what this is?'

'Yes, sir,' said Alex Dan Crichton from Point.

'What is it, Crichton?'

'The belt, sir.'

'But not just any belt,' said Watty. 'This is Whang-ho, Crichton. The real Lochgelly. Take a good look at it. In a minute you're going to feel it.'

He told Johnina Smith to stop blubbering and sit down. Walking on the points of his toes and pushing a pram that wasn't there with his arms, he crossed the floor of the classroom and planted both hands against the windowpane. 'I can't teach with this racket going on,' he raged, above the clatter of the jackhammers on Springfield Road. 'How can I teach with this racket going on?' He turned on Catherine Margaret Macleod (B) from Tolsta, who was in the first desk by the window. 'You've a lovely smile,' he told her. 'A lovely face. God in his mercy lent her grace. For three years now, I've been admiring that face. But can it speak? That is the question. I don't know. It hasn't, up to now. Not to me. Not in three long years has it deigned to utter one single, solitary word to me. Well?' Catherine Margaret Macleod (B)'s lovely face went bright red. She smiled nervously at him. 'Take out your vocabulary book,' Watty told her. *'Learn words. Learn to speak. Learn English. All of you!'* He spread his arms out wide. *'You're the cream of Lewis youth! Ye gods and little fishes!'*

THE REBEL

'The Rebel?' said Colin. 'He's nothing.'

'He's strong, though,' said John Angie.

'*Strong?*' said Colin. 'The *Rebel?*' He passed the cigarette to John Angie and watched as John Angie took a long drag from it. The glow from the red end of the cigarette lit up John Angie's face. John Angie handed the cigarette back. It was their last one.

'He doesn't bother *me*,' Colin said.

'He threw six full containers of beer into the back of the lorry with one hand,' John Angie said. 'Kenny Dan saw him doing it, outside the Crit.'

'How do you know they were full?'

'What?'

'The containers of beer.'

'They were for the Habost bothan,' John Angie said. 'What else would they be but full?'

'They could have been empty.'

'I never thought of that,' John Angie said. 'He could have been outside the Crit loading six empty containers of beer for the Habost bothan into the back of the lorry. I never thought of that.'

'He doesn't bother *me*,' Colin said again. 'I'd like to see him try.'

Colin and John Angie were at the junction of the village road and the main road, leaning against the glebe wall. The night was clearing now, and clean-smelling after the rain; a fresh wind blowing, the moon racing behind rainclouds. They were waiting for the boat bus from Stornoway, which carried the newspapers. The newspapers came over from the mainland every night on the MacBrayne's steamer *Loch Seaforth*. This was before the plane started carrying them. The bus then took them over to Ness. They were a day late. There was a wooden box with a felt-hinged lid at the end of the road for the newspapers, and during the week the bus would stop and the conductress would get down and put the newspapers in the box, but at weekends things were different, at weekends the bus, swaying like a galleon, with steamed-up windows and a wail of Gaelic song from the back, would hurtle past the road-end without stopping, the white, cylindrical roll of newspapers, tied with twine, sailing from the driver's window and landing with a thump in the road, or – more often – the ditch. Colin and John Angie were at the road-end to make sure that the newspapers didn't land in the ditch, which was flooded with two days' rain. The report of the Marciano–Don Cockell fight would be in the paper, and they were looking forward to reading it. Maybe there would be photographs of all the knockdowns.

'The thing about the Rebel,' said Colin, 'is he knows who to take on.' He handed the stump of the cigarette to John Angie and started pacing up and down on the road. 'If someone's drunk. Or old men like Geordie. Or the Golightly. People like the Golightly.'

'He had a fight with John the Quarry,' John Angie said.

'When?'

'Last weekend. Friday night. You weren't home last weekend.'

'Where?'

'Down in Cross. In front of the post office. They were arguing who was the better driver . . . Do you want the last drag?'

'No,' said Colin. He paced up and down, then asked 'Who won?'

'The Rebel,' John Angie said.

The Rebel was the same age as Colin and John Angie, and lived with his grandfather and uncle. His parents had been killed during the war in one of the German air raids on Clydebank; because of the war, they'd left the Rebel behind in Lewis with his grandparents. His granny used to take a stick, a new rope, anything she could lay her hands on to the Rebel, but couldn't keep going very long because of breathlessness; and when she died (the same year as Colin's father), an aunt came to take the Rebel to live with her in Newtonmore on the mainland, but the Rebel refused to go, preferring to stay with his grandfather, a small old man with a limp and close-set eyes, who sat all day in front of a peat fire tending a litter of blackened cooking pots and hawking gobs of spit, at precise intervals, into the fender and ashes. The Rebel's uncle was the local butcher; he kept ferrets. It was not a house for casual visiting.

The Rebel, Colin and John Angie had gone to Cross school together, had been on the same class for the first two years, before Colin jumped a class. Then Colin had gone to the big secondary school in Stornoway, and the Rebel and John Angie to the local secondary school in Lionel. Colin was still in school, and came home every second weekend. The Rebel worked for his uncle. Mainly he drove the big butcher's van, at terrific speeds, while the uncle, a jittery alcoholic, bobbed up and down in the front passenger seat, taking quick sips from a half-bottle and keeping an eye out for the police. The Rebel could drive – he also went into the bars in Stornoway; more than once, Colin, in school uniform, had seen him come strutting out of the Royal or the Caley among the grown men. The Rebel also had a girlfriend on the west side, whom he mounted regularly in the back of the big butcher's van, among the carcasses and sheeps' heads on hooks and buckets of blood and intestines. He played for the Ness football team, and walked always with a rattling of change in his pockets. John Angie was on the dole.

'John the Quarry must have been drunk,' Colin said.

'I don't know,' John Angie said. 'Anyway the Rebel put him down three times, they were saying.'

'John the Quarry must have been pissed out of his mind.'

'The Rebel's strong, man,' John Angie said. 'You can't deny it.'

'Strong my arse! Is it the man that fainted in the canteen at the sight of blood? Remember that? When Ross the dentist was in the school, and Roddy Ivor put out the gob of blood into his mince, and the next thing the Rebel fell off the stool, like that –' he leaned backwards, demonstrating. 'Out cold. His eyes nowhere to be seen. Remember that?'

'Yes.'

'Well then?'

'I wish I had a smoke,' John Angie said.

'Do you know what *I* would do,' Colin said, 'if the Rebel ever tried anything on with me?'

'What?'

'I'd go for his guts.' He stood before John Angie in a boxer's stance, up on his toes, and explained in a tight voice: 'First with the left, feinting. To put him off balance. See? Then a right to the solar plexus. That was how Fitzsimmons beat Corbett,' he added, breathing out.

'Yes,' said John Angie, 'but what would the Rebel be doing all this time?'

'He would be doing nothing,' said Colin. 'Nothing. Because there would be nothing he *could* do.'

They were silent for a while then.

'We get boxing in the hostel,' Colin said. 'With gloves. It isn't strength that counts but skill. Look at Dempsey and Tunney.'

'What about Marciano?' John Angie asked.

'Marciano? Marciano's a freak. Walcott nearly beat Marciano.'

'Yes, but he didn't.'

'Yes, but he nearly did. Like Sugar Ray and Maxim. Sugar Ray would have won, but his legs gave out in the heat.'

'Sugar Ray was the greatest of them all.'

'He said Randy was his toughest opponent.'

'Someone's coming.'

Two figures were approaching on the village road. They were smoking. Their cigarettes made little red points in the dark. They came up. 'Has the boat bus come yet?' the taller of the two asked. It was Donald, John Angie's brother. With him was the Rebel. There was a strong smell of beer.

'Not yet.'

Donald bent down and peered into Colin's face. 'You're there,' he said.

'Aye.'

'Any fags on you?' John Angie asked his brother.

'Not for you,' Donald replied. He dropped what was left of his cigarette on the road and ground it out with the point of his shoe. The Rebel laughed.

'Where have you been like this?' Colin asked.

'Up in the bothan,' Donald said. 'Drinking.'

'Eight pints,' the Rebel said, speaking for the first time. 'That's a gallon, isn't it?'

Colin snorted.

'Eight pints one gallon,' the Rebel recited, laughing. He had a merry, brimming laugh.

'Did you stay up to listen to the fight on the wireless?' Donald asked Colin.

'Yes,' Colin replied.

'Colin's a fighter himself,' the Rebel said.

'It was a good fight,' Colin said, to Donald.

'Anything you want to know about boxing, ask Colin,' the Rebel said. 'He's a boxer himself.'

Donald took out a packet of cigarettes and gave one to the Rebel. The Rebel struck a match, cupping the flame in his hands against the wind. They lit up.

'Aren't you?' the Rebel said, turning, grinning, to Colin.

'What?'

'A boxer.'

'What do you mean?'

'Listen to his voice trembling!' the Rebel exclaimed gleefully. He turned back to Colin. 'Say something else,' he urged. 'Go on.'

'No.'

'Go on.'

'No.'

The Rebel stood in front of Colin, soft laughter spilling out of him, and belched straight into his face. 'Eight pints,' he said. Colin pressed back against the wall.

'No papers,' said Donald. 'Let's go back to the bothan.'

'Wait,' said the Rebel. 'We might hear something.'

'Come on,' Donald said. He started walking back into the village.

'All right.' The Rebel set off after him, flicking his cigarette away over his shoulder as he went. It described a red arc in the air and landed on the road, where it rolled a little way, then stopped, glowing and sparking in the wind.

Their footsteps, their voices, receded.

A merry laugh came back on the wind. It was the Rebel.

They were gone.

John Angie went over and picked up the cigarette. He sucked greedily at it.

'Want a drag?' he asked.

Colin didn't answer.

The moon broke out of the clouds; bright and buoyant, it raced across the sky. Looking south, John Angie could see, against the sky, like a searchlight, the glare of a moving vehicle. He listened as hard as he could, but it was still too far away for him to tell what kind of an engine it was.

When the hullaballo was over, and Godfrey, geometry abandoned, had stalked, still purple in the face, from the room, and Chumbo's nose had stopped bleeding, and Norrie Bachles had retrieved Chumbo's jotter and maths box from the floor, and the blackboard duster had been retrieved from underneath a radiator by Susie, and the twenty-four green ink exercise books had been retrieved from different parts of the room by different scholars and reassembled in their original pile on the teacher's desk, a piece of paper, folded twice, was passed along the class to Colin. The paper was from Prof, a boy with square horn-rimmed glasses and a hollow in the back of his neck, who lived in a posh part of Stornoway and never took gym. This is what the paper said:

Given: Godfrey.

Required: To prove that Godfrey is mad.

Construction: Upon blackboard in centre of classroom, facing class, describe a circle containing quadrilateral ABCD as shown. Let the given Godfrey stand at point P, right hand corner of classroom, at an angle of 80 degrees to the horizontal, facing class, staring at point Q, left hand corner of diagonally opposite ceiling.

Let Donald Roderick Macleod (Chumbo) sit at point R, left hand corner of classroom, in desk, back row, head in hand, facing blackboard, facing Godfrey.

Let the given Godfrey, from right hand corner of classroom, point P, direct the following words – 'Prove quadrilateral ABCD is a cyclic quadrilateral' – at left-hand corner of ceiling, point Q. Let these words be heard by no one except Muriel Mary Martin (Split), at point S, left-hand side of classroom, in desk, front row, nearest to Godfrey, and in position EFGH as shown, EF perpendicular to FG, GH perpendicular to FG, state of nervous apprehension.

Let the given Godfrey, in addition to the foregoing words, further direct at point Q, left-hand corner of ceiling, the word 'Macleod'. Let the word 'Macleod' be heard by no one except Muriel Mary Martin (Split), at point S, left hand corner of classroom, front row, in position EFGH as shown, angle EFG equals angle FGH, state of acute anxiety. Let the word 'Macleod' not be heard by Donald Roderick Macleod (Chumbo), at point R, left hand corner of classroom, back row, head in two hands, abstracted from mathematical considerations by memories of his father's bullock.

Draw the straight lines PS, PR, RP.

Proof: Let the given Godfrey proceed in an agitated manner along the line PS, his progress sharply arrested at point S by sudden unsought contact of his left shin with right-angle of wood and metal at corner of desk (point X) occupied by Muriel Mary Martin (Split), his progress subsequently delayed by demonstration of violent improvised semaphore above head of Muriel Mary Martin (Split), in position EFGH as shown, EF parallel to GH, state of nervous collapse. Proceeding along the line PR to point R, let the given Godfrey commence to belabour Donald Roderick Macleod (Chumbo) about the head with heavy clubbing blows, accompanied by open-handed slaps, causing the nose of Donald Roderick Macleod to issue with scarlet fluid, the eyes of Donald Roderick Macleod to assume a glassy appearance, the cheeks of Donald Roderick Macleod to be likened unto the sun at dusk declining into Loch Roag, and the hair of Donald Roderick Macleod to stand in contrary directions upon his head. Let the further ministrations of the given Godfrey at point R consist of flamboyant flingings of various inanimate objects from desk of Donald Roderick Macleod (Chumbo) to floor beneath, item, one mathematics jotter (dog-eared), item, one box of mathematical instruments comprising compass with stub of pencil inserted, pair of dividers, protractor, set square, six-inch wooden ruler, blue Gillette razor blade and scrap of paper torn from back page of obsolete Science notebook with D.R. Macleod, Class 3A, written on it in dubious copperplate. Returning along the line RP, bypassing at point S Muriel Mary Martin (Split) in position EFGH as shown, EFGH a straight line, state of mortal terror, let the given Godfrey stand at point P, right hand corner of classroom, at an angle of 70 degrees to the horizontal, and direct incomprehensible ululations at point Q, left hand corner of diagonally opposite ceiling, before continuing along semi-circular curve PvY as shown from point P to Y, where Y represents the teacher's desk. Halted at point Y, let the given Godfrey direct at the topmost of twenty-four green ink exercise books upon the desk the words, 'Here is a boy who can't spell Tuesday', and imitating the action of hammerhurlers at Highland games, launch said pile of exercise books at an indeterminate area of the ceiling in brief but doomed defiance of Sir Isaac Newton's First Law of Gravity. Let this action be complemented in rapid manic sequence by the following actions: (1) erasing from blackboard of circle containing quadrilateral ABCD, (2) hurling of blackboard duster against partition wall, whence, describing short arc EFG as shown, it came to rest underneath a radiator, (3) writing upon blackboard with squealing chalk of six problems in the discipline of algebra, (4) exiting in wrathful silence through parallelogram LMNO (door).

Wherefore the given Godfrey is mad.

THE FUNERAL

The door of the chemistry lab opened, and the secretary's face appeared.

'Sorry to disturb you, Mr Macarthur,' she said.

'Not at *all*, Miss Finlayson,' said Wobbly, swiftly lowering the flame of the bunsen burner, then raising his arms in happy surrender and giving a little writhe like a hula dancer from the knees upwards.

'Colin Murray,' she said. 'He has to report to the rector's office.'

'Has *he*?' said Wobbly in a high, jocular voice. 'What have you done *now*, Murray?'

'Nothing, sir.'

'Get along with you, then,' Wobbly shouted, throwing out one arm like Mark Antony over the body of dead Caesar. 'Don't keep Miss Finlayson waiting.'

He fancied Miss Finlayson. Everyone could tell.

'Why does Fatso want to see me?' Colin asked the back of the secretary's head as he anxiously followed her down the stairs.

'You're asking,' she replied. 'Moby's been summoned an' all.'

'You're going to a funeral,' the rector said.

Colin and Alan looked at one another.

'A relation of your father's,' uncle Myles, who was sitting on the other chair in the rector's office, told them. His black hat was on the rector's desk, on top of some papers. 'Norman Macaulay.'

> Lars Porsena of Clusium,
> By the nine gods he swore,
> That the great house of Tarquin,
> Would suffer wrong no more . . .

'So you won't be coming back to school this afternoon,' the rector said.

Outside the main school gates, they saw their other uncle, Dan.

'I'm waiting for the reverend, boys,' he said. He looked odd in a black coat and a collar and tie. He told them where the house was, and how to get there.

'Who was Norman Macaulay?' Colin asked Alan. They were on their way up Matheson Road to the hostel at dinnertime.

'How should *I* know?' Alan replied sharply, over his shoulder. 'Related to your father. That's all *I* know.'

'Never heard of him,' said Colin. 'Never knew I had a relative living in Stornoway till now.'

'You haven't,' Alan snapped, and Pedro, who was with him, laughed. 'I'll tell you something else,' Alan went on. 'You're not coming with me to any funeral in that brown suit of yours.'

'The Grousehunter,' said Pedro.

'But that's the only suit I've *got*,' Colin protested.

'Get another.'

'Who from?'

'Anyone.' And Pedro, after landing a punch on his back that put him to his knees on the hostel steps, also said:

'Get another.'

He got a suit from Wally.

It was a blue single-breasted suit with thin white stripes, and lined on the inside with stuff like silk. A clean white handkerchief was folded into the breastpocket, and the trousers were sharply ironed, with no bulges at the backside or knees. Only one thing was wrong with it – it was far too big for him. He looked at himself in the wardrobe mirror.

'What'll we do?' he asked Wally.

They put braces on the trousers and pushed the buckles up over his shoulders and halfway down his back. This caused the trousers to hang at half-mast and press up into his groin, forcing him to walk with a high, hobbling gait, one leg stepping out from his body when the other one wanted to go straight; at the same time, the trousers were so loose about the waist that he needed two belts to hold them in – Wally's leather belt, in which they made a new hole with the leg of a compass, through the loops, and his own red and yellow snakebelt underneath. 'With a thick jersey on under the jacket you won't look so bad,' Wally said, taking a step away from him and frowning.

'Two thick jerseys,' said Neeawgy.

'Hen Broon models Charles Atlas,' said Angie Brommy, from the bed.

'You'll be wearing a coat,' said Wally, 'won't you?'

> Shame on the false Etruscan,
> Who lingers in his home,
> When Porsena of Clusium,
> Is on the march for Rome . . .

'*Now* I know who he is!' Colin informed his own reflection in the wardrobe mirror.

'Who?'

'Norman Macaulay. The man who's dead. Norrie Aulay he was called. A wild man.'

'You can't wear brown bumpers with a blue suit,' Wally told him.

'His name comes up whenever my mother goes into a rage at us. In the same breath as Black John and Tammy Toronto.'

'Who were *they?*'

'Brothers of my Habost granny's. Wild men.'

The funeral was at two o'clock. At half-past one, he was walking with his brother Alan beside the Acres playing fields. 'Get a move on,' Alan said. 'Why are you walking like *that?*'

'Uncle Dan,' Colin told him, 'said ten to two would be early enough.' 'Just get a move on,' his brother said. They turned a corner, into a street of council houses. On the pavement outside one house, men with hats and coats were standing, talking in low voices. They all had Stornoway accents. One of them came over and started talking to Alan about football. Alan was a famous footballer on the island. He played inside left for the school team. He'd already been capped for the Lewis Select. Inside the house, in the livingroom, they started singing a psalm. When the singing stopped, there was a movement behind the window of people getting to their feet, then the front door opened and a man in a black coat came out: Archie Macrae, the undertaker. Uncle Dan came out behind him. He saw Colin and Alan and beckoned them over. 'Here are the boys, Archie,' he told Archie Macrae. 'Right, Dan,' said Archie Macrae. Uncle Myles came out, accompanied by a tall man in a long grey coat who kept whispering into his ear. Then two men came out carrying a light-brown coffin between them. A bier had been set down in readiness on the path; they placed the coffin on it. One of them showed Colin his hands. 'Have a dekko at that,' he said. His palms were bright orange with the dye from the coffin wood. He went off to show them to someone else.

'Yourselves and your brother at the front, minister,' Archie Macrae murmured respectfully to uncle Myles, 'the two boys behind you,' and then, in his normal voice, to Colin and Alan: 'Right, lads?'

Alan and Colin stood behind uncle Myles and uncle Dan; Alan behind uncle Myles, and Colin behind uncle Dan. They were the chief mourners. Four of the men who had been waiting outside the house filed up the path, on a signal from Archie Macrae, and took up positions beside the bier. The windows and doorway of the house were filled with women's faces. On another signal from Archie Macrae, the men picked up the bier, carried it awkwardly through the gate and let it down on the road. The other men had moved away from the gate into the roadway and formed themselves into two lines. Archie Macrae checked that everyone was in position. 'Right,' he said, and nodded his head. The men picked up the bier again. Inside the house, a woman started wailing. They moved off.

Uncle Dan was smaller than uncle Myles. But he was as hardy as the steel. Beside him, uncle Myles looked puffy and soft. Uncle Myles was the oldest of the family. He was a minister in Inverness-shire, in a place called Knockglass. When uncle Dan came up to Dell to visit them, their mother would sit him on a chair under the light and go in search of a pair of scissors to clip his eyebrows. When uncle Myles came on a visit, he would put his hat among the basins in the scullery, allow their mother to help him off with his coat and tell her to send one rascal to Alex MacFarquhar's for barley meal, Mary dear, to make bannocks, and the other rascal to Sandy's for a ling, perhaps, or perhaps a haddock or two. 'I'm tired,' he would say then, moving up to the kitchen and settling himself in the armchair in front of the Modern Mistress, 'Very tired . . .' A voice came from behind them, low at first, then louder, and when they turned round they discovered they were fifteen yards ahead of the rest of the funeral. They had to halt and wait for them to catch up. The sun went in and came out again. It was a warm afternoon. Ahead of them, on the road fronting the primary school, a hearse and three shiny black cars were waiting. A bus was there too, the driver sitting at the wheel with one arm out of the window. He nipped the end from his cigarette when he saw the funeral approaching. Alan, Colin, uncle Dan and a man with a hat and a strong smell of drink from him were put into the second car. Uncle Myles and another minister who had appeared from nowhere were in the first car. Not many went into the bus. It wasn't a large funeral. The hearse moved off, and the three cars and the bus followed, along Sandwick Road, to the cemetery.

A long, grassy strip of grass was rolled up at one end of the grave. At the other end, a man in a dungaree jacket and trousers, and wellingtons with the tops folded down, stood waiting. A green tarpaulin covered the grave. Short wooden battens lay across it. The coffin was placed on the battens. The men removed their hats, and the man with the dungarees his beret, and uncle Myles uttered a short prayer in Gaelic. When he had finished, the cords tied to the handles of the coffin were unloosed, and Archie Macrae put one of the cords, with a tassel attached to it, into Colin's hand. A shiver went through Colin when he felt the touch of the tassel on his hand. His skin prickled. Uncle Dan was beside him: he was glad. He saw Alan's white face across from him, on the other side of the grave, a tasselled cord in his hand also. Norrie Aulay had been fifty years of age. On his knees, the man with the dungarees removed the battens and tarpaulin from the mouth of the grave, and the coffin was lowered down. Colin let go his cord along with uncle Dan. The grave was deep. Someone threw a bunch of flowers, wrapped in cellophane, down on top of the coffin. Then the other minister spoke. They were gathered here this day, in this place, he said, for no trifling reason, but for the solemn purpose of committing one of their fellow-creatures to the ground. Although they were now alive, it would not always be so with them, and this day, late or soon, awaited them all. He spoke in a grudging, crabbed voice, and finished in no time at all. The man with the dungarees put the beret back on his head, and Colin heard the first shovelful of earth thudding on to the coffin. And another, and another. The men stood around the grave, heads bowed, motionless, until the earth began to fall with a softer sound; then slowly, in ones and twos, they started to sidle away from the graveside. The minister who had spoken last was back at the cars before anyone else.

Going back into Stornoway, the man with the hat and the strong smell of drink from him was with them again in the car. 'Norrie Aulay?' he said to uncle Dan. 'One of ours!' Before the car reached the house, he leaned forward in the back seat and told the driver to stop. 'You lads carry on,' he said. 'I'm going a wee message first, down Newton the way.'

Entering the house was like entering an oven. The first thing Colin saw, on top of a tray of teacups and saucers, was uncle Myles' hat.

'Take off your coats,' an old woman told them, 'and go up to the fire.' The kitchen was full of women. It smelled of warm pancakes and Mansion Polish. The livingroom was even hotter than the kitchen. Colin sat between Alan and uncle Dan on a small sofa. He was so squashed, he had to sit with his arms folded. 'Is this the minister's relations?' a woman's voice asked behind them. He couldn't turn his head round to look at her. 'Yes,' another woman's voice answered. Norrie Aulay's sister came round with the tray of cups and saucers. Uncle Dan told them who she was. Norrie Aulay had lived with his two sisters. The one with the tray – Maggie – was big and bustled about, attending to people, but the other one – Marion – sat looking into the fire. Like Martha and Mary in the Bible. When uncle Myles appeared in the livingroom, all the women stopped talking and concentrated their attention on him. There was no sign of the other minister. 'Tired . . .' said uncle Myles, seating himself on a soft, proffered chair with armrests in the centre of the room, '. . . very tired . . .' accepting a cup of tea in one hand and a plate with a scone on it in the other, '. . . O holy and everloving God . . .' bowing his head and sighing a lugubrious grace into his clerical bib, '. . . for Christ's sake, Amen . . .' raising his head and taking a large, semi-circular bite out of the scone. 'Tired . . .' he said again, and took a sip of tea. Beside him, Colin heard uncle Dan's stomach starting to rumble.

Uncle Dan took a jar of Maclean's Powder from his pocket and asked Maggie could he have a teaspoon. Uncle Dan had a bad stomach. He'd been a prisoner of war in Poland for five years. Uncle Myles looked across at Alan and Colin. 'My brother's boys,' he said. Maggie asked uncle Dan would he take milk to help down the breadsoda. 'I won't, a 'raidh,' he replied. 'How old are you now?' uncle Myles asked Alan. 'Sixteen,' Alan replied. Colin could feel Alan getting tense. He felt a smile coming to his own face. 'The same age as my son Jacob,' uncle Myles told the room. 'Jacob is a holy boy. Are you a holy boy?' he asked Alan. Alan didn't reply. 'Do you go to church on Sunday? Do you seek the Lord while He may be found?' 'No,' said Colin. Alan's elbow went into his ribs. The livingroom had gone quiet. Colin couldn't keep the smile from his face. Everyone

151

was staring at him except uncle Dan, who, after swallowing the Maclean's, sat burping softly, covering his mouth with one hand. The old woman who had taken their coats made a face and shook her head at him. When he saw this, Colin wanted to laugh out loud. He sat, arms folded tightly, shaking with suppressed laughter. 'We go to church sometimes,' he heard Alan's voice saying. 'We have to, in the hostel.'

'Thank you, a 'raidh.' Uncle Dan gave the teaspoon back to Maggie.

'My brother's boys!' uncle Myles suddenly cried out, a muted wail at the back of his voice, when everyone thought the conversation was over, and little murmured exchanges had started up again in different parts of the room. 'Who must – in their own words – *sometimes* – go to church. What a penance –' he turned to Alan and Colin '– what an *ordeal* – that must be for you! To have to go, against your will, to God's house, on God's day, among God's people, to hear God's word. To have to sit in God's house, not willingly, not gladly, not with proper humility and awe, but resentfully and grudgingly, with stopped ears and closed minds, blind eyes and obdurate hearts; where you feel restless, ill at ease, trapped as in a prison, until the service is over and you can return to those haunts you find more attractive than God's house, those pursuits you consider more profitable than listening to God's word. And as *you*' – he spoke directly to Colin – 'conducted yourself not a minute ago here in the house of death, so have I seen you conduct yourself in the house of God. Let me remind you, then, of where you are, and why you are here. This is a house of mourning. It is also the house of God. Where two or three are gathered together in my name, there am I also. So you will do well to remember that here you are in God's presence, and that this his house is a holy place.

But why should *you* go to church, I hear you ask? Why should *you* be forced to attend a place of confinement, where nothing you see or hear touches you? A church is no place for you! You are too young to go to church. God, sin, death – what are these to you, in the morning of your days, with all of life before you? Time enough to go to God's house when you are old, and have nothing better to do. Time enough for God's house then.

And time is what you have, is it not? So much time is at your disposal – you have all the time in the world – limitless it stretches ahead of you, hours and days and weeks and years of it, a broad highway of shining prospects, unreeling and unwinding ever outwards, into a never-ending future. What a joy it must be, to know yourself possessor of such a bounty! To assume, with such careless certainty, that all future time is yours to inherit and keep! We are told that the great queen of England, Elizabeth Tudor, cried aloud on her deathbed: *All my possessions for an hour of time!* And she had many possessions, she was a great monarch, the riches of all the known material world were hers, from north, south, east and west, that mortal hands could bestow. But she was willing to give it all away for what you have, she set no value on any of her possessions against what you possess, she estimated her worldly treasures at nothing against an instant of that time that you, here, this afternoon, enjoy freely and unthinkingly, her cry in her death agony that night, more than three and a half centuries ago – the cry of a great monarch going to meet a greater – is far from your lips, and farther still from your understanding.'

He looked over his shoulder towards the window and sighed. A woman sitting next to him answered his sigh with a sigh of her own. Up in the balcony, no one stirred. *Kreek*, went the clock on the mantelpiece. *Kreek-klunk* . . .

'The afternoon light is fading,' he turned his face back on Alan and Colin, 'this sad day is almost at an end. Soon it will be night. And I would be failing in my duty as your father's brother and my greater duty as God's poor servant if, in the little time left to us together, I did not put one question to you. For who knows where we shall meet again, or when, or in what circumstances. My question to you is this. What if this coming night were to be your last on earth? Our cousin Norman was alive three days ago. Now he is in his grave. Death the great leveller comes without warning, draws no distinctions, is no respecter of persons; young and old, strong and weak, proud and humble, the mightiest monarch and the meanest

153

beggar – Death puts his hand on all alike, all are equal in his sight, and all go down before him to the darkness of the grave. What then, if this very night, you too are summoned to appear before the great throne of judgement and required to render account to the God who created you? What will be the last cry on *your* lips? It won't happen, you say. Not to you. Will it not? Where is your warranty for such a conviction? Show me your guarantee. Death is something that happens to other people? To old people? It won't happen to you? If that is what you believe, my young friends, then listen to me now and listen carefully. There is but one certainty in this world: the certainty of death. Equally and in common with all other creatures, you are marked for death. Between the breath you expel from your mouth and the next breath you living breathe, Death has set up his camp. He is as close to you as that. You may know, or you may think you know, many things; but there is only one certain and sure thing for you to know in this world – and that is, that you will leave it. Here you are not a permanent resident. Here is no continuing city.

His anger endureth but a small minute. So consider this also, both of you, in the small minute that I have left. The coming night, were it my last on earth, would hold no terrors for me, or for any Christian. For the Christian, the night of death is the morning of eternal life. But for you, my young friends, this minute that I have left to remonstrate with you could be the only minute that you will ever have, and makes up the sum of all your minutes from now on, and your hours, and your days, and your weeks, and your years, because this minute is your eternity, and your eternal salvation or damnation depends upon this minute. And in this minute, your last and only minute, God is here, the living God, in this room, he is speaking to you, he has not yet turned his face from you, he awaits your civility in spite of all, and he will listen to what you have to say for yourself, because this minute is all you have. And as you shall answer before him on the great day of judgement, so you must answer now. This is a decision that cannot be deferred until tomorrow. For you, there is no tomorrow. God is long-suffering, slow to wrath; but his spirit will not always strive with you. Come to him now; he will receive you. His love is infinite; his mercy boundless. Those that truly seek

the Lord, he will in no wise cast out. Deny him, and you do so at
your everlasting peril. How often has he knocked before, and you
have not opened unto him? Now he knocks again. Spurn him again
now, and you spurn him forever. *I cried, but you would not hear; but
you shall wail, and I will not hear* . . . And do you deny him still?' his
voice rose to a tremulous, singsong wail. 'O sinner, lost beyond recall!
Go your ways, then, despising him still, rejecting him still. Crucify the
living God anew. Yours is the choice: you have made it. For good,
evil; for life, death; for heaven, hell; for God and his peace, the devil
and his works and pomp. Go your ways; follow the road of your
choosing. Find and keep fast to a like-minded company; mock God's
people; play the freethinking swaggerer, the violent atheist, and let
the laughter of fools be your sanctuary and solace. Be sure to keep in
the daylight, you will be brave as a lion there. Do not waken in your
bed at midnight, in the dark, alone; for your boldness will desert
you then, and your quick tongue cleave to the roof of your mouth
in terror. And I, your father's brother and least of God's servants,
bear witness against you in this, as I shall bear witness against you
on that final day, when he comes, no longer God the all-forgiving,
no longer God the all-merciful and forbearing, no longer the God
who so loved the world that he gave his only begotten son, that
whosoever believeth in him should not perish but have everlasting
life, but God omnipotent, God almighty, the God of justice and of
vengeance, provoked and offended deity, the God of Abraham and
of Isaac and of Jacob, in the glory of his being, to judge the quick
and the dead. How will it fare with you on that day, when you come
before his dread presence and see God face to face? Where will all
your arrogance be then, when you fall on your knees, on your face,
and cry aloud to the hills to fall down and cover you from his
wrath? Of what avail the atheist's laugh, the scorner's approval, on
that terrible and final day, when the firmament is sundered, and the
sea gives up the dead which are in it, and the sun and the moon are
one, and you hear God's voice pronounce upon you the sentence
most terrible and final of all: *Depart from me, ye accursed, into the
lake of fire prepared for the devil and his angels* . . . ?'

*   *   *

Leaving the house, uncle Dan said something to him at the door, but he didn't hear properly what it was that he said. Alan then took off so quickly that he couldn't keep up with him. They were at the bottom of Matheson Road before he slowed down. 'Wait for me,' Colin said. 'What's wrong with you?' 'You!' said Alan, lashing out viciously at him with the buckle of his coat belt. 'You and your mouth . . .'

'The breeks stayed up, then?' Wally asked, when he gave him the suit and the leather belt back; and Looper, who was in the same dorm as Wally, started laughing. How could he do that? Didn't he know anything? 'Here, cove,' said Looper. 'I saw your identical twin down at Mossend, in the middle of a turnip field. He had a crow on his head.' Wally laughed loudly when Looper said that. He didn't know either. They were both laughing. Everything was still the same for them. He watched Wally examine the suit for cigarette burns, hang it on a hanger, hang it in the wardrobe. Why did he do that? What was the use? Why did he carry on as though nothing had happened and everything was the same and the world hadn't changed?. . . In his bed that night, in Dorm 12, after Boily had put the lights out, he knew that whoever was going to sleep, it wouldn't be him. For him, sleep was a thing of the past. He tried to pray, but no words would come. Uncle Myles' face, bodiless and suspended at first, appeared in the dark, above his bed. With him was the man with the hat and the strong smell of drink from him who had been in the second car with them at the funeral, only the man with the strong smell of drink from him was wearing uncle Myles' hat, and uncle Myles the hat of the man with the strong smell of drink from him. 'We're off down Newton the way,' the man with the strong smell of drink from him said, putting his arm around uncle Myles' neck. 'Tired,' said uncle Myles. 'I'm very tired. . .' In the morning, he walked up Matheson Road to school in the company of Mabel and Johnina, two girls from Stornoway who were on the same class as him. They teased him about Annabel Graham, and little ragamuffins from Manor Park, on their way to the Clock School, wolfwhistled after them, and not one of them threw a stone. It was a lovely morning; the sun shining, birds singing in the hedges and treetops. The madman who taught them maths was still off school, and they were told by Oggy, the deputy rector, to do whatever they liked for the first two periods, as long as they didn't make a noise. After that, the boys in the Gaelic choir – Colin among them – went over to Betty's for a practice, in the Francis Street seminary, after that he got permission from Watty to go and work in the library, where he carried on reading *The Old Man and the Sea* by Ernest Hemingway; and what with one thing and another, it was getting on for twelve o'clock, and the morning almost over, before he remembered that he was a lost sinner, and that the pit of hell was waiting for him.

In his final year in school, Calman entered for a bursary competition.

'The same essays come up year in, year out,' he explained to Colin. He had laid the old test papers out in a row on the dressing table in Dorm 12. 'See?'

The test papers had *The Flora MacConnachie Trust* printed across the top in capital letters, and a shield with the cross of Saint Andrew on it underneath, and underneath that *English, Paper 1, Essay. (One hour)*.

'See?' Calman jabbed at the papers with his index finger. 'Year in, year out the same.'

'"*Judge not that ye be not judged*"?' Colin read out.

'Never mind the proverbs,' said Calman. 'What do *you* know about proverbs?'

'"*A walk by the seashore*"?'

'That'll do. Lots of description.'

'How long?'

'Three pages.'

'Ten bob,' said Colin.

'Ten *bob*?' Calman was indignant. 'Come off it, cove!'

'It's for a bursary,' said Colin. '*You* come off it.'

In the silence that followed, Sergeant Macdonald, in police uniform and diced cap, emerged from his end of the end council house across the road, marched down the front path, paused at the gate to contemplate his flowers, marched in a stately manner down Ripley Place, turned into Robertson Road, vanished.

'OK,' said Calman. 'But it had better be good.'

'Right,' said Colin.

'When'll you do it?'

'Tonight at studies . . . Can I have the ten bob in advance?'

'You can *not!*' Calman was indignant.

'Five bob, then? Half a dollar?'

'You most certainly can *not!*'

After supper, Calman and Colin went up the baggage room stairs to Dorm 12, and Colin gave Calman the essay. Calman started reading. His face, suspicious at first, gradually relaxed.

'This isn't bad, cove,' he said. 'What does *effulgent* mean?'

'Shining.'

'. . . *now, however,*' Calman read on, '*winter with his grip of iron had yielded to the balmy zephyrs of summer, and the mound was mantled in a rich livery of green grass, embroidered with a profusion of daisies, buttercups, wild carrots, clover, vetch and fragrant thyme. He heard the fluting, insistent cry of an oystercatcher among the barnacle-encrusted rocks below, and observed the lazy flight of the startled heron. Out on the ocean, the black cormorant, with neck outstretched, hurried on his vigil to the tide-lapped Red Skerry, or the lion rock of far-famed Ronan. Across the waste of waters skimmed the tireless solan goose, or, poised aloft, with folded pinions, dived headlong into the cobalt sea in a cone of silvery spray . . .*'

'Good,' said Colin, 'isn't it?'

'"*. . . Deep among the aromatic riot of poppies, clover, thyme, yarrow, wild carrot and clumps of harebells, he caught sight of the gorgeous hue of the flitting butterfly. Delicate, beautiful, nimble, celestial . . .*"'

'Can I have my ten bob now?' Colin asked.

Daveena stopped him on Cromwell Street, outside Tolmie's.

'How many Highers did you get, then?' she asked him.

'Four.' Colin stared at her. Daveena had never spoken to him before. 'And two lowers.'

'More than enough to get into university. I suppose you'll be going back up there –' meaning the school '– for a sixth year?'

'Yes, well, I –'

'Don't,' she said. 'Leave now, at the end of fifth year. That's what your cousin Alex Norman did, and none the worse for it.'

Daveena was Miss Stewart. She was a tall, skinny woman, who smoked and taught French. She'd never spoken directly to him before.

'Get a job,' she said. 'Dig holes in the road for a year. Do anything. Grow up, for goodness' sake. Don't be the fool they all think you are. Listen to me, for goodness' sake –' she tugged at the lapel of his blazer. 'Don't go back up there for a sixth year. When will you be sixteen? July? Go to the Labour Exchange, for goodness' sake, and get yourself a job. Earn your daily bread among honest people. Become a human being. Then go to university. That's my advice to you. Of course you won't take it.'

Colin made to move off. Daveena stared into his face as if she wanted to memorise every line and freckle in it. He could smell the tobacco from her breath. Her hand still clutched his lapel.

'Some people up there don't like you, you know,' she said.

THE HIT PARADE

Two new teachers came to the hostel to replace The Lisper and Boily when Colin was in sixth year. The names of these two teachers were MacKechnie and Twatt.

They weren't very long in the hostel when Snarler said:

'Thuh-this place isn't funny any more.'

MacKechnie was a tall, baby-faced man who smelled of aftershave lotion, and combed his hair back from his forehead with a centre parting in the style of English footballers like Tommy Lawton (Notts County) or Swift (Manchester City), the goalkeeper. His backside stuck out when he walked, so he was nicknamed, in Gaelic, Cameron Bigarse. His first name was Cameron. If he had Gaelic, he never let on. He taught music. A woman from Poolewe, who was married to a missionary from Baggamealie's village in South Lochs, was supposed to be his aunty, and this woman had Gaelic, and knew

Big Oggy, the deputy rector and head of Gaelic, who was also from Poolewe or thereabouts, and whose voice, booming out the poetry of Alasdair Mac Mhaighstir Alasdair, could be heard through three partitions. But if MacKechnie had Gaelic, he never let on.

Twatt was short and thickset, with a flat, brown face, small, unblinking eyes and a mouth, when he spoke, that didn't seem to move. He taught technical subjects, and wore polo shirts and cardigans. He had a crewcut.

'Thuh-this place,' said Snarler, 'has guh-gone to the dogs.'

They were in Calum Iain's dorm. The entire dorm had just been belted by MacKechnie.

'The matron came in,' Snooks told them, 'with Bigarse in tow, and said this dorm was a disgrace. So –'

'So Bigarse gave us all two of the belt,' Iain F. said. 'For untidiness.'

'Including Calum Iain,' said Snooks.

'Guh-good Lord!' said Snarler.

'I'm a prefect.' Calum Iain, his face white with shock, sat on the chair beside his bed and studied the palms of his hands. 'I'm seventeen years of age. I've never been belted before. Not like –' he jerked his head at Colin, then looked down at his hands again.

'Guh-good Lord!' said Snarler.

Calum Iain was the quietest boy in the hostel. He was also the best scholar. He'd been dux of the school in fifth year. If you were stuck at a problem in maths or science, you went to Calum Iain, and he could explain it to you without losing his temper. He was learning Russian out of books from the public library, and used to sneak down into the hostel cellar sometimes, not to smoke, but to examine the boilers with a Woolies pocket torch. He knew about boilers.

'Belting senior boys,' said Iain F. 'Unheard of!'

'Not even in primary school,' said Calum Iain, speaking very slowly and still studying the palms of his hands. 'I've never been belted till now.'

'Well,' said Colin. 'I'll say this . . .'

He stopped. Calum Iain had raised his head and was looking at him.

'What?' said Calum Iain.

'I don't know,' said Colin. He'd just noticed how angry Calum Iain was. 'He hasn't belted *me* yet,' he said.

'He wuh-will,' said Snarler.

'*You?*' said Iain F. 'You're a cert, cove.'

'So what?' said Colin. 'I'll bet he isn't much use with the belt anyway.'

'He'll do me,' said Snooks.

'The Lisper,' said Colin. 'That was the man that could pull a belt. Once belted by the Lisper, boy' – he found himself talking straight at the top of Calum Iain's head – 'you didn't go back a second time. I remember when he caught myself and Dandy coming in the baggage room window at two in the morning . . .'

'Wuh-well,' said Snarler, moving to the door, and indicating to Colin, with a jerk of his head, that he should come with him. 'I'm shuh-sure you'll soon be in a pa-position to cuh-compare the two. Cuh-compare and cuh-contrast. Whuh-what do *you* think, Cuh-Calum?'

But Calum Iain, in the chair beside his bed, looking down at his hands and shaking his head, didn't say anything.

'Ah fahnd ma trio . . .'

(Looper sang, pretending to accompany himself on a guitar)

'. . . on Blueberry Hee-il . . .'

'It's thrill,' Colin said. 'Not trio.'

Looper stopped singing.

'It's "I found my thrill",' Colin told him. 'Not "I found my trio".'

'OK,' said Looper. He started again:

'"Ah fahnd ma trio . . ."'

'That doesn't make sense,' said Colin. 'Trio doesn't make sense.'

'Who says?' said Angie Brommy.

'Maybe it makes sense to Fats Domino,' said Looper. 'Maybe trio means something else in New Orleans.'

'Like sked in Stornoway,' said Angie Brommy.

'If you heard Fats Domino singing "I found my sked, on Blueberry Hill" it wouldn't make sense either,' said Looper.

'*Unless you came from Stornoway,*' said Angie Brommy.

'*And then it still wouldn't make sense,*' said Looper.

'*Maybe in New Orleans,*' said Angie Brommy, '*trio means sweetheart.*'

'"*O to be in Doonaree, with the trio I once knew*",' said Looper.

'*It's thrill,*' said Colin. '*You know it is. And Fats Domino doesn't play a guitar,*' he rushed on. '*He plays the piano. Honky-tonk piano.*'

'*Lonnie Donegan plays the guitar,*' said Looper.

'*Banjo,*' said Colin.

'*So does Elvis,*' said Looper. '"*Going to rock around the gleoc tonight*",' he sang in a Lewis accent.

'*That's Bill Haley,*' said Colin.

'*It could be trill,*' said Angie Brommy. '*As in larks.*'

'*It's thrill,*' said Colin.

'*Unless he was on a boat,*' said Angie Brommy. '*A drifter called Blueberry Hill. Then it would make sense.*'

'*What?*'

'"*I found my sked, on Blueberry Hill*".'

'*She would have to be called The Blueberry Hill,*' said Looper.

'*Then it wouldn't rhyme,*' said Angie Brommy. '*Hui!*' he asked. '*Where are you going?*'

'*Out of here,*' said Colin. He turned at the door to deliver an opinion. He had to revert to Gaelic.

'*Cuiseachan-chac,*' he said.

He came out of the masters' common room, and the other boys were waiting outside Study One and on the steps. They followed him along the corridor in a milling, excited bunch, noisily jostling and shoving against one another, but without bumping into him or touching him in any way, as though he had a barrier of invisible glass for a foot's space all round him; one or two, more inquisitive than the rest, darting on ahead and then walking backwards, like over-anxious cameramen, trying to see up into his face. He stopped in the main hall, and stood with his back to a radiator. He wouldn't look up. The others formed a semi-circle round him and gradually fell silent.

'How many?' Looper asked.

'Twelve,' said Iain F. 'We heard twelve strokes.'

'Twelve of the best,' the Magpie said, and laughed.

'*You're* here are you?' Looper said, turning on the Magpie and making a grab for him. But the Magpie dodged easily out of reach. It was almost impossible to catch the Magpie; and once caught, it was almost impossible to hang on to him, he wriggled and twisted about so much. Disgusted, Looper turned away. Immediately the Magpie started pulling faces at him, behind his back.

'Let's see your hands, Colin,' Toby said, and some of the other boys also said, 'Yes, let's see your hands, Colin. Show us your hands. Go on . . .'

Wincing, he raised his arms and held his hands out, palms upwards, to their gaze; his face, as he did so, tightening with pain and draining of all colour. As one, they craned forward to have a look. The fingers of both hands were crumpled and trembling, cramped together like an old man's claw, the finger-tips almost touching, and trembled even more when he tried to straighten them. There were raised, red weals across each palm, hot-looking and stinging, as though he'd been chasing with his hands among nettles. A line, thin as a razor slash, beaded with red, ran straight across his left wrist, where the edge of the belt had cut into it, across the blue delta of veins, the flesh on either side of the cut already swollen and discoloured. 'Keep your hand *up!*' MacKechnie had bawled, after hitting him on the wrist. But his hand had not moved. It was MacKechnie himself whose aim had been wrong. And MacKechnie knew it; and that was why he had bawled at him to keep his hand up. Because his own aim had been wrong.

'That's diabolical!' one of the boys kept saying. 'That's really diabolical.'

His hand had not moved. Even after hitting him on the wrist, his hand had not moved.

'And for no reason,' Satch said. 'No reason at all.'

'You never did anything, Colin, did you?'

'He looked at the matron, that was all.'

163

'She kept staring at Colin all through the tea. Didn't she, Looper? From the moment she came into the diningroom. All through the tea, she never took her eyes off him.'

'For no reason,' Satch said.

'For no reason. Then, the minute Colin looked at *her* . . .'

'He shouldn't have looked at her,' Iain F. said. 'That's what she was wanting him to do. You shouldn't have turned round, Colin.'

'That's all she was *wanting*, you see,' Toby explained vehemently, looking about him with large, serious eyes, to make sure that everyone was listening to what he was saying. 'That's all she was *wanting*, was for Colin to turn round and look at her.'

'What she was waiting for,' said Iain F. 'Herself and Bigarse.'

'Then, as soon as he *did* it . . .'

'You shouldn't have looked round at her, Colin,' Rusty said. 'That's what she was waiting for.'

'I told him not to,' Looper said. 'I warned you not to look round,' he said to Colin, 'didn't I?'

'He's not supposed to give you twelve of the belt either,' Rusty said. 'That's against the law.'

'That's right,' said Toby. 'Six is the limit.'

'He's not supposed to hit you on the wrist either,' the Magpie piped up from the back of the crowd. 'That's against the law an' all. If I was you, Colin, I'd go straight to the rector's office tomorrow morning and show him that. I would.'

'Yes, *you* would, wouldn't you?' a sarcastic voice remarked.

'I would. I wouldn't wait till tomorrow morning either. I'd go up to his house this very minute.'

'Why don't you go and shove your finger up your arse this very minute?' the same voice suggested.

'O yeah?'

'Yeah.'

'Who's going to make me, then?'

'I'll make you. Right now.'

'O yeah?'

'Yeah.'

'Better put your wrist under a coldwater tap, Colin,' Looper said.

Nobody was paying any attention to the Magpie and the other guy. They knew nothing would come of it. People were always threatening to hammer the Magpie. 'Before it comes up any further.'

'Come on,' Iain F. said, putting a hand on his arm.

He started like a nervous animal and shook his head.

'Aah, come *on*, man,' Iain F. said. Looper touched him awkwardly on the other arm. Between them, they urged him along the downstairs corridor towards the bathroom at the far end. They were his pals. They weren't really. He didn't have any real pals. He attached himself to Iain F. and Looper because he couldn't be alone, and because he needed an audience. And he was wary of Looper, because Looper was as quick-tongued as himself. Looper and Iain F. were pals. He only tagged along with them.

No one was in the bathroom but Wally, combing his hair at one of the mirrors. He came over while Looper was running the tap, and had a look at Colin's wrist. He was two years older than Colin. He was senior prefect in the school, and captain of the football team. Colin had borrowed a suit from him once, to go to a funeral. 'How many did he give you?' Wally asked, and a look of distaste came over his face, like someone who sees a cat with a live mouse between its jaws. When he saw the look on Wally's face, Colin almost started crying. 'Twelve!' Iain F. said angrily. 'He gave him twelve, Wally.' 'You'll need to put something on that cut,' Wally said, frowning. He stood holding Colin's sleeve and thinking aloud. Looper turned off the watertap. 'No use going to the matron, you're not exactly ...' 'She'd probably give him a dose of castor oil and two aspirin,' said Looper. 'I've got some germolene,' said Wally. 'Maybe Foxy ... Hang on,' he said, and went out. He came back with Foxy, who was carrying a big, square tin box under his jacket and scowling. The box, when he opened it, was full of medicine things – pills and bottles and tubes – all sorts of things. There was even a miniature bottle of brandy. 'What are *you* gawking at, cove?' Foxy asked Looper, and gave him a rap on the head with his knuckles. 'Ow!' said Looper. Foxy never looked anyone straight in the eye, he always focused on a point somewhere above their heads and to one side, his eyes slanting vaguely and his mouth agape, as though he were trying to recall something not very pleasant that had happened to him the week before. That was why he was called Foxy. Really he was looking at you all the time. The teachers never came near him. He now cocked his head at Colin. 'Have you washed out the cut?' he asked. 'With red soap? Very well.' He poked among the jumble of stuff in the box with his index finger, like someone trying to find a washer in a boxful of nuts, hissing softly through his teeth as he did so; finally selected a tube already wrinkled and twisted out of all shape, unscrewed the top of it and squeezed a minute blob of pink ointment on to his finger. 'More than that,' said Wally, who was watching Foxy's performance with a huge grin on his face. 'This stuff costs money, you know,' Foxy protested, pouting vaguely at the ceiling. 'More,' Wally said, grinning, and digging Foxy in the ribs. Foxy seemed to amuse him a lot. 'Stop that!' said Foxy. He squeezed a pink worm out of the tube, smeared it across Colin's wrist. 'Now put this round it,' said Wally, offering Foxy a clean, white handkerchief. 'Do it yourself!' Foxy exclaimed, in an aggrieved tone of voice. 'Come on, Angus,' Wally urged him, calling him by his first name. 'You're the medicine man here. The man with the know-how.' 'O, very well . . .' Giving Looper another knock on the head first, to relieve his feelings, he arranged the handkerchief around Colin's wrist and fastened it neatly with a small gold safety pin, which he found after some more poking about in the box. 'Why didn't you go to the matron, cove?' he asked Colin. The scowl had never left his face. 'Why didn't you put yourself and your injury in the capable hands of Miss MacVicar?'

'You know why, Angus,' said Wally.

'The ministering angel,' said Foxy. Iain F. and Looper burst out laughing. Scowling, Foxy closed the tin box – it had a picture of Edinburgh Castle on the lid – and tucked it back under his jacket. None of the teachers ever came near him.

'Keep the sleeve of your jersey over that,' he said to Colin. 'And I want the pin back.'

Going out of the bathroom, they heard him asking Wally: 'OK if I have another go at hypnotising you tonight after studies?'

*   *   *

At the end of the corridor were two doors. One was the door of the rector's office, the other the door of the deputy rector's. On the morning of his expulsion from school, he was summoned down to the rector's office, and told by Miss Finlayson, the secretary, that he had to wait outside. Miss Finlayson kept giving him embarrassed little glances as she delivered this message, before disappearing into her cubbyhole, and a class, clattering downstairs between periods, slowed down and fell silent for a moment when they saw him and where he was. They knew why he was there.

A mad March day. Over the pale, grainy wood of the doors, the sun kept coming and going. He stood waiting. The sun kept coming and going; over the silent door, and over the door with the rise and fall of voices behind it – the voices of two hostel teachers and the hostel matron, the voice of a Deputy Director of Education, the voice of his uncle Myles, the minister – then a single voice, high and enraged, outsoaring all the others, going on and on and on . . .

The silent door opened, and Big Oggy, the deputy rector, came out. Like a bear lumbering out of his den, glasses on the end of his nose, he made a clumsy rush straight for Colin, stood over him, clapped him heavily on one shoulder, went 'Urrghr urr,' and with the sun coming and going on the back of his Harris tweed jacket, clumped back into his office and shut the door behind him.

Behind the other door, the voices were still going on, rising and falling. He wasn't afraid of them any more.

He could feel the fear draining out of him, out through his fingernails. What was there to be afraid of?

Big Oggy had cracked leather patches on both elbows.

Like a fool, he thought he would never be afraid again.

Heroes

THERE HAD BEEN A football match in Stornoway the night before, Ness v. Back in the semi-final of the Eilean an Fhraoich cup, and on Saturday morning his brother Alan had a hangover. He was still in bed at midday, in the small room above the kitchen in their granny's house with the skylight and the jacob's ladder going up to it. Colin went up the ladder, carrying a mug of tea, and opened the door of the room. Alan's clothes were folded tidily over the back of an armchair. There was a white enamel bucket beside the bed, and a smell of oranges and lysol. 'I hear you scored a hat-trick,' he said to the shape underneath the blankets. 'Beat it,' his brother mumbled. 'Give us half a dollar then,' Colin said, putting the mug of tea on the bedside table. 'I haven't had a smoke all morning.' 'Piss off,' his brother mumbled. He poked his head out as Colin was leaving. 'I met a pal of yours in Stornoway last night,' he said. 'In the Royal. A fat guy. MacDougall. He said to you to go over and see him.' 'How,' said Colin, 'in hell's name, can *I* go over to Stornoway? . . .' Late that night, long after the bars had closed and the last bus gone, he was with MacDougall on the Laxdale road. Holding MacDougall by the lapels.

'We live from day to day, MacDougall,' he was explaining. 'One day at a time, that's all. Where did you get that coat any-way?'

'Dunn's,' said MacDougall.

'One day at a time, that's all. Up she rises and down she goes. You think about it.'

'What are you laughing at, MacDougall?' he asked then. 'I see nothing to laugh at. Where did you get that coat anyway? . . .'

Later, they were in the Black Glen.

'We must take positive action,' MacDougall said, sitting on a low wall and unscrewing the vodka bottle.

Later – out at the Water House – he said:

'Start hitching from here.'

'Going to walk it,' said Colin. 'Son of a Gael.'

'Heesht . . .'

'Son of a Gael. Going to walk it.'

'Here's a pound,' MacDougall said, 'you're not working. Thumb the first thing that comes along.'

'Never!'

He set off at a great pace, swinging his arms. This was the thing to do, by God! By God, yes! The road stretched out before him, into the moor, a faint grey ribbon. There it was. He couldn't see it very well. Never mind. On both sides of the road was black night. He strode on, the wind in his face, swerving violently back into the centre of the road whenever his foot hit against one or other of the verges. He was walking home! Twenty-four miles! Twelve to Barvas, twelve after that to Ness. Nothing to it! His granduncle Norman used to do it all the time, in the old days.

Not twenty-four now anyway. Twenty-four was from the centre of town, he was at least a couple of miles from the centre of town where *he* was, yes and more. More. Nine, ten miles of moor, and then Barvas. After that it would be all plain sailing: houses all the way.

And his mother wouldn't give him a row tomorrow morning either . . . He was seeing the road more clearly now. Not when he told her he'd just walked from Stornoway. He laughed to himself, his feet went even faster, thinking of what his mother would say tomorrow morning, when he told her what he'd done.

'You *what?*' she would say. 'Walked from *where?*'

He laughed out loud in the dark.

'Weren't you afraid of *ghosts?*' she would say.

MacDougall, he thought. He stopped and looked back. Couldn't see a thing. He stood peering into the night. Was that the Water

House? – that vague, black thing? He'd come a good distance already, if it was. Be home in no time at this rate. It was the Water House all right – what else could it be? To the left of it, on the skyline, rose the glow of the town. MacDougall would be on his way back in there. Further left again were the lights running out to Sandwick, the lights on Point . . . he was on the high, level stretch of road, then, coming out of the moor, before it turns down into the Black Glen. There were no cars on the road out of the Black Glen. No cars on the road out of town. At this time of night, Saturday going into Sunday, there would be no cars anyway. Not going to Ness anyway. Anyway he was going to walk it.

It was pitch dark; the wind blowing out of the moor. The moor was open and wide on both sides of the road. He couldn't see it. He could smell it, though, a damp, peaty, heathery smell – the smell of the moor at night. He walked on into it, the grey spool of road blurring and unwinding out of the darkness ahead; trying to walk at a steady pace and keep to the middle of the road; swinging his arms. Not thinking now; intent now only on keeping going and putting the distance behind him.

The road went uphill in a series of curves, the wind freshening against his face as he climbed, the moor still falling away in the dark on both sides of the road. Then for about half a mile the road was level, and then he started going downhill, faster and faster, his feet slapping hard on the tarmac, jolting his body with every step, before the road levelled out again as, almost running, he came into the dip. It was quiet in the dip – he slowed down, staggering a little, and then came to a panting halt. Everything was quiet. He was out of the wind; all round him was silence. In the silence, he could still hear the echo of his own feet. He listened. A stream lipped and babbled in the dark, underground. A sheep coughed, startling him. This was the moor – he inhaled deeply. The real moor. Black and close on either side, and all round him. He could feel it in the dark, black and close on either side, and all round him. It was huge. It seemed to be moving in on him; touching his clothes. He listened again; but there was nothing. Only the pounding of his own heart. Then he started up the next brae. His hands were tight, his feet slapped loudly. He must keep going.

So long as he could make out the road. That was the main thing. He'd be all right, so long as he could make out the road. Sometimes, out at night, it was so dark you couldn't make out the road. You couldn't see anything. It was frightening then. But tonight he could make out the road.

He'd come over in Ivor Deedo's van, the Rebel driving, at five o'clock. While his mother was out at the shop. Taking a pound note from the pink teapot on his way out. The Rebel had waited for him, with the van, out of sight, behind Angus John Tully's house, until the coast was clear. Ivor Deedo and the Big Barney were in the van as well. The Rebel had given him a screwtop of beer from a crate under the driver's seat. He'd sat in the back all the way over, on a spare tyre. Drinking the screwtop, looking out at the evening. It all seemed to have happened a long time ago. It must be two in the morning by now. Sunday morning. The thing was to keep going.

He came to a bridge; crossed it. To his left, from the top of the next brae, he saw, out in the moor, a black, glinting stretch of water with a blacker island in the middle of it. He now knew where he was. John Troop from North Dell had once gone into this loch with a lorry. The water made a quick, lapping noise in the dark, as he passed. Next would be a bridge with iron railings, after that the first of the bridges with whitewashed cement pillars. When he came to that bridge, he'd be halfway across the moor. The glen of the Barvas river would be over to his left, the Barvas hills beyond. Just then the road and moor ahead were swept from right to left by a swift-moving beam of yellow light, then everything went dark again, and turning, scarcely believing, he saw the lights of a car moving in a dip behind. Someone was coming.

He kept walking. The car came on, travelling fast, the beam from the headlights going up and down on the surface of the road in long, smooth, yellow waves. To Colin, it sounded like the engine of a van. It went past him with a roar and a whoom of wind that almost knocked him off the verge. It was a van, a Bedford. Fifty yards up the road, the rear lights started pulsating, as it slowed down and stopped.

The offside door of the van slid open as Colin ran up. A light went on inside.

He stood outside the door, blinking.

The driver sat behind the wheel, looking out at him. He was a big-faced, cheerful-looking man with curly black hair. 'Hallo!' he said. He had a dark suit on, and a white shirt open at the neck.

'Where are you heading?' he asked.

'Ness,' said Colin.

'*Ness?*' The driver put both hands on the steering wheel and burst out laughing. The backs of his hands were covered with black hairs. 'You're walking to *Ness?*'

'Yes.'

'God help us!' And he burst out laughing again.

'Well,' he said at last, slowly shaking his huge, curly head. 'Now I've heard everything.'

He sat grinning to himself.

'Well,' he said. 'You better jump in.'

'I missed the last bus, you see –' Colin started to explain.

'You need to give it a good shove,' the driver said. He leaned across Colin and slammed the door shut with his left hand. His breath smelt of whisky. 'What part of Ness are you going to?' he asked, grinning into Colin's face and still retaining his grip on the doorhandle. Colin felt his own face breaking into a grin.

'Dell,' he said.

His face was burning after the night wind. It wouldn't stop grinning. He looked away from the driver, out of the window, then back at the driver again.

'And I thought I knew everyone in Dell.' The driver leaned forward, scrutinising Colin's face: his eyes went narrow. He shook his head. 'I can't place you.'

'I'm one of the Boxer's sons.'

'Which one?'

'Colin.'

'Ah!' The driver straightened up, as though he'd suddenly remembered something, and settled himself sideways in his seat.

'You were in school in Stornoway, weren't you?'

'Yes.'

'You know Iain Don Macleod, class 3?'

'Yes.'

'My nephew.'

Colin stared at him.

'Are you his uncle Dan? Black Dan?'

'That's me.'

'Jesus!' said Colin.

He got very excited.

'Jesus,' he said, 'I remember you. I used to watch you playing football when I was a kid. My father used to take us, myself and my brother John. You used to play centre half.'

'That's right.'

'You used to play right back too. Left back was John Dood. The greatest Ness team ever. I still know all the names off by heart. Gog was centre. I remember the night you broke the Point fellow's leg down at Lionel, and the Point team refused to play on.'

The driver laughed.

'Jesus!' said Colin. 'I can hardly believe it.'

He looked quickly at the driver, who was still sitting sideways in his seat, grinning at him, and away again.

'You were some player,' he said. 'I remember you fine.'

'Colin,' the driver said. 'Aren't you the one they put out of the school?'

'Yes.'

'You got back in, though?'

'To the school, yes. Not the hostel.'

'What was it? Some carry-on with a maid?'

'No,' said Colin. 'What happened was, I went up to the maids' quarters to see Bellann – she's my cousin –'

'Bellann!' The driver straightened up in his seat and laughed loudly. He stopped. 'What are you going to do now?' he asked. 'Go to university?'

'If I get in,' said Colin. 'I haven't heard anything yet.'

There was a silence. Something in the van made a metallic click.

'Well,' said Colin, leaning forward and rubbing his hands together between his knees, 'I'm glad you came along tonight.'

'No bother,' said the driver. He reached up, switched off the rooflight and turned the ignition key.

'Didn't I see you in the Royal earlier on?' he shouted, above the roar of the engine. 'With a fat fellow with a fur coat?'

'Yes,' Colin shouted back.

'Who is he?'

'Who?'

'The fat fellow.'

'His name's MacDougall,' Colin shouted.

'I know,' the driver shouted. 'I know him.'

'O?'

'I passed him on the Laxdale road back there. A white fur coat trailing to the ground.'

'That's right,' Colin shouted. 'He came with me as far as the Water House.'

'Taking the whole road!' The driver took both hands briefly off the wheel. 'I nearly ran over him.'

'What?'

'A boozer,' the driver shouted.

'Well –'

'Alcoholic. Pure alcoholic. Drank his way through two businesses.'

'He's not an alcoholic,' Colin shouted back. 'He can stop if he wants to.'

'Two businesses,' the driver yelled, waving one hand up and down. 'Four vans he had on the road one time. All gone. Gurgle. Down his throat.'

'Well –'

'A fool,' the driver yelled. 'Could have made his mark in the island. Nothing to show for it except a belly. Two bellies.'

They were approaching Barvas. The road was wider here in places, where a council squad was working on it. They went past a steamroller and a digger. Some of the stones turned up by the digger were a milky-white in colour. They went past a huge, grey boulder, on its own, a little way from the roadside.

'Angus Graham's stone,' said Colin. 'I wonder did he really shift it?'

'He's a bad influence,' the driver shouted. 'A bad influence on a young lad like yourself.'

'Who?'

'MacDougall.'

'Barvas,' said Colin.

'That didn't take long,' the driver said, 'did it?'

'Haven't you got a girlfriend at all?' the driver asked, changing down gears as they came to the road junction. 'A good-looking lad like yourself. Instead of boozing with the likes of MacDougall. Surely you've got a girlfriend?'

'No,' said Colin.

'Not even one?'

'No,' said Colin, embarrassed.

'Has our Iain Don got a girlfriend?'

'I don't know,' said Colin. 'I wasn't *on* his class.'

'He's a good-looking boy, our Iain Don.'

'O yes.'

'Clever too.'

'O yes.'

'When I was your age, I had I don't know how many girlfriends. How old are you?'

'Seventeen.'

'When I was seventeen, I had girlfriends all over the district. Dell and all. You know Babs from Aird?'

'Yes.'

'Cathy Handy? Dena? Maggie Sheoc? There's three for a kick off.'

He laughed.

'Myself and Murdo Meek from Eorodale, who's now in New Zealand. What a man for the women! Wouldn't take no for an answer! Up to Dell on the bicycles . . .' he laughed happily. 'One night Murdo Meek would go to Babs' house, and I'd go to Dena's or Seoc's. In the scullery door, take the shoes off and up through the house in your stocking soles. Dena? Do I remember *her?* Next night we'd swap round.' He laughed again. 'Them were the days.'

'I wouldn't like to live in Barvas,' said Colin. 'Nothing but stones.'

'A lot of plump ones on the west side,' the driver said. 'What about that family of girls from Shader? The ones that sing? Why don't you try one of *them?*'

'I don't know.'

'No pluck,' said the driver. 'That's the trouble with young lads nowadays. They've got no pluck.'

'Well . . .'

'Now I don't mean *you,*' the driver put a heavy, reassuring hand on Colin's knee. 'No no. Anyone who's ready to walk from Stornoway to Ness at night – across the Barvas moor – must have plenty of stuff in him. No no.' He took his hand away. 'Do you believe in ghosts?' he asked.

'No.'

'I don't either,' said the driver. 'But I'll tell you this' – he slowed down to avoid a sheep lying in the middle of the road. The sheep half-turned her head, calmly chewing the cud, and didn't budge; her eyes glassy-yellow in the glare of the headlights. 'There's something in it, all the same.'

'Probably.'

'No probablies about it. You've got the education, maybe, out of books, you and our Iain Don and all the rest of you, we never got the chance at. That doesn't mean we're dummies.'

'Of course not.'

'At fifteen I was working on the breaker in the Dell quarry. Seventeen, I was sailing the seven seas. That was *my* education.'

They drove up the long brae out of Barvas, into the bend at the White Cairns where Angie Raggy crashed the blue Mitchell's bus, and through the long, blacked-out, sleeping villages of Baileantruiseil and Airidhantuim and Shader, travelling fast now, past the Shader schoolhouse, past the loch with the rylock fence in it, down towards

Borve. The driver had stopped talking. It was warm in the van. The heater was on. They were travelling fast. Colin's eyes kept closing. His head ached, his mouth was cracked and dry. The hum of the engine was making him drowsy.

'. . .' the driver said. Colin sat up with a jerk.

The van had stopped. The driver was sitting sideways, in the dark, looking at him.

'What is it?' Colin asked. 'What's the matter?'

'Nothing.' The driver switched on the rooflight. His face was shining with sweat. 'Not a thing.'

'Why have we stopped?'

'I've got to go into a house here,' the driver said, rubbing his forehead.

'Where are we?'

'Borve.'

'*Borve?*'

'I won't be long.' He switched off the rooflight, pulled open the door of the van, letting in a small rush of cold air, and went out, sliding the door shut behind him, and Colin heard his shoes crunching the gravel at the side of the road, then the latch of a gate opening and closing, and the sound of footsteps receding up a path. It was too dark to see anything through the window. Colin sat and waited. He'd soon be home. Six miles. It was very quiet in the van. It was dark. He leaned over and turned the ignition key. The dashboard panel lit up. He turned it off and sat back. After a while he heard footsteps coming back. The door of the van opened and a man put his head in. The head went away, and the driver climbed heavily in and started the engine. 'Too late,' he said. 'He's fast asleep.'

'Who?'

'Tom Tom.'

'Who's he?'

'He sells insurance. Don't you know Tom Tom?'

'No.'

'You don't know what you're missing,' the driver said, and burst out laughing. He was quite cheerful again.

'Who was the other fellow?' Colin asked.

'Where?'

'Just now. At the door of the van.'

'O him?' said the driver. 'That was John Murdo. From Melbost. Never mind him.'

'Were you at the game yourself last night?' he shouted, when they were on their way again. 'I mean Friday night?'

'No.'

'Why not?'

'No money.'

'Your brother played a stormer,' the driver shouted. 'What a player.'

Ahead of them was Galson bridge, and the lodge.

'Do you play football yourself?'

'Sometimes. I'm not much use.'

'Why doesn't our Iain Don play football?'

'I don't know.'

'Your brother. Is he still going on trial with the Hibs?'

'I'm not sure. He never said.'

'A great player.'

'So were you.'

The driver laughed.

'You're nearly home,' he said. 'There's the lighthouse flashing.'

'One mile,' Colin said.

Coming to the junction of the village road and the main road, he said:

'Well . . . thanks very much.'

'No bother,' the driver said.

'You can let me off here.'

'That's all right,' the driver said. 'I'll run you home.'

'There's no need,' said Colin. 'I can easily –'

'Many's the time I've been on this road,' the driver said, turning in to the village. 'Myself and Murdo Meek. After the Dell girls.'

'Is it OK if you don't stop at our house?' Colin said. 'I mean at the gate?'

'Why?'

'In case my mother hears the van stopping and gets up. I mean she'll hear the van anyway. She never sleeps. But if –'

'No bother,' the driver said. 'That's John the Battler's shed, isn't it?'

'Yes. You can let me off here,' Colin added. 'There's no need –'

'I know my way around these parts,' the driver said. He turned left at John the Battler's shed and drove the van down to the gate at the end of the Aird road. There, he ran the van a little way down Donald Dod's brae, braked, put her in reverse and turned her nose towards the village.

'That'll do,' he said.

He switched off the engine and lights.

'Well,' said Colin. 'Thanks once again.'

'That's OK,' the driver said. 'Where are you going?' he said.

Colin had opened the door.

'Hang about,' the driver said cheerfully. 'Five minutes.' He leaned across and slid the door to with his right hand. 'There's no hurry, is there?'

'I better go home,' Colin said. 'My mother –'

'It's nearly morning anyway. Here –' he reached into the inside pocket of his jacket and took out a half-bottle of whisky.

'O well . . .'

'The genuine moorhen.' He unscrewed the cap from the flask, and handed the flask to Colin.

'Good health,' said Colin.

'Down the hatch,' said the driver.

'That's good stuff,' said Colin, shuddering and swallowing hard as his mouth filled with water.

'Have another,' the driver said. Colin shook his head, still swallowing hard, and handed the flask back to the driver. The driver tipped the flask up to his mouth and tilted his head back. 'Slainte,' he said. The whisky made a brisk, glugging noise going down his throat. He handed the flask back to Colin. 'Go on.'

'All the best,' said Colin. He shuddered again and swallowed once or twice, before he felt the warm glow starting to go through him.

'I can see you're a drinking man,' the driver said.

'That's good stuff,' Colin said.

'Have another.'

'Ah, no . . .'

'Go on.'

'O well . . .'

'That's the way. Get it down you while you're young.'

'Better than vodka,' Colin said, and sat back suddenly in his seat.

'Is that what you were drinking in the Royal? Vodka?'

'Vodka an' orange,' said Colin. His voice sounded thick when he spoke. His tongue seemed to have swollen. He handed the flask across to the driver.

'You keep that,' the driver told him. 'You'll need a livener for the morning.' He shifted abruptly in the dark, causing the back of the seat to creak, and asked, 'Why were you thrown out of the hostel? Having a go at one of the maids, wasn't it?'

'No.' Colin shook his head slowly. His voice sounded thick. 'No, what happened was –'

'I'll give you a laugh,' The driver shifted again, causing the seat to creak again. 'Up in this village one night,' he said. 'Myself and Murdo Meek. What a man! We're at Noony's peatstack, with the bicycles, wondering what to do next, when who do we see coming along the road, all by herself, but Smeets' daughter, Annie, the one they called the Swan. Very snooty and high-minded the Swan was, ate herring and potatoes with a knife and fork, wouldn't speak Gaelic, wouldn't speak to any of us. Anyway, there she was, on her way home, carrying a bottle of milk. "The Swan!" says Murdo Meek. "Let's get her!" So out with us from behind Noony's peatstack, and next thing Murdo Meek has his hand over the Swan's mouth and we're dragging her, still clutching the milkbottle, into that empty house next to your granny's the airmen were in during the war. I'll say this for the Swan – she put up a good struggle at the beginning. We had her there till four in the morning. We heard poor old Smeets out on the road at one stage, looking for her, so Murdo Meek put his hand over the Swan's mouth again till he went past. The Swan wouldn't stop crying. Not so snooty any more. Four in the morning before we let her go. The milkbottle got broken.'

He reached up and switched on the roof light. His face was shining with sweat.

'Here,' he said, taking the half-bottle out of Colin's hand and tipping it to his mouth. When he stopped drinking, the flask was empty. He wound down the window on his own side and threw the flask out. It made a little chinking noise against the ground when it landed. The driver wound the window back up. He turned and put his hand under Colin's chin.

'Smooth as a baby's bottom,' he said. 'Don't pull your head away.' He caught hold of Colin's hand by the wrist. 'Feel that,' he said, rubbing it against his cheek. 'I started shaving when I was twelve.' He turned Colin's hand over, studying it. 'You've the hand of a girl,' he said. He let Colin's hand go.

'Why don't you come down the road a spin with me?' he said. 'We'll go to my house. There's no one in it but myself now, since my mother died. I've got a bottle of whisky. We'll drink it. I'll show you photographs of the old Ness teams. I've got them all. What do you say?'

'I can't,' said Colin.

'No?'

'No,' said Colin. 'I'd like to,' he said. 'But I can't.'

The driver switched off the rooflight. He leaned forward, resting both arms on the steering wheel, and put his head on his arms.

'On you go, then,' he said.

Colin sat up and slid open the door of the van. He had to use both hands. The driver hunched, black and bulky, over the steering wheel. He seemed to have fallen asleep. Colin stood outside the van.

'Thanks for the lift,' he said.

He closed the door of the van behind him.

Outside, it was still dark. He walked slowly down Donald Dod's brae. He hoped Scott, the dog, who was kept out in the barn at night, wouldn't hear his footsteps and start barking. There wasn't a road out to Donald Dod's house, only a cart-track. Donald Dod was always talking about getting the County Council to put a road out to his house, like the road going in to Aird. Everyone else in the village knew that the Council wouldn't do it. He cut between Alan's park and Angus John Tully's, taking the short way home. A smell of dew arose from the grass; a cold breeze was blowing. The driver had been right – it was nearly morning. Once on the road to their own house, he felt easier – he turned and looked behind him. The van had not moved.

At the gate of the house, he stopped and leaned weakly against a gatepost. He didn't want to go in yet. The village was asleep. On the windows of all the houses in Dell facing him, the blinds were down. In Aird too, on all the windows that he could see, the white blinds were down. But the morning was coming; out from the Butt, as he watched, a faint pencil line of grey appeared between the sea and the sky. He did not look again in the direction of the van. It was cold – he thrust his hands into his trouserpockets. To his astonishment, there was a pound note in one of them. Opening the gate of their house, he felt a truth enter (where she had not been sought) and touch his heart lightly, with cold, light fingers.

The student calendar

He is gone on a long voyage over perilous seas, Colin, son of Angus, son of Alexander, son of young Murdo. Where he lisped in infant numbers, had his first fitful erection, grew to pimply young manhood, knows him no more. Long shall the brown bog lament, long the black eye of creation bubble in molten sorrow. The sure shank of him, the keen nostril, the screwed-up eyes and the tickler-sucking mouth. Blow, wind from the west, bringing all the smells to him and all the sounds; and rain from the west, fall gently on him, in the grey granite city where he lies.

'If there's a wetter place on earth than Kyle of Lochalsh,' said Chrissie Joan Mackenzie, 'I wouldn't like to see it.' The big train hissed in the dark. They couldn't get into it. It was five in the morning. It was raining. It was cold. The big train didn't leave till half-past six. The waiting room was locked. The station unlit. They stood in a group underneath the sloping tin roof, listening to the rain. They were students, going to Aberdeen. Down at the quayside, the *Loch Seaforth* went *Waa-waa* and churned on to Mallaig with the students going to Glasgow and Edinburgh. 'Maybe Niagara Falls,' said Chrissie Joan Mackenzie, shivering.

Names of stations in the dark and the half-light and the day: Duirinish, Plockton, Duncraig, Stromeferry, Strathcarron, Achnasheen, Achanalt, Lochluichart, Garve. The big train creaked, squealed, jerked to a halt at each one, jolting the sleepers to consciousness, hissing steam. At Lochluichart, a woman handed the guard, through the window, a cardboard box containing a hen. The hen looked wideawake. Dingwall.

'My aunty was in the hospital here,' he said. 'She was the matron.'

Muir of Ord.

'There's a golf course here,' he said. 'I was on it.'

Inverness. A two-hour wait. The Bridge Restaurant.

'Between Inverness and Aberdeen,' said Coonsey, 'there's nothing but green fields with black cows in them.'

'It isn't dinner by the way, cove,' Norrie Scouts told him. 'This is lunch you're eating.'

'Where's your digs?' Coonsey asked him.

'Jamaica Street.'

'Never heard of it . . . Hui, Storky,' he shouted across the restaurant, 'where's Jamaica Street?'

'Donno.'

'You'll have to get a taxi at the station, then,' said Coonsey. 'You're all right,' he told Donald Angus Graham, who had digs in Powis Place, 'you can come off the train with us at Kittybrewster. But he'll have to go all the way in to the main station.'

Aberdeen,

Friday.

Dear Bro. ~~Ian Iain John~~ Eoin Baist',

Woill, here's me in the big city, c/o Bruce, 2 Jamaica Street, and there's you in the even bigger city, c/o Morrison, 68 White Street, and hope this finds you as it leaves me, how is everyone in Glasgow, how is everyone from Hull in Glasgow, how is things in the oilskins and galoshes business, a clerk isn't it? Lift your photograph in a studio with a palm tree and send it to me.

Bruce is Bob (known as Aal Bob) and Margaret (Meg). We communicate. Me: Well . . . I'm off now. Meg: Fessen the pints o' yir sheen, loon. Me: Pardon? Meg: Yir pints is lowsed. Me: What? Aal Bob *(at window):* It's fair abeen. Me *(wary):*

Aye ... Enter Watty, husband of Maud, son-in-law of Meg and Aal Bob, they live upstairs, a mechanical genius. Watty *(holding aloft right hand dripping with blood, thumb sticking out at obtuse angle)*: Far's the aye-a-deen? Aal Bob: Michty begod, Watty min, fit's adee? Watty: I wis knypin' on atat Fordie, ken, an' gied it a richt yark. *(howls at ceiling)* Maad! Me *(exiting discreetly)*: Well ... cheerie the now ... *(tripping over shoelace in doorway)* Jesus! ...

It took me some time to get my bearings in Aberdeen, and I got lost twice – once by night, when I walked for a long time in a southerly direction (going to the Students Union) and fetched up at the Bridge of Dee, and once by day, when I walked for a long time in a northerly direction (going back to the digs) and fetched up at the Bridge of Don. This is an inherited talent; my grandfather (your grandfather too, old chap) was famous for it. He got lost once between Oban and Fort William and it took the combined police forces of Lochaber and Lorne three days to find him.

In University I'm doing (taking) English, British History and Moral Philosophy. Moral Phil, as we students call it. You can call it that too, every Thursday dinnertime, as pleading poverty you hungrily roam the Dumbarton Road and ponder the mutton pies of Patrick. Moral Phil., you can say to yourself. It's all in the mind. Must go now. Write. Do bh. ~~Col Colin~~ Cailean Caillt 'An Micheil.

Outside Kings College library, at the Unicorn, a jowly, densely bearded fourth-year student, Young Oggy, motioned to him to halt.

'If you're not sure at night where you are in this man's town, cove,' said Young Oggy, 'remember that the street lights in Union Street are upright, in George Street they stick out sideways. Furthermore, if you get lost again in broad daylight, remember that all buses in Aberdeen go into the city centre. Finally, try not to stick your bobban gansey inside your trousers, thus betraying your origins to the entire world. And get rid of the snakebelt.' He blew fastidious cigarette smoke out of his nostrils. 'Do you think you can remember all that, cove?'

... Women women everywhere. I don't know where to look next. There must be one for me, I'm tired of pulling my wire and glancing furtively over my shoulder in case the Lord is watching from above. I still consider myself a virgin, in spite of the sweaty shenanigans with Lillian Margaret Hutcheon (hayloft in 33), Dohag (Dell Bridge) and Cathy Caruso (Snarler, myself and Evans, Castle Grounds last year). Noticed one with my atrocious face early in the week, found her beside me in English literature, she nearly dropped a pen, I nearly picked it up, she smiled, I bared my teeth in ghastly approximation of same, so far so bad. To look at: pleasant, delicate, innocent. I have known it before. Rather like Lillian Margaret Hutcheon, in fact, and so, undoubtedly, there is below the fire and brimstone, the sulphurous pit, thunder and lightning, stinking cod, fie fie fie. Maybe I'm a poof.

Two Shakespeare plays first term, Bad *King John* (bad play) and *Antony and Cleopatra* (a doddle). I read it with Watty (not Watty in the digs, he of the torque judders and hardy spicers, but Watty in the school, the good old Nicolson, he of the moustache and tackety boots). In sixth year we read it, and I wouldn't mind a night with Charmian, Iras wouldn't be slack either, unfortunately they both end up dead, but plenty more where that came from (how do you fancy Egypt?). Can also confirm that British History is the same over here as it was over there. Nothing fresh on Lambert Simnel or Perkin Warbeck. And Mary Queen of Scots was still alive the day before the day she was beheaded, all six feet of her, in silken hose and fancy French slubbars.

Moral Philosophy, on the other hand, is a deep, dark subject, concerned with knowledge and understanding, the minds of Plato and John Stuart Mill, the existence of God, etc. To one nurtured on such substantial works of literature as Josephus, Spurgeon, *The Pilgrim's Progress, The Days of the Fathers in Ross-shire* and *The Shorter Catechism*, a word like utilitarianism holds no terrors. The professor, Mackellar, wears trousers at half-mast, cardigans with the buttons in the wrong holes, one sock black one sock red, he snorts, champs, growls, eats lead pencils raw, has eyes rounder, eyebrows hairier and a forehead bigger, shinier, more impressive by far than Plato's. If you wish to see Plato's forehead (the eyebrows are missing), seek him out in Partick public library, Everyman edition of his works. I was going to do (take) Psychology first, and went accordingly to a lecture. I sat there for an hour, listening, not understanding. Psychologists have a language of their own; brave new words: 'stimuli', 'response', 'conceptual', 'motor'. The last-mentioned did it for me. Motor, by God. Motor. That's it. The crowning blow. Baffled, I hastened to the Old Brewery Building, Wrights & Coopers Place, and the room of my Director of Studies, MacCluskey, pink of pluic he, snub of snout, scant of hair, a cherub, a angel, a young Mr Pickwick, his first name is Doctor and he said, Well, devil take it, Colin old chap, I mean to say, why not do Moral Philosophy instead then, Colin old chap, I mean to say, you've got the bone structure for it and all the accoutrements, devil take it? So there you are.

NOVEMBER

Today a football team from Motherwell with a forward line of irresistible midgets defeated Aberdeen FC 5–0 in the gloom at Pittodrie. I watched the whole game, from beginning to end, in the company of a long, tall expert from Easter Ross, James Ross Mackay. In the gloom of the Pittodrie Bar afterwards, he insisted on pointing out the multitudinous deficiencies of the home side, in a piercing Ross-shire accent, to assorted savages in red and white scarves and toories, who, after listening briefly to his harangue, commenced to growl and gibber at him and enquire fa the fuck he thocht he wis, the lang cunt? Burying my nose in the pintglass (Gaelic: plosgartaich), I told myself I wasn't there, that I was on the Galson moor, heading for Loch Mhor Shanndabhat, and resolved never to drink again except on special occasions, New Year maybe, or weddings, and then only lager and lime. Got back to Jamaica Street at 8 p.m., a thing of shreds and patches, and I have been sleeping off and on since.

*   *   *

'When's your next class?' Donald Angus Graham asked him.

'Twelve o'clock. English.'

'Thought you had British History at ten?'

'There isn't a register. Besides, I've done all the stuff already in school.'

'I've got Gaelic at eleven,' said Donald Angus Graham. He took a loud slurp of tea from his mug. 'Nineteenth-century prose. Really boring.'

They were in the Pavilion, a café above the changing rooms at Kings with huge, sloping windows looking out on the playing fields. Henderson and Charles Froggart and the beautiful blonde who went about everywhere with them came away from the serving hatch with their cups of coffee and sat at the next table. Henderson and Charles Froggart were in Colin's Moral Phil. class. They were arguing, as usual, and the beautiful blonde, as usual, kept looking from the one to the other, like someone following the ball at a tennis match, tossing back her long, blonde hair and restlessly shifting her long, honey-coloured, nylon-sheathed legs.

'Loving God, you say?' Henderson guffawed. 'God so loved the world etc.? But in this day and age, the concept of a loving, omnipotent, omniscient Being is an absurdity. Utter absurdity!'

'Not at all! Not at all!'

'Absolute and utter absurdity!'

'And what, if I may be permitted to ask, is the alternative? Aha! Yes? –'

'Alternative? Logically speaking –'

'The alternative is annihilation. That's what you were going to say. Evolution! Fortuitous concourse of atoms! I can't accept that.'

'Why not? It's more . . . how shall I say? . . . *reasonable* . . . than the Garden of Eden.'

'Reason? Aha! Yes! Reason! I thought you'd say reason. But we must go *beyond* reason –'

'I wish merely –'

'There are areas beyond which reason cannot go. Where our rationality must be suspended.'

'In which case, my dear fellow, you are denying the faculty that principally distinguishes you from the beast –'

'Faith! The substance of things hoped for! –'

'You say faith. But what, basically, is faith? –'

'The evidence of things not seen!'

'My dear Charles, that is a patent absurdity! Patent absurdity!'

'Now *that*,' said Donald Angus Graham, 'is what *I* call a conversation!'

He shook his head irritably.

'That's what we came to university to do. To learn new things. To learn to speak like that.'

'We'd get off with the beautiful blonde too,' said Colin, glancing at the next table. He turned back to Donald Angus Graham's pouting, irritated face. 'Anyway, why worry?' he said. 'It's not your language.'

'What do you mean, cove?'

'What?'

'*Your* language, you said.' Donald Angus Graham's face had gone dark red with anger.

'What do you mean, *your* language?'

'*Our* language, then.'

'That's not what you said. You said *your* language.'

'I meant *our* language.'

'No you didn't. You meant me, *my* language. Gaelic-speaking plodder. That's what you meant.'

'I didn't, Beefy.'

'You didn't mean yourself. You didn't include yourself. English is your language, not Gaelic, and you're so good at it.'

'Gaelic is my language too.'

'No it's not.'

'You're wrong, Beefy.'

'No I'm not. I'm not wrong at all.'

'. . . responsibility for one's actions, Charles,' came from the next table. 'Surely you must accept that?'

'But on what principle? You forget Kant's Categorical Imperative.'

189

'*Au contraire!*'

'Act only according to that principle of which you can will that it becomes universal law –'

'To which I am bound to reply –'

'I'm sorry, Beefy,' said Colin. 'You just picked me up wrong.'

'No I didn't,' said Donald Angus Graham. 'I didn't pick you up wrong at all.'

DECEMBER

In the Union refectory, watching the skin forming on his cup of coffee, when Alice Ann Morrison sat down beside him. She'd been on his class in school. He didn't know her very well. She was a plump girl who laughed a lot.

'Colin!' she said. 'Do you mind if I join you?'

'Not at all.' He gave a nervous little jump.

'Well?' she said. 'And how are you?'

'Fine,' he said. 'Great.'

'You got over Friday night, then?'

'The Dive Night, you mean? Sure.'

The Dive was a cellar in the Students' Union. The Dive Night was held there once a month, by the Celtic Society. They ate salt herring and potatoes, and drank and danced and sang.

'You were very rude to me,' she said. 'Do you remember?'

He felt the blood rushing into his face. He shook his head.

'Will I tell you what you said? It was very rude.'

He looked at her and looked away. She laughed.

'My legs aren't that fat,' she said. 'You were rude to Chrissie Joan as well. And to Young Oggy's girlfriend.'

'O God!'

'Better drink that coffee,' she said, 'it's getting cold. Want to come to the Annual Dinner and Dance with me? As my partner?'

'Me?' He looked at her. She laughed. Her face had gone red as well. He felt embarrassed and a little frightened.

'Only if you promise to stay sober. You're very nice when you're sober. Well?'

'Sure,' he said.

... We come from bad stock on the Habost granny's side. My mother says I take after them. Old Amos, church elder, also said so many moons ago, when he caught me in his carrot patch, his pride and joy. And Kate Stanton said it was in my head but not in my hands when I couldn't do the raffia thing at handwork, and granduncle Norman said, 'What do you expect, Mary, of someone who jumped into the river after a trout?' And I stuck a fork in Maggie Mary's cat, and got a kick in the arse from Sinclair the policeman for breaking the cups on the telegraph poles. Jesus, the days I've seen.

Last night was the night of the – take a deep breath – Aberdeen University Celtic Society Annual Dinner and Dance. I went with Alice Ann Morrison, who is big and ungainly, black wires grow on her head, a great one for laughing but unfortunately she doesn't drink, open her legs or permit you to fondle her tits. At first, everything was most enjoyable. I ate all that was put in front of me; I drank, with Alice Ann's approval, a glass or three of rather cheeky sack. I made her laugh. We danced – waltz, old fashioned, which I can do very well, and eightsome reel, primitive. I drank a pint of lager for the thirst. I told Alice Ann I loved her. On her back, under the red velvety material, my hand encountered a lump, and a declivity where the bra strap was, and another lump. I drank a golden doubler of whisky. Alice Ann came into the bar, saw me, smiled, saw what I was doing, stopped smiling. Left. I ordered another. A Uistman was grating in my lug. What do Leodhasachs know about Gaelic poetry? he wanted to know. Where's Alice Ann? I asked him. Long gone to Kentucky. The Uistman sang a song about a battle on a beach in the sixteenth century. How's that for poetry? he wanted to know. Me: Another round. The Uistman: Where will you hear the likes of that in Lewis? Me (*drunk*): Waal ... since ma baby left me ... The Uistman: A Dhia m'anam! Me (*drunk and introspective*): It is myself that is under sorrow at this time. Dram will not be drunk by me with cheer. A worm is gnawing at my vitals – The Uistman (*alarmed*): Go to the bog! ... At the crack of day, I was immersed in conversation with a flaxen-haired, yellow-fanged woman in a long, sleeveless dress. Wife of Professor O'Sniogh. Her upper arms wobbled. Was she Irish too? No – flashing the fangs – English, actually. And me? Welsh. I am Daffyd ap Gwilym, and I love none but married women. That'll do, said a face, possibly O'Sniogh's, on the other side of her. Hands joined by a circuitous route to the face made fists like turnips on the table top. I am Organ Morgan, and I'm leaving.

(Sunday). Alice Ann. Guilty there. I think I love her. Since the Friday night debâcle, I can't get her out of my head. She is coming between me and Bishop Butler's sermons. I must make it up with her, pronto. But how?

Glad you're out of the oilskins and welly boots, and into a chob at Singers with good boodle, canteen facilities, your own locker, free boilersuit plus spare, time and a half Saturday and two weeks' paid holiday a year. What more could heart desire?

Next week it is swotting like mad, and the week after it is exams.

So yous a Singerman now, boss,

Lawd lawd,

Yous a sewingmachineman now.

Colin, his ruins.

JANUARY

Isle of Lewis, isle of heroes,
Twelfth Night.

There was merriment for a while: 'Air do shlaint' and those jolly old, jolly jolly evergreens: "Nuair a fhuair sinn uil' air bord innt', 'Ho-ri, ho-ro, mo ni-nag' and 'An 'eid thu leam, a Mhairi?' (Does anyone know what Mairi said?) Now it is cold everywhere, white and frozen. The bottles are empty. The heroes have departed.

Your big brother Alan, melancholy, magnificent, the first to go. In a scarf with the stripes of the University of Edinburgh, and a blazer with the badge of the University of Edinburgh, and flannels with a crease from the emporium of Shamus Mackenzie, and shoes with a gleam from the catalogue of J. D. Williams. Of me he approves not at all ('no moral fibre') and before you start preening and casting coy, sideways glances at yourself in the two-winged mirror on the dressing table of the back bedroom in the flat on the first landing in the tenement in White Street, he doesn't approve of you either ('neurotic'). Third-year Political Economy (Polly Con) is where he's at, he is somewhat hypochondriac, doesn't drink, plays football for the University First Eleven, also an activity called squash involving rackets and a hard little ball that you hit against a wall and then retrieve, or rather your opponent does, before hopefully doing the same to you. It sounds as though it might have been invented, on an off-day, by a chain smoker with piles and a mean streak. Asked by the dwellers in 33 what (under the sun) Polly Con was, he resorted to ear-splitting English: 'gross domestic product ... spatial and temporal variations in the rate of ... in the United Kingdom,' after which aunty Annie: 'Chan eil sinne tuigs' durd a tha e 'g radh!' On Saturday he departed, in his Vauxhall, the biggest Vauxhall in the world. Good luck, was all I could say, good luck, Alan, ancient of days, may God keep you from slow leaks in the fastnesses of Rannoch, preserve you from the avalanches of Donnchadh Ban country. The last of the braves (i.e. me) is leaving tomorrow night (i.e. Sunday) on the van of Robert (i.e. Robert).

At home, no change. My mother hacking in her harvest time, busy every day, it is necessary I think but I am not sure. I have never been busy. Annie oscillating in her slipstream with a duster and a couple of pimples. She's going to be a nurse. The sooner the better, say I.

When I get back to Aberdeen I'm going to start doing deep breathing exercises and press-ups, attending all lectures (even British History), beavering at the books and going to the library in the evenings – anything to keep my nose out of alehouses. A week now (nearly) since I touched drink, and I have resolved not to drink again. Resolved as in resolution as in New Year. All very well for other people to speak of going for a pint, but from where I am (and you), going for a pint is meaningless. Going for ten pints, yes. And then there is a complete collapse of communication – with me, I can't see beyond my own bloody nose when drunk, loudly trying to impress people (Christ knows why), not aware of other people's feelings, hardly aware of their existence except as receptables for my high, nonsensical words, and if they attempt to say anything, I interrupt or 'listen' impatiently. All of which is a dead loss, utter waste. Most alarming, though, are the mental blanks, when you wake up and can't remember what you were saying or doing. This is more or less what happened at New Year. In the evening (early), I went down to uncle Dan's – very enjoyable until roughly 2 a.m., by which time I had swallowed a bottle of whisky. Uncle Dan sang me his songs, Marion and Norma sang, Tidy sang. I believe D. S. and Mairead can sing too. They're all singers. Anyway, 2 a.m., 4 a.m. wd. be nearer the mark, I insisted on going to the bothan for more, met Tidy, my long-lost bosom crony, on the road and we went to Habost, to the House of Hector, more whisky, Tidy and Hector fell asleep, one behind the sofa, one in the fireplace, but one of the Archies appeared out of the night (TT he) and I went with him in his van to bothan Adabrock. After pints and whiskies, I got a lift back to uncle Dan's house, and after that I can remember nothing. Only that uncle Dan was still in bed, that I was looking for whisky in his sideboard, and that Norma took me back to Dell. My mother told me I was a 'sad and sorry sight' when I appeared, that my language was vile and that I reminded her of Black John and Tammy Toronto in their heyday. That's it. Disgusting. Now I am on the wagon and thinking of writing a play, full of heartbreaking lines, which will make no sense at all, and which I will send you for critical approval. The clock on the mantelpiece has struck once. It is midnight. It is the Sabbath. The frost performs its secret ministry. And so to bed.

Aberdeen, Friday, in the evening, early . . .
Your letter today, at last. Why didn't you reply sooner? Have you washed your hands off-a me, offal? Well, anyway . . .

A preliminary missive, this. Writing it in the digs. Stew and potatoes, I think, on the hob in the kitchen of Aal Bob and Meg his wife, and a new lodger sharing my room and my bed, not female, alas, not Alice Ann (that name!) or Bella Maggie from Portrona, but a large, slow-speaking Lewisman, Murdo Angus Macleod, and he's from Loch-a-Ghainmhich, you don't know where that is, neither did I, it's on the west side, near Breasclete, not far from Callanish, close to Tolstadh-a-Chaolais, a stone's throw from Achmore as the seagull flies. What Murdo Angus is doing in Aberdeen is an advanced course in marine engineering in the College of Navigation in King Street, he's a marine engineer in the Merchant Navy, and in the College of Navigation in King Street in order to become a bigger and better marine engineer in the Merchant Navy, he's 30, engaged to be married to a nurse from Shader, and only in 2 Jamaica Street until the company find a flat for him, let it be soon, let it be now. Mind you, he has a portfolio of dirty photos in his big sailor's suitcase which he allows me to pore over to my heart's content and even take up to the bog with me, one slant-eyed acrobatic lump of a girl in particular (how do you fancy Singapore?). The one he's engaged to has a pleasant, Alice-Ann look to her. He has *her* photograph under plastic in his wallet. She must know about his feet.

This business with the Oilskins and Galoshes people sounds awful. How much money do they want back from you? Will they arrest you, send you to prison, to Barlinnie, solitary confinement? And will I be allowed to visit you there (I would bring a Macgowan's Highland Toffee with a file in it)?

Just been through to see Aal Bob, who is this very day out of hospital and sitting ben the hoose with black wheels round his eyes, assorted lumps and cuts about the face, a sheepish grin and a leg in plaster. It seems that on New Year's morn, Watty, the son-in-law and mechanical genius, turned up on a large, loud motorbike and invited Aal Bob to get on the pillion, they'd go for a wee spin, clear the cobwebs. So off they went, vroom bang, Meg and Maud in the door, protesting. Out about Udny, Aal Bob, in a state of high excitement, demanded a shot on his own. He'd never driven a motorbike in his life before. What happened next, in his own words: 'I caaed the hunnel, the caaf cam' fleein' oot its erse, and next thing the neuks wis comin' up at a hoor of a lick . . .'

Stew and potatoes, I was right, yes, and maybe a pint or three tonight with Murdo Angus in the Butcher's Arms, I'll air my views, out-pint him, puzzle him with Gaelic songs from the district of Ness. Good-O!

A hurried letter, this.

Passed my exams. If I told you what I got in English, you wouldn't believe me.

Very pleased. I wanna go tell it on Bennachie.

Tails up. Chin to the grindstone. C.

PS 'Her feets was wet.' (line from an old Blues song)

FEBRUARY

Here is another letter. Here goes then. Here it goes.

Allan Alabaster: Quiet.

Erchie: Something coming? Something doing?

Allan Alabaster: Quiet.

Erchie *(excited)*: Something up?

Descartes *(sad)*: Oui et non.

A deep silence, during which they look at the door.

A long silence, during which they look at the window.

A deep silence, during which they look at the door.

The door opens.

Alex Dan comes in.

He is dressed in a white, double-breasted suit of many buttons, with the following Gaelic symbols – a peat, a swede turnip, a black wellington with the top folded down, a Hattersley loom, a peatiron, a tractor, a headscarf, a swagger coat, a pair of bootees, a bunch of bogcotton, a sprig of heather, an English stranger, a butterdish (Present from Yarmouth), a tin of sheep dip, a packet of size, a distemper brush, a tweed bonnet from Buth Allan Martin, a bobban stocking, a Bible, a wireless accumulator, a dynamo and three-speed, a pair of Lybro dungarees, a poke of bachelor buttons, a canister of black striped balls, a tea caddy, a tin tray, Mac an t-Sronaich's cave in the Bens of Uig, a screwtop of MacEwan's Pale Ale, a half-bottle of Spey Royal, a hairless dog, a headless hag, a half-sleeping hero up on one elbow, a tobacco knife, a Port Line gansey, an Ayrshire

cow, a black hat, a Sunday suit, a chamberpot, a pan loaf from
J. & E., an Albion van minus the wheels sitting on concrete blocks
and converted into a henhouse, a bottle of M&B tablets, a Kerr's
pink potato, a sack of drowned kittens, a stob, a strainpost, a can
of 3-in-1 oil, a *Shorter Catechism*, a split haddock, a salt herring, a
three-legged pot of crotal dye, a tilley, a battery torch, a waterbutt
and a necklace of limpet shells – deftly sewn into the fabric by
nimble, needle-threading fingers.

Alex Dan: I thought so. I thought so this morning when I
 opened my eyes, you would be here plotting and planning,
 planning and plotting, it isn't Roderick the Potato Boiler, I
 said to myself, he's got the pension now, it isn't Roderick's
 Uncle Alan, he lost his legs and a lung and an eye and an
 ear and half of his chin and all of his teeth in the Great War
 and he's got as many pensions as you like because of it. Now
 I am a fundamentalist, always back to one and one, Descartes,
 and I said to myself, speaking as a fundamentalist, I said, well,
 where do we, I said, where de we go from here, America
 was discovered by an Irish monk long before Columba or
 Columbus was it, long before Columba's Uncle Allan who got
 a pension for a jaw, and long before Roderick the Potato Boiler,
 the question big question is where do we go from here?
The others attack him.
He falls.
The curtain falls.

The curtain rises.

Alex Dan: Savages.

The curtain falls.
End of scene one.

SCENE 2

A room. A tall figure, dressed in black, is standing in the middle of
the room. From the left, a second figure – short, fat and dressed in

a white, double-breasted suit of many buttons and Gaelic symbols –
hastily approaches the first. It is very dark, it is winter, where they are.

Tall Figure *(sadly)*: Is it you, Alex Dan, at last?

Fat Figure *(truculently)*: Not here the hissing of the barnacle
    pot or the singing of kettles. But mouldy bannocks, and kipper
    bones the lamp unlit.

Tall Figure *(sadly)*: Is it you, my hero, is it you?

Fat Figure: I, Alex Dan, stout as a Borve bullock. Fierce
    and terrible in the field of conflict, proud and generous
    in my lofty halls. Many a skull have I cracked, many a
    belly sliced open. Kings and princes have welcomed me,
    beautiful women have . . .

Tall Figure: I, Knox . . .

Fat Figure: . . . loved me. Yet for me the skies were grey and the
    days, in the wake of the dancing, were cold. O great was the
    rejoicing of the widows when I was finally brought low.

Knox: They chopped off your head. I was there.

Alex Dan: My noble head, toothless and unshaven, in a barrel
    of lime.

Knox: I saw it all. I had a ringside seat.

    (Enter Erchie, Allan Alabaster and Coleridge)

Erchie *(trembling)*: Who goes? Who goes there? Who . . .
    who?

Coleridge: It is the frost and the wind in the trees.

Allan Alabaster: Take it easy, Coleridge.

    (Exeunt)

Alex Dan: Quietly now. Heeesht! I know my man and I shall
    follow him.

Knox *(low)*: In your white double-breasted suit of many
    buttons and Gaelic motifs?

Alex Dan *(truculently)*: So?

    End of scene 2.

These are the first two scenes of a play I shall never finish. If you
give me big big encouragement, I might very well write a third
scene. And if you persist – who knows? – I might even out-Webster

Webster. It is, as you can see, a revenge play, and there should be a great deal of blood later on. Maybe I could revise Alex Dan's very important speech in Scene 1, patch it up a bit here and there. Go to the Marischal Library, engineering section, and start again from scratch. Engineering – it is important. Maybe I could invent a machine while I'm there, if I get stuck between scenes, a printing press with a difference, different from the run-of-the-mill sort of kind of. If I get stuck between scenes. Someone at the door. To be continued.

Two hours later. It was Watty, clutching manual of mechanics from his night class and wanting Murdo Angus's address. Murdo Angus is here no more, he is now in a Company flat in King Street, across from the fire station. I insisted on helping Watty with his mechanics problem. No need to go to King Street, I told him, allow me to have a deek, all perfectly simple really, question of plain commonsense, who got Higher Science? – and as a result of my efforts, Watty is now heading, slightly bewildered, for King Street on his bicycle (the motorbike has been confiscated), manual of mechanics strapped to the carrier, leaving behind him, on the table, my page covered in mathematical squiggles and a diagram resembling a mediaeval battleaxe with a currycomb dangling from it.

Now at 9 p.m., having risen from my armchair, negotiated the wardrobe (which takes up half the room; a family of Japanese could easily set up house in it), turned sharp right to my table, sat upon the wobbly wooden chair and taken pen in hand, I resume. Such small writing, such a long page to fill, so finely lined and with two holes at one side in case you want to file this letter for posterity. But I will get round the holes, unless ... What if Watty should return, now, even now, from King Street, problem solved, should now come to my door again and come in and say things? I would be obliged, as before – bowing obsequiously, waving an arm – to offer him my good chair and perch on the wobbly, agreeing, acknowledging, thinking of what to say next and what of the letter then?

Still not drinking, but speaking at faces is becoming more and more difficult, especially academic faces. Yesterday was painful.

Today I wanted to scream like a pressure cooker because of the pain I inflicted upon me yesterday by going to a Celtic Society lecture on Gaelic placenames in Aberdeenshire and Banffshire, and sitting silently afterwards (sweating, trembling, going to pieces) bang in the middle of correct conversation:

'It was really a most interesting and informative lecture . . .'

'And fascinating to think how many parts of the region – indeed, almost all – were Gaelic-speaking. *Do* have another piece of cake . . .'

Great gloom upon me as I wended my way up George Street to the digs, and I nearly swerved into the 524 (a pub), but didn't, then thought of packing the brown suitcase and bolting to Sutherland and the moors, but I paused and asked myself: 'Is there a shop like Disher's on the moors?' The answer, in a word: No. Then I asked, 'Have you a fishing rod to catch fish?' The answer: No. 'Have you a spade?' No. 'A philosophy of life?' No. Stood where are you, then. So I went early to bed, wanted to wallow there, not stay awake too long in case of bad thoughts, not sleep too soon in case of bad dreams. (And sleep seems such a waste – eyes shut, open again – another day with a name to it.) Alice Ann came into the room, lay beside me in the big MurdoAngusless double bed. Her eyes were calm. She smiled at me. 'You're all right, Colin,' she said. 'Everything's all right.' We started doing godawful things to one another, and I woke up in the dark, everything far from all right, damp and crying. I am only to the chin in the green slime, but smiling, smiling . . .

A good house this, nevertheless. Quiet, very quiet, out of the swing of the sea. Nobody bother. I go on, thin like a pin, dodging the holes. Up in the morning 7.30, my halesome parritch with Aal Bob, my Aberdeen buttery and mahogany tea, followed by my crap and a tiny prayer for Calman, who is making it somewhere. The achieve of the thing. After that, things go downhill rapidly. On the insistence of the Uistman MacDonald (he of the poetic prejudices), I joined the Hares and Hounds – *Nothing like a five mile run,* he said, *for getting the shite out of your system* – and so, last Wednesday afternoon, I trotted out of Kings College in his wake, down a grey street, across a golf course, along a beach, over the Brig of Balgownie (with nary a bonnie Scots lassie to be seen), through a park, up a long bloody hill, down another street (this one cobbled) and back into Kings. Wheezing and dying on a slatted wooden bench, I watched the Uistman, through a fluid, roaring haze, remove the running shoes from his feet and a vicious-looking stick from his locker, put on football boots and a yellow and black striped jersey, and clatter out of the dressing room on to the shinty field. Later, from the safety of the Pavilion, I saw him having an altercation with a large madman from Kiltarlity who is doing Agriculture. Scary. I was never very good at games. Going over the buck at PT took a lot out of me, but not as much as it took out of Goggles. Maybe you don't remember Goggles. He was a wicked presbyterian with pimples and pores.

Now it is time to stop. I shall, in my orisons, remember you, for I know that you don't pray, and how on earth are they going to deal with you in heaven if you don't pray? So I shall mention you tonight – briefly – in the many things I have to say about myself. Briefly – quick as I can – because I'm the big shot in the prayer. C.

MARCH

Month of the mad hare and the black cockerel, whose blood, they say, is a specific against shingles. But what is shingles? And who is they?

I found this translation from the Irish in the Stack Room at Kings.

Maine Athramhail went to him; he went to Leogh first. Whose man are you? he said, but Leogh did not answer him. Maine spoke to him like that three times. Cu Chulainn's man, he said, and do not pester me, in case I happen to cut your head off. This man is angry, said Maine, as he turned away from him. After that he went to speak to Cu Chulainn. Cu Chulainn had taken off his shirt and the snow was all round him up to his waist as he sat and the snow had melted for a cubit around him because of the intensity of the warrior's heat. Now Maine asked him in the same way three times, whose man he was. Conchabar's man! And do not pester me; but if you pester me any longer I shall cut your head off as one takes off a blackbird's head. It is not easy to

*talk with these two, said Maine. Then Maine went away from them
and told his tale to Ailill and Medhbh.*

The sleuths of the Clydesdale Bank, Union Street branch, have
fallen upon certain complications with regard to the account of one
No. 2348700 XX Name, Murray, C. Consequently I shall be unable
to repay you the swatch you so kindly sent until the sun and the
moon meet in yonder glen, or the beginning of next month (April),
whichever comes first, when/or/at which time (delete as necessary)
I expect a windfall from the Macaulay Trust and/also from Ross and
Cromarty Education Authority, because Carnegie paid my fees last
year because I wasn't going to get a grant from Ross and Cromarty
because I wasn't going to get into university because I'd been expelled
from school and only reinstated because I'd already sat the Highers
and Fatso told them all that in his reference and plenty more besides
but I got in this year but the fees from last year still stand so Ross
and Cromarty owe me 32 quid (I think). Is that clear?

A spectacular fall from grace at the end of last month. Murdo
Angus, of Loch-a-Ghainmhich and the Ben Line, threw a party in his
new flat in King Street – a housewarming, it was called. Buddies from
the College of Navigation, cousins from a hydro scheme up north,
seafaring men with three legs and a wagonload of voluptuous nurses
from the Southern General Hospital, Glasgow, with Murdo Angus's
intended at their head. Had I not drunk too much too quickly, flaked
out and ended up in the casualty department, Woolmanhill, having
my stomach pumped, an eye the size of a duck's egg dressed and two
broken ribs strapped, I'm sure any or all of the nurses could have had
their way with me. Polish vodka was the cause of my downfall – one
of Murdo Angus's cousins kept feeding me Polish vodka. How I came
by the eye I'll never know. It wasn't a fight. Feeling somewhat weak
but also vaguely heroic after my release from hospital, I carried on
drinking all day Saturday in the Marischal Bar, then back at Murdo
Angus's flat, then back in the Marischal Bar and finally in some
house. Woke up Sunday morning on the steps of a church at the
top of George Street, a man – come to open the church, go ding
dong on the bell – asking me if I'd been there all night? Told him

yes and was he the minister? If so, that it was my wish to discuss fine points in theology with him. Go home, he said, staring at me. Where do you live? Go home. I realised then that, harled in green puke, hair frozen on my head and sporting a dirty pink eyepatch, I didn't cut the most dapper of Sunday morning figures. Bruised all over, freezing pain, gash-gold-vermilion, flashes of fire, I made it across George Street and along Calsayseat Road to my digs, and spent all next week (last week) in bed, very ill, very down. Weeping a little, looking for the loophole. Meg and Aal Bob found out about my doss on the church steps. *Yir an affa Colin*, Meg told me. Aal Bob, the Geoff Duke of Jamaica Street, swinging about the room on one leg, informed me that I was lucky to be alive. My last drink, and this time I mean it. Lochaber no more. Otherwise I'm kaput, and here endeth the lesson.

God, it's cold. Went just then and eased myself, with goosepimpled apprehension, on to an arctic toilet seat, but nothing doing. Weather so cold you can't crap. East wind, shrivels the sphincter, numbs the brain. Scraping ice from the inside of the windowpane this morning, I remembered that next Wednesday, at the latest, I must hie me down to Kings with three essays – the Moral Phil. one cribbed entirely from books which Prof. Mackellar will have read, perhaps even written, using a pseudonym. No shure about this Moral Phil. at all, cove, to tell you the truth. The musings of some lank bastard in a hairshirt who slept in his own coffin and was a stranger to the lavatory are not what I need at the moment. And I still seem to suffer from hangovers – my euphoria, when I wake up thinking I have a hangover, then remember I haven't been drinking, is brief indeed. Dreams as well. Not good. Also end-of-term exams in a fortnight's time. But I'll do the essays. I'll sit the exams. Go home for Easter. My eye is almost back to normal. An infection, the old doc. on Calsayseat Road said. Stop drinking, he said. He took the strapping off my ribs. Ribs heal by themselves, he said. Suffering is good, he said. Which is consoling if I ever again fall backwards off a high barstool, which is what happened, I believe, so one or two grinning winks and elbows have informed me. God, it's cold.

Reading. Apart from the academic stuff, I have read (on Alan's recommendation) *The Good Companions*, by J. B. Priestley. Dickens without the genius. Not worthwhile. Much better to read the Russians, who are, as you said, and I agree, the best. I am reading *The Brothers Karamazov* – magnificent. Since I spent last year at home reading idle books (as uncle Myles would term them), westerns ('He's a feisty, jug-whisky old hellion with a loaded bullwhip an' mule-kick fists,' said Curly. The tense quiet was broken by the sound of hoofbeats outside. Then Curly was boiling out the door, oblivious to the rain. 'Jesse! You skunk-eatin' Siwash! You green-gilled old gallywumpus!') and the other unprofitable trash that affords you the pleasure of tearing it to shreds, what I am now looking for in books is honesty and simplicity. The Russians (Chekhov, Tolstoy, Dostoevsky) offer it, and the Bible and Tagore. I could tell you what I think true poetry is – not clever, not sensational, not remarkable in any way. Beauty and poetry derive from simplicity and honesty. Eliot is not a poet, he is a preacher. Most of the so-called poets I have read are like this, or else they are trying to say something we all know in a very clever way – sensational, breathtaking, clever. The Russians are magnificent.

Well ... that's it. De Profundis and also In Tenebris. Dean cail no brochan dheth. I am running out of gas. He is running out of gas. Say your prayers. Colin the Damned.

Alice Ann ignores me in Kings, avoids me in the Marischal, cuts me dead in the Union. I thought, on the strength of her kindness to me in dreams, that I would venture a smile, a word, tentatively, nervously, by way of expiation, but nothing doing. My dream agent is a cruel trickster. So that's that. Pity.

A-PRAL

Thank you for letter to Dingley Dell.

I'd been down on 33's croft all morning with uncle John and Boy, the faithful hound, chasing sheep – me doing all the chasing. Uncle John was 'with his leg', and Boy chased rabbits, his own tail, the shadows of seagulls – everything except sheep – kept stopping when told to go and going when told to stay, and finally, after an eruption of abuse from the master that must have been heard in Cape Wrath, ran away home.

Got back to the house and my mother said, 'Letter for you.' 'Where?' 'On the mantelpiece.' 'Who from?' 'How should *I* know?' I opened the letter and started reading. She sat across from me. 'From John,' I said. 'He's fine. No news.' 'That's what *you* think,' she said. 'Read further down, where he lands in prison.' As if to confirm this, the kettle on the Modern Mistress gave a steamy purr. Skip the barney that followed. Now you know what happens to all mail sent to your mammy's.

I had quite a good holiday this time, in spite of aggravations like (supra). White wind, flying sun and rain. The Atlantic roaring, the earth stirring. People there are well – eating, sleeping, answering the postman's whistle. And in the evening, nodding by the peat fire and you don't need to put that light on yet. Much of the conversation has to do with death – how they died, what they said. Lambing at present – soon the plough and the peatcutting. I was in a crew that went out on the first of April (quite an appropriate date) to cut Old Peter's peats (a quid each we got from his wife, and our dinner in the house and two teabreaks). On the leading iron, tough, oilskinned Wee Angus Maciver from Aird and the red, rubbered hands and face (goggled-O) of John Angie; on the second, John the Battler and Ally ('I don't know') Batch, North Dell; and floundering in the boggy boggy blackstuff in their wake, myself and the Big Barney ('Maclean to captain! Horse on to Abadan!'), who was very funny all day, hilarious at times, spoke a seamless mixture of Gaelic and English and intends to marry a divorcee from Shader, Cathy Golly, aged 45. Wind north by north east, followed by sun, followed by snow turning to sleet, followed by sun, followed by wind south by south west, followed by rain, followed by a flat calm. The sort of day, the Big Barney said, you wouldn't know what to pawn. We had bananas and pana-cake at the teabreaks. There was duff and tomatoes and a Scribona sponge and bread and ham and bread and cheese and buns and strawberry jam also. But I stuck to pana-cake and yellow banana. By lowsing time, the Big Barney's face was rather hard to make out – I mean, what sort of thing it was – I mean, brown anyway from sailing in foreign climes, and white-eyed, and smeared about the mouth and chin and forehead with black peat – I mean, Genghis Khan lives! My mother told him he should soak it (his face) for a fortnight in a pail of water and washing soda. And what's wrong with girls your own age? she asked him. With the older ones, no words necessary, he replied, grinning all over his gleeful Mongolian pan.

Tales from the Peatbank:

(1) John the Battler, Willie Hearach and Dodo from Swainbost in a bar in the London docks. Cockney whore to Dodo: 'Buy me a drink, ducks?' Dodo to cockney whore: 'Yas, I'll buy you a drink.' Shouts up the bar, 'Large whisky for myself and a bucket of water for this cow here.' Cockney whore removes shoe, buries stiletto heel in Dodo's forehead. John the Battler and Willie Hearach take Dodo to nearest casualty hospital. Stop off en route at an all-night photographer's to have photo taken, Dodo on chair with whore's shoe stuck in his forehead and holding mock-Bible, John the Battler and Willie Hearach on either side of him, each with a hand on his shoulder. Does John the Battler have the photograph? Are you mad? Chrissie would murder me. So who's got it? Donno. I think it went to New Zealand.

(2) 'What's Cathy Golly like?' I asked at the first teabreak – the Big Barney gone out into the moor to smash the eggs of skuas nesting on Leine Shiabhat. 'Not bonny,' said Ally Batch. 'Have you ever,' said John the Battler, 'seen a skinny westsider at the fanks with buck teeth and a wen on his nose? Well, that's Donnie her brother, and he's considered chief in the family for looks.'

(3) The new Sewerage Scheme. It is well known that the water supplied to the west side of the island is very often dark brown in colour and undrinkable. Many believe this is caused by sheep carcasses which find their way into the loch, Loch Strianabhat. Domhnall Malt from Borve said: 'A sheep's ear came out of my tap and it had Aonghas Dhomhnaill Chalum's markings on it.'

(4) Old Peter's wife has installed an inside lavatory. Before that, Old Peter used to crap along a section of the glebe wall next to the Barneys' shed. (His wife used to squat in the middle of the living room and drop currants on a Scottish *Daily Express*). Through the

week, according to the Big Barney, Old Peter's turds resembled the criss-crossed handles of three hoes. But on Mondays, after the big Sunday dinner, 'you could have used them for pitprops.' He doesn't think the new lavatory will cope.

(5) Passing Dan Babsan's house one dark night, Wee Angus Maciver's uncle Murdo heard someone coming out and letting off a fart at the gable end. This was the noise the fart made: *Wick. Waag. Baralalou. Bup.*

(6) Neilly (N. Dell) was deeply in love with little Margaret Mary Finlay, Benview. He used to watch her comings and goings through the binoculars and send her conversation lozengers. Planting Alex MacFarquhar's potatoes last year, he was coming behind her in the drill when she suddenly farted, and the prevailing wind carried the fragrance of it to his nostrils. Love died on the spot.

All I have to say is that if you must go bawling and swaggering along the Dumbarton Road on a Saturday night in the company of Corrags, Whosays, G. K. Graham and Duff, you must also expect to run into the forces of law and order there, and that's all I have to say, and I think it very decent of the desk sergeant in the Marine to boot you all out of it at 6. a.m., instead of letting you languish there the livelong Sabbath, and not charge you either, and that's all I have to say. From Back, you say he was? Now do try and keep little anecdotes like that out of your letters home from now on, why don't you?

On the Saturday before I left, I had an enjoyable evening with uncle Dan. He was to have an operation on the following Wednesday, to remove a stone from somewhere. Operations are not new to him. Many stories about Ness eccentrics, history of Ness etc. I was at ease for a change (given the glowering presence of the sideboard, in which I can vaguely remember rummaging for hooch on New Year's morn) and even contributed quite a lot to the conversation. Glad, glad I went. He was standing alone, outside the house, when I emerged nose-first from the Rebel's van, and his face lit up when he saw me.

'I thought you weren't coming.'

The Rebel, having covered most of the loose females in our end of the district, is now probing with the butcher's van out in darkest Skigersta. Smelling like an abattoir with a brewery in the loft, he is rough-wooing the daughter of John Someone – Nick? Dick? – a large girl, whose like hasn't been seen in these parts since the days of Kennag Mor. Both are red-raw with love bites, and the butcher's van can be seen violently rocking, any old night, at the end of the old Skigersta road, in the Dell quarry, on the breakwater at Port or out at the Butt of Lewis. Peripatetic fucking.

It was with a baggy and apprehensive eye that I left Dell on Sunday night in Robert's van; my face, in the mirror of the *Loch Seaforth* lounge, told me to look out for squalls on the trip to Aberdeen, but nothing much happened until Elgin, when a woman with four shrill, clammy, snot-nosed, sticky-fingered children burst into the carriage where Donald Angus Graham and myself were dozing in the arms of Morpheus. After flinging God knows how many items of luggage into the overhead racks, she set up, before our very eyes, in the middle of the carriage, a small canvas folding table and a high chair for the baby, emptied a couple of message bags of their contents, and the children, who had by this time introduced themselves as Joyce (aged seven), Kate (nearly six), Danny ('he's three') and the baby, started having a picnic.

'Hope you don't mind?' the mother said, pouring milk and juice into cups, unwrapping packets of sandwiches, opening tins of biscuits.

'Not at all!' said Donald Angus Graham, beaming a welcome.

'Joyce!' she shouted. 'Take your hand off the other gentleman's knee!'

'Quite all right,' said Donald Angus Graham, before I could speak.

'Are we having our tea in Aberdeen with you, Mummy?' Kate (nearly six) asked her.

'No, you're having your tea at your granny's.'

'Joyce, we're having our tea at our *granny's!*'

'Ooooh, *lovely!*'

'I'm having tea downtown with Mummy's friend,' she explained to them. 'I'll come out to granny's tomorrow morning.'

'I don't want you to go away,' Danny ('he's three') said, jutting out his lower lip.

'O, stop that nonsense!'

'I don't want you to go away . . .'

'Eat your sandwich,' she said, trying to shove it into his mouth.

'Don' want it,' he muttered, into his jersey.

'Come *on* . . .' she coaxed. 'Mmmm . . .'

'Don' want you . . . go away . . .'

'Look, Mummy, Linda's throwing her piece at the *man!*'

'Will you *stop* that! . . . Little monkey . . .'

The baby looked at her, round-eyed. She started crying. At once, Kate scrambled down from Donald Angus Graham's knee, and around the table. 'Aw, poor Linda,' she soothed. 'Poor little Linda. Don't cry, poor little Linda . . .'

'Now look here,' the mother began, in a high, rapid voice. 'That's *quite* enough from all of you! *Quite* enough! Are you listening to me, Danny? *Are* you? . . . Sorry about that,' she added, addressing me directly.

'No bother,' Donald Angus Graham reassured her, before I could open my mouth.

'Don' want you . . . go away . . .' Danny muttered.

'O *stop* it! And you stop crying, baby. Here –' She gave Linda a plastic cup of juice. 'Now listen to me –'

'I want juice *too*,' Danny muttered.

'Right. Now then. I'll come out to granny's as soon as I can tomorrow, with something for everyone who's good. You get back to your place, Kate. Yes. But only if they're good and go to bed when granny says, Danny.'

'I want a talking doll, Mummy,' said Kate promptly. 'Like Helen Pirie.'

'I want –'

'I want a car.'

'Danny wants a car, Mummy.'

'I want a dress – no – shoes – yes – Mummy, I want a pair of red and yellow shoes.'

'I want shoes too, Mummy.'

'No you're not, you're getting a talking doll.'

'Mummy, Joyce says I'm not getting shoes.'

'I want a tractor.'

'I want shoes *too*.'

'No you're not. You're not getting.'

'Yes I *am*, Joyce.'

'No you're not.'

'I want a car and a tractor.'

'Yes I *am*.'

'No you're *not*, then. Is she, Mummy?'

'Yes I *am*, Mummy. Mummy, Joyce says –'

'Look, Mummy, Linda's pouring her juice on the *man!*'

'Ooooh *Linda!* . . .'

'I want a car and a tractor and a *tank*.'

'Look Mummy, *Linda!*'

'Mumm*ee!*'

'Look, *Mummee!*'

'Sorry about that,' the mother said, handing me a teatowel.

'Not to worry,' said Donald Angus Graham, before I could utter one word.

Passed English and British History, as expected. Moral Phil. so-so. 55 out of 100. Nothing else worth the telling. Went to the Charities Ball first week back, I don't know why. Not to be missed, they said. I suffered terribly: alienated, as at school socials and dances in the ATC hut at Adabrock. Moreover, the girl I took there was utterly indifferent to everything – totally unresponsive and depressing. I should have taken the wardrobe in my room instead; the wardrobe would have been much more inspiring. And Alice Ann was there – a suave lecher in a monkey suit and a bow tie draped all over her. 'Hallo, Colin. Do you know David Leith?' But I was glad they didn't sell booze there. It was soft drinks only.

Aal Bob (his leg still isn't right) has taught me a rhyme about two dogs, which his granny used to say to his oldest sister Annie as she dandled her on her knee, and Aal Bob learnt it from Annie. It goes as follows:

Doggies to the mill and catties to the sill,
Heigh Doggie Batty and heigh Doggie Sim.
Them twa made a ploy, and he ower him
And he ower him again, and he ower him.
Tak' a lick oot o' yon man's pyock,
And a drink oot o' the dam,
And hame gin even,
Hame gin even.

MAY

In the merry month of May, one could be treading barefoot in the morning dew, pu'in' the gowans fine, trysting with milkmaids at the yowe-butts or even studying for one's degree exams (less than a fortnight away), so what better than a dose of the clap to be going on with?

It all began exactly one week ago, when our hero (me), after a plain but filling repast of bradie, beans, chips, Balgownie Bakery baps and tea, left the digs for Kings College library, but instead of going over the small stone railway bridge at Erskine Street and then down Bedford Road, which would have taken me (him) to Meston Walk and Kings, his (my) feet, for some reason of their own, continued up the Great Northern road to Woodside. Thursday evening, six of the clock: a tired hour. The streets blank and empty; bits of newspaper and the fine stour of the day shifting apathetically along the pavements. Entering the Tanfield Bar, a hot, smoky roar of voices broke about our hero's head. He placed the briefcase (property of his late father) containing his Eng. Lit. and Moral Phil. notes carefully on the floor next to his foot, and a small Aberdonian at the counter said:

'Colin! It's Colin!'

'Hallo, Dod.'

'Fa?' another small Aberdonian asked.

'This is Colin,' Dod said.

'Colin fa?'

'Colin! You ken Colin! Student!'

'O aye. Colin.'

'Hallo, Budgie.'

'Met you . . . Marischal Bar, wis't?'

'Fit you drinkin', Colin?'

'I'll get them.'

'Na na.'

'No' for me,' the second small Aberdonian, who was called The Budgie Lemon, said, raising a full pintglass to his mouth. 'Needin' awa' hame for the tatties.'

'Fit wye?'

They were trawlermen. Our hero envied them.

He'd been in the Tanfield Bar before, with Murdo Angus. Murdo Angus, being a seaman, always went to bars like the Tanfield. Sawdusts, he called them. He didn't like lounge bars.

'Three weeks, sivvan hunner boxes,' The Budgie Lemon was saying. 'A richt trip.'

'See the boat we wis in?' Dod said. 'She wisny fit tae ging up the Dee, nivvar mind Greenland.'

He wanted to be a trawlerman too. Fuck Moral Philosophy.

He looked at his own face in the bar mirror. Stern and manly, the face looked back at him. Yes, the face said. This is the place to be. Fuck libraries.

Who goes to the library on a Thursday night anyway?

'Me?' said Dod. 'Nivvar!'

Students. That's who.

He drank down the rest of his pint.

Swots, that's who. Girls from Lewis, in coats, doing ordinary degrees.

He had another.

'A' the best . . . Colin, is't?' The Budgie Lemon said.

The Budgie Lemon was still here.

'Cheers.'

He raised his arm to attract the barman's attention.

(. . .'I'll give you a tip for getting on in the big city,' Murdo Angus said. 'Get to know all the head barmen.')

'You!' The Budgie Lemon said to Dod. 'You've mair patter than a herd of elephants.'

'Awa' an' shite an' I'll hae a Bacardi.'

'Mair patter than Donald Duck's feet.'

They were showing off for him. Wanting to make him laugh.

'Two Bacardis?' he said. 'Wanting beer?'

'Nae haein' a nip yersel'?' Dod asked him.

'No, I'm sticking to the beer.'

'Fit's adee, like?'

'Hae a nippie,' The Budgie Lemon urged him. 'It's my round onywye. Ernie!' he shouted. 'When you've time!'

Norrie Aulay had been a trawlerman. His late relative. He'd gone to university, packed it in, gone on the trawlers, gone to the dogs.

'Drink up, Colin,' Dod said.

'Away you raj!' a short man with a red beard and a pointy nose shouted at his drinking companion. 'You fucking *raj*, Johnston!'

'Now now now,' the barman told him. 'Mind the language, Ron.'

'None o' that now, Ron,' the other barman told him.

'Listen . . .' the man with the red beard made fists and puffed out his chest. 'I'm fast, you know.'

'We ken that, Ron,' the barman said.

'Mac!' the other barman shouted. 'Answer that fucking phone! Fit wis you needin', lads?' he asked.

'Twa Bacardis,' The Budgie Lemon said. 'Nippie o' whisky. Pint for the boy. Bottilie o' coke.'

'Fa?' the barman shouted. 'Tommy?' A man at a table playing dominoes looked up, shook his head and carried on playing. 'He's nae here, tell her,' the barman shouted. 'Hinna seen him a' day.'

> You're free to go . . .
> Darlin' . . .
> I'll break the ties that bind . . .

an old woman croaked into The Budgie Lemon's face.

'Who is this vision of loveliness?' Ron asked. 'Ooochya!' he grunted, as the old woman put her hand between his legs. 'I'll give you a fortnight to stop it.'

'Nae'hin' there,' the old woman cackled. She put her face back into The Budgie Lemon's:

> Somehow . . .
> The dreams we planned . . .
> Have gone astray . . .

'Fa's that singin'?' a fat man in a suit shouted from the till at the far end of the bar.

'Nae singin', Lil,' Ernie told the old woman. 'Boss' orders.'

'Tell him to kiss ma dock.'

'Now now, Lil. *You* ken better'n that.'

'Richt, darlin'. If you gie's a rum an' pep.'

Kenny Dan from Garyvard, who'd been in the hostel with him, left school at fifteen and went on the trawlers. Last known address: Fleetwood, Lancashire. He buttonholed Norbert, the history teacher, the day he left, and advised Norbert not to be about and abroad on the streets of Stornoway if ever he, Kenny Dan, was back in town. And the other guy from Shader with the fair hair, Chewgo . . .

'Fower whiskies, Stan.' The barman dumped four glasses on the counter. 'Fit wis *you* needin', Ron?'

'Large Dewar's, potboy. Quickly now.'

'Cried *fit*?' Dod asked.

'Chewgo.'

'Hear this, Budgie?' Dod laughed. 'Hear fit the boy's sayin'?'

'Rum an' pep,' Ernie said. 'Fa ordered a rum an' pep?'

'Me,' The Budgie Lemon said. 'Here you go, Lil.'

'Six pints, Mac,' a man shouted.

'I canna, I canna . . .'

'Bloody murder in here the nicht.' Dod swallowed down a Bacardi, and shook the remains of it into his pintglass.

'Hey, Ernie!' the fat man at the till shouted. 'Get that berrypicker out of here!'

'Budgie here's ma darlin', are you, darlin'?' Lil said, putting her arm around The Budgie Lemon's neck.

'He's barred, I said,' the fat man shouted. 'Get him *out!*'

'Listen, Johnston!' Ron said. 'I'm the funny man!'

'I never said a word!' Johnston protested.

'Away and take a rugg, Johnston.'

'What's wrong with you, anyway?'

'Away and take a rugg of my starboard tit!'

'There's that fucking phone again,' Ernie said, coming back from the door. Colin turned round and realised, with a shock, it was still daylight outside. Beside him, the red-bearded Ron laughed loudly. 'Shipping them green over the fo'c'slehead!' he shouted, and pushed Johnston in the chest with the flat of his hand. 'Here you go, pal,' the other barman said, putting a nip glass of whisky on the counter beside the two full nip glasses that were already there. 'Who's this from?' Colin asked. 'Never mind that,' said Dod. 'Get it down you. Wantin' water?'

'No.'

'Speir the boy here,' The Budgie Lemon was urging an old man called Dirty Abbo. 'He's at the university.'

'Ask me what?'

'Go on! Ask him! His heid's fulla brains.'

'Fulla mince, mair like.'

'Seven nips, Jack,' a man who had pushed up to the bar shouted. 'Three of Watson's, four of whisky.'

'Tommy Booth!' The Budgie Lemon said. 'It's Tommy Booth!'

'Far's the dog, Tommy?' Dod asked.

'There's nae glasses, nae glasses . . .' the barman called Jack shouted.

'I'll bet you,' another man who had followed Tommy Booth to the bar said. 'Four nothing.'

'I've heard shite and I've heard shite,' Tommy Booth said. 'But that's the biggest heap of shite I ever heard.'

'Four nothing!' the other man insisted. 'Four nothing, and there's a sheet on it.'

'You're on. Hear that, Stan?'

'Fa's rum an' pep's this, lying?'

'That's mine,' Dirty Abbo said.

'Aye, is't?' said Lil, and punched Dirty Abbo in the face. 'Pig tapper,' she said to Colin. 'This is Margaret,' she said. A girl with black hair had appeared.

'Hallo, Margaret.'

'Hallo.'

She was wearing a green coat with an imitation leopard-skin collar. Where had she come from?

'A round here, Ernie,' Dod said, 'what are you for, Lil?'

'Bacardi, darlin'.'

'Margaret?'

'Gin and bitter lemon,' the girl said. 'You coming home?' she said.

'Rum to you, Abbo?' Dod asked.

'Aahn.'

'Aye, he's saying.' The Budgie Lemon interpreted the noise. 'He's bit his tongue.'

'That's three Bacardis, a whisky for the boy, a gin and bitter lemon and a nippie o' Watson's, when I've time, Dod.'

'And one to yersel', Ernie.'

'Listen, Johnston!'

'Far's he gettin' a' the money, Lil?'

'Don't give us the shit! Just don't give us the *shit*, Johnston!'

'Jesus!'

'I'm not Jesus. I just look like him.'

'Stornoway,' the girl in the green coat – Margaret – said. 'I know someone from there.'

'Well,' he said, 'I'm not really from Stornoway, I'm from Ness, that's at the north –'

'Aye aye aye,' The Budgie Lemon, who was listening closely, rapidly nodded his head.

'Mac,' the girl said. 'He's on the boats.'

'Fa, Big Mac?' The Budgie Lemon said to her. '*He* winna ken Big Mac.'

'Three pints, Jack,' a voice roared behind his head. 'Twa rums, one wi' blackcurrant.'

'Four whiskies, Ernie.'

'Sideburns like Elvis,' the girl said. 'He's on the *Ben Ledi*.'

'*He* winna ken him,' The Budgie Lemon told her.

'Same again, Jack!' Tommy Booth was back at the counter. 'Murder, is't?' he said to Colin.

A bell like an alarm bell started ringing loudly.

'Last orders, gentlemen, *now!*' Ernie shouted.

'Nae that time already, is't?'

'Last orders, now!'

'Christ!' said Colin, as The Budgie Lemon tipped what appeared to be a doubler of whisky into his glass. 'It was my round.'

'Behave yirsel',' The Budgie Lemon said.

'Yir nae gaun,' Lil told Dirty Abbo.

'Mnahn!' he protested.

'Yir nae gaun an' that's it.'

'Ernie!' a man croaked. He clutched the bar with both hands. His face was shining with sweat. 'Six whiskies, six Exports, Ernie,' he croaked. 'Coupla cigars.'

'Got glasses for the Exports, Mac?'

'Aye.'

'Fucking say so, then.'

'That's the final now, Tam, Jack, Ernie, hear me?' the fat man at the till bellowed above the noise of the bell. 'That's it!'

'Leech on the arse of society, Johnston,' the red-bearded Ron loudly informed his drinking companion. 'What are you?'

'Drink up now, lads, *if* you please now,' Jack shouted.

'Caan a hoy?' Sticky rivulets of blood from the corners of Dirty Abbo's mouth commingled with dribblings of foamy spittle on his chin; as Colin watched, he swiped them away on the sleeve of an antedeluvian jacket. 'Haan?'

'He's wanting to ask you something,' Margaret said.

'What?'

'Id od eee aid oh a an ann?'

'I don't know,' said Colin. Dirty Abbo held him in a fierce and challenging stare. Colin shrugged his shoulders.

'Odd aw,' Dirty Abbo mouthed contemptuously at him. He went away.

'You, Johnston,' Ron shouted, 'couldn't knock the stew off a bap.'

He pushed Johnston in the chest. Johnston staggered backwards.

'That's enough now, Ron,' Ernie said.

'Here . . .' Ron turned on Ernie, 'I'm fast, you know.'

Dod came back from the gents, buttoning his trouserflies as he came. 'That's some spew in the lavvy,' he told Ernie.

'*If* you please now, lads,' Jack shouted.

> There's no ring . . .
> Of shinin' gold . . .
> So strong . . .
> That it can hold . . .

Lil sang, her head on The Budgie Lemon's shoulder.

'That's some spew,' Dod said, 'and no kidding.'

> A heart . . .
> When it longs . . .
> To be free . . .

'Fa's that singin'?' the fat man bellowed. 'Ernie!'

'Stop greetin', Abbo.'

> The lips are cold . . .
> Darlin' . . .
> That once said yes to me . . .

'Here a rum to you, fae Colin.'

'*Come* away, lads! . . . Ernie! Tak' that fag oot yir mou' and gie a *shout!*'

'Time, gentlemen, *please!*'

'*Come* on, lads!'

'Right, lads! Right, Stan! Come away now, boys, that's the stuff!'

'Drink up, lads, we've had your money.'

'*If* you please now . . . *Come* awa', Ron min!'

'Away . . . and take a *rugg!*'

'*Come* away, now . . .'

'. . . bobbies'll be here in a minute . . . Come *on*, you crowd!'

'Drink up, now . . .'

'*If* you please, lads . . .'

'Time, gentlemen, *please* . . .'

'. . .*and* Lil . . .'

'Time, lads . . .'

'. . . see you the morn's morn, lads . . .'

'After time now . . .'

'Time . . .'

Midnight. Our hero is in the Seaton Park.

What is that he has in his hand? Is it his briefcase?

No.

Who is that stretched on a green coat with an imitation leopard-skin collar under him? Is it Alice Ann? Ruby Murray?

No.

Now there's no need to take them *off*, she said.

Uh?

Push them over to one side.

Ah.

Puddling between her legs after this instruction, our hero suddenly found the thumb, chiseller, long gun, abbot's feather and money pinkie of his left hand engulfed in a warm, slippery, cavernous hole. He fluted with his fingers. It made a noise like a burp.

Never mind all that, she said. Put it in.

Right.

Fumbling blindly, he made a grunting lunge. Stopped. Beneath him, Margaret – for it was she – shifted.

I don't think it's in, you know, she said.

He made another lunge, and lay prone on top of her. He couldn't feel anything. Craning his neck in the dark, his face came into contact with a rhododendron bush.

I still don't think it's in, you know, Margaret said.

No?

Wait! . . . She put her hand down and took hold of him.

I'll put it in, she said.

Canted confidently over a Shanks porcelain in the Students' Union the following Saturday evening (John Thomas a bit tender to the touch, but after the heroics of Thursday night before, what could one expect?), find I can't piss. Bursting for a piss, can't start. As happens if someone stands next to me at a urinal, or a queue forms behind me after the pictures. Finally plant myself on seat, still no go, pull overhead chain, listen to bowl flushing below, cistern filling above, plink plink plink stop, try and relax, think of Dell river in spate, of Kyle of Lochalsh at five in the morning, here it comes and O Jesus! – I nearly levitated bodily off the pan and rocketed through the roof. Imagine a red-hot knitting needle inserted into the eye of your penis. Imagine pissing Jeyes' Fluid, sulphuric acid, bleach. Worse was to come. After a repeat performance on the bog in the digs, and then gingerly bathing the offending member with warm water and red carbolic soap at the washhand basin in the bedroom, I fell into the virtuous couch and a feverish, nightlong slumber. Woke at 7 a.m. glazed in a thin sweat, my lips tasting of salt and my cock stuck fast to the bottoms of the nearly new Paisley pattern pyjamas (sent from home: ex-Alan). Some Niagara of a wet dream? Surely I would have remembered? Stumbling panic-stricken over to the washbasin, succeeded with cold water in detaching head of cock from atrophied swamp of yellow matter, to which cock responded by promptly discharging long, viscous snake of pus, with some venom, against tiles of basin. Christ O God O God! What'll I do now? Sweet Jesus help me! Aal' Bob on the move in the kitchen, hobbling between the porridge pot and the table. I can't ask him. Can't ask anyone. I'm fucked. Dead.

Two days later, head in pieces, my rotting groin wadded in industrial bogroll, I moseyed bandily down to the East Neuk Bar, King Street, where I knew Murdo Angus would be refreshing himself at midday after a hard morning's slog at the logarithms. At first I couldn't see him. Maybe he's in Walker's? Then I saw him at a table, with two leery dotards from the model lodging house. *Well an diabhal orms'*, he drawled. *Look who's here! Sit down. You're a bit out of your road.* Can't Got to speak to you. Excuse us, lads. Thass a' richt, Murdy. He got up, carrying his nip and his half-pint glass. *De tha cearr ort?*

I told him.

'Get away,' he said.

'What'll I do?'

'You haven't *done* anything about it?' He stopped grinning. 'Is that what's leaving you here?'

'A' richt, Murdy?' one of the dotards drooled anxiously, clutching his empty nip glass.

'Hardly,' said Murdo Angus. He swallowed his whisky and chaser, and took the empty glasses back to the bar. 'Come on,' he told me.

'Where?'

'Where do you think?' Frogmarching me through the door and along King Street to the taxi rank at the Kingsway, he opened the back door of the front car. 'Get in,' he said, and got into the front seat himself. 'Pox clinic,' he told the driver.

On the way to Woolmanhill, he only spoke to me once:

'I hope they box the compass with you,' he said. 'I hope you're sitting on hot *water* bottles for the next three months.'

In the Special Clinic waiting room I met the creature that modelled for the face on the back of the Creamola packet sitting, arms folded, knees apart, placidly beaming at everyone and everything, all he needed was a leather football between his feet; the three-man crew of a small coaster who'd caught a dose team-handed in South Shields off a woman called Nancy; and a law student, Kennedy by name, sitting austerely apart, who addressed me thus: 'What are *you* doing here, Col? You weren't screwing Theresa Lightfoot, by any chance?' Will I describe the rubber-gloved doctor and his crabbed questions and his bloodsucking syringe and his Dracula sneer? Pale, sang dumb and giving at the knees, I stood before him, trousers and underpants about my ankles. I was lucky, though. For who hove into view, in the middle of all this humiliation and horror, but John Angus Smith from Borve, fourth-year medical student, doing his practical stint in the infectious diseases, and he took over, thank God, fetched me into a side room, calmed me down, told me it was like catching the common cold or the curam, gave me a couple of hefty penicillin injections in the arse and a hailstorm of pills in a bottle, *Lay off the drink with that lot,* he said, *and come back in a fortnight, I'll still be here,* he's the finest man in the world, if I ever

have a son I'll call him John Angus, not that I ever will as I've sworn
off sex for life, and I'll call the second one Murdo Angus.

Now it is five to twelve a fortnight later and I'm chust back from
the Special Clinic and I've got the all-clear and my wireless is here
and I am here and I am going to switch it on and listen to it.

First exam – British History – next Tuesday. English week after.
Moral Phil., last but not least, on the glorious sixth of June.

I've written a Gaelic play and sent it to BBC in Glasgow. Subject:
One Soule's Progresse through this Vale of Woe. Style: *Allegorical/
Fantastical.* Title: *Noggans.*

Must to the books. What have we here? *Agriculture in Tudor
England.*

My cup runneth over.

JUNE

2 Jamaica Street. Wednesday.

I know the date too, it's on the wall, on a calendar.

Last exam yesterday. Moral Phil. Hard to say. English and History
OK, I think, thanks to your prayers. *Cogito ergo sum*, arsa Descartes,
the Queen of Sweden made him get up early in the morning to
give her tutorials, froze the balls off him, you didn't do Latin did
you, Virgil Cicero Livy, Caesar right back, Ovid deep-lying centre
forward like Hideguti, you did Gaelic didn't you, Fair Duncan of the
Songs, Alasdair Son of Master Alasdair, An Ciaran Mabach stopper
centre-half like Willie Woodburn, you fell out of your pram as a
child, didn't you?

Went to the Marischal Bar last night to celebrate end of exams,
deliverance from clap etc. so I'm right back in the shite once more
as far as money is concerned, counting coppers with an agitated
forefinger and thinking of approachable faces, they're all gone, like
birds on the wing, snow on the river, far away and o'er the moor,
back to the croft, the cot, the bothy, the but and ben, the cosy neuk,
the single end, the semi-detached, the auld hoose, my ain hoose, our
house at hame, am bothan beag coir, the house where I was born,
the House with the Green Shutters, Tigh a' Ghearraidh, Tigh Dubh

Arnol, the Bonnie Hoose o' Airlie, Mo Dhachaidh, Bleak House, Heartbreak House, the House of Shaws, the House of Usher, the house that Jack built, the Wee House amang the Heather, Tigh Mor nan Uinneag, Tigh na Galla, Tigh na Beetch, Granny's Heilan' Hame, Castle Perilous, Castle Dangerous, The Castle Doune, Caisteal a' Ghlinne, the Brows o' Ben Connal, the Hills of Glenorchy, Mull of the Cold High Bens, Gala Water, the Waters of Kylesku, the Banks and Braes of Bonnie Doon, the Bonnie Bonnie banks of Loch Lomond, the Birks of Invermay, the Bush abune Traquair, the Birks of Aberfeldy, the Braes of Tulliemet, the Broom of the Cowdenknows, the Haughs of Cromdale, the Howe o' the Mearns, the Dowie Dens of Yarrow, the Green Hills of Islay, the Far Cuilinns, Bonnie Strathyre, Bonnie Glenshee, Dark Lochnagar, Caddam Woods, The Gallowa' Hills, Rothesay Bay, Tobermory Bay, the Nick o' the Balloch and the Back o' Bennachie. Swipe of dockleaf, swipe of sorrel and seven fleeings to their backsides.

Page 2.

I was writing this letter & came to the bottom of the page & stopped & went out away a wander to the Butchers Arms & now back can't find page 1 which was chockful of wisdom insights proofs but there is nothing to be done so I'll just (chust) start again. I am not drunk – no no no no NO NO!!! Was it you was asking about Donald Macdonald (B) he was we were in the same desk on 2A & his face was glossy pink and his hair was combed? Who was it then?

I am anti-BBC because they didn't even acknowledge my play the bastards also because they're all bloody not Lewis – Uist and Skye bastards. But OK. Fog follow them, horseflies light on them, condors crap on them, drunks like me turn up on their doorsteps nightly. Don't know what now. English and History exams OK. No money. Aberdeen leaving Friday. Don't know what then. Might come and see you. Long summer ahead. Let me, tell me, what you think of. What you think. I don't think, I was told. Cousin Jacob told. You don't think, he told. That's your trouble. You don't speak, Bro. Alan told, face tight with apprehension, outside student flat in Edinburgh where posh party was. You don't listen, Norbert told, uncoiling cruel-looking forked tawse. Sage advises. *Here*, Norbert told, *is a boy . . . what cheats! . . . at history.* No laughing, no talking, no moving, you're out.

Now that you are there, in your very own rented room in Hillhead – your bog on the landing and stairs to climb – you should be well out of the way of irate Gaelic landladies who know your mother and doors locked against you at 11 p.m. forever more. Urinating in the close was very wrong, of course, as was vomiting out of the bedroom window, it isn't easy to remove high-density puke from an exterior wall when you're three floors up, you need a long scrubbing brush with a rotating head and a flexible handle, not to mention rubber gloves and strong detergents. Why can't you vomit on the carpet like everyone else?

When I come to see you – there is a floor, you say, a flat surface for me to sleep on? – I shall wash out the fissures in the morning, before the segment of grapefruit, the porridge, the soft-boiled pullet's egg, the kedgeree, the toast, the coffee, the cod liver oil pluc, the energy tablet – And when you emerge, like Odysseus, from the stormy blankets, we will walk down Byres Road, together, smiling, to the alehouse y-clept the Aragon. On the way back, many hours later, I'll topple over (in the middle of my song) – poor fellow, what an end – never *could* take it, you know.

To continue, not thinking, continuing. My exam in Moral Phil. Well, the first paper was cruel to me. MacKellar, I might add, is certainly stepping on very thin ice because I might take a grudge against him I might just begin to dislike him although he is a decent old bod, quite quite, take umbrage and umbrella him to the very heart. There is a painter here now, Wattie's brother Jim, papering Aal Bob's back room – we spoke at great length about lowers and highers, he has a quine at the academy, fine, OK. The second paper was easy, O very. Verily.

Back to BBC. Well, I fired off letter to Gaelic Department – Uist and Skye bastards – asking for play back, no answer, so I phoned reverse charges & got genial smooth-talking Fred M. & Fred M. said genially, Well, he said, heh-heh, I ignored your letter, it is lying here somewhere & I have no intention of sending play back, in fact I'm sitting on it even now as I speak, heh-heh, it is warming nicely under my genial Uist arse well he didn't say that actually but words to that & if you promise to shut up from now on, he said, stop sending misguided missives reverse charge phone calls to BBC, then we can all go ahead get on as we did/do with things, life. And so I don't hold anything against F. Mac., never did actually, & as the Uistman up here of the heroic bardic verse and caman-smiting proclivities said . . . what . . . donno, forgotten, gone, shiubhal e, chaochail e . . . here comes Jim the painter whistling, we're going to not a pub but a club for afternoon beverage Portland club I knew it had something to do with cement. Jollity, jollity, jollification. Glee.

(Next day, early)

How many pints yesterday? But I slept. Didn't get up through the night, not once.

Sunny morning. Birds and lorries.

My way is not affected by the weather – no moods – same mood all the time. Sun might burn till it rot.

How my thoughts run in the morning.

How the morning breaks.

How wonderful to think: I have slept & this is a new day.

I am old, like the map of Mexico.

Best blessings on your croppy paw. Colin.

Er-hum. I may probably appear in Hillhead before this letter.

Dell, Monday.

When I say this is my fifth attempt to write back to you, I am merely trying to indicate that those powers (or whatever) that facilitate communication are even now holidaying in St Kilda and Rockall. (If you don't believe me, try reading that sentence again.) You yourself must have experienced the frustration of sitting down to a blank sheet of paper, pen full of ink, navel in order, Adam's apple in its proper place, to discover six hours later that you have only succeeded in perfectly excavating the left nostril, chewing off the left thumb and smoking 2ozs of Golden Virginia. In a word: nothing. And now, having slept, risen from sleep, pissed and passed a stone, here I am again.

I shall proceed carefully. Once upon a time, in the public bar, Kyle of Lochalsh, I met one – Neil Stewart MacGregor – who obviously suffered from a persecution complex. I asked him if he had ever been to Lewis. Whereupon he looked round suddenly, furtively, at the other boisterous patrons, planted one foot on top of mine and brought a horny finger to his lips. 'No,' said he, 'sssshd, sssshd, but . . . sssshd . . . I am going there sometime . . . sssshd . . . carefully.' Carefully, then – carefully – I shall proceed.

I'm not quite sure how to take your letter. This bit about *raining* is beyond me – 'your fog-laden face and your raining heart.' What do you mean? Are you trying to become a bad poet? That I am very sad is true, but more frequently (as you may have noticed) I am depressed. These are not to be confused. Sadness is something which can be beautiful, peaceful, and in some way associated with loss of innocence. It is not at all a wholly selfish thing – the world is a sorrowful place, and we who are in it have lost something. But, like Deirdre's song, there is beauty in our grief; whether that grief is expressed or felt, there is beauty in it. Depression, on the other hand, arises from other things – self-loathing, above all, in my case, and a sense of being utterly insignificant, useless, frustrated, isolated. If you think this makes me sound like a candidate for the loony-bin, you're wrong, because I am convinced that each of us, everyone, has his shortcomings, with this difference that some are more aware of them than others.

First of all, then (plunging in at the deep end) I loathe my body. It lets me down all the time, mirrors all my repulsiveness and vileness, and discloses a weakling, a coward. Twitching, quivering inadequacy. That is why I don't like to visit people (as you know) and why I find arrangements, appointments, introductions, social functions etc. unnerving. I have suffered much because of this (e.g. at meals, interviews). Now, when I have to meet people, the whole business of preparation – the scrubbing under the armpits, the powdering of the testicles, the polishing of the teeth – not to mention the swallowing of large whiskies beforehand to placate me, and the subsequent sucking of Polo mints in order to delude whoever I'm meeting that strong drink has not passed my lips – strikes me as painfully ridiculous and pathetic. Especially the latter. Followed by desperate, repulsive behaviour, hysterical attempts to impose myself, to make an impression, to 'take over'. Which is even more pathetic, because it is not worth it and I am not worth it. This is what happened with Alice Ann.

It doesn't mean that I am alone. I have one or two friends, I think. But when (as now) I am depressed (perhaps it is hereditary; my uncle Myles is nearly always like this, I believe) it is necessary for me to keep away from people. The sort of bloody depressions I suffer from are contagious, and I should bear with them and work through them on my own, smoking my ticklers, looking at the wall. If I am depressed in company, then, like it or not, this is another way of imposing myself. And that is why things went so badly wrong between us in Glasgow and why there was such a drastic breakdown in communications. I should never have gone down there in the first place. I should have stayed away.

Passed all three exams (did I say?) in spite of losing my father's briefcase and all the notes therein in a pub called the Tanfield in Aberdeen, the night I caught the clap. My mother has enquired once, and will again, about whereabouts of briefcase ('Is it in the pawn?'). Difficult. All I can do is live quietly under her roof, carry low sails, in all things give her sway, cross her in nothing, and try and keep what Aal Bob, my landlord, would call a 'calm sough'. The moor is still out there.

Invitation to Murdo Angus's wedding next month. Carloway Free Church, and reception in Stornoway Town Hall. I can't go. Booze is to be avoided at all costs. The curse of icebound hell light permanently on me if I touch another drop this year.

Purdy is a brave, brazen fellow. Although I do not disapprove of him running away with his brother John's wife (quite a feat, good luck to him) it is beyond me how he can then go back to Dell, with her or without her.

I cannot understand people like Sherpa Tenzing and Purdy.

I am cross-eyed with exhaustion. The monsters were after me last night in dreams.

Colin.

PS My black eyes, swollen nose. Heart lurching in dismay, I now seem to recall small angry fists beating a tattoo on my face in the Hillhead dark, as pissed and resigned I lay on my back on the floor in your room. Was it you? The pity of it, Iago! . . . Or did I really, as we agreed in the morning, fall on my face over a bench in Great George Street?

JULY

Dell, Sunday.

Dear John L. Sullivan,

The story of the stag party, the wedding and the piles.

Murdo Angus, surname Macarthur, is a chief engineer in the British Merchant Navy, and plies his trade between London (in England), Singapore (in Singapore) and points east. Manila rejoices at his coming; Yokohama hears his siren's song and is glad. He understands engines and boilers, shafts and sprockets, and would gladly tell you everything about them. $dy/dx = [(x-q-p) + 4PY - 94f \log3 HN] (1-y)$. Home from the College of Navigation before the wedding and the happy holiday, he was assailed in his demesne on the west side by his colleagues the cog people, the piston-and-screw people, the bad, bad boiler people. This is what they did to him. First of all they deprived him of his bright and tidy outerwear, his shirt and his underwear, and clothed him in a woman's nightgown. How humiliating, you will say! How awful, the person reading this over your shoulder will say! How I agree with all three of you! Then they locked him – the wretches! – in a cage, put the cage on a trailer, put the trailer on a tractor, and rumbled him over the old Pentland road to Stornoway, where, after trying to choke him with flour (Lofty Peak, I suppose), adorning him with a mixture of rotting vegetables and a barrelful of offal from Tigh nan Guts, finally baptising him with old engine oil and sump sludge, they left him on Number 1 Pier for all to see. An Englishman said: 'Is this a tradition?' An American said: 'Is it some kind of protest?'

Now, a digression. On his way home from the whalers, Geordie (not the one from Swainbost, the one from Fivepenny) wandered into a car showroom in Glasgow and bought himself a Humber

Super Snipe. It arrived in the island last Friday night, on the *Loch Seaforth*, and Geordie was there in person, on the quay, to take possession of it, accompanied by his admiring cousin, Disciple Dan, and two bosom cronies, Sambo and Nellie's Boy. After a modest refreshment in the Caley, followed by another modest refreshment in the Royal, they set off for Ness in the new car, Geordie at the wheel, Disciple Dan in the front passenger seat and Sambo and Nellie's Boy in the back. Somewhere in the deeps of the Barvas moor, the Humber Super Snipe turned a somersault, went along for about ten yards on its roof, turned another somersault that landed it back on its wheels and pointing in the right direction, and Geordie carried on driving. No one said anything for a mile or two. Then Disciple Dan turned to Geordie and asked: 'What did you do that for, George?'

The stag party on Monday night was not really a stag party at all because a number of fat wives, giggling, corseted, broke into the house in the early morning. One of Murdo Angus's tunnel-tigering cousins and myself got very drunk on whisky, sang 'Ho ro 'se poit-mhuin na caillich', decided to poach salmon, and staggered back from the Grimersta river at daybreak to our John West salmon sandwiches and more whisky. Later, on the way, the bumpy way to Airidhantuim, I finished a whole bottle ('do shlaint', do shlaint''), with the brother of the bride, another sailor and a man of infinite accomplishment and dexterity who drove one-handed. We stopped for a piss and talked to some cows in a field of dew. In Airidhantuim I talked incessantly until the half-past one bus to Ness. The half-past one bus and Taramod Lasdaidh.

Wednesday, the wedding day, O wedding day. The Free Church, the spiritual refreshment, the tremor in the back of Murdo Angus' head. Give him a typhoon in the South China Seas any day of the week. The largest and curliest cousin (first name: Kenneth; nickname: Tarbh an Ach) was the best man. The back of Tarbh an Ach's head.

I took the west-side bus to the reception, but I didn't know anybody, and waited alone in Stornoway for the Royal to open at five o'clock. One morning here, at exactly eleven, Dodo from Swainbost looked at the clock. 'Up spirits!' said he. 'Up spirits, Dodo!' said I to myself outside the Royal, hearing the screech of the doorbolts. I went from there to the Criterion (which is close to the Town Hall) and drank whisky until five minutes to six with Corrags and Biffo Dubh of the Civil Service. In the queue outside the Town Hall I spoke to faces I had spoken to at the stag party – 'O yes, O tha, bha, bha 'm party math dha-rireabh, bha-bha . . .' Something happened, somebody coming, slowly, easily, along narrow Point Street. O miracle! O maragan dubha! It's the Uistman! 'Ancient acquaintance of the doorjambs, is it really you?' 'Dia, Dia, a Leodhasaich . . .' Back to the Criterion and more whisky. 'Woke up this morning, said to myself, "Murdo Angus's wedding." Got the plane to Stornoway and staying in the Lewis hotel. When I comes, a Leodhasaich, I comes.' Chicken soup, chicken, peas, peaches and cream, whisky. Whisky. Slaint'. Here's how. Over 250 guests. After the food, speeches, reading of telegrams etc., the lights go dim. I can remember finishing bottles of whisky in a corner of the Town Hall with the Uistman, the cousins, the bride's brother and a few others. I can vaguely remember going with the Uistman and one of the bridesmaids to the Carlton – 'everybody is in the Carlton' – and nothing else until six or seven in the morning, when I am found in Shader again, arguing with the bride's brother about God knows what – something to do with football, Lewis football and the football brain of my brother Alan. The argument was approaching a climax. I said: 'Going to Lewis Hotel, see the Uistman.' Bride's brother said: 'Going to bed. Bed here for you.' I said: 'No no. Going the Lewis Hotel.' And off I went, zig zag, Stornoway twelve miles, and the dew, the foggy foggy dew.

I was wearing my suit. A new suit. I've got a new suit now. And a white shirt. And two labourers in a van said: 'Leum a-steach, a dhuine.' And I said, 'No no – mise coiseachd dhan a' Lewis Hotel.' But they convinced me that it was much more comfortable to sit in the back of a van and be driven to town. I sat in the back and delivered a furious monologue to the backs of their heads. In Stornoway I crossed a river and sat on a bench, wet with dew, in Willowglen. I was tired, very tired, and I slept. 'Have you slept there all night?' A woman's voice, Stornoway voice. I sat up, didn't open my eyes, and said, 'Yes yes, all night.' 'Butter go to town and get a cup of tea.' 'Yes yes.' When I was quite sure that she had disappeared forever out of my life, I opened one eye slowly, saw that it was still early, got up, and felt strange pains in the region of the anus. Forget it. The Lewis Hotel. Start walking. In front of Lipton's, standing solidly on the other side of the street, was a policeman. I had met him at the wedding, a cousin of Murdo Angus'. We went to the Lewis at ten past nine, myself and the policeman. We used back doors and weird corridors. I had two pints of lager, the policeman had three bottles of Export. Halfway through my second pint, I asked one of the girls to waken Mr MacDonald, that Mr Murray was waiting on him in the public bar. She returned, nice wench. Said Mr – What's his name again? – had left ten minutes ago, had gone to the cycle shop and was going to buy postcards. I was looking at her eyes closely. She explained with many gestures where the cycle shop was – do you think you'll find your way there now? I said no, calmly, why don't you accompany me to it? The policeman said, 'I'll show you' – and we found the Uistman buying a half-bottle of whisky in Henderson's in Bayhead. We returned to the Lewis after greetings, salaams and so forth, sat in the lounge bar all morning drinking whisky and eyeing the barmaid. I congratulated the barmaid on her presence of mind, her tits and what I could see of her arse. She said she was Nighean Allan Bhig from Cross Skigersta. In the club I sang 'A Pheigi a Ghraidh' loudly. We fed the seagulls at the quay, ate fish, bought bananas in Lipton's and the Uistman bought another half-bottle of whisky. In Lipton's, a lot of women with message bags and headscarves gathered round us. The Uistman recited a poem for them by Iain MacCodrum, and I told them I was an old Canadian from Ness. (I've got a crewcut these days.)

Got back home nine o'clock. The Uistman stayed for two days, sheared sheep for my uncle John. Sweat the poison out of my system, he said. He doesn't tie their feet. He's an expert. After the shearing they all went to the bothan. They were still there at eleven o'clock the next morning. I couldn't go. I was ill. I had piles. The Uistman made a great hit with the boys in the bothan. He sang, said his long poems, played on a tin whistle he carries about with him and told several entertaining whoppers. My piles are OK now. What a bloody thing. I would tell you a great deal about piles, but I am getting bored with this letter. The sun is shining. Noise of seagulls and bluebottles.

Colin.

SEPTEMBER

Singing in the Rain.

He sat inside the doorway of the old barn, under the dripping lintel, singing.

> A ribhinn a bheil cuimhn' agad . . .
> (he sang)
> A ghruagach dhonn an cluinn thu mi
> A ribhinn a bheil cuimhn' agad
> An oidhche mas do sheol mi . . .

Rain rained through the roof of the old barn. Shiny pools of it formed on the black earth floor. Wind whined through the gap in the end wall, wrinkled the pools, flailed among the rafters. He unscrewed the top of the whisky bottle and took a swig.

> 'S fhada, 's fhada thall tha mi . . .

'Why are you sitting there?' a little girl asked him in English.
'I don't know.'
'Are you tired?'
'Tired, yes.'
'Are you *very* tired?'
'Yes, very tired.'
'We get that song in school.' She spied the bottle. 'Is that juice?'
'Grownup juice. Eil Gaidhlig agad?'

'No,' she said. 'My mammy says grownup juice is horrible.'

She ran off, splashing through the puddles, a little fair-haired girl. Belongs to the English family that moved into Tigh a' Ghlinne. From Sheffield or somewhere.

A little fair-haired girl sat beside him on his first day in school. Jessie Morrison from Cross. She could put her wellingtons on by herself. A book lay open on the desk between them.

> I see a kitty
> I see a ball
> Kitty sees the ball . . .

Their foreheads bumped. He loved her. Then he loved Catherine Macleod from Swainbost. On class 4 he loved Betty Mackenzie who loved Murdo Maclean who loved Miss Gilchrist who loved the man who drove Tweedie's lorry. After class 4 he didn't love anyone.

Miss Gilchrist was from the mainland. She had funny Gaelic. 'All stand!' she stand. They sang:

> Indians are high-minded
> Bless my soul they're double-jointed
> They climb hills and don't mind it
> All day long.

She wasn't long in the school. She taught them 'The Auld Hoose'. Swaying ecstatically on the pouffe by the kitchen range, he sang, over and over again, the first verse of 'The Auld Hoose':

> O the auld hoose, the auld hoose,
> What though the rooms were wee,
> When kind hearts were dwelling there,
> And bairnies full of glee . . .

Voices, very loud, from the bedroom. His dying father is astir.

'Where are you going? Get back to bed!'

'Out of my road!'

'For God's sake get back to bed!'

'Out of my way till I strangle the auld hoose!'

Two travelling music teachers came to the school. A nice one and a bad-tempered one. The nice one was called the Major. He had a xylophone. He let them all have a shot on it.

> Ho ro eileanaich o gu,
> Plink plink plonk plink plonk plink plong . . .

The bad-tempered one was small. He stood on the piano stool. Scowling, he raised his arms and described little circles with his forefingers. 'And . . . NOW!'

> What shall we do with the drunken sailor,
> What shall we do with the drunken sailor,
> What shall we do with the drunken sailor,
> Early in the morning?
>
> Hooray the speedway riders,
> Hooray the –

Down with him from the piano stool. Bristly moustache. Twitching nostrils.

'Are you trying to get under my skin, boy?'

'No, sir.'

'Are you? You wart? You unspeakable pimple?'

'No, sir.'

The king died. King George the Sixth. Between them, Donald Ham and Dubba the janitor carried a mahogany wireless into the classroom. Dong, went a bell in London, followed by two minutes' silence.

> Abide with me, fast falls the eventide,
> The darkness deepens, Lord with me abide . . .

It was the king's favourite hymn. He wore an electrically heated boilersuit to keep warm. But death was not deterred.

> Help of the helpless, O abide with me . . .

On Coronation Day they got a mug and a New Testament each.

Was he in the big school in Stornoway then? . . . He unscrewed the bottle and took a swig. No he wasn't. Their mother put his mug and his brother John's mug into the china cabinet, to join the butterdish commemorating the coronation of Edward, Duke of Windsor, who didn't last long, and the teaplate with the purple rim commemorating the coronation of George the Fifth, who did. 'Oir fhearg cha mhair ach mionaid bheag . . .' she precented to herself in the sunny Sunday morning scullery, peeling potatoes for the big dinner, considered a sin. 'Trath feasgair fos . . .' she sang, repeating the line. 'Ulapul . . . Ulapul . . .' went the brothpot on the kitchen range. 'Poliu . . . Poliu . . .' the pan of Creamola replied.

Thig aoibhneas leis an latha . . .

John the Battler next door came home from sea with a large electric wireless. The first in the village. Floob-loob-loob went the needle along the short wave band. It stopped and harangued them in a foreign tongue. 'That's the Rooshian language,' said John the Battler, and turned the knob, with a clunk, to medium wave. Radio Luxembourg, 208 metres! Saturday night, nine o'clock – Scottish Requests! Peter Jock MacMadron! O my name is Mackay and my home is in Skye! Keep right on to the end of the road! Before that, at half-past six on the Home Service – Scottish Dance Music! Jimmy Shand and his band! The daddy of them all!

Daddle a dum dee daddalum, da dum dee dah . . .
(What about Bobby Macleod, then?)
Da daddle deedle dahlum, deedle daddle dah . . .

On class 1A in the Nicolson Institute, he loved Enid Elizabeth Hepburn (unattainable), and on class 3A a scrawny, sun-peeled girl from The Battery, Babs Tough, followed him about town in the company of her pals, cornered him in shop doorways, asked him to the Guides' Social (he wouldn't go). In the Playhouse cinema on Saturday mornings, before the lights went down and the curtains whirred open, they played 'O Mein Papa'. Eddie Calvert and his Golden Trumpet. The Yellow Rose of Texas.

235

There's a yellow rose in Texas,
That I am going to see,
Nobody else could miss her,
Not half as much as me . . .

Sprawled in the wooden ninepennies, he asked Calum Gogs for a shot of his specs during the Sunblest Bread commercial and discovered he was short-sighted . . . very short-sighted . . . blind as a bat. Sprawled as in the wooden ninepennies, he contemplated the slanting stone lintel above his head. It seemed to tilt, as he watched; to flutter slightly. Optical illusion. Nothing to worry about. Mere trick of the light, refraction through rainy air. Who got Higher Science first go? And if it should fall and crush him, in spite of the science? Then it was an act of God. The moon by night thee shall not smite, nor yet the sun by day.

O the moon shines tonight on Charlie Chaplin,
His boots are cracking, for want of blacking,
And his old baggy trousers will need mending,
Before they send him, to the Dardanelles.

They sent his granduncle William to the Dardanelles on a battle-ship, HMS *Majestic*. He swam about in the Aegean after she was sunk, favouring the breaststroke, and was rescued. Grand-uncle Norman was on HMS *Orama*, off the coast of Africa. The youngest brother, his grandfather, was on HMS *Clan Macnaughton*, lost with all hands on the third of March, 1915, forty miles north of Shetland. Heroes three, they had the proof in writing; but only two came back, in 1919, to the land fit for heroes to live in.

Down to Glasgow to visit the brother. High noon on Dumbarton Road. In Wilson's, a wee man with bib overalls, tartan bonnet, merry eyes: *You look like an educated man, son. Up the road at the university, are you?'* Yes, first year. Clever fellow. No working with the tools for him. He goes to Ibrox on Saturday to watch the Rangers.

> I love to go a-wandering,
> Along the Copland road,
> And as I go I love to sing,
> The sash my father wore . . .

On a black, dampish treestump on the banks of the Kelvin, they took alternate swigs from a half-bottle. The Kelvin was brown, the colour of bootpolish. 'Nae lessons the day, son?' the wee man asked.

'No.'

> Comb your hair, paint and powder,
> You act proud and I'll act prouder,
> You sing loud and I'll sing louder,
> Tonight we're settin' the woods on fire . . .

'Yir no' a bad chanter, son,' the wee man said.

'That's Hank Williams,' he said. 'The finest . . . the greatest . . . Died at twenty nine. The greatest . . . the finest . . .'

To a bar called The Smiddy at five o'clock, to meet the Singersman. The Singersman not pleased he drunk ower him. That's not why he gave you the sub. When did you start? he asked, putting his cascara features on him. Where? Who were you drinking with? Did you get the messages I asked? Later that night, in Hillhead Street, snarling incoherently above you in the dark, he will pound and pummel your face with his small, crabbed fists. I'll get him for that if it's the last thing I do. Break his teeth in his mouth . . . We'll just go to the Royal for a quick one, he told Alice Ann, outside D. D. Morrison's. She had a woman on her arm, her mother. *O, the Satan!* the woman exclaimed, making a clicking sound and revealing her top false teeth. No we won't, said Alice Ann. Don't you ever stop drinking? Wine is a mocker, strong drink is raging, he murmured, looking Alice Ann straight in the face. Her eyes on him: dark brown. *O the Satan for my life,* the mother exclaimed, *and he has the Bible on the tip of his tongue!*

> I'll cry myself to sleep, and wake up smiling,
> I miss you, but no one will ever know . . .

Her eyes on me: dark brown.

> I'll even make believe, I never loved you,
> And no one will ever know the truth but me . . .

Good old Hank. Daddy of them all.

Why was I in Stornoway yesterday? O aye. List of prescribed reading for second-year English (Hons). Go git 'em, cowboy. MacGregor the librarian handed me back the list, coldly fixed me with his gurnet's eye, silently pointed to the door. Well: daingit! All my good intentions come to nought. Might as well drown my frustration in a pint. His mother asked: *Should someone have met you off the bus with a wheelbarrow to carry all these books?* Good one, Mary! *Your eyes are swimming in your head,* she added. *Would that be the strain from too much reading in the Stornoway library? . . . Stand still, you tramp!* she bawled then, removing the remains of a sherry bottle from his inside pocket. He didn't mind. He knew where, in the peatstack, a whole bottle of whisky was located. *Where did you get the money, you tramp?* she bawled. *You tramp and you liar.* Well: daingit!

Dounchadh Ban made a song in praise of whisky. She wouldn't be so ready to put her hand in Donnchadh Ban's pocket and confiscate his bottle. So did Uilleam Ross. Burns couldn't take it. All mouth. Who else? He sat up, trying to remember. The rain had stopped; turned to mist. He uncapped the bottle. Drank. All was grey before his eyes – land, sea and sky blurred and coalesced to one neutral colour. He couldn't tell where one ended and the other began. The same weather conditions prevailed inside his head. Vaguely, because he knew they were there, he could make out the wavering gable end of a house, a shadowy henhouse, the shapeless weight of washing on a line. Beyond that, nothing. Out on the invisible Butt, the foghorn moaned. His heart contracted at the sound. So it moans on Girdleness, when the grey haar creeps in from the North Sea, haloing the northern lights of old Aberdeen. Where I am going back in two weeks' time. *Now I love Aberdeen and I love my queen, happy as we can be . . .* Hurry up, boys, said Maud. Don't want to be late. Going to church with Maud and Watty. They're Baptists.

Half-cut on vodka, not supposed to smell the breath, he sang with the best of them:

> There is a fountain filled with blood,
> Drawn from Immanuel's veins . . .

Tears came to his eyes. Hymnbook held aloft in both hands, swaying in the pew, he bellowed at the roofbeams:

> Then in a nobler, sweeter song,
> I'll sing thy power to save,
> When this poor lisping, stammering tongue,
> Lies silent in the grave . . .

A tug at his arm: Calm down! It was the poetry, he said afterwards. I got carried away by the poetry. *You liar,* a voice said inside his head. *O, you liar!* A woman's voice, not old. *How can you sing about love?* the voice continued. *You don't know what love is.* It wasn't Alice Ann. He uncapped the bottle, drank fiercely. *With the roaming, in the gloaming* . . . Above him, the lintel fluttered. *On the banks of the silvery Dee* . . .

After the next drink he tried to sit up, not sure why, possibly to address the foghorn, and fell back inside the doorway, coming to rest with his left arm under him and his head up against the doorpost. Drunk as an owl. Drunk as a boiled coot. Seinn O ho ro seinn . . . He felt with his free hand the back of his trousers. My bum's wet, Mammy. Seinn O ho ro leanainn . . . The doorway smelled of mud and sheepshit. The doorposts were rotted; the door long gone. The old barn not a barn any more. Nothing was stored there now. Nothing had been stored there for years. Nothing would ever be stored there again. It had seen the two days, the old barn. What are you doing up there with no trousers on? I fell in the dam. I mean the river.

> Way down upon de Swanee river,
> Far, far away . . .

Come down from there! his mother said. *This minute! You too!* she told the demure face, slow-blinking eyes and dirty knees of Lillian

Margaret Hutcheon, over from Tarbert Loch Fyne on her summer holidays.

> All de world am sad and dreary,
> Everywhere I roam . . .

A sudden, violent bout of coughing stopped the song in his throat, shook his entire body, turned his eyes to glass. Irritation of the trachea. Take Dr Henderson's Cough Mixture, teaspoonful, thrice daily. Who, from an early age, used to con Black's Medical Dictionary in his father's bookcase? Colour diagrams of your insides, front and back. Red heart, purple liver. Fawn intestines. Who, from an early age, knew where his stones were located? A brightness exploded inside his head, behind his left eye. O God! he said, and keeled over slowly, on to his back. The bottle, where was it? Raindrops formed, shivered on the stone lintel above his head. *Plink*, they fell in the blank light. *Plink plonk . . . plink!*

He lay on his back, under the dripping lintel. What matters is dancing.

> Seinn O ho ro seinn . . .

His right hand fumbled briefly in the mud.

> Seinn o ho ro leannain . . .

On the night of the third of March, 1915, on her road home from Aird, his great-grandmother heard the sea give a weighty groan, and knew one of her sons was dead.

> Seinn O ho ro seinn . . .

He lay on his back. Sang dumb.

A serious case

B Y THE TREMBLING IN his legs, he knew that he couldn't make it up the stairs, not with the bus moving, so he went and sat in the lower deck, on the long seat at the front, with his back to the driver; and no sooner had he sat down than a woman with a message bag in the seat opposite frowned at him, pointed to the No Smoking sign above his head and told him to put his cigarette out. She continued to frown at him after she'd spoken, as did one or two of the other passengers, so he turned his head away from them and looked out of the window. Tall, grey Aberdeen buildings went by, the sun, from the North Sea, dazzling on the granite, and then a pub with a blue lamp outside it. He'd been in that pub one night. He couldn't remember a thing about it. It was a pub for art students. He thought he remembered tartan walls and a glass table going over on its side. But maybe that was another pub altogether. He was barred from two pubs in Aberdeen – the Volunteer Arms, for vomiting on the carpet in the lounge bar, and the Frigate, for falling downstairs on top of a silver wedding party. But maybe he'd been all right in the pub with the blue lamp. Maybe, in the pub with the blue lamp, he hadn't put a foot wrong.

'Kings, is't?' the conductor asked.

He held out a threepenny bit and nodded.

'Mind an' get aff at the richt stop this time.' The conductor, who was not a young man, tore a ticket from his machine, handed it to him, and then said to the woman in the seat opposite, but loudly enough for the rest of the lower deck to hear: 'He's an affa loon, this, for falling asleep on public transport.'

The room of Dr MacCluskey, his Director of Studies, was in the Old Brewery building. A lecturer he wanted to avoid – Harrison – also had a room in there. So did Hendry and Mungo Maclaren. Hendry had already chucked him out of Scottish History for non-attendance. Mungo Maclaren had written him a letter, which he hadn't answered. Harrison, he knew, wouldn't say anything to him, even if they happened to bump into one another – a mild enquiry, at the most, as to why he hadn't submitted any written work this term, or attended any of his Middle English lectures. But he still wanted to avoid him. The other lecturer he wanted to avoid – Mackie – had a room inside Kings College itself, and he had no intention of going in there.

The morning was already hot. He checked the time on the big clock at the front of Kings after coming off the bus, then crossed the road, and keeping his head down, dodged under the pointy arch with the university shield on it and set off up the path to the Old Brewery building. Ten o'clock, MacCluskey had said. He was forty minutes late. So if MacCluskey wasn't in his room, who could blame him? Why *should* he be there? Did MacCluskey – a senior lecturer in Modern European History – have nothing to do all morning but wait for *him*? 'Ye gods!' a voice said. 'It's himself!' He halted. Two females were barring his way. One was Chrissie Joan Mackenzie. The other one was from Wester Ross, Alina something. He didn't know her. 'What's leaving *you* down here?' Chrissie Joan asked. 'We all thought you'd left. Didn't we, Alina?' 'Going to see my Director of Studies,' Colin said. 'That's never a beard you're trying to grow?' Chrissie Joan teased him, and then her voice changed. 'You look awful, Colin,' she said. 'What on earth's happened to you? You look really terrible.'

After pushing at the door of the Old Brewery, he tried pulling the handle towards him, and so entered the cool gloom of the building. Small wooden stairs were in front of him. He climbed them slowly, holding on to the rickety bannister with his right hand. At the top, he halted, puffing heavily, and wiped his face and neck with a handkerchief, and the palms of his hands. Then, with shrinking head, he dodged along the dim passageway until he arrived at MacCluskey's door. He hesitated, and knocked lightly. No answer. MacCluskey wasn't in. Why should he be? That was that, then. He felt relieved. Should he knock again? No. He started back along the passageway. The sound of a door opening behind him caused him to quicken his footsteps. A voice called out:

'Mr Murray?'

It wasn't for him. He kept going.

'Mr Murray!'

He halted. Turned round.

'I was . . . I thought you weren't in.'

'Do come back.'

'I'm sorry I'm late.' He stood in front of MacCluskey, trying not to breathe on him. 'My bus . . .'

'Do go in.' MacCluskey's mouth tightened and twitched at the corners as he waved Colin into the room. 'Please sit down,' he indicated a hard chair in front of the desk. 'One small matter to attend to,' he said, starting to close the door from the outside, 'and then I'll be with you.'

MacCluskey's room in the Old Brewery building had one white-washed stone wall with a small, square window in it, three walls panelled with wooden V-lining and a low, raftered ceiling. Harrison's room further along the passageway was just the same. By stretching upwards, you could have grasped and then swung from the three unplaned spars bracing the rafters. The uneven wooden floor, made shiny by feet, studded with flatheaded nails, gleamed where the sunlight, slanting through the small window, fell on it. The same sunlight caught the backs of MacCluskey's books, packed in dense rows on the shelves behind the desk; history books, reference books, dictionaries: most of them hardbacked. Long spills of paper stuck out of some of them, folded over; one tome on the desk, double-columned like the Bible, had a sheet of paper covered with MacCluskey's minute, squiggly handwriting (impossible to read upside down) beside it. There was an oppressive stillness in the room. 'This room is for studying, and for people who wish to study,' cousin Jacob informed him, the only time he went to visit him in his digs. Holy Porky, who shared the room with cousin Jacob, was there as well, dug in at one end of a table behind a rampart of books. Cousin Jacob's chair, briefly vacated, cousin Jacob's books, briefly abandoned, were at the other end. 'I only came,' Colin whispered, 'to ask could you lend me a quid till next term?' 'I'm afraid not,' said cousin Jacob. 'Now, if you don't mind, Donald and I are working . . .' MacCluskey's room had the same air of heavy, studious silence. Where had he gone? Had he gone to fetch Harrison? Why was he taking so long?

The sun, through the small, square window, filled the room with hard, white light.

On the hard chair, in the hard light, Colin sat forward with his forearms resting on his spread knees, his fingers laced tightly, his hot, beating face turned to the floor. Outside the window, in the trees, birds were singing. A faint hum and bustle of traffic from the High Street. Footsteps went by down below, tramping on gravel. Someone shouted, and then laughed. Out there, the day was going on as usual. It seemed remote and unreal to him, where he was. He was sweating again. In his ears, his heart pounded. Feeling sick, he took the already damp handkerchief from his pocket and wiped his face. His hands trembled when he used them.

He closed his eyes. Behind his eyelids, pale suns quivered; blood-red honeycombs went up and down, up and down. Waves of weakness came over him, wave upon wave to overwhelm him, and he sat up with a terrific jerk, stopping in his throat an involuntary cry of desperation. His vision blurred and went black and came swimming back, and he was back in the room, on the hard chair, in the hard light, bewildered and blinking. His heart lurched and raced, his head sang. MacCluskey was speaking to him.

'. . . kept you waiting.'

He stood up carefully; his head at a rigid angle. The bright dizziness came and went. He didn't want to make any sudden movement, or try to speak –

'. . . not feeling *well?*' MacCluskey's voice asked him.

He nodded, speechless, then felt his legs starting to fold under him and grabbed for the back of the chair.

'Are you sure?' MacCluskey's small face looked concerned. 'Do sit down,' he said.

'Thank you.'

'Can I get you anything? Glass of water, or . . . ?'

Colin shook his head. 'I'm fine,' he said.

MacCluskey sat down in his own chair. He had a small, round face, plump cheeks and a bald head, fringed about the ears with sparse, sandy hair. He always wore a bow tie. He studied Colin across the desk. Speak to him, Colin told himself. Say something.

MacCluskey spoke.

'Perhaps we could begin?' he said.

'Fine,' said Colin. He sat up in his seat, to show how fine he was. His head started singing. He sat back again. Say something, he told himself. Speak.

MacCluskey spoke.

'Tell me, Mr Murray,' he said. 'Are you still a student at this university?'

Colin looked at him.

'I ask,' MacCluskey continued, 'because you never seem to *be* here.'

'Not this term, no.' Colin spoke quickly, his voice shaking. 'But I can explain that. I –'

'Not last term either,' MacCluskey interrupted him. 'Let me see. You sat a first-term exam in Anglo-Saxon for Mr Harrison. After that, nothing. I've just come from Mr Mackie, who has no idea who you are. Two essays for Dr Maclaren – one on Chaucer, one on the metaphysical poets. Very good essays – outstanding, even – but according to Dr Maclaren, you didn't take the trouble to come and collect them. He wondered what had become of you. That would appear to cover your progress in Advanced Special English, or have I omitted something?'

'No. But the reason –'

'You stopped attending Mr Hendry's lectures in Scottish History early in first term. Your reason at the time being that you felt you'd taken too much on. Latin was abandoned soon afterwards, for the same reason. For two terms, in other words, you have done no academic work of any kind. Nor have you kept any of your appointments with me. I had no idea where you were or what you were doing until you telephoned me last night. Where were you telephoning from, by the way?'

'The Students' Union.'

'It didn't sound like the Students' Union. What was going on in the background?'

'It was a bit noisy, yes,' Colin said. 'Agriculture students.'

'Why did you leave 2 Jamaica Street?' MacCluskey asked.

'Well, it's a while ago now . . .'

'January,' said MacCluskey. 'I called round there one night, looking for you, and Mr Bruce told me you'd left. He didn't know where you'd gone.'

Colin didn't say anything.

'There was some mail for you. Mr Bruce didn't know where to forward it.'

Colin didn't say anything.

'Did you have a particular reason for leaving 2 Jamaica Street?' MacCluskey asked. 'You seemed to be quite happy and settled there.'

'No,' said Colin. 'I mean yes. I was.'

'You should have notified me, you know . . .' MacCluskey produced one of his small white Director of Studies cards. 'So where are you staying now?'

'Well, I'm not staying anywhere actually at the moment . . .'

'No?' MacCluskey slotted the cap back on to his Parker 51 pen.

'No, I'm sleeping on a friend's floor at the moment . . .' He stopped and waited for MacCluskey to speak.

'You're a difficult chap to get hold of, Mr Murray,' MacCluskey said. 'In fact, I haven't set eyes on you since the night you appeared at the students' party in my house and put your head into the pot of curry. Last November, that was.'

'I'm sorry about that night –'

'You went next door first. Professor and Mrs Simpson's house. They wanted to call the police.'

'I'd like to apologise for that night –'

'Then you literally fell into my house, appropriated a gin bottle for yourself –'

'I'm really sorry about that night, Dr MacCluskey, I was –'

'– sang a long Gaelic dirge, wept, stumbled through to the kitchen and put your head in the curry pot. November last year, that was. Six months ago.'

'– very drunk that night, I'm afraid, I know that's no excuse, I tried to write your wife a letter of apology, yourself too, of course –'

'My wife, Mr Murray?'

'Yes.'

'Mrs MacCluskey is not my wife.'

'But I thought –'

'I'm not married.'

'But then –'

'Mrs MacCluskey is my mother.'

'O.'

'Which brings us back to the question: Are you still a member of this university?'

Colin looked down at the floor. He looked across the desk at MacCluskey, who frowned slightly at him, then raised his eyebrows in mute enquiry. 'I don't know,' he muttered.

'Do you remember *why* you telephoned me last night?'

'Yes, I –' He stopped.

'Someone else was at the telephone with you.'

'Was there?'

'Your voice was very loud. Understandable, considering the uproar in the background. Another voice, not so loud, kept telling you what to say.'

'Perhaps they were waiting to use the phone?'

'I don't think so, Mr Murray. I don't think so because the telephone was taken from you at one stage, and the voice in question addressed me directly.'

'O God!'

'Shetland, the voice said it came from. It hoped I was hanging plumb, and asked me to arrange for you, its friend, to receive vast sums of money on loan from the university, which the voice insisted I was in a position to do. What does hanging plumb mean?'

Colin shook his head.

'There *is* a contingency fund in existence, within the university, which students in temporary genuine need can borrow from – your friend from Shetland was right about that. And yes, I could approach the Fund Committee on your behalf. But you would need to show me good and sufficient reason before I went ahead. Squandering your grant in pubs and doing no work at all over the past two terms' – MacCluskey's mouth went up briefly at the sides – 'hardly qualifies.'

'No, right . . .' Colin started to get to his feet. MacCluskey motioned him back into the chair, and then stood up himself.

'You don't know if you want to remain in university? Is that what you said?'

'No. I mean yes.'

'No, you don't know, or yes, that's what you said?'

'Yes, I want to remain in university.'

'Obviously you can't be presented for any degree examinations this year.'

'I know.'

'Would you go and see the university doctor? If I made an appointment for you?'

'What for?'

'Just for a chat. Do sit down,' he said, as Colin started to his feet. 'May I be quite frank with you?'

Colin nodded.

'You're a serious case,' MacCluskey said. 'A student in name only. As your Director of Studies' – he threw out his arms, palms upward; a hopeless gesture – 'I have nothing to direct.'

'But I thought, if I came to see you, and then went to see my English lecturers – Mr Maclaren – and explained to them –'

'Explained what, Mr Murray?' MacCluskey sat down again. 'Do you want my advice or not?'

'Yes.'

'Then go and see the doctor. A very good man. Tell him what's been happening to you.' He pulled the telephone on the desk towards him, raising his eyebrows in mute enquiry.

'All right.'

'Extension 24,' MacCluskey spoke into the mouthpiece. He waited, rolling his eyes to the ceiling and tapping with his fingers on the bow tie. 'Dr Anderson? Dr MacCluskey here. Could I speak to Dr Anderson? Thank you.' He waited, then said: 'Dr Anderson? Yes. That matter we spoke of earlier. That's right. I don't think so. I would say not. Thank you so much.' MacCluskey put the phone down. 'That was Dr Anderson,' he told Colin. 'He'll see you straightaway.'

'You mean now?'

'That's right. You know where the medical department is?'

'Yes. I was there before.'

MacCluskey nodded politely.

'When I fell on the black ice. I had to get stitches.'

'You know where it is, then. Do co-operate with Dr Anderson. A very good man. He'll help you sort yourself out. A psychiatric assessment, I should think, followed by a period of hospitalisation. Then, when you're quite fit again – perhaps six months, perhaps a year – you may reapply to repeat second year.'

A hooter went off, somewhere in the city; a high, prolonged whine, dying down and then rising again. It was midday.

'Let's face it, pal,' said MacCluskey, vaulting lazily out of his chair and swinging in the blazing, dazzling light by one arm, from a rafter. 'You're up shit creek without a paddle.'

What he really said, opening the door, was: 'Do keep in touch, Mr Murray. Let me know how you get on.'

'Yes,' said Colin. 'Thank you.'

The door of MacCluskey's room closed with a click behind him.

He padded quickly back along the passageway, towards the stairs. With every step, he felt easier; he no longer had the hot, breath-stopping constriction in his chest, the dry agony in his throat. And a feeling of exhilaration was mounting in him – he wanted to whistle, to sing, to laugh out loud. He'd gone to see MacCluskey! He'd done it! He thumped confidently down the stairs and pushed open the door at the bottom, almost hitting a man – not a student – on the other side, who drew back, startled, to let him come out. Colin winked at him in passing – a light, witty toss of the head. The man took no notice.

Outside, on College Bounds, he stood with a grin on his face, breathing in the bustle of the street, his eyes narrowed against the glare of the sun. The heat from the pavement was coming through his shoes. The High Street, with the medical department, was behind him. He set off swiftly in the other direction. In front of Kings, and along the paths, the trees were in bloom. Green and still in the heat; not a leaf stirring. Students were sitting under the trees in small groups, or stretched out sunbathing on the grass. The girls were in summer dresses. Chrissie Joan Mackenzie and the other one had been wearing coats. If, from Ness, on a hot day, you can see the mountains of Wester Ross risen above the horizon, it means bad weather. He hurried past Bishop Elphinstone's tomb and the entrance to Kings, keeping his head down, crossed University Road and headed up the Spital. He now knew where he was going. The Spital was narrow, with high walls and buildings trapping the heat. From now on, the road went uphill. He hurried along. Someone shouted and waved to him from the doorway of a small newsagent's on the other side of the road. Without his glasses, he couldn't make out who it was, but he waved back anyway, but didn't stop. To be stopped now would be disastrous. He went past a shopfront with no sign and nothing in the window. Behind it, out of sight, a concrete mixer was churning . . . All right. He pushed open the door of the Red Lion and went in.

Inside the bar was nice and cool. The counter lined with lunchtime drinkers. He stood at the end nearest the door. The barman came down.

'A pint of lager.'

The barman held the glass at a slight angle under the mouth of the tap. The lager, pale green with a foaming white head, rose in the glass and overflowed, frothing, down the sides.

'Wantin' lime?'

'No.'

He carried the glass over to a table. The condensation beaded cold on the outside of the glass. He sat down. He felt fine. He wasn't thinking about anything. The darts thudded into the soft cork of the board: tok, tok, tok. The voices of the other drinkers came and went. Faintly, from outside, came the put-put-put of the concrete mixer . . .

He raised the pintglass to his mouth and closed his eyes. Slowly, his head tilted back. He drank without haste, pausing between swallows, but without taking his mouth from the glass or opening his eyes. When he set the glass down, it was almost empty. Circles of froth went down the inside of the glass, marking the spaces between swallows. He sat back, well at ease, and looked round the bar. It was fine to be in a bar. It was a very fine day . . .

Ah, but the storm that was coming . . .

The letter

WHEN ANNIE WENT OUT to the byre at nine o'clock to milk the cow, the gale was at its height; a wind from the north east driving in from the Butt, raging against the house, rattling the doors and windows; threatening, with every rain-laden gust, to tear the very slates off the roof. The weather forecast had been right after all. But up in the living room it was bright, it was warm, where the rest of the family were grouped about the fire and watching a programme on the television: Isobel half-asleep on the settee; John, the oldest, very red in the face, to one side of the fireplace with a cushion at his back and his sore leg up on a pouffe; their mother, aged ninety-one dozing in her own armchair among rugs and balls of wool and *Christian Heralds*; a white knitted shawl over her shoulders and a white knitted pixiecap on her head. Breathing out, her mouth made a small, popping noise; in her lap, her hands and her knitting lay idle. The peat fire in the hearth flamed red and yellow, flickered on the black silk of her gown and on the glass panels of the china cabinet and on the polished oak face of the sideboard. Rain lashed the windows; the wind, moaning in the chimney, caused the picture on the television screen to shake. It was a night for staying indoors.

Out in the byre at the rear of the house, Annie was milking Maddy, the cow. Crouched on a three-legged milking stool, her forehead resting against Maddy's brown and white flank, she pulled at the firm dugs with easy, expert fingers, holding in her other hand, tilted, a tin mug, into which the first jets of milk went squirting with a high, mewing sound, which changed as the warm, foaming liquid rose in the mug, to a sound like muffled purring. When the mug was full, Annie would empty it into the big milkpail beside her, crooning gently to Maddy as she did so in a nonsense language of her own, while Maddy switched her tail from side to side and tossed her head, to show she was listening, rattling the loose chain around her neck and sending great clouds of breath steaming into the dark night air of the byre. Set in a cobwebbed window above Annie's head was a small paraffin lamp, and whenever the wind gusted against the window and underneath the door of the byre, the pale-yellow, half-moon flame of the lamp would rise, flickering, in its globe, and send agitated shadows moving along the walls and rafters. Other creatures were in the byre. Across from Annie, on the other side of the cement runnel, Charlie, the six-month old calf, had already settled in his stall for the night. Snuffling noises came out of the deep dark at the upper end of the byre, where Tag, the ram, in a reinforced pen of his own, rummaged and butted through an evening feed of hay, sliced potatoes and sliced turnips. And on the top rance, shiny with age, of the flake that separated the byre from the barn proper, three cats – Big Tom, Nellie and the Nightowl – like a row of familiars, sat waiting.

Most nights, Annie took her time over the milking. She loved being in the byre, among the smell and the feel of animals, talking to them, stroking them, and as often as not Isobel (or Margaret, if she was at home) would open the barn door from the kitchen side (the house, barn and byre were all connected) and shout at her was she going to be up there all night, and what did she think she was doing, taking so long to milk one cow? And Margaret (if she was at home) would usually add why didn't she make her bed up there with the animals while she was about it? But tonight, Annie was in a hurry. It was cold in the byre; gloomy – and she had a lot to do before bedtime. Tomorrow, for the first time in five years, she was going over to Stornoway on the nine o'clock bus, to get the rest of her bottom teeth pulled out. She had four left. Dr MacAulay had made the appointment for her himself, over the telephone, from the surgery. He spoke to the dentist on the telephone, leaning back in his big chair as he spoke, and he called the dentist Hamish and not Mr MacRitchie. Annie, sitting up very straight in her good coat and hat on the chair opposite, couldn't help listening. Dr MacAulay spoke in English, of course, and he told Mr MacRitchie all about her four remaining bottom teeth using words that Annie had never heard in her life before; her eyes, as she sent the quick threads of milk hissing into the mug, still went big at the memory of them. '*Stay* there!' she exclaimed suddenly, as Maddy, sensing her hurry, grew restless and shifted her hindlegs, almost knocking over the milkpail. 'Stay,' she said, more softly. 'Stay now . . .' After the dentist's, she had a long list of messages to get in the Stornoway shops for Isobel and the neighbours. Then, at dinnertime, Isobel had arranged for her to go to cousin Zena's in Goathill for a lie-down. Zena's daughter Cathie was meeting her outside Woolies at one o'clock. Before that, though, and before everything else, she was going to the big post office on Francis Street with her letter.

The letter was to her nephew Colin. No one knew she had written it. Secretly, over the past two nights, when the rest of the household were in bed and she was sure she wouldn't be disturbed, Annie had settled herself at the kitchen table with pen and ink and a writing pad with lines on the square-patterned oilcloth in front of her, and with much audible sighing and furrowing of brows at first (for the pen was not a familiar instrument), and then with more and more confidence, she had composed a letter. She didn't know Colin's address – only the town where he'd last been seen. That was why she was going to the big post office on Francis Street. Because she didn't know what more to put on the envelope. Asking in the village post office was no use – Allan John's wife would only laugh and make a mockery of her and give the gossips a field day. But the people in Stornoway wouldn't do that – the people in the big post office on Francis Street. They wouldn't even look at her letter. There was a big letterbox outside the post office with two mouths – one for island letters and one for mainland and abroad, so she would post her letter from there. And she had read somewhere, or heard Isobel telling it, that sometimes letters were posted with nothing but the name on them, and still they arrived at their destination. And also letters from foreign countries, with the address in a different language. But she already had Colin's name for them, and the name of the town he was in – Southampton. That would give them a flying start.

He'd been seen in Southampton by three lads from the district, on their way home from sea. He told them, when they stopped him, that he had a job there as a bus-driver, and that today was his day off. He wouldn't come for a drink with them, he was in a big hurry, and so they never got a chance to ask him how he was or when had he learned to drive or where had he been hiding for the past two years? But he looked well, they said – the same as ever. No change at all in him, that they could see.

The milking done, Annie eased herself up slowly from the stool, groaning out loud from the pain of having sat so long in the one position. She stood for a minute stroking Maddy along the side of her neck, scratching her behind the ears. 'You nearly knocked it over,' she murmured in mock reproval. 'You nearly managed it that time, didn't you?' Maddy tossed her head and huffed out a response. 'But I can't stand here talking to *you* all night,' Annie told her. 'People will be wanting their supper.' Bending down again with a small grunt, she picked up the milking stool through the hole in its centre and placed it against the door of the byre, and kicked in with her feet the sacking that acted as a draught excluder at the bottom of the door. She picked up the tin mug and the milkpail in one hand, and the lamp in the other and stepped carefully over the runnel, holding the lamp away from Charlie's stall in case the light should disturb him. She stopped at Tag's pen; leaned over to have a look. 'Tag mor,' she whispered. The great, all-battering head came up; baleful eyes glared up at her. 'Go to sleep, Tag mor,' she whispered. She pushed open the flake with her foot and went through into the barn. The cats arched and purred about her feet. She set down the lamp on a killing-stool next to the door jamb, closed the flake with her free hand and turned the sneck. A scythe hung from dooks on the wall. Green glass fishing floats; hanks of rope. There was a smell of creosote and turnips. Opening the door that led into the kitchen set up a shrieking draught of wind in the passageway, so that the door, hinged backwards, was flung instantly out of her grasp, into the wall of the partition. Carrying the mug and the milkpail, she went into the kitchen. The cats followed, purring loudly. She put the milkpail on the table and switched on the electric light. She had to stop for a few seconds to let her eyes become accustomed to the sudden brightness. Then she went back into the barn, fetched the small paraffin lamp, and after a short but strenuous tugging match with the wind, managed to pull the door to, behind her. Screwing down the wick, she placed the lamp on the top shelf of the dresser, where it popped and puttered fitfully for a while, and then went out.

Clean muslin cloths hung in an overlapping line on the front rail of the stove. Annie felt them with her hand; they were dry. With the tin mug, she filled the cats' feeding dishes straight from the pail; the Nightowl's head came sneaking into her own dish – the bottom of an old Fray Bentos pie tin – while Annie was still filling it. Annie contemplated the sleek top of the Nightowl's head for a moment, then took hold of her by an ear. Immediately the Nightowl stopped lapping and flattened herself out along the floor. She started snarling. 'What did you do with the starling?' Annie asked. 'What did you do with her?' The Nightowl flattened herself even further along the floor, tail twitching furiously, and keeping up a low snarl. 'Don't think I didn't see you,' Annie told her. 'Don't think that for a second, leddy.' She peered into the Nightowl's face, which was flecked on the mouth and whiskers with milky foam. 'You little murderer,' Annie told her. 'And never mind that bad temper.' She let the Nightowl go, and collected the muslin cloths from the stove rail. Two deep white earthen bowls and a large milkjug were already lined up on the table, along with John's coronation mug for 1937 and three smaller mugs, presents from Arran, with blue and white stripes. She stretched the muslin tightly across the rim of the milkpail. Tipping the pail, she strained the milk into the bowls first, and then into the milkjug. Then, from the milkjug, she filled the four mugs. After that, there was still enough milk left in the pail to refill the milkjug to the brim. Maddy was a good cow. She put the two large bowls and the milkjug away, into the press of the dresser, took two round barley bannocks, wrapped in a teatowel, from one of the drawers, and cut each one carefully into four segments. She set out the four mugs of milk and the pieces of barley bread on a tray. Under the sink tap, she rinsed out the muslin cloths, the milking utensils. She was finished. But she made no move to go up to the living room. She stood at the sink, staring out of the window, very still; a small, plump woman; as though waiting for something, listening for something, above the onslaught of the gale. But her eyes were faraway; and her voice, when she spoke, full of sadness. She was speaking to Colin. 'Where are you tonight?' she asked. 'On such a night. Where are you?' Over and over she asked; but the wind, with all its clamour, the rain that drummed and fretted in the darkness on the other side of the glass, gave back no answer.

Up in the living room, they were still watching the television. 'Close that door after you,' her mother told Annie, when she appeared with the tray. 'You're letting up a draught.' 'Isobel!' said Annie. 'Wake up!' 'I *am* awake,' Isobel said, annoyed. 'Give your brother his supper,' her mother told Annie. 'John!' said Annie. 'Sit up!' 'I wasn't asleep,' said Isobel. 'Resting my eyes. That's all I was doing.' John sat up, very red-faced and irritable, and took the coronation mug from the tray and two wedges of barley bread. 'Even though my eyes were closed, I could hear everything that was going on,' Isobel said. 'Hold your tongue,' John told her. 'No one here wants to listen to your blathering and nonsense.' 'Your brother's talking to you,' her mother told Isobel. 'Who were *you* talking to down in the kitchen?' Isobel asked Annie. 'I wasn't talking to anyone,' Annie said. 'Yes you were,' said Isobel. 'A woman of sixty. We could all hear you.' 'Talking to herself,' said John. 'Gone doolally.' 'Who's that dancing on the telly?' Annie asked, sitting down. 'Italians?' 'Italians!' said Isobel. 'Do they *look* like Italians?' 'What are they, then?' Annie asked. 'Russians!' said Isobel. 'Shut up, then, gawdammit, two seconds, the pair of you, and watch the thing,' John said, and his face went redder than ever. 'Hallo!' said Annie. 'He's getting the steam up!' She was the only one in the family who could tease him. 'A bad man!' said Isobel. 'Stop provoking your brother to wrath, the two of you,' their mother told them. From under the pixiehood, she frowned at Annie with hard, bright eyes. 'She's looking at me again!' Annie whispered, delighted, to Isobel.

'Look! Her eye is on me again!' She started laughing. 'What'll I do?' she whispered. 'What'll I do, where'll I go?' 'Doolally,' said John. 'Gone doolally . . .'

Overhead, the tramping of feet, the creaking of joists and floorboards, had stopped. They were all in bed.

My dear nephew, Annie read –

(the writing pad held away from her, at a slant to the light; her lips moving silently, shaping the words; eyes going warily along the line –)

. . . all so happy when we heard Iain Ban, mac Dholly and the other boy from Habost saw you in Southampton after all this time not hearing from you or knowing where you were Isobel said she knew you were alive all the time that God told her but no word or message from you why didn't you give the boys your address why didn't you write to anyone for the past 2 years and more did you lack pen and paper on your travels? Anyway heres a letter from your old aunty Annie and hope it finds you Im sending it to the main post office Southampton with your name on the envelope hoping it will find you from there please write back to me. Please come home.

Excuse chewing on corner of page as Boy had the writing pad in his basket with him hes our new dog as old Boy died he had to go (chewing doorposts and knobs Off the sideboard) and weve got another dog in his place your uncle Dan (Swainbost) Sheila thats his mother hes only a puppy yet 3 months black with a white breast and one white paw your uncle John has started to train him but I wont say anything about that (mas can mi cus).

According to Iain Ban youve grown a beard. Take off the beard. Come home. Miracle of miracles the boys ever met you in the first place as their ship wasnt supposed to go to Southampton at all.

Well dear I hope your well all well here so far except your granny (aged 91) and down with a bad cold from sitting in a draught at the scullery window and confined to bed since two days with her back and 2 bottles but gets Up to the fire at night for the telly she likes Sports the snooker (the Welshman) and boxing whenever its on we sent for Dr MacAulay he came he gave her pills (green) Now says he youve to stop drinking so much milk sitting on the end of the bed your grannys eye on him I know you still are holding up the specimen bottle because it turned pink too much milk is bad for you says he shes got cant spell the thing sugar as well says he as well for him to be addressing the bedpost who spends every waking hour shes up in the bottom of the dresser among the bowls and milkjugs hes putting me over to Stornoway on Friday (Dr MacAulay) to the dentist so will post this then at the big post office in Francis street everyone else well no change your mother chasing sheep as usual now you write her a letter shes not against you no matter what you think or what she said and never was your brother Alan the same hes just the way he is now you write to your mother.

Well dear all very pleased to hear you got a job and Good Wages Alan Angus over the road says bus drivers get good wages (hes the same as ever) and big money (where and when did you learn to drive?) so you stick in at your job this time and nevermind the rest not like the day and a half you did between school and university on the road squad before you fell out with Cox the gaffer and got sent home keep yourself to yourself thats always the best way and if your in any trouble however small just keep your tongue still and your hands by your side no matter how hard sticks and stones may break my bones but names will never hurt me (theyre the losers not you) remember when you threw the stone at me behind the old sheepfank?

(Because she wouldn't give him half a crown. She sat back, remembering. He was thirteen years old at the time, home from Stornoway for the weekend, and he'd been following her about all afternoon – from the house to the Co-op van, from the Co-op van to the shop – trying to wheedle half a crown out of her to buy cigarettes. A Saturday afternoon. She was taking the back way home, she still hadn't given in to him, he was trailing about fifty yards behind, when suddenly, with a yell of rage and frustration, he bent down, straightened, and threw a stone after her. It went straight up into the air. They both halted then, equally astonished, to see what would happen next – he up at the old stone fank, poised like a petrified discus thrower, she half-turned, with a bag of messages in each hand, in the drybed hollow of a stream. Up and up the stone went, almost disappearing from view; when it started to come down, she stood where she was, watching it; even when she realised the stone was coming straight for her, she still stood there ('Why didn't I move?' she used to ask afterwards in a voice full of wonder. 'I saw it coming and I didn't *move*. . .') It came with a rush like a slingshot, whispering out of the sky, too late she let go the message bags, vaguely, from the direction of the old fank, she heard a high yelp of alarm, before, blotting out the day, the stone cracked into her forehead . . .)

She stopped laughing, wiped her eyes, sighed and read on:

Everything at home the same no change we got terrible weather yesterday (Monday) gale force winds no one able to do a hands turn outside the sea rising over Cros a Bharagi white so high we could see it from the house and 2 sheep stranded on Eilean Glas since 3 days with weather and cant get Off the lees black up to the fences at the bottom of the crofts the 2 sheep were from Habost (Tullys) poor things Maggie Dods haystacks blew away with the wind as far as the river she never put ropes or anchors on them I told her to Weather? she says what weather? the sheafs scattered with the wind as far down as the river the second time its happened this year to the same family Charlie over the road lost the slates Off his roof as usual he was here in the afternoon in the middle of the gale himself and Alan Angus wanting your uncle John to give them each a haircut your uncle John saying he never saw the likes since the great gale of 1954 when the Clan Macquarrie *went on the rocks at Borve but this time wasnt so big a gale as that time but it was a big one all the same.*

(Wednesday 11 p.m.)

New writing pad I got today from Bean Allan John in the post office Lady what can I polish next as you used to call her she hadnt one with lines look how crooked my hands going already Write a letter? Id rather clean out a henhouse any day of the week also the pen keeps going at a slant on me as I got (2) fingers jammed in the door of the barn holding it for your uncle John putting on a new hinge so excuse handwriting. I wasnt watching and he put my (2) fingers in the door on me. So excuse handwriting. I was watching Allan Angus next door through the barn window trying to go up on the roof in the gale drunk instead of watching what your uncle John was doing the thumbnail black a miracle if I dont lose it I says to him then seeing he was on his feet what about breaking the septic tank at the back of the house for me In this gale are you mad? he says remember the septic tank he hasnt broken it yet 3 years last April since we got a bathroom I wish I was a man of course I blame my mother myself always letting him Off with everything putting his socks on his feet for him thats why hes the way he is and then if he gets started on anything he always makes a perfect job especially if its for someone else as this district well knows its getting him started thats the problem he went over to Stornoway with Charlie and Allan Angus a week last Monday in Charlies big van to the slaughterhouse with 7 mults (wedders) and Charlie (3) well you know them the usual gallivanting in and out of pubs after the sale (remember the year you and him went over and drank a wedder a piece on us?) so anyway they arrived back home about 10.30 p.m. after breaking a pillar of cement on Galson bridge.

We were all waiting there arrival to see what price did they get your uncle John got 48 grading on 5 and 52 on the 2 that was on grass all summer but Charlie never got a grading on his ones at all nothing on them but the head and the backbone Mac D. D. told him so Charlie took them out of the ring.

So about seven o'clock the chops and potatoes are in the fryingpan my mother at the scullary window looking out for the van thats where she got the draught 8 p.m. no signs of them 9 p.m. no signs finally Charlies wife comes in to see was your uncle John arrived home by himself Off her head O pray to God Charlie doesnt give the wheel to Allan Angus O God be with us all this night O God if he gives the wheel to Allan Angus.

However going on 11 p.m. we saw something appearing with only one dim headlamp my mother and I were outside on the path and the big van passed at a terrific speed with one side the side facing our house torn Off your uncle John and Charlie in the back sound asleep among the wedders and Allan Angus on the wheel.

Murdos (Murchadh Iains) wife in hospital very ill since 3 months poor girl Isobel went to see her when she was over she was asking after you old Sandy on the Leig died since you were home last and Smeets the oldest girl the Swan home from America for her fathers funeral but didnt stay in the house but in the Royal hotel Stornoway no other news no news is good news one of Flocks daughters (Melbost) getting married again once not enough for her thank heaven for blessed singleness Shonag Flock shes related to you on your fathers side as Flocks mother and your fathers father was first cousins Maggie the Curer the rest of the family went to Canada to Manitoba so your third cousins shes getting married in November to a widower from Lochs twice her age with 3 grownup children and the shock to her mother was sudden and severe she met him in Harris when she was working as a house and table in that castle in Harris and thats where she met him. And Gunn home from Hartlepools in August with a car and a wife and a dog like the dog on the telly for Dulux paint they stayed a week hes grey in the head already (aged 26) and never paid us a visit (nach cac e). However they did pay a visit to the 3 old uncles in their mansion with the nettles growing out through the roof and first thing on entering a hen lighted on the wifes head mistaking her hairstyle for a nest the first old uncle says Hallo Jock to her the second Merry Christmas and the third (Finlay) shook her hand and asked why did she have the scale of the herring in her eyes she had those things in her eyes instead of glasses so that was the new wife from Hartlepools meeting the husbands relations.

Well dear all v. happy to hear your working and not on the tramp as some people said now you stick in at that job no matter where you are theres always something to avoid and some people will cause trouble but you tell yourself No I wont before you do anything (look before you leap) your granny always including you in her prayers she got a text for you (the years eaten by the locust) and Gods promise your going to be a good man one of these days.

Keep away from drink.

Remember you can be very stupid with drink the worst I ever saw no wonder you appeared with a bashed nose once upon a time.

As for your brother John I wont say anything its between yourselves another fool with drink Im only sorry what happened happened brother rising against brother you were so nice with one another when you were little boys coming down to our house every morning hand in hand in your pixies but maybe youll be friends again come time who knows I know hes sorry now for all that happened drink no excuse hes starting in the university this month (Glasgow) you wont know that he left Singers and did the highers he lacked and next week hes starting in Glasgow university and back staying with Norman Gunn and his wife in White street Partick they took him back in spite of setting fire to his bedroom when he was there before and annoying other people in the tenement going into their houses late at night drunk and keeping them up talking.

After 1 a.m. so Ill stop writing everyone else upstairs in bed long ago with their hotwaterbottles and chamberpots and bibles a wild night here again tonight rain banging on the windows no end to it the wind wheeee the minute you open a door lifting the carpets the picture on the telly shaking our aerial must be kaput Robert Dougall on the news of course your uncle John saying what a strong man look at the shoulders on him look at the hands thats the hands of a strong man Kenneth Kendall the same of course he never saw a single person in his whole life that wasnt a giant in strength and size and drinking a pity Robert Dougall isnt here to break the septic tank I said but he never let on he heard me.

Well dear remember to write back to me whenever this reaches you and I know you will your granny when she heard youd been found started knitting a pair of socks for you so please come home plenty good food and fresh air and no one to bother you all that forgotten long ago we made (maragan) last week I was thinking of you one without onions also a suit of Alans lying idle in the wardrobe do you want it sent say if you do and Ill send it in a parcel along with your grannys socks. Well dear Ill close now so goodnight dear please write to me and may God keep you from your loving aunty Annie.

She thought for a minute, then picked up the pen and wrote:

Thursday 12.30 p.m. PS.

In the afternoon today in spite of the wild gale and high seas your cousin Dolly and cousin Malcolm and Mac Tully got the 2 sheep from Habost Off the eilean at low tide with ropes your cousin Dolly swam out against a third wave when his mother (bean Uilleam) was carrying him she was down in the shore one day and a bull seal came out of the

sea and walked beside her everyone knows that and then your cousin
Malcolm made a harness with loops in it on the (rope) and cousin Dolly
on the eilean caught the sheep and put them in the loops one after the
other and the other two hauled them ashore and that was how they
got the poor sheep Off.

PPS.

Your uncle John appeared in the scullary door after dinner with the
7lb Ord Mor for to break the tank.

He said come on then so we both went Off.

He stood looking at it and said well what now with my leg so I
told him to go inside the big tank and hammer hard he said No. This
other tank will need to come Off first as its stuck to the other I said O
heavens no.

So finally he put the Ord Mor on his shoulder and disappeared over
the road into Charlies garage and we saw him no more till teatime.

She sat back wearily and rubbed her eyes. The letter was finished.

The alarm clock on the dresser said one in the morning. Down
in Australia, the potatoes would be on the boil.

Purring, the Nightowl rubbed against her leg. 'Hrrruf' went Boy,
fast asleep in his basket, on his back, forepaws twitching.

She took an envelope from behind a tea caddy in the dresser and
printed carefully on it:

COLIN MURRAY

Leaving a space, she then printed:

SOUTHAMPTON, ENGLAND.

She fetched her good handbag from the living room, found her
purse and took a pound note from it.

On the first page of the letter, in the top left hand corner of the
page, she wrote:

pound tip for fish suppers my other pension hasnt come yet as its
every 3 months.

Carefully she folded the pound note inside the letter and put the
letter inside the envelope. She sealed the envelope and put it into
her handbag.

Carefully she cleaned the nib of the pen with a torn-off piece of the *Daily Express*, and made sure the lid of the ink bottle was screwed on tight. She put the writing pad, the pen and the bottle of ink away, into the left hand drawer of the dresser. The gale was still blowing as hard as ever. But it would die down by morning, the forecast had said.

She put the light out and went to bed.

She came back from Stornoway, laden with message bags, on the quarter to six bus; even though Zena, seeing how ill and white she'd looked down town all afternoon, had wanted her to stay in Goathill for the night; holding a bloody cloth to her mouth all the way over and speaking to no one at all; the pain from her torn mouth going up both sides of her head, now the anaesthetic had worn off, hurting her ears and behind her eyes, so that she couldn't hear or see properly. But she had posted her letter, and she was happy. And that night, warm and drowsy in bed after taking the aspirins the dentist had given her (Isobel had been putting hot-water bottles in the bed since early afternoon; and Maggie Dodo had come over at nine o'clock to do the milking) she had a dream about Colin.

She dreamed that she was back in their old black house, on a summer's morning, and coming out of the doorway she hit her head against the low stone lintel, and there at the front of the house was Deena, the black mare they used to have, her coat shining in the sun. And then she had a lot of other dreams that ran into one another that she couldn't remember, but not bad dreams, she wasn't afraid – and then she must have woken up, it was towards morning, the skylight was growing grey ... And when she fell asleep again, she saw Colin.

He was standing high above her on the prow of a great ship, among a crowd of people, and she was down below on the quay, among herring barrels and Calor Gas cylinders, looking up at him. It took him ages to notice her, but at long last he did, and he asked her what on earth she was doing down there, all alone, so far from home, and he said he was glad to see her. He told her that he was getting on very well now, and that he would soon be coming home.

He kept talking so much, and the crowd around him kept making so much noise, she couldn't get a word in edgeways, not even to tell him that she'd written him a letter, or to ask why he was wearing that big white bandage around his head? For before she could do any of that, a siren wailed in the night overhead, and the great ship started to move. Rows and rows of yellow lights were along her sides, high up in the night, the lights of her portholes; round and yellow, hundreds of them in rows above her, going farther and farther away in the dark, as the great ship moved out, leaving. But when she tried to follow, the herring barrels and cylinders of Calor Gas kept getting in her way, hitting her shins. So she stopped. And when she looked up again he was no longer there, there was no sign of him, or of anyone, there was only the great ship leaving, going farther and farther away, and she saw the name on her stern, in high, white letters, and she knew then what ship it was; it was the greatest ship in the world, it was the *Queen Mary*.